Everyday Lies

Everyday Lies

LOUISE GUY

Text copyright © 2017, 2020 by Louise Guy
All rights reserved.

Previously self-published in Australia in 2017.

Published by Lake Union Publishing, Seattle

www.apub.com

Amazon, the Amazon logo, and Lake Union are trademarks of Amazon.com, Inc., or its affiliates.

ISBN-13: 9781542015950
ISBN-10: 1542015952

Cover design by Sarah Whittaker

Printed in the United States of America

For Ray
Thank you for your love, support,
encouragement and belief.

Chapter One

EMMA

Emma shivered with anticipation as she stepped off the escalator, sidestepped the chaos of the crowded linen section and made her way toward homewares. Never would she have believed something so simple as acquiring a centrepiece would cause her heart to race. Her lips curled into a smile. *Acquire* – the perfect description for her unconventional shopping methods.

She passed by appliances and glassware and headed toward the tables boasting fine china, candlesticks and an assortment of other ornate pieces. It was a finishing touch she was after. The menu for the dinner party was set, she knew exactly which table linen, cutlery and serving platters she would be using, but she had one final item in mind to complete the table.

She should have been an event planner. Her husband's expectations for their dinner parties were high. In their early days together she had suggested they employ an expert. Daniel had said no, building a successful investment company was something he wanted to achieve as a team. So he'd encouraged her to become the expert, and over time she had. It certainly hadn't been instant, though. Emma's expertise had been born of trial and error; like the time she'd decided to turn their outdoor entertaining area into a winter wonderland. She'd placed almost two hundred candles, having given no thought to the fact it was a windy night. Their guests had been treated to a spectacular sight when the table linen had caught fire and the outdoor space had been reduced to a pile of ashes.

Emma fingered a lace tablecloth as she moved toward the centrepieces. She didn't want anything elaborate, just something that showcased her discerning style. She grinned. *Style.* That's something she definitely had.

Less than five minutes later, heart thumping, Emma strode toward her car, revelling in the familiar feeling of excitement. The centrepiece had slipped easily inside her bag. Of course she knew it was wrong, that she should stop. But the anticipation, the rush it gave her, was all too addictive.

Emma sighed and cast her favourite Donna Karan aside in favour of the Gaultier. She'd prefer something casual but securing Andean as a client tonight was important, and she needed to make the extra effort. With her honey-blond hair piled high on her head in a French bun, the tiered slip dress ensured a modern, sophisticated look. Perfect for entertaining on a warm Brisbane night.

Daniel's wolf-whistle as he entered their bedroom suggested the Gaultier was the right choice. 'Gorgeous, Mrs Wilson. You are absolutely gorgeous.'

Emma smiled as Daniel wrapped his arms around her.

'How did I get so lucky? Not only are you incredibly talented but you're sexy, too.' He slipped his finger through the strap of the dress and pushed it off her shoulder. 'Why don't we take this off for just a minute? Don't want it getting messed up before dinner.'

Emma laughed and swatted him away. 'Come on, there'll be plenty of time for that later. You need to shower and get dressed.

Your thoughts should be completely focused on Di and impressing her and the others from Andean. Million-dollar deals don't fall in your lap every day, so use your charm on her to get this contract secured. Then you can work on me.'

Daniel stood to attention and saluted. 'Yes, ma'am. Charm will be reserved at all times for the sole purpose of client manipulation, as directed.'

Emma rolled her eyes and shooed him in the direction of the en suite. 'Go on, glam up. I expect to be impressed.'

Daniel grinned, planted a quick kiss on Emma's forehead, and headed into the shower.

The eight guests expressed the usual oohs and aahs as they were led from the front door to the dining room. With high ceilings, marble floors and spacious living areas, Emma's home, while opulent, retained a relaxed and inviting feel. The interior designer who'd worked on the house five years earlier had been right: the art deco furniture and finishings were impressive and provided great talking points.

Now, after a delicious entrée and main course, Emma finished serving the dessert of raspberry soufflés amid the laughter and chatter of their guests. She took her own seat and gazed at Daniel as he moved around the table and refilled wineglasses. His new, clipped haircut disguised his receding hairline and made him look incredibly young and sexy, and the fitted design of his azure shirt not only highlighted the blue of his eyes but, pulled taut across his muscular chest, left no doubt that he looked after himself.

'Oh, how beautiful. Is it a sooty owl? I saw one just like it up at the Bunya Mountains last Easter.'

Emma's thoughts were broken by Di, the managing director of Andean. She'd picked up the new centrepiece and was examining it.

Emma's heart raced, as it had when she'd left the department store. Would anyone suspect? She smiled at Di. 'I'm actually not sure. It was passed down from my grandparents.' She ignored Daniel's raised eyebrows. 'It's been in the family for a long time.'

'Really?' The surprise in Di's voice was obvious. 'It looks brand new, you've looked after it very well.'

Emma swallowed. Why did she say it had been passed down? She was lucky she'd remembered to take the price tag off. 'I've had it restored recently.'

Di nodded. 'They've done a marvellous job.'

Emma's heart rate slowed. Of course no one had suspected. Why would they?

'I've been a mad birdwatcher since I was ten.' Di smiled at Emma. 'I'm guessing by your choice of centrepiece that you may have worked out my interest in birds already. Owls are my favourite, of course, which the company name suggests.' Di went on to explain her encounter with an Andean pygmy owl when she'd been travelling in Venezuela.

It was close to midnight when the last of the guests left. Daniel turned to Emma as he shut the front door. 'You were fabulous tonight.' He pulled her toward him. 'If they sign the deal, it's because of you and your sooty owl. That was amazing, Em. How did you know Di was so keen on birds?' He laughed. 'She went on about her owl encounter for close to an hour. Did you see her husband's eyes glaze over?'

'And just about everybody else's.' Emma grinned at Daniel. The centrepiece had been the perfect choice. She'd had no idea about Di's bird interest, or the fact that Andean was named after an owl. However, the piece had jumped out at her when she'd been shopping for a reason.

'Did your grandparents really give it to you?' Daniel asked.

Emma lowered her eyes and shook her head. 'No, sorry, that was a stupid lie. I have no idea why I said that. It sounded better than saying I'd gone out shopping for it.'

Daniel chuckled. 'Good choice. She'd think we were trying too hard if we were buying birds to impress her.' His hands travelled slowly up the sides of her dress, causing a shiver of anticipation to run down her spine. There was a softness in his eyes, a gentleness in his smile as he pulled Emma toward him, his lips brushing her ear. 'You are an amazing wife. We make such a great team.'

His lips met hers briefly before he slowly pulled away. 'How about you go and relax while I clean up the kitchen? You've done enough tonight.' He winked. 'Then I plan to whisk you to bed and show you my appreciation for your efforts.'

Emma smiled as Daniel walked back to the kitchen. He was such a good man: so loving, so generous. He adored her. Her thoughts flicked briefly to the owl. How would he feel if he knew? She pushed the thought out of her mind and concentrated instead on the delicious sensations travelling through her body. The fact that her husband still turned her on after fifteen years was a true sign they were made for each other.

She moved into the dining room. She'd give him a hand before she went upstairs. The table was strewn with empty coffee cups and dessert plates, and as she stacked the dishes she found herself glancing at the owl. Its eyes drilled into her, full of accusation.

She should be thankful to it; the dinner had been a success and Daniel was delighted with her. But the more she stared, the more uneasy it made her feel.

Emma picked it up. Making her way through the dining room to the laundry she walked out of the internal door to the triple garage. She manoeuvred her way past Daniel's BMW and opened the sliding door to an enormous storage cupboard. The boxes were all neatly labelled, most of them marked 'Kitchen Supplies'. She removed the lid of the nearest box and placed the pewter owl on top of a crystal vase – another item acquired from Danes, the large department store. When she looked at the boxes she realised how many items had come from Danes in the past five years. She needed to get smarter, diversify. Twinges of guilt stabbed at her gut. This time she couldn't push thoughts of Daniel out of her mind. She shook her head. Diversify? Was she kidding? Imagine Daniel's disappointment if he discovered her secret. What she needed to do was stop.

Chapter Two

LUCIE

A line of volcanoes hung from a string across the classroom, each representing a child in the Year Two class. The walls were adorned with colourful drawings and a mixture of handwritten stories showcasing contrasting writing styles, from beautiful, well-formed letters to letters of inconsistent sizes and some that were almost illegible.

Lucie peered out of the window as she pegged the last volcano in place. They had fifteen minutes before the bell rang. The schoolyard was its usual mayhem: filled with the laughter and screams of at least a hundred small children while parents wove their way between the multitude of handball games that were taking place.

Lucie turned as the door opened and Anna, the class teacher, arrived. Lucie had worked as a teacher's aide in Anna's class for the past two years and enjoyed the friendly banter that had developed between them. What she'd give to have Anna's shining, straight blond hair; she looked like she'd just walked out of the salon. Lucie wished her own black bob would straighten so perfectly. It didn't matter how long she spent on it in the morning, by the time she arrived at school the humidity had it curling at the ends.

'Morning,' Lucie said.

Anna waved, a coffee cup firmly planted to her lips. She moved over to her desk and dumped her bag in the middle, setting the coffee cup down next to it. 'Saw you staring out the window. Did Tara Green's killer heels catch your attention?'

Lucie smiled and turned to look out of the window again. 'No, I didn't see her. What was she wearing this time?'

'The usual lady-of-the-night outfit.'

Lucie stifled a giggle. 'Jesus, you can't say stuff like that.'

'Why not?' Anna moved to the window. 'Look, there she is. Her skirt hardly covers her bum. Not exactly school-drop-off mate-rial. And look how she walks. No one walks like that unless they've been extremely busy all night in the bedroom. Perhaps that's how they afford the school fees?' She grinned at Lucie.

Lucie moved away from the window and started to take the chairs down from the top of the desks. 'I think you're terrible! The poor woman probably has some posture issue and you're turning her into a whore.' She returned Anna's grin. 'God, I hope she's not. If she was I'd probably be jealous.'

Concern crossed Anna's face. 'Tom's got a few nice, single friends. We could organise a dinner or something?'

Lucie shook her head. 'No, I'm not ready. It's too soon and Noah's still so little – he's not even six yet. I couldn't do that to him. He's been through so much already.'

'Luce, it's been three years. Do you really think it's still too soon? Wouldn't Matt want you to be happy?'

'I can't be happy until I'm ready.' She put the last of the chairs down. 'Quick, skull that coffee – bell's about to ring.'

Anna opened her mouth. 'But—' She was cut off. On cue, the bell rang and the door flew open. Chaos, in the form of twenty-eight seven-year-olds, had arrived.

At five to three Lucie slipped out of the classroom and made her way toward the prep rooms. She sent a private thanks to Matt's parents for insisting they pay Noah's school fees.

'It's what Matt would have wanted,' Walter, Matt's father, had insisted.

Lucie knew this one act meant a lot to Matt's parents. It was part of their grieving process and she was truly grateful. After everything Noah had to deal with, being there for school pick-up was important.

She smiled at the prep mums who were gathered outside the classroom. At exactly three o'clock, three classroom doors opened and an avalanche of small children poured out. Noah's face lit up the moment he saw her.

'Mum, Mum, look what I've got.'

Lucie grinned and scooped him into a big cuddle. 'I think you'll have to introduce me.' She held her hand out to the bear Noah had tucked under one arm.

'This is Mr Hamlet.' Noah held the bear's hand out so Lucie could shake it. 'He's the class mascot. You get him when you've done something amazing and then you have to keep him for the whole weekend and take photos and write a diary.'

'And you got him? What did you do that was so amazing?'

Noah's chest puffed out as he looked up at Lucie. 'I stopped a bully. He teased Emily and I stopped him.'

'Really? Did you tell Mrs Winthrop?'

'No, he did one better.' Lucie looked up to see the teacher, Jane Winthrop, standing behind Noah. Jane rested a hand on Noah's shoulder. 'I overheard him tell the bully to leave Emily alone. He took Emily's hand and ran with her to the playground where they took turns on the slide. He showed what a good friend he is and also exerted wonderful confidence. I am very proud of him.'

Lucie smiled. Noah's cheeks were pink as he beamed. She pulled him close for another hug. 'Well done. You really are amazing.'

'Noah,' Mrs Winthrop said. 'Why don't you go and put Mr Hamlet in your bag while I have a quick chat to Mum?'

Noah smiled and headed off to his bag hook.

Lucie watched him go before turning back to face the teacher.

'So,' Jane said. 'How are you going?'

'Me?'

'Yes, you.'

Lucie was surprised at the direct question. She didn't know Jane very well, she'd really only had contact with her this year because she was Noah's teacher. 'I'm fine. Why? Is there a problem with Noah?'

Jane shook her head. 'Not a problem exactly, but I've noticed that he seems a lot quieter than usual. I wondered if anything had changed at home or if he might be worrying about something?'

Lucie reflected on the last few weeks. Noah had certainly been more difficult than usual, but she'd put that down to him testing boundaries. 'Not that I'm aware of.'

Jane nodded. 'I thought that might be the case. We've been doing a unit on family this term. Would that cause an issue, do you think?'

A lump rose in Lucie's throat. Of course it would cause an issue. She wanted to kick herself. There was no excuse. She hadn't made the time to read through this term's curriculum for the preps.

Jane touched her arm. 'I'm sorry. I'm guessing from your face that this would be the problem.'

Lucie nodded. 'Yes, I imagine it is. How much emphasis has been placed on dads?'

'Some. They've had to draw their family, including extended family, and write a few sentences about each person. Noah included you, his grandparents, some aunts and uncles and his cousins. I kept an eye on him and he seemed fine. He put more detail into his drawings than any other child and seemed happy enough doing it. But earlier this week I noticed he seemed quite withdrawn. I wondered if it might have stirred up some feelings.'

Lucie looked over to where Noah was busy chatting to Mr Hamlet. 'I'm sure it has. I'll talk to him tonight. Thanks for letting me know.' She attempted to smile. 'I feel awful. I should have read the curriculum, been on top of this.'

Jane shook her head. 'We're all busy, we can't do everything, so don't blame yourself. Read through the curriculum when you get a chance and keep in touch.'

Lucie nodded. 'I will, and thank you. Now, we'd better get to swimming.' She called to Noah. 'Come on, we need to pick up Liam and Ruby. You don't want to miss out on the diving.'

Lucie took Noah's hand in hers and together, with Mr Hamlet tucked into Noah's bag, they hurried toward the car park.

Lucie navigated her way out of the crowded aquatic centre, grateful for the hour of silence she could now enjoy before Kate dropped Noah home. Having swimming lessons with his cousins and sharing the drop-offs and pick-ups was a definite advantage, even if it meant she had to put up with her sister-in-law. Ten minutes later Lucie pulled into her driveway. She sighed, taking in the long grass and overgrown flowerbeds. She needed to make time to tidy the garden. Maybe it was a project she and Noah could tackle over the weekend. This had been Matt's area; if he were here it would be immaculate and probably have all sorts of vines and flowers growing over the little weatherboard cottage to hide its age and ugliness. But he wasn't.

Lucie unloaded Noah's schoolbag and stopped to collect the mail before letting herself in through the worn wooden door.

She made her way to the kitchen, dumped Noah's bag, switched on the kettle and sat on a stool. She flicked through the mail. Bills: electricity, phone and internet. She opened the electricity bill. Her stomach dropped. She knew it had gone up a lot, but almost double? Their usage wasn't that much more than this time last year but the cost was huge. It would throw her budget right out. God, she hated this. When Matt was alive money hadn't been an issue. Employed as a wine distributor he'd earnt a good salary and with her wage too they were very comfortable. They'd eaten out every weekend, gone on holidays at least twice a year and paid a good amount off their mortgage. Now, she could barely manage to buy Noah new clothes when he outgrew them. Even working full-time wasn't quite enough to cover their basic outgoings. Matt had promised to set up life insurance but had never got around to it. Instead, he'd left her grieving, with hardly a cent to her name.

The kettle hissed, jolting Lucie from her thoughts. Tea was not going to cut it. She pulled herself up off the stool and opened the fridge. The bottle of sav blanc she'd put in the night before was nicely chilled. Wine. That was all she had left of Matt. Cases and cases of wine; half the garage was home to his passion. They'd invested in a number of boutique wineries in South Australia and, as part of the contracts, Matt had insisted on receiving two cases of each new vintage. She smiled; he'd turned her from tee-totaller to wine drinker – white and red. She could now taste a wine and easily identify many of the flavours. She poured herself a large glass and took it through to the family room. Until three years ago, she had never had to stress about money in her life. She attributed the grey hairs she'd recently plucked to money – or lack of it. She took a sip and closed her eyes, her thoughts returning to Matt. He'd be smiling at her, watching her enjoy his wine. It was her connection to him; the time of day when she could relax, think about him, share her problems and news about Noah. She never would have imagined a simple glass of wine could bring him back to her.

As Lucie finished her wine, the ringtone of her phone broke into her thoughts of Matt. She sighed when she looked at the caller display: Kate.

'Lucie, I'm held up. Can you pick up the kids?'

Lucie put her wineglass down and glanced at her watch. Kate should have picked the kids up ten minutes ago. 'Their lessons have already finished.'

'It's no big deal; Ruby will look after Noah. Just go and get them, would you?' Kate hung up.

Lucie clenched her fists and took a deep breath. She'd never understand Kate. Bossy, self-centred, self-important. She'd done her very best to upstage Lucie and Matt at their own wedding by announcing her pregnancy during the toasts rather than congratulating the bride and groom.

She bit the inside of her cheek. What if she wasn't available to pick the kids up? Kate hadn't even bothered to wait to find out.

Lucie hurried into the kitchen and grabbed her bag and keys. She eyed the wine bottle. It was a third empty. She'd only had one glass, but it was a large one. She hesitated. Should she ring Matt's parents, see if they could pick them up? She shook her head. No, Jan would be at her art class and have the car. She took a deep breath; she felt fine and, as she couldn't afford a taxi each way, there was no other option.

Avoiding the temptation to speed, Lucie was careful to stay a reasonable distance from the car in front. After a third of a bottle, she'd probably be over the limit. She pulled up in front of the aquatic centre. Liam was sitting on the ground, his swim bag next to him. Lucie jumped out of the car and hurried over to him. 'Where's Noah?'

'With Ruby. She's *organising* him – whatever that means.' Liam rolled his ten-year-old eyes. 'I'm starving, did you bring food?'

Lucie ignored him and walked straight into the centre. Her eyes scanned the pool deck and stopped at the entrance to the toilets. There they were. Bloody Kate. How could she leave a five-year-old on his own? She raced over to Noah and Ruby and hugged them to her.

Noah struggled from her grip. 'What are you doing here? Aunty Kate's picking us up.'

'She got held up. Are you okay? Were you scared?'

Noah looked at her as if she was mad. 'Why would I be scared? Aunty Kate's always late. Ruby and I had our showers. And look' – he pointed to his clothes – 'we even got dressed.'

Lucie smiled. Her sister-in-law might have let her down, but her niece certainly hadn't. 'Thanks, Ruby. I'd forgotten how responsible you are.'

Ruby blushed. 'That's okay, you don't have to worry. I'm old enough to look after Noah. Mum says that even though I'm eight, I'm going on thirty.' Her face shone as she replayed her mother's words.

Lucie smiled. Ruby was so innocent, so naïve.

'And we had fun, didn't we, Noah?'

Noah nodded. He adored his cousins. He might not have any siblings but his older cousins were the next best thing.

'Okay then, let's get you all home, shall we?' Lucie grabbed their swim bags and led them back out the front to find Liam.

She took a deep breath as the kids piled into the car. She wished she'd only had a small glass of wine. Driving herself was one thing, but putting three children in danger was another.

'Come on, let's go home, it's late.' Lucie backed out of Kate's driveway. It was with relief that she'd delivered her nephew and niece into the hands of their babysitter. She was furious with Kate for abandoning the kids at the pool. Kate was still at work; so was Brad, her husband. Some days she wondered whether moving to Queensland after Matt's death had been a good idea. She'd done it for Noah, so he could be closer to Matt's family. To give him grandparents, aunts and uncles and cousins to grow up with. If she'd moved back to Canada, to her own family, she would only have had her two brothers. Her parents were both dead and there were no cousins for Noah to play with. But there were times when she wondered if being closer to Matt's family made it harder. The Andrews family were constant reminders of Matt.

'What did you say?' She realised that Noah was talking and she hadn't listened to a word.

'I'm hungry. I'm hungry. Why didn't you bring me any food?'

The whine in Noah's voice grated on Lucie's nerves. She took a deep breath. He was tired and she was already on edge. 'I wasn't expecting to pick you up tonight, love. Aunty Kate was held up so she rang me at the last minute.'

'So, you should have brought me something. I'm starving.'

'I told you to eat a banana on the way to swimming. Next time, perhaps, listen to me.'

'I hate bananas. I want McDonald's. Take me to McDonald's, now.'

Lucie's hands tightened around the steering wheel.

'McDonald's! I said McDonald's!' Noah was shouting.

Lucie glanced in the rear-view mirror. His face was red, his mouth set in his trademark pout.

She spoke calmly. 'Stop shouting. We'll be home in a few minutes. The spaghetti won't take long. You know that's what we eat after swimming, not McDonald's.'

'I hate spaghetti. Hate it. I want McDonald's.' Noah started to cry.

Lucie stopped at a traffic light and tried to ignore the wails that were coming from the back seat. Noah was beyond reasoning with; she just needed to get him home.

She looked in the mirror again and her heart started to pound. 'Noah, be quiet.' She used her loud, strict-teacher voice, knowing it would get his attention. 'There's a policeman behind us. What do you think he'd say if he heard you talking to me like that and then crying because you didn't get your own way?'

Noah's sobs quietened. He wiped his eyes. 'He'd think you were horrible for not taking me to McDonald's.'

Lucie kept her eyes on the mirror. Were they going to pull her over? Her heart raced as the light turned green. She moved forward, following the car in front. No sirens. Her turn-off neared. At the same moment she put on her indicator the flashing light of the police car filled the back window. Her gut churned and she thought she was going be sick. She turned off the main road into her street, hands trembling as she pulled over to the kerb and stopped the car. She opened her window and gulped in some fresh air in an attempt to settle her stomach.

'Why have you stopped, Mum? Have you changed your mind? Are we going to McDonald's?'

Lucie shook her head. 'No, I think the policeman wants to have a chat to me.'

'What policeman? Where is he?'

She glanced in her mirror. The road behind was empty. She sank down, her head resting on the steering wheel. The flashing lights hadn't been for her. Jesus, she'd nearly had a heart attack. Bloody Kate, it was all her fault. She could just imagine her holier-than-thou reaction if she had been breathalysed.

'Are we going to McDonald's?'

Lucie turned to face Noah. She took a deep breath.

'No, love. Let's go home, make some dinner and enjoy some stories, shall we?'

The hope drained from Noah's face and it screwed up in anger. He lashed out and kicked the back of Lucie's seat.

'Stop it,' Lucie said, as the small feet pushed into her back again and again.

'I won't!' Noah screamed.

Lucie turned away from him and faced the road. If Kate had picked the kids up as planned she'd be at home with dinner ready for Noah, enjoying a glass of wine. She was about to restart the car when the full force of both Noah's feet pushed into her back.

'Ow!' Lucie's face scrunched up in pain. His foot had managed to press right on the section of her shoulder blade she'd strained lifting a heavy box earlier in the week. She turned and faced Noah. 'Stop it immediately!'

Tears ran down Noah's face as he kicked at her seat again.

Lucie grabbed his leg and squeezed it. 'I'll let go when you agree to behave. Do you hear me?'

He continued to cry.

She increased the pressure on his leg. 'I said, do you hear me?'

Noah nodded, his eyes wide as tears continued to stream down his face.

'We are going to go home. You will eat your spaghetti and you will stop this awful behaviour, do you understand?'

Noah nodded again and pulled at Lucie's hand. 'You're hurting me, Mummy. Let go.' He looked at her, his eyes wide. 'I'll behave.'

Lucie released her grip, noting the red marks on his leg. Her stomach churned again. She turned away. She'd hurt her son, actually hurt him. Something she'd said she'd never do. She'd have to make it up to him. He was pushing her buttons, but she'd never resorted to anything physical. Her hands trembled as she fumbled with the key to start the car. The day was not turning out as she'd planned.

Minutes later they pulled into their driveway. Lucie pushed open the front door and Noah ran past her straight to his room.

'Dinner will be ready in ten minutes,' she called. She walked into the kitchen. The bottle she'd opened earlier still sat on the bench. The wine, which had been a major contributor to her stressful afternoon, was exactly what she needed to calm herself down.

She picked it up and poured herself a glass. It was warm. Opening the freezer, she added a few ice blocks. Sacrilegious, Matt would say. Lucie thought back to the nightmare car ride. There were so many times throughout the day she needed more than the memory of Matt. She needed his help to parent and Noah needed his never-ending patience and understanding. He was so much calmer than her. Even when Noah was two and throwing himself on the ground for the sixth tantrum of the day, Matt would wait it out. It didn't ruffle him in the least. She sighed. How was she going to manage Noah when he was a teenager if she couldn't manage him now?

Chapter Three

EMMA

Emma slipped her phone back into her bag and signalled to the waitress.

'What's the hurry?' Cass asked. 'We're supposed to be having a long, lazy lunch.'

Emma smiled. 'It's almost four thirty; I'm pretty sure what we've just had constitutes a long, lazy lunch. Sorry, lovely, I'm going to have to go. I need to talk to Daniel.'

Cass frowned. 'What's so important that it can't wait?'

Emma bit her lip; she wasn't sure she wanted to go into this with Cass. 'It's my parents. I had a text from my sister about their wedding anniversary. It's next weekend and she wanted to check we were coming.'

'We?' Cass's eyes widened.

'Yes, we. That's why I need to talk to Daniel.' Emma placed her platinum credit card on the small tray and watched the waitress retreat to the service area. She turned her attention back to Cass. 'Look, I haven't mentioned it to him yet. I wasn't even planning to go myself but Simone's putting pressure on me. It's their fortieth anniversary so we should be making a big deal out of it. I was just going to send a gift, but Simone thinks I should be part of the celebration.'

'Of course you should,' Cass said. 'I know you don't see them often but this is important. Do you think Daniel will go?'

Emma shook her head. 'I'd say it's very unlikely. I just hope he won't be upset that I'm going.'

'For God's sake, they're your parents whether he likes it or not. Of course you're going.'

'It's not that simple.' Emma shuddered, thinking back to their last visit. Visiting their home town brought back too many painful memories for Daniel. He wouldn't talk to her about them, instead he withdrew, spent as much time on his own as possible. It had taken five weeks last time for him to come out of what she thought was a kind of depression. She didn't want to take him there again.

'It should be. Even though you haven't seen them for a while, you still love them and get along, don't you?'

Emma nodded. 'Yes, of course. The problem is, it brings up his past. Life would be a lot simpler if we came from different towns. It's really the only thing that causes problems between us. Without our background issues we'd always be happy.'

'Happy?' Cass put her wineglass down and stared at Emma. 'This from the woman who runs her life according to her husband's wishes and normally dresses to his specifications.' She pointed at Emma's plate. 'Eats rabbit food to stay slim, doesn't work because he won't let her and is denied the one thing she really wants – a baby.'

It was as if she'd been slapped. She stared at Cass. 'Do you really think that's how it is? That Daniel treats me that way?'

Cass shrugged. 'That's the impression you've always given me.'

A heaviness settled in the pit of Emma's stomach. She knew she'd spoken to Cass from time to time about some of her frustrations but she hadn't realised she'd painted such a horrible picture of Daniel. 'What about all the good things I've told you? How he showers me with flowers and presents, surprises me with romantic weekends away? He adores me, Cass, I know that. He doesn't tell me how to dress or what to eat; and work and a baby, they're just not a priority right now.'

'For him, maybe. But what about what you want? And then there's your family. That's a huge part of who you are and he's asking you, or should I say *telling* you, to leave them all behind.'

Emma sighed. 'Again, it's not like that. It's a hard one. His past comes with so much baggage. He can't deal with it. The fact that my family are part of his background is just too difficult for him. I knew that from the start. This isn't something he's just dropped on me.'

'And you accepted it?'

Emma nodded.

'From where I sit you should stand up for what you need. Things change; what we need changes. At the moment it seems that everything's on his terms. Look' – she held up her glass – 'it's probably the wine talking, ignore me.'

Easier said than done. Was she really that weak? Was Daniel in charge? No, she'd known from the outset that their background was the one area that was going to be difficult. Daniel's father, the town of Golden Bay and the people in it, were something he needed to leave behind, and she needed to detach herself, too, for their relationship to work. He hadn't demanded it, it was just how it had to be. She loved Daniel. They'd built his success together. They were a team. He acknowledged and respected that. Talk of their families was generally the only time that issues arose between them.

She thought of her father; he wasn't like Daniel. He was a gentle man, and if anything her mother was in control of that relationship. She couldn't remember a time she'd ever seen him demand anything. That was one of the things that had attracted her to Daniel – he was so different from her family. He was driven, ambitious, successful. Running a fish and chip shop as her parents had for forty years wasn't her definition of success. Yes, she'd love him to agree to let her work, or have a baby, but she knew he wasn't saying no, he was just saying not right now. He wanted the business to be bigger, for him to be able to step aside, employ a manager so he could be more hands on when they did have a family. She could hardly argue with that.

'What's happening for the wedding anniversary?'

Emma was relieved by the change of topic. 'I don't know much, other than it's at the golf club. Simone's arranged everything.'

'Your sister? Is she older or younger?'

'She's four years younger than me. My only contribution so far has been opening my chequebook so I'm hoping she's got it all under control.'

'Daniel doesn't want you going but he's okay with you spending money on it?'

Emma hesitated, grateful for the interruption of the waitress returning with her card and receipt. She signed the docket and stood up. 'Come on, I've got to go. If I'm going to this thing I need to get organised.'

'Good,' Cass said. 'You need to live your life, too, not allow the world to revolve around Daniel.' She leant forward and hugged Emma. 'Thanks for lunch, let's catch up for a coffee during the week. Make sure you remind yourself that you're equal partners in your marriage. Don't let Daniel dictate what you can and can't do.'

Emma smiled, giving her a mock salute. 'Yes, boss.' She watched Cass cross the car park. When it came to having a rational discussion about their families and hometown, Cass's instructions were easier said than done.

'I don't want you going.' Daniel opened the fridge and pulled out a Corona. 'We discussed this before and we agreed. Our families are our past – our unpleasant pasts.' He opened the bottle and took a swig.

Emma stared at her husband and considered her options. Which tactic would upset him the least? 'Look, I understand you want nothing to do with your dad, but my family's different. I'm still in touch with them and I want to see them every now and then. This is a really special day for Mum and Dad and they want us all to be there. I certainly don't expect you to come.'

Daniel snorted.

'I'm going to head up on Thursday and help with the organising. I'll be back Sunday night. It's only a four-hour drive.'

Daniel's face seemed to be getting darker with every word that came out of her mouth.

'The next big one is their fiftieth so there are a lot of years without obligation in between. I'm due to visit, it's been ages.'

Daniel shook his head. 'No, you aren't. You haven't seen them in years and don't need to now.' His eyes filled with pain as they searched Emma's.

She swallowed. Cass was wrong; this wasn't about Daniel controlling her, it was about Daniel avoiding the pain that these discussions and visits brought with them. She knew it was tough for him but she needed to go and she hoped to be going with his blessing. She moved closer to him and stroked the front of his shirt. 'Come on, babe. I'll be away a couple of days, that's all. If I don't go they'll be really upset.'

Daniel closed his eyes as Emma's hands moved down to his legs. She applied more pressure as her hands moved behind and cupped his bottom. He hardened against her and groaned. 'God, you know how to talk me into anything, don't you?'

Emma laughed as her hands moved to the front of his pants and unzipped him. 'If only I'd realised how easy you were.'

Daniel opened his eyes and his faced softened as he took Emma's hands in his. 'Go, but remember, from my perspective Golden Bay and the people who live there don't exist. I don't want to know anything about it, Em.'

Emma nodded. The pain in his eyes was real. This wasn't about control, it was about self-preservation.

Emma's stomach churned as she drove past a new sign welcoming visitors to Golden Bay. She was nervous. It had been at least two years since she'd visited for her mum's sixtieth. Although she shouldn't feel guilty. There was nothing stopping her family from visiting her. They were quite capable of making the four-hour journey. A vision of Daniel, his arms crossed, face dark and unsmiling, popped into her head. Okay, so maybe there was one rather large and intimidating reason why her family might not feel comfortable enough to visit. He'd withdrawn from her since their discussion about going to the party. She just hoped he would have put it out of his mind and returned to his normal self by the time she returned on Sunday.

Emma drove down the main street and slowed, noticing the improvements that had been made to the town. It was quite a transformation. The old shopfronts had been replaced with new signage. There were at least three cafés in the strip; the last time she had visited there were none. Tables and chairs sprawled out on to the widened footpaths and people laughed and chatted, enjoying their coffees in the afternoon sunshine. Golden Bay looked modern.

Emma continued down the main street, past the bakery and the fruit shop and on to the butcher's, owned by Harvey, Daniel's father. She wondered if he was busy serving customers. She was married to his son yet hardly knew him. She'd met him once prior to their wedding, and then on her wedding day when he'd briefly attempted to welcome her into the family. Daniel had kept the conversation short. Then he'd told her that his family included just the two of them, not his father or anyone else from their past. It was a surprise he'd even agreed to invite anyone from their families to their wedding. Initially he'd wanted to elope, to avoid the issues of having to deal with them, but when he realised how important the wedding day was to Emma he had given in.

To Emma, Harvey seemed like a nice man, but she was married to Daniel and respected his decision to leave his past behind. To a lesser extent she'd felt the same way when she'd left Golden Bay at the age of seventeen. She'd moved to Brisbane with a girlfriend and they'd both picked up temp work. Emma smiled at the memories of those two years when they lived, worked and partied together. She'd met Daniel at the races toward the end of her second year in Brisbane. He'd later told her his first inclination was to run the moment she mentioned she'd grown up in Golden Bay. But with six years between them, though they had vague memories of each other growing up, they'd been at different stages in their schooling and moved in different circles of friends. So he hadn't run; he'd told her she was so damn sexy it just wasn't possible. The feeling had been mutual.

Emma slowed as she approached the fish and chip shop – her parents' livelihood. She pulled over, amazed at the transformation that had taken place. Any resemblance to the old family business, including the big red sign that had boldly announced 'Fish and Chips', was gone. In its place a new aqua and black sign, announcing 'The Café', glistened in the sunshine. Chairs and tables adorned the footpath and the line to order spilt out of the front door. Their clientele appeared to be mainly teenagers dressed in school uniform. Some had chips but the majority were holding juices. She hadn't noticed a juice bar in the main street but Golden Bay had really moved with the times. She restarted the car and drove past the shop. The crowd in front of the counter prevented her from seeing if her parents were there. She would go to their house rather than dropping into the shop. She didn't need the whole town witnessing her homecoming and turning it into small-town gossip.

When Emma pulled into the driveway of number forty-four she found herself smiling. The rest of Golden Bay might have been modernised but the family home looked the same. The old Queenslander stood high on the hill overlooking the headland and turbulent waters of the surf beach. She made her way up the stairs toward the front door, noticing one of the walls had patches of different colour paint slapped on it. Paint samples? Perhaps the house was about to get a facelift. She remembered it being painted the current cream with green railings when she was in high school. She'd probably been about fourteen so it made sense that, twenty years on, the paintwork looked tired and in need of some work.

The front door was flung open as she stepped from the top step on to the verandah. She was enclosed in a tight hug before she'd even had time to say hello. The smell of Charlie perfume told Emma she was home. It was strangely comforting. What wasn't so comforting was her mother's body. Hugging Maggie was usually a challenge, her wobbly belly making it almost impossible. But today Emma's arms not only went around but she could feel her mother's ribs through her shirt. She pulled back, looking her mother up and down.

'You're so thin. You look so different.' Emma had been going to say 'amazing', but looking at her mother's face she wasn't so sure. She looked tired, her skin pale. 'Are you okay, Mum?'

Maggie laughed. 'Here I was thinking you'd like the new and improved me. A lot of work's gone into changing my shape, you know.'

Emma smiled, not quite sure whether to believe her mother's jolly mood. 'So you're okay?'

'I've been a bit unwell here and there, but I'm in my sixties, it's expected. My new figure is down to my fitness regime.' She took Emma by the hand. 'Come in and say hi to Dad; I'll tell you all about my new lifestyle later.'

Emma allowed her mother to lead her into the family room where her dad sat, eyes closed, in his favourite armchair. His eyes sprang open as they entered the room and he leapt to his feet, rushing to engulf Emma in a bear hug.

'Ems, my lovely Ems. You don't know how good it is to see you. We're so pleased you came.'

Emma's chest tightened. It had been easy sitting at home in Brisbane to convince herself that her parents probably didn't care if she visited or not. Her dad's overwhelming welcome suggested they did.

Ten minutes later Emma sat across from her parents, nursing a strong cup of tea. The only way to have it, according to her mother. 'The town looks amazing. So does the fish and chip shop, or should I say *The Café*. When did all the upgrades take place?'

'When Andrew Myers took over the town.' Maggie laughed. 'Isn't that right, Brian?'

'Sure is, love.' He turned to Emma. 'Andrew Myers, well, Drew as he likes to be called, is a young hotshot from Sydney. He came into the shop when he first arrived asking for a good spot to surf, so we had a chat. He's a marketer, whatever that might be. Long story short, he decided to stay. Got caught up with small-town life but then decided we all needed to be brought into the twenty-first century, so he got things rolling.'

'It's been eye-opening,' Maggie added. 'He held a meeting in the town hall and outlined his vision.' She turned to her husband. 'That's the word he used, isn't it?'

Brian nodded.

'Anyway,' she continued, 'everyone assumed he was crazy. Imagine trying to get the townsfolk to spend money on our shops, which were perfectly good as far as we were concerned. But he did. He worked so hard for all of us. He organised a number of government and community grants for doing up the streets and shopfronts. The only contribution the shop owners have had to make was the renovations they've done on the inside.'

'Really?' Emma asked. 'What was in it for him?' It seemed strange that someone with no links to the town or any financial interest in it would go to such an effort.

'Nothing,' replied her father. 'He said he had a vision for living in a small town that offered some of the modern conveniences of the city but couldn't find what he was looking for. When he stumbled across Golden Bay he decided he'd fix it to his own liking.' Brian chuckled. 'And fix it he did.'

'The town's reaction has been wonderful,' Maggie said. 'Once the footpaths were widened and the shops tarted up, the shop owners wanted his ideas on how to improve the insides. You'll have to go in and have a look; we've really been transformed, all thanks to Drew.'

'Mind you, not everyone jumped at the idea to start with,' Brian added. 'It took nearly a year of planning and convincing. The pharmacy, greengrocer's and newsagent's only came on board once they saw the improvements that were being made to the shops around them. They realised they were missing out.'

'What does this Drew do, when he's not saving run-down old towns? How does he finance his lifestyle if he's going around doing everything for free?'

'We're not sure,' Maggie said. 'Of course there's been a lot of speculation. That he's inherited a lot, made his money on the stock market, has investments. Who knows? When it comes to his personal life he's quite private. He loves a chat about the surf or his other passion, birds, but other than that he keeps to himself.'

'Well, I can't wait to see inside the shop. It was packed when I drove past. Although to be honest, most of the kids out the front were drinking juices, taking up your seats. Is there a juice bar in town?'

Brian laughed. 'No, but you can get juices. Another of Drew's great ideas. He's turning the town a bit healthier, too.'

'I'm surprised he hasn't shut you guys down. I doubt fish and chips fall into his idea of a healthy town. Better watch out or he'll turn you into a health food shop before you know it.'

Emma caught the look that passed between her parents. She put her tea down on the side table. 'You're kidding – it's still a fish and chip shop, isn't it?'

'Yes, of course, but we have updated the menu a bit,' said her mother.

'Might not find that old Chiko Roll you used to love on the menu these days,' Brian added. 'We still do the basics – fish, chips, burgers – but we've added a whole new line. Sushi, salads, a few vegetarian dishes and of course the juices, which you saw. It's been incredible for the business; we owe him a lot.'

Emma's mouth dropped open. 'Sushi? Juices? How long have I been gone for? How come you've never mentioned any of this?'

Her parents exchanged an uneasy glance, her father becoming the spokesperson for the two of them. 'Em, you're usually busy when we chat, love. We enjoy hearing what you've been up to but by the time you've filled us in it's usually time for you to head off to something. We weren't sure how interested you'd be. We know you've never been too keen on the shop.'

Emma swallowed. Did she really show no interest in her parents' lives? She rang them every few weeks, usually while Daniel was at work, and yes, she often talked more about what she was doing, but that was because she assumed they were doing the same old thing they'd always done. She did her best to smile at them as her stomach clenched. Was she that self-absorbed? 'I'm here now and I can't wait for you to show me inside the shop.'

Maggie covered her mouth as a coughing fit wracked her body.

'Are you okay, Mum?'

Maggie nodded. She stopped and stood up. 'Of course I am, just need a glass of water. I'll get that and then I need to sort out some things in the kitchen for dinner. Why don't you two have a chat while I get organised?'

Emma nodded, lost in her own thoughts. Her parents' lives had completely changed and she'd missed the entire transformation. Although she imagined they could argue the same about her. Had she made them feel excluded and unimportant too? She blinked away the tears that threatened. It was easy to avoid thoughts of her family when they were at a distance, but sitting here with them it was a different thing altogether.

Brian pulled himself up out of his chair. 'How about I go and get your bags, love? You can settle in before we have dinner. It'll just be the three of us tonight. We invited Simone and Johnno but they couldn't make it. Tomorrow we can show you around the place and then Sunday's the big event.' He rolled his eyes. 'Sim's gone a bit over the top we think.'

Emma snapped back to the present and smiled at her father. 'Over the top? Forty years is a big one, it *should* be over the top. How is Simone?' Emma had hardly spoken to her sister since Maggie's sixtieth. They exchanged Christmas and birthday wishes, usually via card or email, but that was all. They hadn't fallen out, they just lived very different lives.

Her father's eyes lit up. 'She's good; you'll see for yourself tomorrow. She would have liked to have come tonight but she was too tired.'

'Too tired?' Simone too tired? That was new. Her sister usually never sat still. She rushed from client to client, chopping their hair and talking a million miles an hour, before dashing off to play netball or tennis or join friends at the pub for drinks.

Brian nodded. 'I'd better get these bags sorted.'

She watched as her father made his way out on to the verandah and headed down the steps toward her car. She sat alone in the family room, its faded wallpaper and worn rugs suggesting not a lot had changed in the past seventeen years. How misleading it was.

Emma caught an image of her reflection in the shop window and closed her mouth. It was quite likely that it had been hanging open all morning. The tour of the town had been a real eye-opener. The fact that so many changes and improvements had been accomplished in a relatively short time was absolutely extraordinary. They'd stopped for a coffee at the local bakery, which now boasted the addition of a quite upmarket café. Emma remembered the days when it was a treat to go to the bakery and buy a heated Four'n'Twenty pie. Now the warming ovens displayed six varieties of pies, huge sausage rolls with their flaky pastry glistening under the lights, and a number of other hot pastries, all made on-site. On top of that they also offered gourmet sandwiches, overflowing with meat and salads, and a large selection of cakes and mouthwatering slices.

'Did you want to pop into the butcher's, say hi to Harvey?'

Emma stared at her father. 'I don't think so. I hardly know him. It would be awkward.'

'I know, love, but he is your father-in-law and he knows you're here. It would be more polite than running into him for the first time at the party tomorrow.'

'The party? He's invited?'

'Of course he is. Daniel may choose to live his own life but Harvey's part of the town, he's part of our lives.'

Emma nodded. Of course he would be, Golden Bay was a small town and her parents knew everyone. 'No, he might be busy. I'll see him at the party, it's no big deal.' No big deal for her, but certainly a big deal for Daniel. She pushed the thought out of her mind and smiled at her father. 'Now take me to The Café. I was blown away by the outside yesterday and I want to see what you've done on the inside.'

If Emma had been impressed by the rest of the town, her parents' business was no different. After admiring the shop's new frontage, she turned to her father. 'Who did the sign? It looks great.'

Brian was standing tall, his chest puffed out. 'We used a contact of Drew's. He brought him up from Melbourne to have a look around the town and a week later a truck arrived with all the new signs.' He chuckled at the memory. 'He called it the big reveal. He spoke about the vision for each of our businesses and then revealed the signs. You should have seen us: the oohing and aahing was instant confirmation that they were a success. We wanted them all put up straight away, but Drew said no. He wouldn't let any of us put them up until the final changes had been made to our shops. He said it would be a message to the town that the shop was complete and they'd better rush in and see for themselves, and of course buy something at the same time.'

'It looks great; so do all the tables and chairs.' The widened footpath hosted eight tables, each surrounded by four chairs. 'They're an improvement on the bench.'

Brian laughed. 'Yes, Drew wasn't that impressed when he first came to see us. I think his exact words were "What, you expect me to eat on a bench?"'

32

Emma laughed. The bench was the waiting area in the shop. Customers placed an order and then took a seat on the long bench. Eating in hadn't been an option, it had been takeaway only.

'We do still have a waiting bench.' Brian held open the shop door. 'Come in and have a look.'

Once again, Emma found herself having to close her mouth. This was not the shop she'd spent her teenage years trying to avoid. Not the shop she'd hated with a passion that had earnt her the nicknames of Battered Em and Olive Oil. Grease Monkey had also been a favourite with some of the boys. She'd spent most of her pocket money on spray deodorants, covering up the greasy oil smells that attached themselves to her hair and skin. This shop smelled fresh and clean. Granted, they hadn't started cooking yet but previously when you opened the door you'd be hit in the face with the smell of hot oil – regardless of the time of day.

A door opened at the back of the shop and her mother appeared carrying two large bowls. 'Hello, love. What do you think?'

Emma shook her head. 'I can't believe this is the same business.'

Maggie laughed. 'I know, neither can I. They practically gutted it during the renovations so I'm not sure if you can really call it the same shop. Take her through, Brian.' Maggie pointed to the door she'd just come through.

'Why? Have you upgraded the parking area, too?'

Maggie laughed and placed the bowls of salad in the refrigerated glass cabinet. 'Sort of.'

Emma followed her father through the door, expecting to step out into the car park. Instead she walked into an industrial-sized kitchen. A huge workbench acted as an island in the middle of the room. The cooking appliances, deep fryer, grill and ovens lined the back wall. Emma turned and poked her head back into the front room of the shop. Sure enough, the fryers were gone. She hadn't even noticed. She walked around the kitchen, admiring the cleanliness and high-end appliances. This must have cost a fortune. How could her parents afford this?

Her father must have read her mind. 'The shop's done okay over the years, love. We decided to invest our money in ourselves rather than risk it to shares or some big business to lose it for us. Our business has increased by forty percent since the upgrades. It won't take us much longer and this will all be paid off.'

Maggie pushed the door open and re-entered the kitchen. 'We even do catering now.'

'Really? People want fish and chips delivered to them for events?' Emma couldn't imagine hosting, or attending for that matter, an event that required her to eat fish and chips. Neither would the wives of Daniel's colleagues. They spent hours at the gym each week and were more likely to have fat sucked out of their arses than allow it to pass their lips.

Maggie laughed and handed her a glossy brochure. 'No, fish and chips aren't usually on the catering menu. You'll see all of the options there.'

Emma read through the menu: five different salads, a variety of sushi rolls to choose from, soup, pastries, sandwiches and desserts.

'We don't do the pastries or desserts,' Maggie added. 'They come from the bakery. We're working with them quite a bit these days.'

Emma stared at her parents. Who were these people? Her country-bumpkin parents, talking like successful business owners.

Brian laughed. 'You look surprised.'

'If I'd been away for ten years and come back to the town all spruced up and the businesses all modern and thriving, I'd understand. But I haven't been away that long; I was here for Mum's sixtieth.'

'Mum just turned sixty-five, love; it has been a while.'

Emma stared at him. Five years? She'd been sure it was only two. 'Sixty-five? I hadn't realised.'

Her father smiled. 'You're busy, we understand that. Daniel and his high-flying career, the city life. This backward little town didn't appeal to you as a teenager, we hardly expect it to appeal now.'

Emma couldn't speak. Tears pricked the back of her eyes. He was too nice. Her father was just too nice. If she ever did get her wish of having children, she could only hope Daniel would be as understanding with his daughter. Her parents had let her live her own life, never once complaining that they'd been excluded.

'Now, why don't I make you one of our raved-about juices. Go into the service area and you'll see them all listed on the blackboard. Let me know which one you'd like.'

Emma read through the list of juices, all scrawled in fancy chalk writing. She wondered who'd done that. It didn't look like either of her parents' writing.

'Simone,' Maggie said. 'That's her handiwork. In fact, the juices were her idea.' She laughed. 'She was on some health kick at the time that we were making changes and suggested them. In all honesty, I think she was sick to death of cleaning her juicer so this was an easy way to get them for free and not have to clean up afterward.'

Emma smiled. 'Simone has always been good at problem-solving.'

Her mother cleared her throat. 'Yes, well, turned out, regardless of her motivation, the juice bar has brought in a lot of business. We added a coffee machine, too, so we could make fancy coffee. I must say I still prefer my cup of Nescafé, but that's just me. The younger people today like things different. Or more likely they just like saying all the fancy names.' Her lips curled at the edges as she put on a deep voice. 'A tall, skinny, mocha, soy latte, thanks, with an espresso shot on the side.'

Brian walked back into the service area to find them laughing. He was carrying a tray with three green juices. 'I decided for you. I've made you our favourite, although I can make something else if you'd prefer?'

Emma took a juice from the tray and eyed it with suspicion. It was very green. She took a sip. 'Mmm, delicious. What's in it? I can taste ginger and lemon with something else. Cucumber?'

Brian winked. 'Plus kale and apple and a few other secret ingredients.'

'It's no wonder the juices are doing well if they taste like this.' She took her drink over to the new bench, which had been set up for customers waiting for takeaway orders. She sat down and ran her hand along the blue fibreglass edge. 'Now this is unique.'

'Drew again,' Brian said. 'It was one of his old longboards. Said he had the perfect thing for us and turned up with this. I told him he was mad. Who wants to sit on a surfboard while they're waiting? Turns out I was wrong; everyone loves it. They are allowed to sit at the tables and chairs while they wait but the majority of the time they choose the board.'

'So, is this Drew coming tomorrow?' Emma asked. 'I'd be interested to meet him.'

'Yes, he should be there. I'll make sure I introduce you.'

Emma nodded. She *would* be interested to meet him. He seemed to have taken over the town. She wondered what his story was. You didn't do this amount of work for no return. 'I'd better head over to Simone's and see what needs to be organised for tomorrow.' Emma stood up and placed her empty juice glass on the counter. 'Thanks for the tour, and the juice. I'm still in shock, I think. The shop's blown me away; so have you two.' She impulsively threw her arms around her parents. 'I'll see you this afternoon, okay?'

'No worries, love. We'll be here until about two and then home after that,' Brian said.

Emma pulled back and stared at her father. 'Both of you? Who's looking after the shop?'

Maggie laughed. 'The staff, dear. We're not required all the time.'

'Yes, of course.' Emma gave her mother a quick kiss on the cheek before heading out to her car. *Of course?* Was her mother for real? Her entire childhood had been spent with one parent or the other always at the shop. With the exception of a rare family holiday, the only day in the entire year they'd spent as a family had been Christmas Day. She was *really* looking forward to meeting Drew Myers – it appeared he could perform miracles.

Emma's black Audi glided into Simone's driveway a few minutes after leaving The Café. She wondered what it would be like to live so close, to be so much a part of each other's lives. She shuddered; it was unlike her to be so sentimental. She knew exactly what it would be like, it was the very reason she'd left Golden Bay. She needed to keep things in perspective: this was the life she detested. Small-town mentality, everyone knowing each other's business.

She took a deep breath before opening the car door. Everything had changed so much in the last five years. From what her parents had said at dinner the previous night, Simone was still working in the same job and still living in the house she and Johnno purchased six years ago. At least one person in the town hadn't changed. Although her parents had exchanged some strange looks when talking about Simone, which they wouldn't elaborate on when Emma questioned them.

The front door opened before Emma had the chance to knock. Simone hesitated and then burst out laughing.

Emma realised her shock was clearly visible on her face. How could it not be? Simone was pregnant. Ready-to-pop pregnant.

'Hey, sis, you're going to be an aunt. Surprise!'

Simone was still laughing as Emma followed her through the house into the kitchen.

'I'm just making a coffee. Want one?'

A stiff drink would be more appropriate, but she nodded. 'Thanks.' She sat herself down on one of the kitchen stools. Why didn't her parents tell her, or Simone, for that matter? This was such big news.

Simone lugged her bulky body across the kitchen to get the cups before turning to face Emma. 'Make yourself comfortable while the pregnant lady waits on you, won't you?'

Emma stood up. 'Sorry. I think I'm in permanent shock or having some weird dream. First the changes to the town, then Mum and Dad, the business entrepreneurs, and now you, pregnant. I feel like I've entered someone else's family and life. How come no one told me what's going on?'

'I rang you and left three messages, told you I had news. You never called back.'

Emma swallowed. She had a vague memory of planning to return Simone's calls but never getting around to it. Still, this was huge news. 'Why didn't Mum or Dad say something?'

'I told them not to – I wanted to be the one to tell you.' Simone shrugged. 'When I didn't hear from you I figured you weren't interested.'

Heat flooded Emma's face. 'What? Of course I'm interested. Imagine if it were you excluded from everything. Being excluded from your wedding was bad enough.'

Simone handed her a coffee cup. 'Bring it outside, the chairs are more comfortable for my elephant body.'

Emma followed her out on to the verandah. A nagging, nauseous feeling had developed in her stomach. She'd always felt like an outsider and having the pregnancy kept from her confirmed she was.

Simone's eyes softened as she looked at Emma. 'You weren't excluded from the wedding, you know that. Johnno and I didn't want one. We eloped; no one was there. For God's sake, our witnesses were two gardeners working at the hotel we were married at. I don't know why you're so shocked about what's happening now. You bolted out of here as quickly as you could and we rarely hear from you. You've hardly shown any interest in Mum and Dad, or me for that matter, in years. What did you think? That we'd all just stagnate, waiting for you to return before we got on with our lives?'

Yes, Emma had assumed they would all remain stagnant in their small-town ruts with no significant changes in their lives, but she couldn't say this to Simone. 'Of course not. Like I said, the changes are just a bit of a shock.' She forced a smile. 'A wonderful shock, mind you. When are you due?'

'In about six weeks.'

'Six weeks! And you're organising this whole party? Why didn't you say something? I could have helped.'

Simone grinned. 'You did help. Don't worry, I haven't strained anything other than my hand to write the cheques for the party. Your contribution was invaluable. In fact, it covered everything.'

Emma stared at her sister then forced a laugh. 'So, the party's on me? Good, that absolves me of any guilt I was beginning to feel.' It wasn't so much guilt as exclusion she was feeling. How could her parents not have mentioned Simone's pregnancy? She did her best to keep a smile on her face. 'Tell me more about the baby.'

Simone rubbed her belly. 'It's a she. Other than spewing my guts up for twelve weeks and now waddling around like a fat duck, all's going well. Johnno's really excited; in fact he can't wait. He's been buying every baby device and toy you can imagine. This is going to be one spoilt little girl. Mum and Dad are pretty excited, too. They assumed you'd be the first one to give them a grandkid so they're chuffed that it's me and the baby will be close by. Guess if you did have one they'd never see it anyway.'

Heat rose up the back of Emma's neck. 'Of course they would.' She'd hardly keep her parents away from their grandchild.

Simone rolled her eyes. 'What, every five years?'

Emma was silent.

Simone relented. 'Sorry. Tell me about Danny. Still conquering the business world?'

Emma relaxed as the conversation moved to safer ground. Half an hour later, Simone pulled herself up and motioned for Emma to follow. 'Come on, I'll show you the nursery. Johnno will be asking you tomorrow what you think about it, he's giving everyone the tour. I told him you wouldn't be interested but he still insisted I show you.'

'Why do you think I wouldn't be interested?'

'Dunno, didn't think you were into babies. Certainly can't imagine you with one. Imagine it puking on that designer shirt – you'd have a fit.'

Emma followed Simone into the bright pink nursery. When had the family labelled her as shallow and materialistic? Her sister couldn't imagine her as a mum and Daniel did everything he could to avoid the topic. Even Cass joked about how it would cramp her style. She tried to swallow the lump forming in her throat. Maybe they were right: perhaps she just wasn't cut out for it.

The sun sank, turning the sky above the hinterland a fiery orange as Emma stood on the balcony overlooking the eighteenth green. A group of four were finishing up their round. A cheer went up as one of the men dropped a putt from at least five metres. She had to hand it to Simone, she'd chosen a good event planner for the occasion. Her parents were overwhelmed at the fuss that had been made of them. Maggie was in tears the moment she'd walked in to find their family and friends, which included most of the town, on their feet, clapping the couple's wonderful achievement. Her mother's sixtieth was the last time Emma had seen her extended family. With them all scattered throughout New South Wales and Queensland it wasn't unusual to go years without seeing them.

Simone had given a lovely speech about her parents. About the family holidays they'd enjoyed as children, that their parents had attended every school event they'd been involved in and how they'd supported her and Johnno through the early years of their marriage and now her pregnancy. Emma was impressed: even at thirty-four weeks pregnant, she'd carried it off beautifully. She'd had to wipe away a tear as Simone talked about the hardworking couple, their selflessness and endless encouragement of their children.

'Beautiful spot here, isn't it?'

The rich, deep voice interrupted Emma's thoughts. She turned to find herself face to face with Daniel's father. She wasn't sure whether to shake his hand or lean in and hug him. She opted to do neither.

'Been a while, Emma. How are you?'

Emma smiled. 'Good, Harvey. How about you?'

He shrugged. 'Can't complain. Shop's doing well, golf handicap's holding strong and the fish are biting most days. That's me about summed up. How's that boy of mine?'

'Daniel's good. Always busy and travelling with work.'

Harvey laughed. 'Don't think I'll ever get used to him being called Daniel. Was called Danny until the day he shot out of here without looking back. Didn't even tell me he was going. Bet you didn't know that. Not sure if he was worried I'd try to stop him or if he just didn't care. Found out from Doreen at the post office. Came in to buy her meat that morning and asked me if I was excited or sad that Danny was off to the big smoke to make his fortune.' The bitter trace in Harvey's voice was replaced with genuine sadness as he spoke.

'It's not easy at that age to go against your parents' wishes,' Emma said. 'Perhaps that's why he didn't talk to you.'

Harvey nodded. 'Loyal, aren't you?' He smiled. 'That's important. My Caroline was loyal. I could have murdered the mayor and she would have stood by me, defending me to everyone who'd listen. Danny's a lucky boy.'

Emma swallowed. Daniel spoke as if his father had no feelings, was a loser. It was one thing to sit in their comfortable home talking about Harvey, but speaking to this well-presented man was a different matter.

'Haven't heard from him since your mum's sixtieth, you know. Not a word.'

'Come on, Harvey, what about your birthday and Christmas? I know it's not much but it is contact.'

'A card from you, while appreciated, is hardly hearing from Danny. Sorry, love, but your beautiful handwriting gives away who's in charge of those obligations. I appreciate the presents by the way, bit flasher than I'm used to but they've been useful.'

Useful? Emma had referred to gifts as *useful* herself, but it generally meant they'd be good to regift.

Harvey touched her arm. 'Anyway, I'd better go and mingle. Heard you were going to be at the party so wanted to say hello. Tell Danny . . .' He hesitated, a mixture of emotions crossing his face. 'Tell him I said hi.'

Emma nodded. 'I will, and I'll suggest he gets in touch.'

Harvey smiled. 'Thanks, love. Won't hold my breath though.'

Emma watched Harvey move back inside the function room, immediately welcomed into a group of men. She couldn't help but feel sorry for him. Daniel was his only family. She would have a talk with him; maybe she'd be able to convince him to come down for a visit. She instantly dismissed the thought.

'Em,' Simone called out to her. 'Time to do the cake.'

Emma stood with Simone and her parents and joined in with the three cheers the guests gave the couple. The smiling faces around them were genuine. Her parents were surrounded by friends and their beaming faces signalled the success of the day. Emma wondered who would come to a party for Daniel and her. Other than Cass, the people Daniel referred to as friends were business acquaintances. They were nice enough couples, but not people Emma would consider friends. It was different here though. Of course her parents knew people, they were part of the community. They'd run a shop in a small town for close to forty years. They'd seen their customer's children grow up, finish school, marry and start their own families. Tears threatened once again. What was wrong with her? She didn't want this life. She'd made that decision when she'd left the Bay at seventeen. She'd further confirmed it when she'd agreed to marry Daniel. She couldn't have them both. It would be too hard on Daniel and he was her choice. Their life was her choice.

Emma told herself the same thing over and over again when later that afternoon she sped past the 'Welcome to Golden Bay' sign. It reminded her that she hadn't set eyes on the business magician Andrew Myers. She wondered whether further changes would occur between now and her next visit. Five years wouldn't pass this time. She'd have to manage Daniel with care, but nothing was going to stop her from returning when her niece arrived.

Chapter Four

LUCIE

'Come on, Noah. Get your things and let's go. Granny and Gramps will be waiting to see you.'

Lucie listened to the bangs and crashes coming from Noah's room and held the front door open. She laughed as he finally appeared, dragging a huge, overstuffed bag, Mr Hamlet's head poking out of the top. 'What's in there?'

'Mr Hamlet and some other stuff. I promised Ruby I'd bring something for us to do.'

Lucie ruffled his hair. 'I don't think Ruby's going to be there, hon. It's just us for lunch today.'

Noah shook his head as he dragged the bag out the front door. 'Yes, she will, she told me so. Granny's looking after her and Liam's going to a friend's house.'

Kate had better not be there, Lucie thought. She was still angry with her sister-in-law. Leaving the kids on their own at the pool was bad enough, but then putting Lucie in a position where she had no choice but to drive over the limit was unforgivable. What if she'd been pulled over or, worse still, had an accident?

Ten minutes later, they stopped outside Matt's parents' home. Walter, Matt's dad, was standing at the geraniums, secateurs in hand, cutting off the dead heads. His garden was his pride and joy. The colours were brilliant at this time of the year. While the surrounding gardens tended to feature palms and semitropical species, Walter somehow managed to have roses thriving alongside petunias, salvias, agapanthus and what seemed to Lucie like a hundred other plant varieties more suited to gardens in Australia's southern states.

Noah jumped out of the car, opened the gate and cast himself into Walter's waiting arms.

Lucie stepped out, smiling as she heard Walter's booming laugh.

'Goodness laddie, it's only been a few days since I saw you. What a wonderful greeting.'

Noah untied himself from Walter's embrace and raced back to the car. 'I need my bag.'

Lucie opened the boot and took out the bag. 'Let me bring it in, it's heavy.'

'Nah, I'm fine.' Noah did his best to heave the bag on to his shoulder and staggered toward the front door.

'Jan,' Walter called out. 'Jan, open the door. Noah's coming through.'

Jan opened the door just as Noah reached it. 'My goodness, what have you got there, a dead body?'

Lucie looked on indulgently. Noah was lucky to have such loving grandparents. With her own parents both dead, her brothers were her only contact with home. She hadn't been back to Canada since before Noah was born. She'd tried to encourage her brothers to use Facebook and Skype but they were not into computers and not great with communication. The annual birthday and Christmas calls were often the only time she heard from them.

'Come on in, dear,' Jan called. 'Kettle's boiling.'

Lucie walked up to the front door, giving Walter a quick peck on the cheek as she passed by.

'Been a while, Lucie. Don't become a stranger now, will you?'

Lucie laughed. 'Okay, I get the hint – we're here too often. I'll try not to be back for at least a week this time, okay?'

Walter winked, his grey eyes twinkling. 'You know I'm kidding. We love seeing you. Move in if you want, would save you some petrol.'

Lucie swatted him on the arm. 'Cheeky bloody thing, aren't you?'

'Bloody? Turning into a real Aussie, you are. Matt would like that.'

The mention of Matt's name made them both pause.

'Sorry, love. Didn't meant to upset you.'

Lucie shook her head. 'Don't be silly, you didn't upset me. Of course Matt would be happy. Be trying to make me eat that Vegemite gunk, too, if he thought I was turning Aussie. That will never happen. I'll stick to my Canadian maple-syrup roots, let me assure you.'

They both laughed. 'I'd better go in and see Jan, sounds like she's getting a cuppa ready.'

Walter laughed again. 'Cuppa – Aussie through and through.'

Lucie left him pruning the geraniums. She'd have to think of some more Australianisms and throw them into conversation; he'd love that.

Jan had the tea laid out on the kitchen table as Lucie walked in. It was hard to believe she would soon be seventy. Trim and fit, if it wasn't for her cropped, grey hair and the few lines that had started appearing around her neck she could be mistaken for being in her fifties. Lucie gave her a hug. 'I wish you'd let me bring something for lunch.'

Jan shook her head. 'You know the rules – it's my lunch and I'll do the cooking. You bring yourself and my gorgeous grandson. You'll be sent home with anything you do bring, so don't even bother.'

Lucie smiled. 'Okay, orders are understood. Where's Noah? It's awfully quiet. He said Ruby would be here so surely chaos should have started by now?'

Jan pointed to the bay window overlooking the back garden. 'Chaos has been directed outside.'

Lucie walked over to the window. In the middle of the freshly cut lawn stood a teepee. 'I assume they're inside?'

'Yes. Noah dragged his bag across the lawn and the two of them somehow managed to get it through the front door of the tent. What on earth was in it?'

'No idea. He wouldn't tell me. Things to play with was all I got.'

'Come and sit down and we'll have a nice chat before the others get here.'

'Others?'

'Yes, Kate and Liam are coming for lunch, too. Their plans fell through and Brad's away so I invited them. It's been a few weeks now, maybe even a month, since we all caught up together, so I knew you wouldn't mind. Now, tell me all your news. What scandals are happening at the school?'

Thank you, Matt. Lucie silently raised her glass and toasted her husband. Not only had he left her with a ton of wine but his parents also had a wine collection that the most astute collector would be envious of. The red they were drinking perfectly accompanied Jan's four-cheese lasagne and took the edge off Lucie's simmering anger toward Kate.

'Top up?' Walter asked, the bottle poised over Lucie's glass.

She hesitated – she didn't want to risk being over the limit. But then again, they would be here for a few more hours so another glass would be okay. She nodded.

'Like your wine, don't you, Lucie?' Kate sipped her own glass of water. 'You should think about doing a detox, give your liver a break for a few weeks.'

Jan laughed. 'Kate, a couple of glasses of wine are good for you, particularly red wine. Lucie doesn't need a detox any more than I do. It's not like we're raging alcoholics.'

Kate shrugged her shoulders. 'It's always good to give your organs a break and a flush-out, no matter how beneficial you convince yourself wine is.' She turned to Lucie. 'What's going on with you? You seem a bit edgy today.'

Lucie wasn't sure if she'd ever get used to Matt's very forward sister.

'Anything wrong? Man trouble?'

'Man trouble?'

'Yeah, well, something's up, that's obvious. Figured it must be a man.'

Heat crept up the back of Lucie's neck. She saw Jan and Walter exchange a look, the hurt in Jan's eyes obvious. 'There's no man,' was all she said.

'Pity,' Kate said. 'You look like you could use one.'

'Kate! That's enough,' Jan said.

'What?' Kate asked. 'I was just saying. Lucie seems a bit off today, that's all. I wondered if perhaps there was a secret man. Was kind of hoping there was; it's been three years. Matt wouldn't expect her to become a nun.'

Lucie took another sip of her wine, trying to calm the anger rising inside her. She put her glass down and looked directly at Kate. 'You're right, I am a bit off today, but it's nothing to do with a man.'

Kate's face lit up. 'Sounds intriguing. What's going on then?'

'What's *going on* is you called me after my son's swimming lesson had finished to let me know you couldn't pick him up. It's not a case of my being "off", but rather angry.' Lucie picked up her glass and gulped some more down. There, she'd said it. She was sick of feeling resentful toward Kate and never saying anything.

'Kate, you didn't?' Jan looked horrified.

Kate rolled her eyes. 'It was hardly a big deal. Liam and Ruby were there with him and when I rang Lucie she said she could go. They would have been waiting ten, fifteen minutes at the most.' Her eyes drilled into Lucie's. 'If it's that big a deal, let's change the arrangement: you pick up the kids.'

'You expect me to take them both ways?'

Kate shrugged. 'That could be your contribution, couldn't it? I can't take them; I don't finish work in time. Your cushy hours allow you to. You're going anyway, so what's the big deal?'

Lucie sat in silence, nursing her wine as her head began to pound. She couldn't afford the fees the pool charged for the lessons so Kate and Brad had given Noah a term of lessons for his birthday. She'd been overwhelmed at their generosity at the time. She now realised the present came with strings attached. She could see Kate waiting for an answer, waiting for her to say, no problem, she'd do it. She wasn't going to fall into that trap. The lessons were a present, nothing more, and she was a single mother. Why should she be the one running around after someone else's kids? While she loved Liam and Ruby, they weren't her responsibility and she wasn't going to let Kate push them on to her.

Walter stood up before she had an opportunity to respond. 'Kate, come into the kitchen with me. I want your help with the dishes.'

'But I'm not finished.'

'I said come, and I mean now.'

Kate dragged herself up and followed her father into the kitchen. Walter's voice lowered to an angry whisper as they disappeared from view.

Jan put her arm on Lucie's. 'I can't believe she's my daughter sometimes. I'm so sorry.'

Lucie smiled. 'It's not your fault. Matt always warned me that Kate was one to speak her mind.'

'And think about herself,' Jan added. 'Now, if you want my help picking up the kids from the pool, just let me know.'

Lucie shook her head. 'Not necessary. I'll work it out with Kate. She can do her share. I won't be bullied by her.'

'Good for you.' Jan smoothed the tablecloth in front of her. 'You know, if there is a man, Walter and I will be happy for you, don't you?'

'Really? You didn't look happy when Kate suggested it.'

Jan's face reddened. 'It took us by surprise, that's all. Of course we want you to be happy. Matt's gone' – her voice wavered – 'but he'd want you to be happy, and for there to be a man in Noah's life. If you need us to look after Noah at all while you and the man catch up, let me know.'

Lucie laughed. 'Firstly, let me assure you there is no man. Even if one fell at my feet, I'm not ready. I'm not sure I ever will be.'

Jan squeezed her arm.

'But,' Lucie added, 'if I ever do feel ready and Prince Charming appears, I'll let you know straight away. Okay?'

Jan nodded. 'Sounds fine. And it doesn't need to be for a man either. If you need a break on the weekend, you just let us know. We'd love to have Noah. He could even come for a sleepover.'

Lucie nodded. 'We'll see.' She hadn't been away from Noah for a night since Matt died. What if it happened again? She still blamed herself. If only she'd stayed home the night of the fire, if only she hadn't insisted she and Noah have a night away, Matt might still be alive. She wasn't sure she'd ever be comfortable being away from Noah at night.

'Let's go out and find the kids, see what Noah had in that huge bag when you arrived.'

Lucie finished the remainder of her wine before following Jan out the French doors and into the neatly manicured garden.

It was close to nine by the time Lucie was ready to tuck a very tired Noah into bed. They'd ended up staying at Walter and Jan's for the afternoon and enjoyed a light dinner before coming home. Noah had begged to stay and play a board game after dinner with his cousins and Lucie had given in.

'Teeth all brushed?'

Noah nodded.

'Mr Hamlet all tucked in?'

He snuggled the bear closer to him, giggling as he did.

'Nighty-night, then.' Lucie leant down to kiss Noah on the forehead.

He immediately moved his head out of her reach. 'No. You haven't read me a story. I want seven tonight.'

Lucie looked at her watch. 'It's already more than an hour past your bedtime. We'll read some stories in the morning, okay?'

Noah sat up, throwing off the bedcovers.

'Hey, what are you doing?' Lucie asked, as her son climbed out of bed and ran to the bookshelf. 'I said not tonight. You've had a really busy, fun day with Ruby and Granny and Grandpa. It's time to sleep.'

Noah ignored her, throwing books off his bookshelf on to the floor behind him. 'Not that one, not that one, not that one.' The discard pile continued to grow. 'Ah, this one.'

'Noah, stop!' Lucie's voice was raised. 'Did you hear me? Put the book down right now and get back into bed by the count of three. One . . . two . . .'

Noah stuck out his tongue, ran, and jumped back on to his bed. He pulled the doona back over himself, grabbed Mr Hamlet and held the book out for Lucie. 'Read.'

Lucie folded her arms, determined not to spoil a lovely day. She often found it easier to handle a classroom of twenty-eight kids over this one, very strong-willed little boy. She took a deep breath and decided to change tactics. She moved closer to Noah and took the book from him.

He rewarded her with a huge smile.

She returned his smile. 'We can read this first thing tomorrow morning if you are good and go to sleep without a fuss now.' She watched as his top lip turned up, his face turning red with anger. She held her hand up to stop him from responding. 'If you are going to make a fuss, there will be no stories and no ice cream tomorrow.'

Noah started to cry. 'I hate you!' he yelled. 'I hate you! Daddy always read me a book. Every night. He wouldn't say no, no matter how late it was. Why did Daddy have to die? I wish it was you.'

Lucie felt like she'd been punched. She still hadn't had a chance to talk to Noah about the family projects they were doing at school. She watched as he hugged his bear close, his chest heaving up and down as he sobbed. She sat back down on his bed and willed him to calm down as she rubbed his back.

At the touch of her hand he flipped over and faced her. 'Get out! I hate you, get out!' His fist rose as he screamed and tried to punch Lucie's arm.

She grabbed his fist. 'You do not hit me. Do you hear me? Never.'

He tried to pull his arm away. 'Let go, you're hurting me. Let go!'

Lucie let go and stood up.

She closed his door quietly and made her way down the hall to the kitchen. She'd talk to him tomorrow. There was so much anger and hurt in him. How had she missed the build-up? What should she have been doing differently? Opening the fridge, she took out a bottle of wine and poured herself a glass. Tomorrow she'd try to talk with Noah, get things back on track. She let out a deep breath and took a sip of her wine. She'd had no idea what she'd signed up for when she'd married Matt. That he'd be taken from them so quickly, that she'd be parenting on her own. She just hoped she could turn things around. Make Matt proud of her, and of Noah.

Two days later, Lucie stopped at the letterbox as she reversed her car down the driveway. She glanced in her rear-view mirror; Noah was fastened into his booster seat, Mr Hamlet on his lap. 'Postie's just been, did you want to empty the box?'

He nodded, unbuckled his belt and pushed the door open. He lifted a pile of letters from the box. 'Hope there's one for me.' He passed them to Lucie.

She flicked through them. Two were addressed to 'The Householder' and she passed them back to Noah. 'Here you go. Now pop your belt on. We'd better get moving or we'll both be late for school.'

Lucie smiled as she remembered her discussion with Noah the previous day. Sunday had been spent talking about Matt and their family. About how lucky they were to have Granny and Grandpa so close by, and Aunty Kate, Uncle Brad and Liam and Ruby. Noah had told her how one of the other kids at school had teased him because he didn't have a dad. Said Matt didn't want a kid, that's why he'd died. When he'd said that Lucie had struggled to control herself. She'd be having a word with that child's mother later today. They'd spent the morning looking at photos of Matt and then Lucie had come up with the idea that Noah put together a poster for show and tell. They'd selected eight photos, mostly of Matt and Noah, and Noah had written some words under each photo. The end result was beautiful. Noah's addition of *I love my dad* in his large childish scrawl was the final touch.

They drove into the staff car park a little before eight. Lucie was supposed to start work at eight but liked to help Noah get organised for his day. They put his lunch in the fridge, unpacked his bag and hung it on its hook.

'Where do you put Mr Hamlet's diary?' Lucie asked.

Noah took it from her and placed the diary on a little blue stool in the classroom's book corner. He gave Mr Hamlet a kiss and placed him on top of the book. 'I love Mr Hamlet,' he said. 'I wish I could keep him.'

She pulled Noah close and gave him a hug. 'I know, but that wouldn't be fair to the other kids. You can see him every day when you're at school. Now, where's your poster? Let's put it on Mrs Winthrop's desk, shall we?'

'No need.'

Lucie turned to find Jane Winthrop entering the room. 'Good morning Mrs Andrews; good morning Noah. Did you have a nice weekend?'

Noah nodded. 'Yes, and I made something for show and tell.' He handed over the poster to his teacher.

She unrolled it. Lucie noticed her swallow hard before she looked up at Noah. 'This is really beautiful, Noah. I think your dad would love it, too. How about we make it our feature for the day? I think this is too special to just be normal show and tell, don't you?'

Noah's face lit up. 'Yes, I do.' He turned to Lucie. 'Can I go and play before the bell?'

She gave him a quick hug and kiss and watched as he raced out of the classroom toward the play equipment. 'I hope you don't mind, Jane? I realise it isn't a topic from the show and tell schedule but it was important to him. I also think it is a good opportunity for him to tell the other kids his daddy died.'

Jane nodded. 'Of course. Did he talk about his feelings on the weekend?'

'Yes, we spent a lot of time yesterday talking about Matt, looking at photos and remembering funny things about him. He was only two when he died so I'm not sure how much he really remembers. I also tried to make Noah understand that we're lucky to have the rest of the family around us.'

'Sounds like you've got it all under control.' Jane smiled. 'I'll let you know how he goes this week. Hopefully the bright, happy little boy who started the year will reappear.' Jane moved to her desk and sat down. 'I'm running a bit late this morning, so I'd better get organised for the day.'

'Of course.' Lucie retreated from the classroom. Was she imagining things or had she just been dismissed? She put the thought out of her mind as she hurried toward the Year Two classrooms.

'Don't even think about it,' Anna said as Lucie hurried into the classroom.

Lucie stopped. 'What?'

Anna put her finger to her lips and beckoned Lucie to come closer. She crossed the classroom toward Anna's desk. What on earth was going on?

Anna's voice came out as a whisper. 'Mrs Cock's standing right outside the window. Don't you dare say anything too loud, she'll hear you.'

Lucie clasped a hand over her mouth. *Mrs Cock!* Anna was outrageous. She dropped her bag on the floor and doubled over with laughter. It was almost a minute later that she realised Anna was staring at her. She stood up and smoothed her crumpled shirt with her hands. 'Sorry, that caught me off guard.'

'Are you okay?'

Heat rose up Lucie's neck. 'Yes, why?'

'It seemed like you really needed that. Everything okay on the weekend? How's Noah?'

Tears stung the back of Lucie's eyes. Her emotions were like a roller-coaster. It had been a hard weekend. Reminiscing about the wonderful times they'd had with Matt had been lovely but it had also stirred up a lot of feelings. That, coupled with Noah's behaviour and having to put up with Kate, was taking its toll on her.

'I'm here if you need to talk, you know that, don't you?'

Lucie nodded. 'Thanks. Noah's been a bit upset about Matt. We're getting through it though.' She looked away. Anna's face was full of sympathy and she didn't want the floodgates to open moments before the bell rang. She took a deep breath. 'Now, what have you got in store for the little monsters this morning?'

The morning flew past with a blend of songs, spelling and artwork. Lucie had to hand it to Anna, she ran a tight ship. The kids, even the naughty ones, responded to her. She was firm but had a soft heart and was loved not only by the students but the parents, too. Lucie took a bite out of her sandwich. The staffroom was relatively quiet for a Monday. The Years Three to Six children were at a swimming carnival and with several of the remaining teachers in the playground on duty, Lucie relished the opportunity to enjoy a quiet half hour. She rummaged through her bag and fished out the pile of mail she'd slipped into it that morning.

There were two letters and about seven leaflets. She put the leaflets aside ready for the bin and opened the first letter, a water bill. That was okay; it was in the budget and, from memory, was around the amount she'd allocated. The second was watermarked with the Queensland Government's logo. She didn't think there was an election coming up and that was about the only time she received mail from them.

She pulled out the letter, her heart sinking immediately. A speeding ticket. Five hundred and sixty-eight dollars. How on earth was she going to pay that? Thirty-four kilometres over the speed limit! She never drove that fast. She pushed her lunch aside and stared at the ticket. It was when she had been driving through the tunnel on her way back from Woolloongabba two weeks earlier. She remembered that tunnel vividly. Noah had been screaming his head off because he hadn't wanted to leave the birthday party they'd been to. She'd had to drag him away and manhandle him into his car seat. He hadn't stopped screaming and by the time they'd reached the tunnel her head was pounding. She'd had enough. If she'd been able to pull over, she would have. Instead she'd reached behind and grabbed his leg. She'd kept one hand on the steering wheel and her eyes on the road. She'd had to yell louder than him to get him to quieten down. She had no idea she'd been exceeding the speed limit at the time. The whole scene happened as if in slow motion, as if he were never going to quieten. She folded the letter and put it back in the envelope. She'd have to find the money somewhere; she had no choice.

Noah's excited face did nothing to lift Lucie's mood when she collected him from the classroom that afternoon. She hardly listened as he chatted on about presenting his poster to the class. It wasn't until they were halfway home that she realised he'd stopped talking. She glanced in the mirror – he had his arms folded across his chest, his mouth turned down.

'What's the matter?'

'You're not listening. I told you all about showing my poster and you didn't listen to any of it. It was about Daddy, it was important.'

Lucie took a deep breath. She was distracted and it wasn't his fault. Actually, it was. If he'd behaved after that bloody party she wouldn't be trying to work out how she was going to pay a speeding fine and buy him presents for his birthday, which was only a few months away. 'I'm sorry. I'm listening now so why don't you tell me again.'

Noah shook his head, his mouth clamped firmly shut.

'Okay, well, let's chat about it over dinner, when I'm not concentrating on driving and can give you my full attention. How does that sound?'

'Shut up! Shut up, you bum head!' Noah screamed the words out, almost causing Lucie to sideswipe the car next to them.

She straightened the car. 'What did you say?'

She glanced in the mirror. Noah had his mouth open, ready, by the looks of it, to launch into another round of obscenities. 'Stop it!' Lucie used her angry, loud voice. 'Stop it right now! You do not speak to me like that, do you hear me?'

Noah placed his hands over his ears and started to cry. 'You hurt my ears, you hurt my ears.'

Lucie sighed. She couldn't win. She braked, realising she was too close to the car in front. Where had it come from? She'd had a clear road ahead only moments ago. She slowed back to the speed limit. It seemed that when she was distracted by Noah her foot pushed down harder on the accelerator. She needed to take more care. The thought of the speeding ticket in her bag caused her stomach to clench.

Moments later Noah's sobs were drowned out by a siren. She glanced in the rear-view mirror, the flashing blue lights causing waves of nausea to flood over her. She pulled over. There was no doubt that this time the siren and flashing lights of the police car were for her.

Chapter Five

EMMA

A crash of bottles drew Emma from a dreamless sleep. The invasive early-morning visit from the garbage truck contrasted to the sunrise kookaburra song she'd woken to in Golden Bay. The truck's noise, accompanied by Daniel's gentle snores, confirmed she was definitely back home.

She slipped out of bed, careful not to wake her husband. He hadn't been home when she'd returned yesterday. He'd left a message on her phone to say he was entertaining clients and would be back late. She hadn't heard him come in so it must have been very late. Other than a few text messages, they'd had very little contact while she was away.

Emma took herself down to the kitchen, poured herself a juice and sat at the breakfast bar. She flicked open the weekend papers, which were stacked on the bench, and caught up on the news.

Half an hour later Daniel appeared. He wore a pair of silky boxer shorts and nothing else. He yawned and stretched his arms over his head as he made his way to the coffee machine. 'So, you're back. Want a coffee?'

Emma nodded. They hadn't seen each other for three nights. Usually when Daniel was away on business they were all over each other the moment he returned. She watched as he busied himself making the coffee, smiling with relief when he filled the metal jug with milk and placed it under the steam pipe. If he was going to the effort of making the foam for a cappuccino, maybe he wasn't so angry after all? She took this as her cue to make amends. She got up from the stool and moved up behind Daniel, putting her arms around his waist. 'I've missed you.'

Daniel put the jug down and turned to face her. He didn't say anything, just cupped her face in his hands and drew it toward him, kissing her tenderly. He drew back briefly, then kissed her again, this time more passionately. Emma could feel her body reacting, and the hardness pushing against her leg confirmed he was more than ready. She moved her hand to his boxer shorts, enjoying the sound of his groan. His tongue was moving deep inside her mouth, but then he suddenly pulled away and turned back to the coffee machine. He was still upset.

She put her arms around him again. 'Everything okay?'

'Big night. I need some coffee before I can function today.'

Emma laughed. 'Seems to me you're ready to function.'

Daniel didn't respond. She unwrapped her arms and sat back down at the breakfast bar. A few moments later he put a coffee in front of her and took his own out through the bifold doors and headed away from the house toward the pool.

She picked up her mug and followed him. He sat down at the poolside table, his gaze focused on the water feature. Emma sat across from him. 'How was your weekend?'

He turned to look at her. 'Good. Golfed with the guys from Andean on Saturday and then we kept going, had dinner and went on to the sports bar at St Lucia.' Daniel yawned. 'It was a late night.'

Emma nodded. 'What did you do last night?'

'Dinner with Jerry and Elise. Elise was disappointed you weren't there.'

Jerry Carter was Daniel's business partner. His wife, Elise, was beautiful, well groomed, dressed by a professional stylist, superficial and mind-numbingly boring. A typical trophy wife. Avoiding five hours of Elise was a definite bonus. 'I'll give her a call, see how she's doing.'

He smiled at her. 'Good, thanks.'

Emma played the game and played it well. She knew how to stroke the egos of the wives who needed it. She didn't love it but considered it part of her job. She took a deep breath. 'I got a bit of a shock at Golden Bay.'

Daniel's face hardened.

Emma didn't let it put her off. 'The town's changed. You wouldn't recognise it. Some hotshot's been in and had them all redo their shops, and he's modernised the main street. It looks amazing.'

Daniel's face remained impassive.

'My parents have reinvented their business. It's a full-on café now – you can eat in, get juices, and they're offering healthy food in addition to fish and chips. Sushi, salads – they even cater for events.' Emma sipped her coffee, waiting for Daniel to say something. He didn't. 'Oh, come on, hon, I want to tell you about it. I'm not asking you to go and visit, I just need to talk. I've been a total outsider all weekend, I don't want to feel like that with you, too.'

Daniel met her eyes. 'An outsider?'

'Yes, everything's changed yet no one's bothered to tell me. I'm not talking little changes either; I mean a major facelift for the town. On top of that my mum's about half the size she used to be and Simone's pregnant, due in a few weeks. If it wasn't for the wedding anniversary I don't know that they would have even told me when she had the baby. They don't seem to think we're worth the effort to keep in touch with.'

Daniel's face softened. 'See, we don't fit in. We never have. That place is not our life any more. We are outsiders.'

'Yes, but they're still my family. They are still a part of me. I chose to leave the Bay when I was seventeen, but I still want to see them.'

'You haven't for the past few years.'

'Five years, according to everyone. The timeframe hasn't gone unnoticed. The last time either of us visited was for Mum's sixtieth.'

'Yeah, well, that was hardly a success. No wonder we stayed away.'

He was right, that had been an awful night. Daniel had written himself off. He'd started drinking before they arrived and spent the entire night nursing a bottle of Jack Daniel's. He'd been rude to everyone who'd tried to approach him, including his father.

'I saw your dad.'

Daniel's body tensed.

'He asked how you were. Said to say hello.'

Daniel nodded. 'Is that all?'

'Yes. We only spoke for a few minutes. He seemed well. Said he was busy with his golf and fishing.'

Daniel stood up. 'Good for him.' He slipped off his shorts and dived into the pool. He surfaced halfway along and swam to the far end.

Emma watched as he powered along, his strokes strong and purposeful. His muscles rippled under the surface of the water. Exercise was definitely a coping mechanism for Daniel. She sighed: her husband was complicated. She knew that was the end of this discussion about her visit to the Bay. But with Simone's baby due in six weeks, it wouldn't be the last.

Thoughts of Daniel and his complex background were foremost in her mind as Emma pushed through the revolving door of the department store out on to the street. She was about to walk toward her car when a firm hand clamped down on her shoulder.

She'd left home intending to visit the sports shop to see if she could get some new goggles for Daniel and do a quick shop at the supermarket. She'd had no reason at all to visit the large department store, but its pull was too great. The moment she'd set foot in the store she'd been overwhelmed by the desire to find something for Daniel, to show him how much she loved him. She'd settled on a pair of cufflinks. Not an easy item to steal, especially as one of the shop assistants had helped her choose them. In fact, she hadn't even considered stealing them until the attendant had left her with them while she assisted another customer. Emma had held on to the box, pretending to browse at other items until she was sure the assistant was too busy to notice. The familiar rush of adrenaline had shot through her and suddenly she was invincible. She had considered adding a tie to her gifts but changed her mind. Once she had an item she liked to leave the store and enjoy the rush as she walked into the sunshine.

'Ma'am, you seem to have forgotten something.'

Emma's stomach contracted. She'd overdone it at Danes. She should have known better.

The woman released her grip on Emma's shoulder. 'I'm store security. Would you please come with me?'

The woman was very polite and the embroidered words on her shirt confirmed she was a security officer. Emma decided to play it cool. 'I'm sorry, I think you might be looking for someone else. I'm in a bit of a hurry.'

'Madam, please come with me. I have witnessed you taking an item without paying for it and video footage confirms it.'

Emma kept her eyes down. Heat crept up the back of her neck and into her cheeks. No doubt everyone was staring at her. She followed the security guard back inside but stopped at the bottom of the escalator. 'Where are we going?'

'Manager's office. You can wait there until the police come.' The woman pointed to the escalator.

Emma inhaled sharply. The police? Did they really have to call the police? It was only a small item. She'd never had a problem charming her way out of anything before – hopefully this manager would be as easy as most men to manipulate.

'Emma?'

Emma's head jolted up. Elise Carter was riding the escalator down from the top floor. Her stomach churned; Daniel could not find out. Elise's face registered concern as her eyes darted from Emma to the security guard. Emma mustered up a smile and gave her a wave.

'Hi Elise. I'll catch up with you soon for a chat. I've got a few things to attend to right now.' She rolled her eyes and gave Elise a conspiratorial wink. Elise's forehead creased in confusion as she smiled back. She'd need to come up with a good story to feed Elise the next time she saw her.

They reached the top of the escalator and the woman walked Emma through the homewares department. Emma gave a fleeting thought to the sooty owl she'd *acquired*. They obviously hadn't had cameras watching her that day. They continued down a threadbare corridor to an office. She led Emma into a room and pointed to a chair.

The tattered carpet and peeling paint were no better than the corridor. It was hardly inviting. They could definitely use the eye of Andrew Myers to fix this place up, Emma decided.

The security guard stood at the entrance of the room, her wide build blocking the doorway. 'Ms Sanders is at lunch. She will be back in a few minutes. You'll need to wait.' She remained standing.

Emma sat and stared at her shoes. Jesus, how had it come to this? She'd been caught shoplifting. She, Emma Wilson, highly respected wife of a successful businessman. Daniel would be so disappointed and embarrassed if he found out. And her family? Imagine if her parents knew. She took a deep breath. She needed to stay calm; there was no reason for them to find out. She had to do something. Charming a woman wasn't going to be so easy. Her best bet would be to try to convince the woman it was all a misunderstanding.

What seemed like an hour but was actually less than ten minutes passed and the woman told Emma to pick up her bag. Emma followed her through a maze of corridors before being ushered into another office. A well-groomed woman stood from behind a glass desk and pointed Emma to a chair. 'Thank you,' she said to the security guard. 'You're doing a great job. I can take it from here.'

The security guard nodded and left the room.

The manager peered at Emma over the rims of her designer glasses. 'I'm Natasha Sanders. There's no need to say anything, the police will be here any minute.' She sat back down at her desk and appeared to be reading something on her computer.

Emma shifted in her chair. This was her chance. The woman looked as plastic as the mannequins in the store, hopefully her looks hid a caring personality. She cleared her throat. 'Excuse me.'

The woman looked up.

'There's been a misunderstanding. I completely forgot to pay for the cufflinks. I'm more than happy to pay for them now.'

'I'm sure you are. Most people are once they've been apprehended.' She returned her focus to her computer screen.

'Look, my husband is quite a well-known investor. I'm sure he wouldn't want a fuss to be made. How about I organise a donation to your favourite charity on his behalf and we put this little incident behind us?'

'I'm sorry, Mrs . . .?'

'Wilson.'

'Okay, Mrs Wilson, let me clarify our store's position. Danes has a zero-tolerance policy when it comes to shoplifting. The police are called every time.'

Emma met the woman's eyes with her own. They were hard, unforgiving.

Before Emma was given any more time to contemplate her options, there was a rap at the door.

Natasha Sanders got up to open it. She smiled at the police officer. 'Sorry to call you in again. We've detained Mrs Wilson after our security guard noticed her leave the store without paying for an item. The video footage will be released to you, of course.'

The officer approached Emma. 'Mrs Wilson, my name's Constable Matthews. We are here to investigate an allegation of stealing. Open your bag, please.'

Emma's fingers trembled as she unzipped her favourite Louis Vuitton. Bloody fingers. Surely they'd believe it was all a misunderstanding. She held it open toward the police officer.

'Please empty it on to the desk in front of you.'

Emma turned the bag upside down and watched as the cufflink box fell on to the desk along with her purse, make-up and phone.

The police officer bent down and picked up the box, the sale tags showing it was from the store. 'Did you pay for this item, Mrs Wilson? If yes, please produce the receipt.'

Emma shook her head. 'No, I accidentally left the store without paying for it. Unfortunately the staff here won't let me make amends by paying for it now.'

'Please empty each compartment of your bag.'

Emma did as she was told. God, this was embarrassing. A complete stranger scrutinising her personal items. Tampons, her foil packet of pill tablets, the photo of her and Daniel posing naked together. She bet the officer was having a good laugh to himself. She emptied the last item from her bag and waited for him to speak.

'Okay. I'm satisfied that the cufflinks are the only item that hasn't been paid for. Are you willing to come with us to the station for an interview?'

Emma's heartbeat raced; did that mean she had a choice? 'I don't know. What happens if I don't?'

'In the current situation we have enough evidence to arrest you if you choose not to come willingly.'

'Look, Constable Matthews.' Emma forced a smile. 'There really has been a misunderstanding. If you'd just let me pay for the cufflinks it would save me wasting your valuable time.' Surely there was no need to take this further? She was an immaculately dressed, well-spoken woman. She was hardly a threat to anyone.

'Collect your belongings and come with us please.' The constable pointed toward the office door, where a second officer stood with a small smirk on her face. She certainly seemed to be enjoying Emma's discomfort.

Emma remained seated in the chair, her hands gripping the armrests. There had to be some way out of this.

Officer Matthews sighed. 'Look, Mrs Wilson, you have a choice: you voluntarily accompany us to the station or we go through the procedure of arresting you. Which will it be?'

Was vomiting an option? That's exactly what Emma felt like doing. She closed her eyes in an attempt to compose herself. This was now out of her control. She opened her eyes and collected her belongings. Head held high, she walked toward the door. This was ridiculous. It was just a small item – less than five hundred dollars. Why they wouldn't let her pay for it was beyond her. Her thoughts flicked to Daniel. Oh God. What would he think of her? He was so proud of her and now she'd let him down. Tears pricked the backs of her eyes. She took a deep breath. She'd get through this. No matter what happened with the police she promised herself Daniel would not find out.

Chapter Six

LUCIE

Lucie's eyes flicked to the speedometer as she drove toward her in-laws' house. She was doing her best to stay five kilometres below the speed limit at all times. She couldn't risk another fine. The cost was one thing, but the demerit points on her licence were the bigger concern. The two tickets she'd received the previous week had cost her nine demerit points. One more ticket and she'd lose her licence for at least six months. She'd spoken to the legal aid office that week to find out what her options were for paying the fines. Even the minimum repayments were going to be a stretch. She couldn't ask her in-laws for a loan, then they'd know just how bad her financial situation was. Her other option was community service. The fine could be converted to unpaid community service as long as she could prove she was struggling financially. She'd filed the application immediately and had heard back that morning that it had been approved and she would be required to complete her work on Saturdays, starting this week. She was required to complete thirty-four hours of community service. Her only problem was Noah: he would need to be looked after.

Lucie walked up the garden path, taking a deep breath as she passed under Walter's honeysuckle archway. It was in full flower and the scent was delicious. As she knocked on the front door, she could hear music and laughter radiating from the house, and when no one answered, she wound her way through the rose garden, following the path that took her into the backyard. She called out as she approached the open French doors leading into the kitchen. The laughter and music stopped abruptly, replaced with muffled whispers.

Two guilty, flour-streaked faces stared at Lucie as she stepped into the house. Her eyes moved from the guilty faces and travelled the length of the usually immaculate kitchen. She assumed it still existed under the piles of bowls and cooking ingredients that were strewn over the benchtops. She tried not to laugh. Jan looked like a naughty child who'd been caught out.

'Hi, Mum.' Noah wiped his face with his sleeve, leaving another trail of flour down his cheek. 'We're making gnocchi. Granny said we could stay for dinner. Can we?'

Lucie smiled. 'Yes, if Granny says we can. I definitely want to try your gnocchi, and then I think we might need to help clean up.'

Jan turned to Noah. 'Speaking of cleaning up, why don't you go down to the bathroom and have a wash? When you get back we'll boil the water for the gnocchi and give the sauce another stir.'

Noah grinned and ran off down the hall, leaving a cloud of flour in his wake.

Lucie started to laugh. 'What a mess. I don't think I've ever seen an item out of place in your kitchen before.'

'No, it's not my usual cooking style.' Jan brushed her hands on her apron. 'But we've had a lot of fun, and when you're five that's what you need, isn't it?'

Lucie's smile faded. Jan's words had been delivered without a smile; she'd chosen them carefully. 'Is there a problem?'

Jan hesitated before bending down to open the dishwasher. 'I'm a bit worried about Noah.'

'Why?'

'He said you were pulled over the other night, that it scared him. It always tugs on my heart when the kids are put in scary situations.'

'It wasn't a big deal. I was only a few kilometres over. The policeman was very kind, especially to Noah. I'm not sure why he told you he was scared.'

Jan stopped loading the dishwasher and rose to her full height, her eyes boring into Lucie's. 'It wasn't the policeman who scared him, it was you.'

'Me?'

'He said you were angry before the police came, yelling at him, hurting him.'

'What?' Tears welled in Lucie's eyes. 'I didn't hurt Noah. I raised my voice to get him to stop behaving so badly, that's all. You know I'd never hurt him.'

Jan stared at Lucie.

'Jan, I'd never hurt Noah, you know that.' Lucie watched as Jan hesitated. She felt sick. Jan actually believed she'd hurt Noah. She turned toward the hall. 'Noah, hurry up, we need to get going.'

'Oh, don't do that. He's gone to so much effort to make the dinner.'

Lucie looked back at Jan's stricken face.

'I'm sorry if I've upset you – I didn't mean to. I was just worried. Noah's usually such a happy little boy, but the past month or two he's seemed quite withdrawn. The fact that he told me he was scared today made me feel like I had a glimpse of what might be going on.'

Lucie wiped a tear from the corner of her eye. 'What's going on is he's five years old and missing his father. His latest school project on families isn't helping.'

Jan's eyes filled with tears. 'I'm sorry, Lucie. I shouldn't have said anything. I know you are doing a wonderful job with Noah, the poor little thing. If only Matt was still here. How much simpler life would be.'

Noah came back into the kitchen. His smile slipped as he looked from Lucie to Jan. 'What's happened? Why does everyone look sad?'

Jan smiled at Noah. 'I'm not sad, love, it's just your mum remembered she had to get home to do something. I'm hoping she'll make a quick call to see if it can be postponed so you can still stay for dinner. She was just deciding if that would work.' She looked over at Lucie. 'What do you think?'

Lucie smiled. Jan was only ever looking out for Noah; she was lucky that Matt's parents cared so much. But the insinuation that she'd done something wrong hurt. 'I think we'll be fine to stay. Let me just go and make that call.' She walked back outside, hoping the fresh air would give her a few minutes to regroup. Before their conversation she'd planned to ask Jan a favour. Now she wasn't sure how it would be received.

Jan hugged Lucie tight as they said their goodbyes. 'Please forgive me. I didn't mean to imply anything.'

Lucie smiled. 'There's nothing to forgive. I know you and Walt just want the best for Noah, and I love you both for that. We're lucky to have you so close; don't think for one minute I don't appreciate all that you do.'

'We're always here, and the Saturdays when you're doing your course are no problem at all. We'd love to have Noah. If you're going to be busy all day learning then you won't want to cook either. Come here when you've finished and we'll have dinner and a glass of wine ready.'

A thickness in Lucie's throat made it hard to swallow. Here Jan was, bending over backward to help her out, believing she was bettering her teaching qualifications by doing a course. She'd never told her in-laws that Matt had left her with nothing. He'd had no life insurance and all their savings had been invested in three new wineries, all of which were still in their infancy and not producing shareholder returns. She'd considered selling the shares but they were worth next to nothing. Unless one of the wineries produced an award-winning wine some time down the track it was unlikely Lucie and Noah would ever see any money from them. She couldn't tell Jan this. Matt was their golden child; he was generous and kind, and he had loved his family so much. She didn't want Jan and Walt's memories of their son to be anything but that.

'So we'll see you Saturday then.' Jan hugged Noah tightly before resting her hand on Lucie's arm. 'Drive carefully, won't you?'

Lucie nodded and reversed out of the driveway. She waited until they had turned the corner before speaking. 'What did you say to Granny?'

'About what?'

'About the other night, with the policeman?'

'Noth-noth-nothing. I didn't say nothing.'

Lucie looked in her rear-view mirror. Noah looked scared, his little face full of concern. Her heart softened. He was five; sometimes she forgot how little he was. 'You're not in trouble. I just wondered what you'd said about the policeman. He was quite a nice man, didn't you think?'

Noah's body visibly relaxed. 'Yes, he was a good cop. Are we going to Granny's on Saturday?'

'You are. I have to do a course for the next few Saturdays, so you can go and play at Granny and Grandpa's, is that okay?'

'Yes. I hope Ruby comes, too.'

Half an hour later Lucie turned off Noah's light after reading him a story and kissing him goodnight. She was grateful that she hadn't had to come home and cook dinner. She walked into the kitchen. A bottle of red wine stood open on the bench from the night before. She poured herself a glass and sank down on to one of the stools. Community service. She never would have believed she'd be doing community service. Still, it could have been worse. If she'd been pulled over the night she'd picked the kids up from the pool she probably would have lost her licence as well. She took another sip of her wine and wondered what Matt would think. They were only speeding tickets but both had been caused by Noah's behaviour. What was she going to do about him? He'd been good today, but that was thanks to Jan and an afternoon full of attention. She needed some new ideas for disciplining him. She'd have a chat to Anna at school – she had three boys, maybe she'd have some suggestions.

Lucie closed her eyes, her body slowly relaxing as the wine worked its magic. At least she had one constant in her life, one thing that was guaranteed to make her feel better. She had a time of day she could look forward to. A time when she could connect with Matt through his wine. If she didn't have this, she couldn't imagine what kind of a basket case she'd be.

Chapter Seven

EMMA

The leafy streets of Indooroopilly welcomed Emma as she brought the Audi to a stop in front of a school crossing. She smiled as hordes of children crossed the road to the school's entrance. Their laughter and smiling faces were a good tonic for the morning. In five years, Simone's baby would be heading into an establishment like this one. Emma sighed – she was getting a bit ahead of herself. Once the road was clear and the crossing guard had taken her place back on the side of the road, Emma manoeuvred the car forward, in search of Chapel Hill. In the six years she'd known Cass, she'd been to her house only a handful of times. They usually met at a café or at the gym.

Emma was grateful for the guidance of her GPS as she pulled up in front of Cass's pretty cottage, situated at the base of Mount Coot-tha. She reached over to the passenger seat and picked up the arrangement of dark orange Asiatic lilies she had ordered earlier in the week. She'd collected them that morning. She owed Cass a huge thank you.

The front door opened as Emma walked up the path and Cass appeared wearing her gym gear. Her face broke into a smile when she saw Emma. 'This is a surprise. What are you doing here?'

Emma moved closer, handing Cass the flowers. 'Came to say thank you. You were a lifesaver the other day, picking me up from the police station. I was far too shaky to drive. I don't know what I would have done without you.'

Cass shook her head. 'It was nothing. You didn't need to do anything, but I'm glad you did.' She brought the flowers to her nose. 'These flowers are exquisite; I've never seen anything like them.'

'It wasn't nothing. If Daniel found out he'd kill me.'

Cass raised an eyebrow. 'Not literally, I hope?'

'You know what I mean. I really need to keep this one to myself. It would be so embarrassing for him if his clients knew his wife had been caught shoplifting.'

'Yes, well, the real question, I think, is why his wealthy wife was shoplifting in the first place? Perhaps we need to get to the bottom of that before we worry too much about Daniel.'

Emma didn't respond.

Cass cleared her throat. 'Look, I'm about to go for a walk around the mountain. Do you want to come? I can loan you some clothes.'

Emma hesitated. Daniel was going to be playing golf most of the day and they weren't going out for dinner until eight. She had the whole day to fill. 'Sounds good. I've got my gym bag in the car, I can change into my own gear.'

Ten minutes later, the flowers arranged beautifully in a vase and Emma dressed in her sports gear, they set off down the driveway and headed toward Mount Coot-tha.

'Let's go this way.' Cass pointed toward the mountain. 'We can do a loop up to the lookout and come back around the other side. It's not a huge walk but there are a few hills that will get the blood pumping.'

Emma nodded and fell into step beside Cass. They walked in a comfortable silence before Cass asked the question Emma had been expecting.

'So, tell me, why did you take the cufflinks?'

Cass hadn't pushed for any information when she'd arrived to collect her from the police station earlier in the week. Emma had been grateful but knew she owed her an explanation.

She didn't meet Cass's eyes. 'It wasn't the first time. It's something I've got rather addicted to doing.' Saying it out loud wasn't easy. 'I've got a ton of stuff all packed away in the garage at home. Daniel would have a fit if he found it.'

'Do you think you want him to find it?'

Emma looked at Cass. 'Of course I don't. Why would you think that?'

'Seems strange to me that you'd keep stolen things at home if you were really worried. Are you sure you aren't looking for a way out?'

'What, of my marriage?'

Cass shrugged. 'Maybe, I don't know.'

Emma laughed. 'I think the psychology professors at the university are rubbing off on you. No, I wasn't hoping to be found out. In fact, I've given little thought to the consequences. It's been so easy, I didn't really anticipate being caught. I certainly didn't expect to be charged, either.'

'What happens now? Do you get a fine?'

'I'm not sure. I have an appointment at the Magistrates' Court on Tuesday. I spoke to a lawyer yesterday. He said it was a first-time minor offence so I'd probably get off with a fine and slapped wrists. He's offered to come and represent me but I declined. Other than being humiliated, it shouldn't be a big deal.'

They made their way to the start of the trail that led up to the lookout.

'If you want me to come with you, let me know.'

'What about work?'

'I'll put in for leave; I'm owed quite a few days.'

Emma was touched. 'Thanks. I think I'll be okay though. Sounds like I can turn up on my own and have it all dealt with.'

'Okay, but if you change your mind let me know.' Cass grinned. 'So, did you steal the flowers you gave me?'

Emma punched her gently on the arm. 'Shut up, you. My life of crime has been brought to an abrupt end. It will all be over after Tuesday and not only will I never do it again, but I won't have to give it another thought.'

They both laughed as they continued in the direction of the lookout. Emma knew she'd had a lucky escape. Daniel didn't need to know about it; she'd pay the fine and then put it all behind her. She'd be relieved when Tuesday was over.

The gentle breeze and beautiful blue sky did nothing to ease the churning in Emma's stomach as she walked away from the Magistrates' Court. Nothing had prepared her for how belittled she would feel. Bloody hell, she'd been spoken to and treated like a common criminal. The moment the magistrate looked at her she realised she'd made a mistake: she'd taken extra care with her clothes and make-up that morning, even earning herself a wolf-whistle from Daniel. In fact, she'd had to remove his hands from her body multiple times. If he'd had his way, her beautiful suit would have been ripped off and left in a crumpled heap on the floor. She'd managed to convince him she was running late for a charity function and they could continue where they'd left off later. Her flawless appearance seemed to say something else to the magistrate, however. The raise of her eyebrows was the first sign that this might not be as simple as being fined. The magistrate dealt with the matter quickly and firmly. The facts were stated and the punishment handed down. It was when Emma, shell-shocked by the speed at which it had all happened, left the courtroom and requested the opportunity to appeal the decision that she was put in her place. The legal clerk's words were very possibly exactly what the magistrate would have liked to have said, but was too professional.

The clerk peered from behind her thick glasses at Emma. 'You seem to think you have some kind of entitlement due to your social standing, don't you, Mrs Wilson? Let me tell you what the community is sick of. They're sick of wealthy women like yourself wasting police time and the court's time. You live in big houses, drive fancy cars, have stylists, cooks and cleaners and, as a result, have nothing to do. You relieve your boredom by shoplifting. Not only does this steal the profits of the business and its shareholders, but it puts the price of items up to cover the store's loss. This affects hardworking people who can no longer afford to shop in these stores.'

Emma wished she'd just signed the paperwork and not asked about appealing the decision. If the clerk was worried about Emma wasting the court's time then this lecture certainly wasn't helping.

She didn't stop there. Her voice raised, ensuring everyone queuing behind Emma heard every word, she began a personal attack on Emma's character. 'You are a disgrace, Mrs Wilson, an absolutely appalling example to society. We can only be relieved that you aren't a mother and that your shame isn't being witnessed by your children. I hope you will learn from this experience and we will not see you in here again.'

This comment brought tears to Emma's eyes. If she had children she probably wouldn't have had the need to shoplift because her life would be fulfilled, she would be happy. Cass's question of why she did it popped into her head. She didn't have an answer at the time, but the clerk's suggestion that it was a good thing Emma didn't have children had hit home.

Other than completely belittling her, the clerk confirmed that the magistrate's decision was final. Converting the community service hours Emma was required to complete into a fine was not an option.

She was sure the clerk's lips twitched upward as she watched Emma's horrified reaction to this news. Her case was closed and the court clerk had great pleasure in providing her with the details she needed for her community service: she had to report to the Department of Corrective Services to be given a work order.

She walked back to her car, already wondering what excuse she would be able to use so Daniel wouldn't question her whereabouts on the community service days. She sighed. So long as it was mid-week there'd be no real reason for him to find out. For now, she needed to get home and pour herself a very large drink.

Chapter Eight

COMMUNITY SERVICE

Lucie's hands trembled as she riffled through her handbag for the third time. Keys, water bottle, breath mints, sanitiser – it was all there. She gave a shaky laugh. For goodness' sake, why was she so nervous? She needed to pull herself together. She was going to an aged-care facility, not to prison.

She'd already dropped Noah off with Jan and Walter, and at ten to nine pulled into the car park of Treetops Retirement Village. Her hands continued to tremble as she turned the car off. At this rate, they'd probably send her off in a straightjacket, rather than put her to work. She locked the car and walked over to the main entrance. Taking a deep breath she went through the automatic doors.

'Prisoner?'

Lucie was confronted by a large, balding man with a clipboard.

'You? Are you a visitor or a prisoner?'

Lucie gave a nervous laugh. 'Is this a joke?'

The man shook his head. 'No. I've got five prisoners reporting to work today and I have a feeling you might be one of them. Let me see, I'm expecting two women in their thirties, one in her late seventies and two men. You're not a man and you're ageing very well if you're nearly eighty. Visiting hours are yet to start so I'm assuming you are either Emma Wilson or Lucie Andrews. Am I correct?'

Lucie nodded. 'Lucie Andrews.'

He ticked her name off the list and handed her a lanyard. The card attached said 'Volunteer'. 'I've asked that they be changed to "Prisoner". Hopefully they will be ready for next week. Take a seat over there.' He pointed to five chairs that had been lined up next to each other, completely out of place, in the middle of the foyer. 'You're the first to arrive. The others will be here in the next five minutes or their sentences will be extended.'

Lucie walked over to the chairs and sat down. Was this guy for real? This was community service; no one doing this had actually committed a real crime, had they? She'd assumed everyone would be here for speeding tickets or other minor offences.

One of the men arrived moments later, covered from head to toe in tattoos. He was dressed very nicely, had even polished his shoes. He gave Lucie a quick nod as he sat down on the seat furthest from her. He was followed by a second man – 'boy' would actually be a better description as he only looked about twelve. Lucie assumed he must be older to have received a court-appointed work order and she wondered why he'd been sent here when he looked more suited to some of the other programs people were allocated to, like removing graffiti or picking up rubbish, rather than preparing food all day.

A grey-haired older lady came in through the door, leaning heavily on a walking stick. Lucie assumed she was one of the residents.

She hobbled over to the man and stuck out her hand. 'Florrie Jacobs, reporting for duty, sir. Prisoner 83819277.'

The guy referred to his clipboard and then pointed her in the direction of the chairs.

The old lady sat down next to Lucie. 'Hello, love, what are you doing time for?'

'Um, speeding tickets.' Lucie hadn't considered anyone asking her why she was here. The old lady looked at her expectantly. 'Oh, sorry, I'm a bit new to all of this. Why are you here?'

The old lady lowered her voice. 'Armed robbery, but don't tell anyone. The judge has gone easy on me because of my age. Should be locked up really, but I think they worked out that was what I was aiming for. Free room and board.' She gave a bitter laugh. 'Didn't quite work out that way though. So they've put me in here, pretty much until I die. Means I at least get a couple of meals a week that are good for me.' She nudged Lucie. 'Look, another crim.'

Lucie looked up to see the other woman arrive. She was wearing cargo pants and a white T-shirt that looked brand new. She hadn't taken off her sunglasses and had a cap firmly planted on her head, pulled down low so it was hard to see her face. Her Louis Vuitton handbag completed her outfit. She was going through the same questioning process by the man in charge.

She snuck another look at the little old lady next to her. Neatly dressed in a navy skirt and floral top she looked distinguished, respectable. Armed robbery? Surely they wouldn't have a speeding-fine offender sentenced to work with an armed robber? And anyway, she was tiny and needed a walking stick, how on earth could she have performed an armed robbery?

'Okay.' The man with the clipboard stood in front of them, demanding their attention. 'All prisoners are in attendance; we will get to work. Firstly, my name is Rodney Faraday, however, you will refer to me as Warden or, if you prefer, sir. I am in charge today. If you want your hours submitted to DCS this afternoon you will do what I say, when I say it. Does everyone understand?'

There were nods from the group.

'I said, does everyone understand? Your response should be "Yes, Warden". Let's try again. Does everyone understand?'

'Yes, Warden!' Florrie's voice boomed over the top of the others.

Lucie fell into step behind Florrie and the two men as they followed the warden down a corridor.

'Is this a joke?'

Lucie turned to face the soft-spoken woman behind her. She'd taken off her glasses and Lucie could now see uncertainty in her blue eyes. In fact, her face mirrored Lucie's own thoughts. 'I'm not sure. I think the guy's on a power trip.'

'He's a complete wanker.' The woman's face transformed as she grinned at Lucie.

Lucie smiled back and stuck out her hand. 'Lucie Andrews, first-time offender.'

The woman took her hand, 'Emma Wilson, same as you. What about the old lady? Is she a resident or actually doing this for real?'

'She told me she'd committed an armed robbery and they'd gone lenient on her.' Lucie laughed at Emma's shocked face. 'I know, I nearly wet my pants when she said that. Here's me thinking I should get the poor old dear a cup of tea and turns out she should be behind bars.'

'I assumed we would all be minor offenders.'

'Yeah, I'd hide that beautiful handbag if I were you. She might decide to steal it.'

Emma's face coloured.

Lucie wondered what she'd said. It suddenly dawned on her. 'Oh, sorry, I wasn't thinking. I'm forgetting we're all crims. I'm speeding tickets by the way – might as well get it all out in the open.'

'Well, that's hardly a crime. Why are you here? Why didn't you just pay them?'

This time it was Lucie's face that reddened. 'I didn't have the money – things are a bit tight.'

The women stopped talking as the warden approached them. 'There will be no talking, do you hear me? You will all come into the kitchen and put on your clothing and hairnets. Then Martha, the head chef, will allocate you a task. You will have a break at eleven and another for lunch at one. You may talk during these breaks but not during the work time. Do you understand?'

'Yes, Warden,' Emma said in a loud, clear voice.

Lucie bit the inside of her lip. She felt like a naughty schoolgirl, ready to burst into hysterics. No one would believe a guy like this existed. The worst thing, considering she'd lied about her whereabouts for the day, was not being able to tell anyone about him.

Lucie opened and closed her hands in an attempt to stretch her fingers. Three hours of peeling potatoes, carrots and beetroots had left them cramping. She hoped she'd be given a different task for the afternoon. She sat outside in the sunshine at one of the two tables that had, according to Rodney, been allocated for the prisoners' breaks. She refused to call him Warden. Wanker, yes; Warden, no. Having spent the morning staring at piles of vegetables stacked on the stainless-steel bench it was a relief to sit out in the sunshine and enjoy the view of the gardens. Many of the residents were sitting at tables or in their wheelchairs, some surrounded by visitors, others on their own.

She pulled the tinfoil off the lunch tray she'd been handed. It was a bonus that they were fed. She bet those sentenced to removing graffiti didn't get a meal provided. The pumpkin soup smelled lovely. She dipped a roll into it and took a bite. It was delicious. No wonder there was a long waiting list for the retirement home.

'How's it going, love?' Florrie plonked her own tray across the table from Lucie and sat down.

Lucie smiled. 'Sore hands, and sore feet from standing so long, but otherwise all's good. How about you?'

'I'm good. They had me delivering the lunches to the residents, so I got to push the trolley around and visit a few people.'

Lucie was surprised. She hadn't realised Florrie had left the kitchen; she'd assumed she was stationed around the corner on a stool where Lucie couldn't see her. 'I didn't think they'd let us mix with the residents, considering we're not even allowed to talk. How did you manage that?'

Florrie winked. 'I'm a regular. They're used to me.'

'Regular?'

Florrie nodded. 'I've been doing this twice a week now for five years. I started off like you, peeling the veggies, working my hands until they were calloused. Not any more. You wait. If you're here long enough they might let you do something else.'

Lucie smiled. 'I've only got to do a few days.'

'Mind if I join you?' Emma hovered next to the table with her tray.

'Of course,' Florrie said. 'All crims are welcome here.'

Emma sat down and examined her food. 'Soup, pasta, bread, salad and dessert. They certainly feed them well. There's no way I could eat all of this.' She put the lids back on to the pasta and dessert and moved the soup in front of her.

'So what's your crime?' Florrie asked her. 'Don't answer, let me guess, I'm usually pretty good at this.' Her eyes twinkled from behind her glasses as she stared at Emma. Finally, she spoke. 'I'd say fraud.'

85

Emma spluttered on her soup. 'Fraud? What on earth would make you think fraud? I think I'd be in jail, not doing community service.'

Florrie gestured to Emma's clothes and bag. 'Well, you're so nicely dressed and made-up, you've got beautiful rings on and carry an expensive bag. Even I can tell it's not a fake. You look very polished and posh. It's not going to be anything you could pay your way out of so I'm thinking fraud.'

Emma shook her head. 'Shoplifting. I got caught shoplifting.'

Florrie looked shocked. 'Really? But why? That's ridiculous. I saw you arrive – that was your beautiful black car, wasn't it?'

'Yes, my Audi.'

'So you're rich and you shoplift. Or' – Florrie had a gleam in her eye – 'you're not rich but steal to create a fantasy lifestyle? Now that would be intriguing.'

Emma laughed. 'Sorry to disappoint you but no. My husband has a very successful business and I am quite well off. I have absolutely no excuse for what I did and, obviously, after this little experience I won't be doing it again.'

Florrie shook her head. 'Don't be down on yourself. You're wrong, you know. There's an excuse for everything we do. We don't go about doing things without some kind of reason. It's working out what the motivation behind our actions is, then we can do something to help ourselves.'

Lucie and Emma both stared at Florrie. She started to laugh. 'I'm a wise old woman. Like I was telling Lucie before you arrived this morning, I'm in here for armed robbery. Yep, a little old lady holding up a 7-Eleven. Can you believe that? And my excuse, or reason if you prefer, is I wanted to go to jail. I wanted someone to look after me in my old age. I can't afford a place like this and have no family so it seemed like a good idea. The joke was on me, of course, cos they wouldn't put me in jail. The gun was a fake, and apparently it had to be real, but I haven't been able to find out where to buy one. Someone said eBay or somewhere like that, but I don't have a computer. Neither of you happen to shop on eBay, do you?'

'Not for guns,' Lucie said.

Florrie looked hopefully at Emma, who shook her head.

'Oh well, I'll get one at some stage.' She turned to Emma. 'You need to work out, if you don't already know, why you like to shop-lift. Once you work that out and do something about it you'll be a lot happier.' She pulled herself up using the table to support her. 'I'm not all that hungry. I might see if they'll put this meal away for me so I can take it home for my dinner.' She hobbled back inside with the tray, leaving Lucie and Emma staring after her.

'Wow,' Lucie said.

'Wow, all right. She's some old lady. Do you really think she's been doing this for five years?'

'To be honest, I'm not sure if I believe anything she's telling us. She reminds me of my five-year-old – full of exciting, imagined events.'

'You have a five-year-old?' Emma asked.

'Yes, Noah.'

'Is he with his dad today?'

'No, his grandparents.' Lucie avoided Emma's eyes as she responded.

'Sorry, did I say something wrong?'

Lucie shook her head. 'No. I still find it hard to tell people about Matt. My husband died three years ago. You'd think I'd have worked out how to handle it by now, but I haven't.'

Emma placed her hand on Lucie's. 'Hey, I'm sorry. I can't even begin to imagine how that would be. If Daniel . . .' She shuddered. 'I'd be completely lost.'

'Thanks. I'm managing, but it can be difficult.'

Rodney stood at the door, his clipboard still in hand. 'Ladies, three more minutes and you need to be back in there and on dessert duty. Do you hear me?'

'Yes, Warden!'

Emma's shout caused Lucie to jump. 'Jesus, would you stop doing that? You're going to give me a heart attack.'

Emma broke off some of her bread roll and laughed. 'Sorry, can't help it. He's such an arrogant little prick, might as well have some fun with it. I'd love to see him in charge of a real prison; I reckon they'd eat him alive.'

A few minutes later the women found themselves back in the kitchen being shown how to make the cake layers for the black forest gateaux being served that night for dessert. At least this was a more interesting task than the morning's vegetable peeling.

At exactly five thirty, as they wiped down the stainless-steel benchtops, Rodney came back into the kitchen. 'Tools down, prisoners. Come and sign this form and then you can leave. I will see you all back here at the same time next Saturday. Florrie, I'll see you on Tuesday. You obviously have more hours to serve.'

Florrie winked at Lucie; she looked like she loved this as much as the warden did.

Lucie waved to Florrie as she collected her belongings. 'Did you need a lift anywhere, Florrie?'

'No, I'm fine, love. My neighbour will collect me soon. You go, get home to your little boy.'

Lucie caught up to Emma as she walked through the front doors out into the car park. 'See you next week?'

'Yep, I'll be here.' Emma glanced at her watch. 'I'd really better get going; need to get out of these clothes before I get home. If anything is going to make my husband suspicious, these will.'

'What's wrong with them? You look great.' Lucie had been admiring the slim-fitting cargo pants, wondering where Emma got them. But knowing she couldn't afford them she hadn't bothered to ask.

'They wouldn't quite live up to my husband's fashion expectations. Anyway, I'm glad you like them as I bought them specifically for this, so you'll be seeing me in them for the next few weeks.' Emma opened her car door, climbed in and gave Lucie a final wave.

Lucie walked toward her own car. She couldn't imagine what Emma's lifestyle must be like – shoplifting for the sake of it, her husband scrutinising her wardrobe. If she'd learnt nothing else about Emma today, she'd learnt that they were living in very different worlds.

Chapter Nine

EMMA

Daniel, dressed in a black dinner suit, was pacing in front of the garage when Emma arrived home. She let out a breath, relieved she'd thought to stop to change clothes on the way home. The clock on her dashboard said it was only six; she had at least an hour to get ready before they needed to leave. She wondered why he looked so agitated.

Daniel opened her car door before she had a chance to do it herself.

Emma smiled. 'Thanks, you're being very chivalrous.'

'Where have you been?' Daniel didn't return the smile. His face was tight, his voice strained.

'Why? Has something happened?'

He relaxed a little and forced a smile. 'No, sorry, I've just been worried. I expected you'd be home by now. We've got dinner tonight, don't forget.'

'I hadn't forgotten – it's with the Chapmans, isn't it?'

'Yes. Jerry and Elise will be there, too.'

Emma swallowed. She'd forgotten all about Elise Carter and their run-in at Danes. She'd meant to pay her a visit, make up something that Elise would believe. She pulled Daniel toward her and kissed him. 'You're looking very handsome. Why were you pacing up and down?'

Daniel hesitated. 'Look, it's probably nothing, but your dad called.'

Emma pulled away from Daniel. 'Dad? He called here?'

'Yes, he couldn't find your mobile number so he called the house. Anyway, he wanted you to know that your mum's been a bit unwell. They've admitted her to hospital this afternoon for some tests. He told me that you weren't to worry, it was probably just routine stuff and he'd call again tomorrow when they knew what was going on.'

A shiver went down Emma's spine. Something was wrong, terribly wrong. 'You spoke to my dad? Had a proper conversation with him?'

'He rang the house, I wasn't given much of a choice.' Daniel frowned. 'What did you expect? That I'd hang up on him when he's in the midst of telling me his wife's been taken to hospital in an ambulance?'

'Ambulance? What? You said it was no big deal!'

'I don't think it's a big deal. She had some chest pains and didn't think it was a good idea to drive herself. Your dad was out and she couldn't get a hold of Simone so she rang an ambulance. According to your dad she said it was the least bother for everyone.' He smiled, his eyes soft and kind.

Emma stared at him. Daniel was being nice about her parents, talking as if they were great friends. It wasn't normal or natural; he was hiding something. 'She's really sick, isn't she?'

Daniel ran his hand over his head. 'Jesus, how did you come to that conclusion?'

'You hate my family, you're completely dismissive of them. Suddenly you're talking like they're people you care about. That's why I'm worried.'

'Okay, let me start again. Your loser father rang to say your loser mother's been taken to hospital for some tests. No need to panic, even though the doctor will be some backyard hack without a clue what he's doing. That better?'

Tears pricked at the back of Emma's eyes. 'You're still being too nice, your voice isn't mean enough. I'd better go and ring Dad.'

Daniel grabbed her hand before she had a chance to walk away. 'Don't. He said he'll be at the hospital all night with her and doesn't have a mobile phone. He'll call as soon as there's any news but thinks it will be tomorrow. If you're still up for it, let's get you dressed and take you out on the town to get your mind off things. And, for the record, I don't hate your family. I just find it easier not to deal with them or anything that stirs up the past.'

Daniel leant forward and kissed Emma gently on the lips before pulling her into a tight embrace.

Hand in hand, Emma and Daniel walked through the brightly lit entrance of the Customs House and made their way to the restaurant at the back of the building.

'The restaurant?' Emma asked.

'Yes, there's only six of us, seemed crazy to book a private room. It will be nice, sitting outside. We can enjoy the river view.'

Emma smiled as the maître d' approached them. 'Ah, Mr and Mrs Wilson, so lovely to see you tonight.' He shook hands with Daniel. 'The staff will be delighted to have you dining with us. I hope you've both had a good day?'

Daniel smiled and clapped the maître d' on the back. 'We have, as we hope you have, too.'

The maître d' directed them to a table out on the balcony, overlooking the Brisbane River. Peter and Helen Chapman were already seated, enjoying a glass of wine. Peter stood as Daniel and Emma approached the table. He clasped Daniel's hand before making his way around the table to kiss Emma. He looked her up and down. 'My, you look beautiful, as always.'

Emma laughed and sat down next to Helen. They'd been friends with the Chapmans for a number of years.

'Hope you don't mind that I've invited Jerry and Elise,' Daniel said. 'Jerry was hoping to have a bit of a chat about investing in some gold and silver. He thinks we should diversify from business investment and I wanted you to hear what he has to say. It seems quite valid and I want you to be in from the start if there's an opportunity there.'

Peter nodded. 'I appreciate it.'

The maître d' arrived at the table with a tray holding a Corona in a frosted glass – Daniel's usual – and a glass of champagne.

'Now this is what I call great service,' Daniel said. He raised his glass and offered a toast to friendship and success.

Daniel and Peter stood again as Jerry and Elise arrived at the table ten minutes later. Elise was all squeals as she air-kissed Emma and Helen. They were soon seated and more drinks organised. The men started to talk golf and moaned about their forever stagnant handicaps. Emma half listened as Daniel moaned as much as the rest of them. She smiled. He played the social game well. He could par the course when he went around by himself, but with colleagues and clients he always blew out his scorecard by ten to fifteen shots. At times he laughed with Emma, saying how he'd had to five-putt the last green to ensure his opponent walked away with the win.

Elise excused herself and made her way toward the ladies' room. Emma saw it as her opportunity to have a quick chat. She excused herself as well and followed after Elise. She was touching up her lipstick when Elise came out of the toilet cubicle. She smiled in the mirror at her. 'Great to see you. I missed out the other weekend when you guys caught up with Daniel.'

Elise turned on the tap. 'Yes, how was your weekend away? Daniel mentioned you'd gone to see your parents.'

'It was lovely, thank you.' She cleared her throat. 'So how have you been? Saw you shopping the other day. Did you buy anything nice?'

Elise's forehead creased. 'Oh yes, that's right. On the escalator. Who was that woman you were with? She didn't look very nice; in fact she looked rather scary.'

Emma laughed. 'Just a woman I was helping out. She has a few issues and needs a hand from time to time. It's some of the volunteer work I do.'

Elise raised her eyebrows. 'Really? What charity is that?'

Emma racked her brains. 'It's not really a charity. I just go into the psych hospital and help out from time to time. They struggle to get volunteers, as you can probably imagine.' Psych hospital? Jesus, where had that come from?

Elise turned and stared at her. 'What, and they let you take the patients out shopping? That one didn't look very friendly at all. Are you sure that it's safe to be doing that?'

Emma bit the inside of her lip. The story was getting out of control. A psych hospital would hardly allow patients to head out shopping with a volunteer. 'Some of them are still okay to go out. That lady was being reassessed this week, so it might be her last outing.' She gave a little laugh. 'I was thinking of helping out at a retirement village instead; it would be safer.'

Elise dried her hands and walked toward the exit. 'I'm surprised Daniel would allow you to go into a mental hospital. There's no way Jerry would let me – not that I'd want to.'

'They're not called mental.' Emma stopped herself – that was hardly the point of this conversation. 'Look, Elise, stop for a minute.'

She stopped and turned to face Emma.

'You're right, Daniel wouldn't let me do that kind of work so I haven't told him. I'd hate him to be worried or upset. I've already stopped volunteering there but I would really appreciate it if you didn't mention it to him.'

Elise nodded, her smile sickly sweet. 'Of course. That's nice of you to worry so much about him.'

Emma relaxed; she didn't like lying, but she didn't have much choice. Thank goodness Elise was gullible.

They made their way back to the table, but just before they reached it Elise turned to Emma. She lowered her voice. 'The two police you left the store with, do they work at the mental hospital, too?' She winked, took her seat and turned to Helen.

Daniel looked over and smiled as Emma sank down into her chair. A shiver ran through her as she forced a smile in return.

Morning sunlight flooded through the bedroom window. Emma stretched and slipped out of bed to close the shutters. Arriving home at midnight the night before, Daniel had insisted they leave them open so they were bathed in moonlight as they made love.

Emma pulled on her robe, smiling to herself. Sex with Daniel was always good. Even when he was stressed or upset it was good. Last night, when he'd been at his loving, caring best, was extra special.

Elise hadn't said anything more about Emma's situation but had made a point of giving her a big wink when they left. Emma had smiled and winked back. Perhaps Elise liked the idea of sharing a secret; perhaps it was something they would bond over? She would just have to hope she kept her mouth shut.

Daniel was snoring softly as Emma slipped out of the room and went downstairs to prepare coffee. She glanced at the kitchen clock – it was nearly nine already. She checked the home phone and her mobile. No messages. She wondered if her dad would be home. She picked up the phone and dialled her parents' house.

She was just about to hang up when her father's voice came through.

'Dad, it's Emma. How are you? How's Mum?'

'She's not great, love.'

A lump rose in Emma's throat. She crossed her fingers: her mum couldn't be sick, not really sick.

'I was going to ring you later this morning. The doctor's found masses on her lungs. They did a CT scan last night and are doing some biopsies this morning.'

'Masses? What, cancer?'

Brian sighed. 'We're hoping not, but it's not looking too good.' The phone went silent.

'Dad?'

She heard her father clear his throat. His voice broke as he spoke. 'Sorry, love.'

A tear escaped the corner of her eye. She'd never seen or heard her dad cry. 'Dad, I'll come down. I should be there just after lunch, okay?'

'There's no need love. I'm not sure there'll be any more news by then.'

'I'm still going to come. I'll come straight to the hospital.'

Emma talked to her father for a couple more minutes before hanging up. She turned to find Daniel watching her from the doorway.

'Your mum?'

Tears rolled down Emma's cheeks. Her mum couldn't have cancer. It wasn't possible. Things like this happened to other families, not her sweet, gentle parents.

Daniel came over and hugged her tightly, stroking her hair.

She pulled away from him, wiping her eyes. 'I have to go back to the Bay. It might be lung cancer.'

'Oh no.' Daniel held her tighter. 'That's awful. Of course you need to be with her.'

'You don't mind? You said you hated me going there. Just two weeks ago you had a fit about it.'

'If your mum's sick you should be there. If something happens and you don't get a chance to say goodbye you'll never forgive yourself. Trust me, I know.'

Emma pulled back from the embrace again and stared at her husband. His eyes were distant, deep in his own memories. 'You didn't get a chance to say goodbye?'

He shook his head.

'But she was sick, you knew that. What happened?' Emma was confused. Daniel had told her his mother had died when he was fourteen. She'd had cancer and after a year of fighting had lost her battle. It was in her bones, too advanced when it had first been detected. He'd never talked about her actual death.

'Why don't I make us some coffee?' Daniel walked over to the kitchen bench and started fiddling with the coffee machine while Emma sat down on one of the stools.

Daniel continued to talk, his back to her. 'My dad was told she was at the end of her journey. She only had a few days to live. It was at the same time as my Year Nine adventure camp.' His voice wavered. 'The bastard sent me on that camp. At the time I was glad to go, glad to have a break from the hospital visits. When I looked back afterward, I realised Mum knew she was saying goodbye to me that last day. The day that all I did was talk about the camp and how I couldn't wait to go on the flying fox and go kayaking. I never thought that would be the last time I'd see her.'

A lump rose in Emma's throat.

'When I got back from camp Dad told me she'd died the previous day. He didn't even come and get me early from the camp. Just met me at the bus and told me on the way home in the car. I later found out he'd brought her home to die. That was her final wish, to be surrounded by everything she loved. It just didn't include me.'

Tears ran down Emma's face as she listened to the hurt and anger in her husband's voice. She'd learnt more about him in the past five minutes than she had in their entire relationship. So many things now made sense.

Daniel turned back to Emma, a coffee in each hand. His face filled with concern the moment he saw her tears. He put the coffees down and came over to her. 'No need to cry, it was a long time ago. The main thing we should learn from it is that if your mum's sick then you need to be there. I know I've acted like a prick about your family. It's not really about them, I just hate the fact that they interact with my father. Your family's a constant reminder of him and that town; that bloody town.'

'I can understand you hating your father, but why do you hate the town so much?'

Daniel sighed. 'It's not so much the town, but the people. Mum was pretty popular, had a good network of friends. It's a small town so everyone knows everyone. Do you know, not one person came over to the house after she died? Not one meal was left for us, nothing. I never understood it. Mum had always been the first to cook and bake when there was any sort of crisis. She'd organise the town to drop off meals for a family in need every day until they were okay. Yet no one did that for us. Dad went to pieces and I was left, at fourteen, to cook, clean and look after him. I could cook toast and put together a bowl of cereal at that age. Those bitches were supposed to be Mum's friends. What a joke.'

Emma pulled her husband close to her. She couldn't believe what she was hearing. 'No wonder you hate them. I can't believe Mum and Dad didn't help out.'

Daniel pushed Emma away and picked up his coffee. 'They didn't. That's enough soul-baring for me today. Let's go out to the pool, drink these and then I'll make us some eggs while you get packed.'

Emma followed Daniel out to the pool, her head spinning. Finally she understood and sympathised with Daniel's hatred for the Bay and everything it represented.

The white walls seemed like they were closing in on Emma as she wound her way through the corridors in search of room twelve. The smell of antiseptic and bleach permeated her nostrils. Her stomach had been in knots the entire drive. Her mother couldn't have cancer. She was too fit, too happy. Her weight loss was a result of exercise, not illness, wasn't it?

'Oh, my goodness.'

Emma heard her mother's cheery voice before she saw her. Daniel had disappeared for half an hour while Emma got ready for the trip and returned with an exquisite mixed bouquet. Emma had been reduced to tears again. Her husband's change of attitude amazed her. The arrangement was so large that it now blocked Emma's view. She sat them on the tray table near her mother's bed and leant down to kiss Maggie. 'How are you, Mum?'

'Better now you and your flowers have arrived. Emma, they're magnificent.' Maggie was smiling but her pale, pinched face gave away the shock and discomfort of the past twenty-four hours. 'Where on earth did you get them? Certainly not from Birds in Paradise; Hilda does a nice job, but not like this.'

Emma smiled. 'Daniel went out and got them this morning. They're from a florist near us. He sends his love.'

Maggie looked up, her eyes wide with surprise. She coughed, her chest racking as she did. She finally caught her breath. 'Well, please thank him for me. They are really gorgeous and quite special.'

'Where's Dad?'

'He's at the shop. I suggested he go in, do a few hours to take his mind off things.' Tears glistened in Maggie's eyes. 'He's trying to be strong and supportive but I know him too well. He's a mess inside. It's not really helping at this point – don't tell him though, will you?'

Emma shook her head. Her poor dad. He'd be lost without her mother, which was probably exactly why he was a mess right now. 'What have the doctors said?'

'Not a lot. The CT scan showed masses on my lungs. They've done some initial tests and we expect the results tomorrow. It depends on the results as to what happens next.'

Emma sat down in a chair next to her mother's bed. 'Do you need anything? Is there anything I can do?'

Maggie thought for a moment. 'Yes, there is. I'd love you to go and get me some of my regular everyday clothes. Your dad brought me some but they are my nicer dresses. He had it in his mind that looking good would help me feel good.' She smiled. 'He's being sweet but not very practical. I've got some comfortable trackpants and a few light jumpers in my wardrobe.' She pulled the blankets around her. 'It's bloody freezing in here – if I don't have cancer I certainly expect to have pneumonia by the time I leave.'

A lump lodged in Emma's throat at her mother's use of the word 'cancer'. It was only a word, but a terrifying one.

Maggie took her hand and stroked it. 'Don't worry about me, love. There's no way I'd let something like cancer beat me. I'm ready to fight if I have to.'

'Let's hope you don't have to,' Emma said. 'Now, should I get your things now or later?'

'Now would be great. Pop in and see your dad on the way. He'll give you a key. There are a few other items I'd like you to get, too.'

Briefly wondering why her mother hadn't asked Simone to get the things she wanted, Emma memorised her mother's list, before leaving and driving past the revamped cafés and local shops along the main street toward The Café. Her hands clenched the steering wheel as she passed Harvey's Meat Emporium. To think, only a short time ago she had been talking to Daniel's dad, feeling guilty that they'd neglected him and thinking of ways to persuade Daniel to make contact with the poor, lonely man. Now she'd like to walk in and slap him hard across the face. To prevent his son from saying goodbye to his own mother was unforgivable. The impact it had had on Daniel's life was enormous. Emma could only imagine the boy he'd been prior to his mother's illness and death. Probably happy-go-lucky, the life and soul of the party. She saw that side occasionally, but then he often closed up, became serious, withdrawn. Harvey had a lot to answer for, as did the women of the town.

She pulled up outside The Café where a few people were sitting outside enjoying a late lunch. As she walked into the shop, she stopped and sucked in a breath. Her dad was behind the counter. He was unshaven, his skin grey and he looked at least ten years older than he had at the anniversary party.

His face lit up when he saw Emma. He finished serving a customer and came around the counter and hugged her. 'Thanks for coming. I know Mum will be pleased to see you.' He gave a small laugh. 'She threw me out; said I was too miserable to keep her company.'

Emma smiled at him. 'No offence, but you do kind of look like a mess.' The deep circles under his eyes were more obvious close up. 'Have you had any sleep?'

101

Brian shook his head. 'Not much. The chair in your mum's room isn't all that comfortable. She's insisted I sleep at home tonight so I'll get a good night.'

Emma nodded. 'Okay. I'll need your keys if that's okay. I've already stopped in on Mum and she's asked me to pick up a few things from the house for her.'

'What?' Her father's voice was filled with hurt. 'Why is she asking you? I could have got them for her.'

Emma touched his arm and lowered her voice. 'Some of it's women's stuff. She might have thought you'd be uncomfortable.'

'Don't be silly, we've lived together for forty years; there's nothing I don't know about her.'

'Then she probably wanted you to have a break from fussing over her. She's more worried about you and how you're coping than she is about herself. You know Mum.'

Brian sighed and fished in his pocket for his keys. He slipped one of them off the ring and handed it to Emma. 'No doubt you're right. I'm planning to leave at about four and head back to the hospital for a couple of hours. Will I see you there?'

'I'm not sure – I'll check with Mum. She might need a rest or prefer us one at a time. I'll play it by ear and see you at home later, if not at the hospital. What do you want me to do about the key?'

'You hold on to it; I've got a spare hidden in the shed.'

'Okay. Can I make a suggestion?'

Brian nodded.

'Go home, have a shower and a shave and put on some fresh clothes. I think Mum would be less worried if you turned up looking like your normal self.' She gave her dad another quick hug. 'She'll be okay; she refuses not to be.'

Tears filled Brian's eyes. 'I hope so, love. I can only hope so.'

Emma climbed back into her car, tears rolling down her cheeks. Her dad looked so old, so lost. She'd never imagined she'd see him like this.

Maggie was sitting up in bed watching television when Emma returned. She'd collected the clothes her mother asked for and also had a bag with toiletries, a book and Maggie's iPad.

'I'm shocked.' Emma put the bags on the bed. 'You have an iPad? When did you get so tech savvy?'

Maggie smiled. 'Do you remember my friend, Patty Davis? She's Joanna's mum – the skinny little girl you played with in primary school.'

'Yes, I remember.' How could she forget? Joanna was the first of her friends to start calling her Grease Monkey and other names.

'She moved to Sydney when Joanna and her husband had children. Wanted to be near the grandkids. I was rather upset at the time. Patty and I were very close. We walked most mornings together and we often had her and Graham over for dinner.' She held up the iPad. 'This was her parting gift to me. She loaded on email, Skype and even Facebook so we could keep in touch. We usually Skype once a week, often in the evening over a glass of wine, and we put photos up on Facebook for each other.' She leant toward Emma. 'To be honest, I've probably seen enough of her grandkids now.' She laughed. 'I'll get my revenge when Simone has her bub.'

'My mother's on Facebook? Now that's a turn-up,' Emma said. 'I thought I'd had all the surprises last visit.'

'You can't go away for five years and expect everything to be the same.'

A slight chill ran through Emma as she caught the bitter edge to her mother's words. It appeared the lovely warm welcome from the anniversary weekend did have underlying resentment. She deserved it, she knew that, but it still hurt to hear. She cleared her throat. 'So, where's Simone?'

'We haven't told her.'

'What?' Emma's mouth dropped open. 'How can you keep something like this from her? She needs to know.'

Maggie shook her head. 'That baby is the only thing she needs to think about right now. I don't want her getting upset and going into labour or something worse. I've sworn the few people who know I'm in here to secrecy. You know what this town's like. And anyway, we don't know anything for sure.'

'Yes, but . . .'

Maggie stopped her. 'No buts. I don't want her knowing just yet. Now, how was your father when you saw him? Unshaven and looking like a bum still?'

Emma nodded.

'I hope you had a go at him, told him to pull himself together?'

Emma chatted with her mother for a little while but noticed she was tiring. 'Why don't I go and leave you to have a rest? Dad said he'd come in sometime after four.'

Maggie nodded. 'Thanks, love. I think I could use a little sleep.'

After kissing her mother goodbye, Emma retraced her steps through the hospital corridor. She had only been here once before and that was to visit Simone when her sister was ten and had broken her leg. She'd been quite jealous at the time of all the fuss and attention Simone had received. She'd even wished it was her getting to stay in a nice room and be waited on by the nurses. The deserted corridors and sterile walls didn't offer the same appeal now she was an adult.

Emma remained deep in thought as she weaved her way through the myriad corridors. She made a final turn into the one that led to the hospital entrance and car park and ran smack into something solid. A male voice cried out as she crashed to the floor and the air rushed from her lungs. She looked up to find a guy, mouth open, standing over her. He appeared to be frozen.

She caught her breath. 'Are you just going to stand there gawking at me, or are you going to help me up?'

'Oh God, I'm so sorry.' He held out his hand and helped her back on to her feet. 'I'm so sorry, I didn't see you.'

Emma rubbed her elbow, which seemed to have taken most of the impact. Her bottom was also hurting but she was less inclined to rub that right now. 'So I gathered.'

His face and arms were tanned, his tight black T-shirt highlighting his muscular arms. Emma could hardly see his face through the mop of jet-black hair that flopped over his forehead and into his eyes. It was a teenager's haircut and looked out of place on a guy who must be pushing forty.

'Maybe you should get a haircut, then you could see where you're going.'

He pushed the hair off his face, revealing warm, caramel-coloured eyes. 'I think you might be right. My mother's always telling me off. If she got wind of this little incident she'd take the scissors to me herself.' He smiled at Emma. 'How's your elbow? I know a good hospital if you need a doctor.'

Emma wasn't in the mood for his humour. She knew this type of guy – all dimples and good looks. She'd dated a few of these types before meeting Daniel. They lived off their charm and thought the world owed them something.

He didn't wait for her response. 'How about I buy you a coffee to make up for my klutziness.'

Emma shook her head. Was he for real? Was this how he picked up women? Trawling the hospital corridors, literally knocking them off their feet.

'No, thank you. How about you watch where you're going next time, and if knocking someone down is your stupid ploy to meet women, I suggest you find another tack.'

Emma felt a twinge of remorse as a look of horror crossed his face. She hesitated. Should she apologise? She shook herself. No! He was the one who was out of line. Head held high, conscious of his eyes drilling into her back, she walked toward the hospital's exit.

Emma wasn't sure whose face registered the most surprise when Simone opened the front door. Surely there was a limit to how big a belly could balloon?

'What are you doing here?' Simone asked.

'Nice welcome. Are you going to invite me in?'

'Um, sure. Of course.'

Emma followed Simone as she shuffled down the hallway toward the kitchen. 'So how come you're back so soon?' She turned to face Emma, a wicked grin slowly appearing. 'Making up for the past five years, are you?'

'Very funny. No, not exactly. But I need a cup of tea. Sit down, I'll make us both one.'

Simone didn't need convincing and sank down into a comfortable chair as Emma moved about the kitchen as if she were a regular visitor. 'You do realise you'll have to help me out of this, don't you? There's no way I'll get up. Johnno thinks it's hilarious, calls himself "the crane".'

Emma smiled. 'You've grown bigger since the party. You look like you're going to explode.'

Simone groaned. 'And feel like it. All those bloody women who talk about their glow during pregnancy and how wonderful it was must have used surrogates. They left out the swollen ankles, sore tits and veins in places veins should not be.'

'I thought you said it was all going well?'

'It is, that's my point. My stuff's minor, doesn't even register on the shit-pregnancy radar. It's a breeze, according to the midwife I've been seeing. Can't even begin to imagine what the birth will be like.'

'So don't. Just go with it. From what I hear, there's not a lot you can do to really prepare anyway. It'll be horrible and then you'll have a beautiful baby and forget all about it.'

'You reckon?'

Emma grinned. 'No idea. Sounded good though.' She poured some milk into Simone's tea and brought the cups over.

'Why are you really here?'

Emma avoided Simone's gaze. 'Oh, was just nearby, thought I'd stop in. Daniel's pretty busy so I was at a bit of a loose end.'

'Em, you were always a hopeless liar. What's up?'

Simone was right. She should have thought through a story before she arrived. 'It's Mum. She's not well and I thought I'd come up and see if she needed a hand.'

'Mum, what? Why on earth would Mum call you if she's not well? I'm just around the corner.' She struggled to the edge of her seat. 'Help me up, would you? I need to ring her. Silly old bat, she must be losing it.'

Emma didn't move to help. 'No, don't. She's not at home; she went into the hospital yesterday. She didn't want you to worry, that's why Dad called me. Actually, she'll be furious when she finds out I've told you. She's convinced you'll go into labour and then she'll miss all the action.' Emma smiled, trying to downplay the situation. 'She can't be too sick if that's her biggest worry.'

Simone sank back into her chair. 'Hospital? What's wrong with her then?'

'They're not completely sure. That cough she had turned nasty yesterday. She was having trouble breathing and chest pains so they ran a few tests. They found some shadows and masses on her lungs, but they could be a number of things. The biopsy will give us a better idea tomorrow.'

Simone's rosy cheeks turned pale.

'Are you okay? You're not going to go into labour, are you?'

Simone looked up at Emma. 'Biopsy? Do they think it's cancer?'

'Not necessarily. It's one of the possibilities, but even if it is they've already said the lumps are contained in the lungs and they haven't found any anywhere else, so it will be quite treatable.' Emma hoped this lie sounded more believable than the last one. It wasn't exactly a lie as they hadn't mentioned finding lumps anywhere else. She just hoped this might lessen Simone's anxiety.

'I should go and visit her.'

'Leave it until tomorrow. I'll come and get you and we can go in together. Dad was going in this afternoon and she was already pretty tired. She really didn't want you knowing, so this will just worry her even more.'

Simone nodded. 'Okay.' She stared at Emma. 'What happened to your elbow?'

'What?'

'Your elbow. You've been rubbing it for the last five minutes.'

Emma dropped her hand. 'Oh. I bumped, literally, into some mopsy-haired idiot at the hospital. He was nearing forty but dressed and acted like a seventeen-year-old. Smashed straight into me. I got the impression he knocks over women as a habit, uses it as a pick-up line.'

Simone laughed. 'God, what a loser. Probably a visitor. The town has its share of idiots but I doubt any would sink that low.'

Emma sipped her tea. 'I was thinking, if Mum's not back on her feet in a couple of days I might need to hang around, help out a bit. There's Dad and the shop, too. I'm not sure exactly how everything runs, or how involved Mum is, but I imagine they might need a hand.'

'What about Daniel? He hates you coming here. Won't he mind?'

'No, he won't mind at all. He spoke to Dad yesterday.'

Simone raised her eyebrows.

'I wasn't home when Dad rang. Anyway, I think it's brought up a whole lot of unresolved issues for him.'

Emma was aware that Simone was waiting for further explanation.

'Let's just say he missed the opportunity to say goodbye to his mum before she died and, as a result, wants me to be here.'

Simone's face was now almost grey. 'In case she dies? I thought it wasn't that bad?'

'Of course she's not going to die. I'm just saying, the whole having-a-sick-mum thing hit home with Daniel.' She grinned. 'You should see the flowers he bought for her, they're so over the top they're almost embarrassing.'

Simone didn't return Emma's smile. 'I couldn't cope if something happens to her.' Her eyes clouded with fear. 'I really couldn't. I've got no idea what I'm supposed to do with a baby. She's supposed to help me.' Tears started to roll down her face.

Emma moved toward her sister and took her hand. 'Oh, Sim. I shouldn't have told you. I didn't want to upset you, but of course I have. I shouldn't have come to visit.' Emma could have kicked herself.

Simone shook her head. 'I needed to know. Don't worry about the tears, they're another side effect of pregnancy; I cry five or six times a day – ask Johnno. The amount of tissues we're going through is ridiculous. It's better I get it out now. Then when I see Mum I can be all strong and tell her she's an idiot for trying to protect me.'

Emma looked at her younger sister. 'You're going to make a good mum. Look at you, all strong and selfless. That's one lucky baby. Come on, let me be useful. What have you got to eat? I'll make up something for dinner and ring Dad, tell him to stop in here on the way home from the hospital. If that's okay?'

'Okay? That'd be great. I didn't think you knew how to cook. I assumed it was all restaurants for you and Daniel.'

Emma was pleased to see the wicked spark returning to Simone's eyes and the colour to her cheeks.

'I'd watch it if I were you, you might actually need to get out of that chair at some stage. Shut up and have a rest or whatever it is you overindulged, whingeing pregnant women do.'

The hospital window ledge overflowed with colourful flower arrangements.

'It's like a florist's in here,' Simone said, leaning down to kiss her mother's cheek.

Maggie laughed. 'Your dad's gone a bit crazy on the flowers, trying to match the arrangement Emma brought with her. Now, what are you doing here?' She glared in Emma's direction. 'You weren't supposed to be worried about this.'

'She needed to know, Mum. We all do.' Emma sat down in a chair beside the bed, indicating for Simone to do the same. 'Tell us what the doctors are saying. Have you had the test results?'

Maggie nodded. 'The initial tests have shown that more invasive testing is required. They won't know what they're dealing with until these are carried out.'

'Can they do the tests here?' Emma asked.

'No, I'll have to go to Brisbane. Just for a day, then they'll let me go home. It's been scheduled for Friday.'

'What exactly are they testing for?'

Maggie and Brian exchanged a glance before Maggie faced her daughters. 'They've suggested it might be small-cell lung cancer. If that is the case they need to know what stage it's at so they can begin treatment.'

Simone's hands gripped the arms of her chair as soon as Maggie mentioned the word 'cancer'. 'Cancer? They really think you've got cancer?'

Maggie gave a little laugh. 'Looks like it might be, love. But other than the cough I feel fine. They say people are usually really fatigued but I haven't been that tired. If it's early days it will be quite simple. They'll operate, remove the tumour, give me some radiation therapy and send me on my way. The biggest pain is the timing, with Bub about to arrive.'

Simone shook her head. 'Don't be worrying about that. I'll be fine. I just need you better as quickly as possible so you can enjoy her.' Tears rolled down Simone's face as she tried to smile. She wiped her eyes with her sleeve. 'Sorry, it's the bloody pregnancy making me all sooky.'

Emma could feel tears scratching the back of her eyes and tried her best to blink them back. They were supposed to be here to cheer their mother up. She looked at both of her parents, who were also teary-eyed, and laughed.

They all stared at her, which made her laugh harder. She bent over, laughing harder still, even though she knew how inappropriate her reaction was. She tried unsuccessfully to pull herself together but then she heard her father start to laugh. He was wiping his eyes with one hand and holding his side with the other.

'They're mad,' Simone said to Maggie, setting Emma and Brian off again. 'We're talking about cancer, what on earth's so funny?'

'It's just the way they cope,' Maggie said. 'Look at them, they're a couple of loons. It reminds me of when Emma was twelve and next door's dog died. She was so upset but couldn't stop laughing.

While inappropriate, it's quite contagious.' She started to laugh. 'I'll tell you what, laughing's a lot more fun than moping around.'

Simone looked on as her family laughed.

Eventually Emma noticed her sister's glare. She wiped her eyes. 'Oh, come on, Sim. We're just being silly. It might make you feel better.'

Simone gave her a weak smile. 'Give me a chance to digest everything, okay? It might take me a while to think the whole thing is hilarious.'

'A long while, I'd think.' A deep voice spoke from the hallway.

Emma jumped to her feet. What the hell was he doing there? It was the loser who'd knocked her down the previous day. Was he following her?

'Can I come in?'

Maggie was smiling at him. 'Of course you can. Come in and meet my eldest daughter.'

He walked into the room and stopped abruptly as his eyes met Emma's. He blushed. 'I think we might have already bumped into each other.' He pushed his hair off his forehead and winked at Emma. 'I've organised a haircut for this afternoon. I hope you'll approve.'

Emma shifted uncomfortably from foot to foot. Who was this guy? She looked to her mother for help.

'Emma, this is Andrew Myers. You've heard us talking about him and all the wonderful things he's done for us and the town.'

Andrew put his hand out. 'Please, call me Drew, and I hope we can start from scratch. I like to make an impression, but not one that has you lying flat on your back.' He grinned. 'Actually, that might not be quite true, I didn't word that very well.'

Emma reluctantly shook his hand. 'I'm Emma. I'm impressed with what you've done with the town. Less impressed with your clumsiness, but I assume that's all part of your act?'

'Emma!' Simone said. 'There's no need to be rude.'

Drew dropped her hand. 'No, she's quite right, Sim. If anything I need to apologise to Emma. I bowled her over yesterday, unfortunately quite literally rather than in my usual charming, witty way.' He grinned. 'Now, enough about that, I just popped in to give Maggie these.' He reached into his bag, pulled out a box of truffles and handed them to Maggie. 'Enjoy. I'll pop back in later for a chat when you're on your own. I don't want to intrude on family time.'

'You're not intruding, son,' Brian said. 'You're as welcome as any other member of this family.'

Drew looked at Emma. Arms folded across her chest, mouth unsmiling; her message was clear.

'I'm not sure everyone quite agrees with that.' He winked at Maggie. 'Now, you enjoy one of those chocolates.' His grin reappeared as he looked at Emma. 'You might want to have a couple of those before I see you again, sweeten you up a bit.' He raised his eyebrows and retreated from the room.

Emma released the breath she'd been holding. 'Well, he tops the list of dickheads I've met.'

Brian laughed. 'Think you might have met your match there.'

'My match? What are you talking about?'

'Don't take it the wrong way, love, it's just that some men find it intimidating talking to a beautiful woman.' He chuckled. 'I don't think Drew's one of them.'

'Let's change the subject, shall we?' Simone suggested. 'A few minutes ago we were discussing your treatment, which got dismissed rather quickly so you could all collapse with laughter and then Emma could flirt with Drew. I think there are more important things to be discussing.'

Emma stared at Simone. She was not flirting with Drew. The guy was an arrogant idiot. But Simone was right about one thing. For one lovely moment the whole cancer situation had been forgotten.

Brian walked out of The Café carrying two juices and a folder tucked under his arm. He placed a juice on the table in front of Emma and sat down. 'Are you sure you want to stay and do this? What about Daniel? What will he say?'

'He'll be fine. I have to head home for a few days over the weekend, so he'll see me then.'

'Oh?' Alarm flashed in Brian's eyes. 'I assumed you'd be here for the weekend. Your mum will be home on Friday and Saturday is one of our busiest days.' He opened his folder and pulled out a staff roster. 'I think I might need to consider getting a manager in for the next month or two.'

Emma avoided his gaze. 'Of course I'll help as much as possible. I just have a . . .' She hesitated, too embarrassed to tell him she had to report for community service. '. . . A prior commitment. I'm sorry, Dad, but it's something I'm obligated to do and it's for the next five Saturdays.'

Her father patted her hand. 'Don't apologise. You're already doing a lot more than anyone ever expected. I'll work out something.' He went back to studying his roster.

Emma sipped her juice. Of course she had to help out, but what was she getting herself into? She knew nothing about preparing food or running a business. Her dad had assured her the casual staff could practically run the place, she'd just be overseeing them and helping out on the days she was in the shop, but it was still daunting. Particularly when she thought back to the number of years she'd spent trying to get away from the place. She wasn't sure how Daniel would take the news but hoped he'd be supportive, particularly in light of the way he'd acted on Sunday morning.

'Look, love, I'll be fine to manage until next week. You can't do anything to help Mum right now. With her in hospital I might as well be in the shop full-time. Why don't you head home, check with Daniel that he's okay with you being here? I know you have a busy life, we don't want to cause any problems.'

'It won't be a problem. Are you sure you don't want me to help out this week? I could stay until Friday.'

Brian looked at the rosters again. 'No, I think we'll be fine. When you get back it will only take half a day to train you up. There's nothing really hard to learn and it's not as if you'll be running the place on your own.'

Emma glanced at her watch. 'How about a different plan? It's only ten o'clock. I could stay until two or even three today. How about you train me up now? That way when I get back I'll be ready to jump straight in.'

Brian nodded. 'Great idea. Okay then, let's head back into the kitchen and find some aprons. It's *training time*.'

Emma smiled. She'd heard her father use that term many times as she was growing up. Every schoolkid they'd employed part-time had to go through training time. She never had as she'd refused to work in the shop. After years of being teased and taunted, at age fourteen she'd faced the disappointed faces of her parents and informed them she'd applied for a part-time job at the pharmacy in the town's main street. Now, twenty years later, her father would finally have the opportunity to introduce her to his infamous training time.

Emma whizzed past the Golden Bay sign, relieved to be heading home for a few days. She'd sent Daniel a message to let him know she'd be home late but hadn't had a reply. He was probably stuck in meetings. She was looking forward to a swim and rolled her shoulders, wondering if she'd have time in the next few days to book in a massage. Her body was tense after the stress of the visit. Her mother's tests were scheduled for Friday so they wouldn't have any results back until at least next week. She'd promised her dad she'd be back on Sunday night in time for her first shift on Monday. That would give her five days at home. One would be taken up with community service but the others she would enjoy with Daniel.

Thanks to roadworks she pulled into the driveway half an hour later than she'd expected. She pushed the button and the garage door opened. Daniel's car space was empty. She smiled. That gave her enough time to have a shower and get changed before he came home.

An hour later Emma poured herself a glass of wine. It was seven thirty and still no sign of Daniel. She tried ringing his phone and once again got his voicemail. If he hadn't heard her earlier message, he might not even realise she was home. She decided to get busy, prepare a meal for when he did arrive. She opened the fridge, pleased to see it stocked full of fresh vegetables. She selected the ingredients she'd need for her oven-baked chilli and basil linguine. It would only take her twenty minutes to prepare and then it could go in the oven until he got home.

Two glasses of wine and an hour and a half later, Emma took the linguine out of the oven. Still no word from Daniel. She served herself up a bowl, added a salad to her plate and decided to sit outside to eat it. It was a beautiful, warm Queensland night. She turned the pool lights on and listened to the chirping sound of the cicadas as she ate.

It was close to eleven when Emma climbed into bed. Her phone rang. She grabbed it. Daniel, finally. 'Where are you?'

'Perth. I just landed, that's why my phone's been off. Bloody long flight, I'm exhausted.'

'Perth? What? Why didn't you let me know you were going? I came home to see you.'

'Hon, I've had this meeting scheduled for months. You weren't home so I didn't see any reason to report in.'

Emma sank back on to the pillows. 'I wasn't asking you to report in, I'm just disappointed, that's all.' She lowered her voice. 'I was looking forward to seeing you, making love to you.'

Daniel cleared his throat. 'God, don't say that; you make me want to get on the next flight home. I'll be home Saturday morning. How about I cancel golf and we spend the day together. My flight gets in early. I'll have to drop into the office first but should be home by nine.' He laughed. 'After catching the red-eye, I'm not sure how much energy I'll have, but if all activities are confined to the bedroom, I should manage.'

Emma ran her hand through her hair, tugging on the ends. 'I don't think I can. I've got that commitment on Saturday. You know, the charity I told you about. They'll be expecting me. It would be rude to have said I'll be involved and then not turn up.'

'Can you cancel? Throw a bit more money at it if you feel guilty and tell them you'll be there next Saturday.'

Jesus, now what did she say? 'I'm not sure—'

Daniel cut her off. 'Sorry, Em, my luggage has arrived and I've got a taxi waiting. Don't stress about the charity thing, they'll survive. I'll see you Saturday, okay?'

'Okay.'

'Gotta go. Love you.'

Emma put down her phone. She'd ring the community service people, find out if she could postpone her work order by a week. It wasn't an unreasonable request. She'd tell them she was sick. They'd have to allow her to postpone. She smiled. She'd been dreading Saturday, now it was a day to look forward to.

Chapter Ten

LUCIE

Noah stood in the middle of his bedroom, his fists clenched, his face turning bright red.

Lucie wanted to hug him. He was doing his best not to explode, to try to talk and reason with her. The problem was his attempts weren't going to change her mind – she'd had no choice but to say no.

'But it's Freddie's birthday. My best friend Freddie. I *have* to go to his party.'

Lucie took a deep breath. 'On Saturday you will be at Granny and Grandpa's. I have my course and I have to go. Grandpa will be out playing golf all afternoon when the party is on so Granny won't have a car. There's no way to get you there, sweetheart. It's not that I don't want you to go, it's that it's just not possible.'

Noah started to cry.

Lucie didn't blame him. He'd only been invited to two other parties this year and the thought of missing a birthday was excruciating. She moved closer to Noah and sat down next to him. She tried to pull him toward her for a cuddle but he pushed her away.

'Get away!' he screamed. 'Get away, I hate you! I never go to parties and when someone finally asks me you wreck it.' He started lashing out at Lucie, his fists pummelling her arms.

She grabbed them and stopped him punching. 'Hey, stop that. Hitting me isn't going to help.'

Noah wailed even louder and, with his hands bound, kicked out, his foot connecting with Lucie's cheek.

She dropped his hands and started rubbing it. Jesus, this kid had some power. She wouldn't be surprised if it bruised. She stood up; there was no point continuing this – he was angry and irratio-nal. She left his room and closed the door as the volume of wails increased behind her.

Lucie pulled an icepack from the freezer before sinking on to a chair in the kitchen. What was she supposed to do now? She'd planned to take Noah out for a treat tonight – they both loved pizza and she had a voucher to get one half-price. She could hardly reward his bad behaviour. She sighed. God, he was hard work at the moment. Of course, it wasn't his fault he couldn't go to the party, but his reaction was out of control.

A crash of breaking glass jolted her from her thoughts. She jumped up and dashed back down the hall to Noah's room and pushed open his door. Noah was hiding beneath his doona. Lucie's eyes travelled to the shards of glass covering the bedroom floor and the large hole in the window. She clenched her fists. How could he have done this? She carefully picked her way over to the window and looked out. Noah's soccer ball lay in the garden bed across from his window. He must have kicked it straight through. Lucie glanced at her watch. It was after five. Getting anyone to fix it now would be impossible. She looked at the lump in the bed. Noah was lying very still, no doubt trying his best to disappear. She pulled back the doona. His face was white. He'd obviously given himself a shock. She sat down on his bed.

'Are you okay?'

Noah shook his head, tears rolling down his face.

Lucie pulled him toward her and cuddled him. His little chest heaved as he cried into her shoulder. She rubbed his back until he'd calmed down. His lip quivered as he pulled away and looked at her. 'I'm sorry, Mummy, I didn't mean to break it. The ball went in the wrong direction. It was the ball's fault.'

'You know you're not allowed to play with balls inside. It doesn't matter what you were trying to do, you shouldn't have had the ball in your room in the first place. You know that.'

Noah nodded, his blue eyes glassy from crying. 'Am I in very big trouble?'

Lucie sighed. 'Let's talk about that later. For now we need to get this cleaned up and organise someone to fix it. Although it's so late I don't know if anyone will be able to do it today.'

Noah's lip trembled. 'I can't sleep in here tonight with a big hole in my window. The monsters might get in.'

She took a deep breath. Pointing out that he might have given it some thought before kicking the ball through the window probably wasn't going to help. 'We'll give Grandpa a call, see if he's got some board or something we can use to block it up until it can be fixed. Come on' – she held out her hand – 'let's go and ring him.'

Fifteen minutes later, Noah was comfortably settled in front of the television while Lucie began the task of vacuuming the broken glass from his carpet. She'd rung Walt and was expecting him any minute. She hated to imagine what this window was going to cost to fix.

Once all the glass was captured, she went back to the kitchen to make toasted sandwiches. Pizza was no longer on offer.

Halfway through preparing his toasted ham and cheese there was a knock on the front door. She called out to Noah. 'Go and let Grandpa in, but look through the window first and check it's him.'

She heard Noah's footsteps run down the hall and the front door open. The voice that greeted Noah was definitely not Walt. She turned the sandwich maker off and hurried down the hall. 'Brad?'

Kate's husband was standing at the front door, a large sheet of plywood in his hands, his toolbox in the other. 'Hi Luce, handyman service has arrived.'

Brad? It was bad enough she'd had to ring Walt, but now he'd interrupted Brad's night, too.

Brad sensed her discomfort. 'Don't worry about it. Walt rang me because he didn't have any board. He was going to pick it up on his way over but I said I'd come.' He rolled his eyes. 'Any excuse to get out of the house is welcomed at the moment. Kate's on one of her rants. How about you show me this window.'

Lucie smiled. 'I'm not sure what to say. Other than thanks, I appreciate you coming.' She led Brad down to Noah's bedroom. He laughed when he saw the hole. 'Practising his soccer goals, was he?'

'Something like that.'

'Well, by my estimation he's managed to kick it directly through the middle, so that confirms he's a good shot.' Brad grinned. 'Bloody kids. Pain in the arse, aren't they?'

'You can say that again. He's a bit out of control at the moment. Getting upset and acting out about all sorts of things.'

Brad opened his toolbox. 'Just so you know, it doesn't get any better. Liam's ten and at times I want to kill him.' He held up the hammer. 'He's lucky I haven't taken one of these to him.' He started chipping away at the jagged pieces of glass sticking up from the bottom of the windowpane. 'I'll just make this a bit safer before I put up the board. The guys who replace it will obviously clean everything up but I think it's worth getting rid of a few nasty pieces.'

'Thanks, Brad, I really appreciate this.'

'No worries. As I said, I was looking for an excuse – *any* excuse – to get out of the house tonight. Unfortunately, this will only take about ten minutes.' He winked. 'Next time tell Noah to make a bigger mess, something that will need a few hours of cleaning up.'

Lucie laughed. 'Don't encourage him. Now, unless you need my help, I'd better get him something to eat.'

'I'm fine. The less help the better; it will take me longer.'

Lucie heard his whistling as she walked back to the kitchen. Brad was such a nice guy, she couldn't imagine why he'd chosen Kate as his partner. There must be another side to her for a man like Brad to have taken any interest in her. Lucie shook her head; if there was, she certainly hadn't seen any glimpses of it.

Fifteen minutes later, Lucie gave Noah his sandwich and was making another for herself when Brad appeared in the kitchen.

'Okay, all fixed. I'd better get back to the dragon's lair. Leave you to your dinner of toasties.' He grinned. 'Kate would have a heart attack if I suggested toasties for dinner.'

'We don't have them very often but my dinner plans followed the ball out the window. I needed something quick.'

'Hey, I'm not criticising, I think it's great. So many times we get home late from things and Kate will insist the kids still have a full meal of meat and veg. The last thing you can be bothered cooking, or eating, for that matter. She doesn't do easy at all.'

No, Lucie was sure she didn't. From what she'd observed, Kate made everything as difficult as possible. 'Do you want one?' she asked him. Brad hadn't taken his eyes off the sandwich she was making. 'You're welcome if you've got time.'

'Yes, please.' Brad put his tools down and sat on a stool across from Lucie.

She laughed. 'I don't need to convince you then? Do you want to give Kate a ring, tell her you'll be a bit late?'

'Nah, I told her when I left I might be a while. I planned to stop at the pub on the way home if the job here wasn't very big. Keep me out a bit longer.'

'Did you want me to make this a takeaway?'

'No, of course not. I'd rather stay and talk to you.' Brad glanced at the fridge. 'Don't suppose you've got a beer?'

Lucie glanced at the clock. It was nearly seven and she should start getting Noah ready for bed. Brad was sitting across the kitchen table from her enjoying his second glass of red and third toasted sandwich. Like the rest of the family, Brad had grown to appreciate Matt's wines and had happily accepted a glass when Lucie broke the news that she didn't have any beer. Lucie had poured herself a large glass as well. She was enjoying Brad's company. Other than on the odd occasion when he'd dropped Ruby off for a play, she'd never spent any time alone with him. They usually saw each other at family occasions when Kate and the rest of the Andrews clan were together. Lucie stroked the stem of her wineglass. 'I have to ask you a question – a personal one.'

'Oh? I'm an open book, ask away.'

'Kate. Has she changed a lot since you first met her?'

Brad laughed. 'Why? Because she can be such a bitch?'

Lucie's face grew hot. 'No, I didn't say that. I just wondered, that's all. She sometimes seems a bit outspoken, a bit self-absorbed. I know some women change once they have kids, I wondered if that had happened to her.'

Brad took a large sip of his wine. 'Nope, she's always been a bitch.'

Lucie laughed. Her hand flew up to her mouth. She was shocked at her own reaction. 'Sorry, that's not funny, it's just the way you said it. So matter-of-fact.'

'It *is* a fact. She's a bitch. I got her pregnant and I got locked into a life that at times I hate. I'm only there for the kids. If it wasn't for them it would've been the one-night stand it always should have been.'

'You're kidding? You stuck by her when it was just a one-night stand? Why?'

'To save my father, the reverend, from having a complete heart attack. It was bad enough I knocked someone up, but if he'd found out I wasn't even seeing her, he would have killed me.'

'But you were a grown man. Surely you had to do what was right for you, regardless of the baby?'

'When Kate tracked me down and told me she was pregnant, of course I didn't want anything to do with her. It was my mum who convinced me to give it a go. This was her grandchild, she didn't want to miss out on it. Rather than tell Kate to get lost, which part of me was keen to do, I asked her out instead. I think she was so shocked that not only did she say yes but she decided she quite liked me. She can be loving and kind, so there is a part of her that I've kind of grown to love; it's just she can be so bristly and mean, too.'

'Have you ever thought of leaving?'

'All the time, but I couldn't do it to the kids. Imagine the damage she'd do to them as a single mum. Even if I got fifty percent custody they'd still be on their own with Kate half of the time. She'd be yelling and screaming, making them feel like shit. She does it now, but then I'm their soft place to fall. Kids need that. You can't take out your frustrations on them and not expect it to come back and bite you later on. I'll leave, but I'll wait until they finish school first. That way they can choose where they live and I doubt it will be with Kate.'

Lucie stared at Brad. 'I had no idea, neither did Matt. He said you were great for Kate.'

'Matt was a good guy. In fact, other than Kate, the whole family is beautiful. I'd miss Jan and Walt if I did leave her.'

'Why would you leave Aunty Kate?' Neither Lucie nor Brad had heard Noah come into the kitchen.

Brad reached out and grabbed Noah's hand and pulled him up on to his lap. 'Hey, buddy. Saw the goal you kicked through your window earlier. Nice shot, but next time take it outside, okay?'

Noah nodded. 'It was an accident. Why are you leaving Aunty Kate?'

Brad laughed. 'I'm not. I was talking about when I have to leave her in the mornings, how I always feel different when I'm not around her. Probably like your mum does when she drops you at school. She probably misses you all day.' Brad winked at Lucie. 'Now, I think it's your bedtime. How would you like Uncle Brad to help you have a quick shower so there's time for – let's see, how about four stories?'

'Four?' Noah's face lit up. 'Really?'

Brad nodded. 'Yep. Now you go and get your teeth brushed and clothes off and I'll turn on the shower for you.'

Noah ran to the bathroom.

'Four? Are you sure you have time?' Lucie was surprised at Brad's offer.

Brad stood up. 'Hey, these are my delaying tactics. Anyway I've probably drunk too much to drive straight away.' He handed Lucie her wineglass. 'Why don't you go and sit down and relax? I'll put Noah to bed and then I'll clean up the dishes.'

Lucie sank down into a chair; she could get used to this. She closed her eyes. Poor Brad. She'd always wondered what he saw in Kate. She'd assumed, or at least hoped, Kate was nicer to him behind closed doors. Lucie must have dozed off as what seemed like only a minute, but was apparently four stories later, Noah rushed into the lounge and tugged on her arm. 'Wake up, I've got good news.'

Lucie opened her eyes, trying to focus on Noah. 'Good news?'

'Yes, Ruby's going to Freddie's party, she's friends with Freddie's older sister, so Uncle Brad can take me, too. I don't have to miss out.' Noah beamed as he told her. 'Isn't that great?'

'Mm, maybe.' Lucie was trying to think and wake up at the same time. His behaviour had been so bad, she really didn't think he should be allowed to go now. 'Let's talk about it tomorrow.'

Noah's face fell. 'But why? I'll tell Freddie tomorrow that I'm going.'

Lucie pulled herself up out of the chair and took Noah's hand. 'Come on, back to bed. We'll talk about it tomorrow.'

Noah refused to walk. He pulled tightly on Lucie's arm. 'I'm going to the party. Uncle Brad can take me. You can't say no now.'

Lucie turned to her son. 'Noah, you behaved appallingly earlier. You even smashed your window. I'm not sure that your behaviour is good enough to go to a party. Like I said, we'll talk about it tomorrow.'

Noah started kicking out at Lucie.

She raised her voice. 'Don't you dare.'

'Noah.' Brad's voice stopped him kicking immediately. 'Noah, come over here at once.'

Noah walked over to Brad, his lip quivering.

Brad got down on his knees so he was face to face with Noah and put one hand on each shoulder. 'We don't hit or kick girls, ever. That includes Mummy. Do you understand me?'

Noah nodded.

Brad continued. 'Your dad will be expecting you to do your best right now. To look after your mum and for her to look after you. He would hate to see you getting angry.'

'But—'

Brad stopped him. 'I know you're upset and you think it's not fair, but your mum said she would talk about it in the morning. That means you say goodnight, you give her a hug and you go to bed, hoping that in the morning you'll be able to think of some things that might convince your mum to let you go.'

'Like what?'

'Let's get you to bed and we'll have a chat. Go and say goodnight to your mum.'

Noah walked back to Lucie, his head hanging. He flung his arms around her legs. 'Sorry, Mum. Goodnight, I love you.'

Lucie bent down and kissed him on the top of the head. 'Goodnight. Sweet dreams.' She watched as he walked back to Brad, took his hand and headed toward his room.

Brad reappeared five minutes later and sat down across from Lucie. 'He's exhausted. I think he'll be out to it in a few minutes.'

'Thank you. What you did back there was amazing – calming him down, making him see reason. It probably would have ended up with me throwing him through a window if you hadn't been here.'

'It was my fault. I shouldn't have told him I could take him to the party. I forgot he was probably going to be punished.'

'Do you think I'm being unreasonable saying he can't go?'

Brad hesitated. 'Look, he's five. He's a passionate little kid, reacts instantly when something happens. I think maybe you need to give him a break.'

'What, let him go?'

'At least give him the opportunity to earn the right to go. I suggested to him some ideas of what he could say to negotiate his way to the party. See what he comes up with in the morning. He knows he's done the wrong thing so the way I see it is you can punish him, make him miserable, or you can give him the opportunity to fix the situation and earn his right to go to the party.'

Lucie nodded. 'Sounds reasonable. These are the kinds of strategies I need to start using with him. Nothing I'm doing is working.'

Brad laughed. 'He's a great kid, so you're doing something right.' He stood up. 'Now, I'd better go or I'll be thinking up strategies to deal with the wrath of Kate. Let me know whether you want me to take Noah to the party. I can pick him up from Jan's on Saturday.'

Lucie got up and followed Brad down the hall toward the front door. 'I will, and thanks for everything tonight.'

'Any time.' He grinned. 'In fact, if you can have more problems, or just want to invent some, call me first. Like I said, I'm often looking for an excuse to get out of the house and now I've tasted your toasties I'll expect a broken tap or leaking pipe soon, okay?' He turned to face Lucie, his deep-blue eyes piercing hers.

Her heart flip-flopped as he stared at her. She'd obviously drunk too much. This was her brother-in-law; she wasn't allowed to be attracted to him. She shook herself. She wasn't attracted to him, she just loved that she'd been looked after so well tonight.

Brad leant forward and gave Lucie a peck on the cheek. He grinned again as he straightened up. 'Now, make sure you get me back here one night soon. I mean it – that's your payment for my services tonight.'

Lucie waved as Brad reversed out of the driveway and drove slowly off down the street. She smiled to herself as she closed the door. She wondered if he'd drive that slowly all the way home in

order to prolong his outing. It had been nice to have a man helping with Noah. It made her realise that he really did need a strong
male figure in his life.

Lucie woke early the next morning to the sound of rapping on
the front door. She dragged herself up out of bed and checked the
clock. It was six fifteen. She'd been robbed of fifteen minutes' sleep.
She pulled on her robe and made her way down the hallway. The
rapping continued. She looked out the window; Kate was on the
doorstep, her hand about to bang the door again.

Lucie opened the door. 'Can you stop knocking? Noah's still
asleep.'

Kate pushed past her into the house.

Lucie stared at her sister-in-law's back as she disappeared down
the hallway and into the kitchen. She closed the front door and
followed after her.

Kate was pacing up and down when Lucie entered the kitchen.
'Are you okay?'

'No, I'm bloody not.' Spittle escaped Kate's lips.

'Did Brad get home okay last night?'

Kate stopped pacing. 'Yes, four hours after he came here to
help put up a piece of board.' Kate pointed a finger at Lucie. 'Why
don't you tell me exactly how it can take four hours to put up a
piece of board.'

Lucie stared at Kate. 'It doesn't take four hours, as I'm sure
Brad's told you already.'

Kate looked taken aback.

Had Brad lied about what he was doing last night? He had no
reason to; other than leaving out the bit about how he was avoiding
Kate, he hadn't actually done anything wrong. 'Your husband was a
godsend to me last night. He helped me with Noah – a completely

129

out-of-control Noah. If Brad hadn't been here I guarantee that little boy would have gone to bed in tears, thinking he was in huge trouble and knowing he'd be missing a party on the weekend. Brad helped me be a bit more reasonable about it all and had a man-to-man chat with Noah. I'm sorry if he was later than you anticipated but I'm still not quite sure why you're banging on my door so early in the morning.'

'Four hours? It took four hours to do all that?'

Lucie nodded. 'I didn't actually check the time but yes, Brad was here for longer than any of us had anticipated, and for that I'm exceptionally grateful.'

'I bet you are. And so this lovely four hours you had together, it was essential to be offering him wine and dinner, was it? Surely you'd realise I had dinner waiting for him.'

Lucie shook her head and walked over to flick the kettle on.

'What, you don't think I deserve an explanation?'

Lucie turned and studied Kate, whose face was red, her body rigid with anger. 'Why haven't you asked Brad about last night if it concerns you so much?' Lucie asked.

'Bloody Brad! I never know whether he's telling the truth or not these days. He's always out at night.' She crossed her arms. 'I'm beginning to wonder if this is where he's been visiting.'

'For goodness' sake, Kate! I rang your parents to see if your father could help me board up the window. Walt rang Brad and the next thing Brad was the one standing on my doorstep. Yes, I offered him some food – if you consider a toasted sandwich dinner. It would have been rude of me not to. He had a glass of wine and we had a chat. He was incredibly generous to help me with Noah and turned an otherwise horrible night into a positive one. I'm sorry if you have a problem with any of this but I can tell you one thing: nothing inappropriate was said or insinuated at any time that Brad was here – by either of us.' Lucie hoped her face

130

wasn't turning red as she had a fleeting thought about her reaction to Brad's kiss goodbye. 'Now, I need to get ready for work as, I imagine, do you. How about you go home and apologise to Brad if you've been accusing him of acting out.'

Kate looked taken aback by Lucie's speech. She was used to walking all over everyone, particularly Lucie, but there was no way Lucie was going to allow it in her own house.

Lucie moved toward Kate. 'Come on, I'll show you out.' She walked to the front door and stopped. 'And for the record, my heart is still completely devoted to my husband – your brother. I've not looked at another man since Matt died and I'm not sure when or even *if* I'll ever be ready to. We both know why you came here this morning and, just so you know, I'm offended by the suggestion.'

Kate's face was red. Lucie had never seen her lost for words before. Perhaps early morning wasn't a good time for Kate – the bitch within must still be asleep.

Kate walked out of the front door and down the path to her car.

Lucie gripped the doorknob, her hands shaking slightly. She was usually the person that tried to make the peace. She wasn't usually so forward or defensive. She wasn't a hundred percent sure if Kate brought out the best or the worst in her. What she did know, however, was that for the first time since she'd known her, Kate had walked away from a discussion with her tail between her legs. She smiled to herself just as Kate turned around to face her.

'Don't invite Brad around here again, Lucie. I mean it. I've listened to your pathetic little tale of woe – poor me, poor Noah, Brad's our knight in shining bloody armour, and I don't for one minute believe you aren't interested in him. The next time Brad disappears in the evening for hours on end I'll be straight round here and I can guarantee you, I'll make sure any relationship you have with our family ends. No more Granny and Grandpa for you and Noah, no more babysitting or help from any of us. Do you understand?'

So much for Lucie having the final word and coming out on top of Kate for a change. Lucie took a deep breath, went back inside and shut the door. Moments later she heard Kate's tyres squeal as she pulled out of the driveway. She instantly felt sorry for Brad. She'd rather be alone than trapped in a marriage to Kate.

Chapter Eleven

Community Service

Emma pulled into the parking area of the retirement village. She slammed her door shut and stomped across the car park to the front door. She was furious. Daniel was going to kill her and it was all this bloody little power-hungry warden's fault. Rodney. Even his name annoyed her. She'd rung the Department of Correctional Services on Wednesday morning to request her community service day be postponed. She'd been put through to Rodney, as he was her supervisor, and the conversation, which had started off with her politely requesting a change of day, deteriorated into an angry shouting match. Actually, upon reflection, she realised she had been the only one shouting.

The warden, as he requested she call him each time she spat the name Rodney down the phone, exercised his full power and arrogance, refusing her request to add the day to the end of her work order. A doctor's certificate confirming illness would be her only option and he made it very clear that the doctor would need to be informed of her commitment on Saturday prior to writing up a certificate. She'd slammed the phone down in the end. Now, standing in front of the arrogant little prick, she wanted to slap him.

He checked his clipboard. 'Good, you made it. Take a seat.'

She remained standing, anger seething beneath her skin. Was it even worth the effort of saying anything? All it would achieve would be to confirm that he had all the power. She wouldn't give him the satisfaction. Instead, she took a deep breath and walked over to the chairs. Florrie was already seated, waiting.

Florrie grinned and patted the seat next to hers. 'Come and sit with me, love, and tell me all about your week. Have you been good or have you added to your haul?'

Emma sat down next to Florrie. 'My haul?'

'Yes. Have you been out shoplifting this week?'

Emma laughed. Florrie's comment instantly relaxed her. 'No, as I said last week, I think being caught and having to do community service has taught me my lesson. I won't be stealing anything else. How about you? Got yourself a gun yet?'

Florrie shook her head, the smile slipping from her face. 'No. Although I haven't had a lot of time this week to look. Been a bit busy. Now, where's that other girl? Considering she's in here for speeding tickets you'd think she would be the first to arrive.'

The old lady was such a character. She had a wicked glint in her eye and Emma would almost bet this was the highlight of her week. 'Here she is now.'

Lucie glanced at her watch as she hurried through the automatic doors.

'Hurry up, prisoner,' Rodney bellowed. 'You're almost late.'

She sat down next to Emma, her voice a whisper. 'Almost late, not late, you little prick.'

'Who's a little prick?' Florrie's voice was loud enough for everyone, including Rodney, to hear.

He turned to face the group. 'Did someone want to add some time to their sentence? I'd be more than happy to make that recommendation to the courts.' He stared at Lucie. 'No, I'm sure you wouldn't like that one bit. Get your things and head to the kitchen. I expect aprons on, hands and arms scrubbed and hairnets fixed immediately.'

Two hours later they were given permission to stop and have some morning tea.

'There's definitely some perks to this.' Florrie licked her lips as she picked up a jam tart.

Lucie's eyes widened. 'Where did you get that from? The warden was very clear that *prisoners* are only to have broken biscuits and one cup of tea or coffee. I'd watch out if he sees you eating that.'

Florrie shrugged. 'I didn't hear any of those instructions. I'm not wasting my morning making tarts if I can't eat some.' She lowered her voice. 'I've put another four in a box to take with me – they're in the fridge.' She nudged Emma. 'Go and get one for yourself and Lucie. You'd be good at sneaking them out – you're a pro.'

Emma grinned. 'You seem to be forgetting I got caught, Florrie.'

'How about you, Lucie?' the old lady asked.

Lucie shook her head. 'No, you keep them, Florrie. You look a bit thin to me; a few tarts will do you good.'

'Now, Emma, love, what does your husband think about your life of crime?' Florrie asked the question and sat back, eagerly awaiting Emma's answer.

'God, don't talk about my husband.'

'He's not pleased then?'

Emma shook her head. 'He doesn't know, and to top it off he's expecting me to be home this morning to meet him when he gets back from Perth. He's not going to be happy.'

'Where does he think you are?' Lucie asked.

'Helping organise a charity event. I've been away all week, too, so haven't seen him since last Sunday. I don't think he's going to be happy finding out I'm going away again on Sunday night.' She went on to tell Lucie and Florrie about her mother being unwell and her offer to help for a while.

'They're family, love. He won't object to you helping family, surely?'

'Mm, I'm not sure. It's a long story, but he could go either way on it.'

Florrie looked at her expectantly. Emma could tell she was dying to hear the long story. She patted her arm. 'Another day perhaps. For now it looks like we *prisoners* are due back inside.' Rodney walked in their direction, looking pointedly at his watch.

Emma gathered the cups and stood, stifling a giggle as Florrie stuffed the rest of the tart in her mouth.

'Hiding the evidence,' she mumbled as her mouth bulged. She got to her feet and hobbled inside before Rodney had a chance to reprimand her.

Emma watched as he pulled his clipboard out from under his arm and made a note. 'What are you writing?'

Rodney looked up. 'None of your business, prisoner. Get back to work.'

The anger Emma had managed to contain earlier rose to the surface. This time she wouldn't let it go. What's the betting the little weasel was writing down that Florrie had eaten a tart? He'd probably make her work extra hours to pay for it. 'How about you give her a break?' Emma said. 'She's an old lady; she shouldn't even be here doing this.'

Rodney's gaze softened as his eyes connected with Emma's. 'That's one thing we definitely agree on. Back to work, please.' He turned and walked toward the kitchen.

Two hours later Lucie sat back down at the table with her lunch tray. Emma was already there, her face pale, looking at her phone.

Lucie wondered what Emma's story really was. She was obviously a wealthy woman, stuck doing community service each Saturday and lying to her husband about it. She wondered what would happen if he found out. Not that she was any better, of course; she'd lied to everyone about her whereabouts as well. Luckily Matt's family weren't interested enough in the course she said she was doing to ask questions about its content.

'Oh no.' Emma's eyes were glued to her phone.

'Everything okay?' Lucie asked.

Emma looked up. 'Not exactly. I've got twelve missed calls and two very worried messages from my husband.' She sighed and slipped her phone back inside her bag. 'I've sent him a text to say I had to do the charity work after all. Hopefully he won't be too upset. He can get a bit worked up sometimes.'

Lucie looked startled, making Emma laugh. 'Not like that; he wouldn't hurt me. I just mean I'll have to listen to him rant and rave for a while. The bigger problem is I've been away all week and need to go again tomorrow night. Seeing him for twenty-four hours in a week isn't enough.'

'You can't delay your trip?'

'No, not without knowing if Mum's okay. Hopefully it's early days if it's cancer.' Emma's voice faltered.

Lucie's stomach contracted at the word. Her own mother had died from breast cancer when she and Matt were living in New Zealand. That was only four years ago and the emotions were still very raw. Losing Matt a year later had left her feeling very alone. The two most important people in her life gone within a year of each other.

'Anyway, there's no point dwelling on what it might be until we know for sure what it is.'

Lucie was jolted back to the present. She nodded. 'You're right. Best to deal with what you know for sure than try to deal with what you assume.'

Emma nodded then grinned. 'That sounded very profound. Actually it sounded like something Florrie would say. Where is she? Our break is nearly half over.'

Lucie turned and craned her neck to see if she could see Florrie somewhere back in the kitchen. There was no sign of her. She turned back and started to eat her lunch. The sandwiches were quite nice, as was the fruit and yoghurt. The residents here were certainly fed well. Emma was absorbed in her phone, rapidly keying in a text message. Lucie wondered if Brad had picked Noah up for the party yet. She'd dropped him over at Jan and Walt's on her way this morning.

She might have been imagining it but she was sure Jan had been a bit funny with her. Lucie didn't have time to check whether there was an issue, but would need to this afternoon. She imagined Kate had been talking about Brad's extended visit the other night. She didn't really care what scenarios Kate would conjure up in her imagination, but she did care what Jan and Walt believed. She'd make sure they knew any problems were all in Kate's head.

A tray crashed down on the table next to Lucie, startling her and causing Emma to drop her phone. Florrie had arrived.

Lucie stood up to see if the old lady needed any help.

'Sit yourself down. I'm old and decrepit but perfectly capable.' Florrie manoeuvred herself on to the bench next to Lucie and took the lid off her tray.

Lucie inhaled. 'Wow.'

Florrie's tray contained a delicious-looking pasta dish, herb bread and a small bottle of wine.

Emma started to laugh. 'Oh my God, how on earth did you manage that?'

Florrie winked. 'You'd be amazed at what a pretend gun can get you these days.' She looked over her shoulder to the kitchen.

With no one watching them she reached into her bag and retrieved a very real-looking gun.

'Jesus, put that away,' Lucie said. 'You can't walk around with that in here.'

Florrie put it on the table next to her lunch tray. 'It's only a replica. Got me a nice lunch. This gun's well worth the thirty dollars I forked out for it.'

Lucie took the gun from the table and pushed it back into Florrie's bag. 'Put it away; I'm going to have a heart attack. What if the warden sees you with that? You'll probably be sent back to court.'

Florrie shrugged and tucked into her pasta. 'Oh, this is delicious. You girls really should try it.'

Lucie and Emma watched as Florrie ate her lunch, savouring every bite. She kept her wine until the end and then sat and slowly sipped it.

'I still have to know,' Emma said, 'wherever did you get that lunch from?'

Florrie grinned. 'It was delivered to one of the residents, Peter – a Saturday lunch treat from a son too busy to visit. I guess he was relieving his guilt by sending in a meal from Peter's favourite restaurant.'

'But how did you get it?'

'Staged another hold-up. I'm getting good at them. This time I got away with it.'

'But surely he'll tell the nursing staff?' said Emma.

'Probably, but as I've eaten the evidence I'm not sure how they'll prove anything.'

'Florrie,' Lucie admonished. 'That poor man has been robbed in his room of his lunch. You probably terrified him.'

The old lady winked. 'Don't worry, love, he has severe dementia so the likelihood of him having any recollection is zilch. I'm not a monster, by the way: I took him my lunch. Really it was just a swap.'

'With a gun involved,' Lucie added.

'Yes, well, that makes it all a bit more exciting, doesn't it?'

Lucie looked at Emma. What had they got themselves into? This old lady was unbelievable. She wasn't sure what to think of her behaviour. Emma, on the other hand, clearly thought it was hilarious. She had a twinkle in her eye and was mirroring the grin that was firmly fixed on Florrie's face. Emma's grin suddenly turned to a frown. She was facing the kitchen so could see everything that was going on.

'Warden prick's coming this way. Florrie, get rid of your wineglass.'

Florrie picked up the glass and drained the rest of the wine from it before placing it back on the table. Lucie wanted to grab it and hide it before the warden saw it. But it was too late. Florrie was already speaking to him.

'Hello, Warden Rodney, having a nice day I hope?' She picked up her glass and held it out to him. 'I didn't realise you offered table service; another glass, please.' Lucie watched as Rodney's face turned scarlet. 'Oh, and my friends here might want something, too.' She turned to Lucie. 'What about you, dear? Feel like a tipple?'

Rodney snatched the glass from Florrie's hand. 'Get back to work, all of you. And you' – he pointed his finger at Florrie – 'you'd better watch it. I've got a good mind to write this up and send you back to the magistrate for a chat.'

Florrie patted his hand. 'Oh, that would be lovely, dear, thank you. Can you make sure I see Graham again? He and I get along so well. I'd love to tell him all about the marvellous job you're doing here.'

Lucie half expected steam to come out of Rodney's ears. Instead she noticed the corner of his mouth turn up. He coughed, trying to hide a smile.

Florrie held out her hand to Rodney. 'Now help me up, dear – that wine seems to have gone straight to my head.' She giggled. 'Not sure I'll be all that much use this afternoon. Might need to go and find a spare bed somewhere and have a lie down.'

Lucie shook her head in Emma's direction as they watched the old lady use Rodney for support on her way back to the kitchen. 'Jesus, what's she going to do next week?'

'She's quite a character, isn't she?' Emma said. 'She's loving every minute of this.'

Lucie nodded. There was something that didn't sit quite right with her about the Florrie situation. She was, as Emma had said, a real character, but Lucie wondered whether it was all a front. She had no family and from the sounds of it she lived on her own. Lucie shook herself, got up from the table and went back into the kitchen. Florrie was not her problem. She needed to concentrate on getting this work order completed and returning to Noah and her regular life. She looked over at Emma, who appeared to be miles away as she began cutting up fruit for the residents' dinner. She reminded herself again that she didn't have the energy to take on anyone else's problems; she had enough issues of her own.

Chapter Twelve

EMMA

The house was dark when Emma pulled into the driveway. She let out a breath she was unaware she'd been holding. This was her husband, she shouldn't be nervous about seeing him. Daniel was probably asleep. The overnight flight would have taken it out of him. That was a good sign: if he'd had a decent sleep he might not mind so much about her not having been here today.

Emma pushed the button to open the garage roller door. Her heart sank. Daniel's car was missing. He wasn't asleep, he wasn't even here. She sighed as she manoeuvred her car into the garage. At least it bought her some time. She'd already changed out of her cargo pants and T-shirt into Daniel's favourite black-and-white striped dress, but an opportunity to shower and refresh her make-up would be welcome.

An hour later Emma came back down from their bedroom. She walked along the hall to the kitchen and stopped. Daniel was seated on one of the bar stools, beer on the bench, a newspaper spread in front of him. She smiled; even with his back to her he looked relaxed, like he would any other Saturday afternoon. She moved behind him, slipped her arms around his waist and nuzzled his neck. Her relief was short-lived. He ignored her, picked up his beer and took a swig.

Emma released her arms and sat on the stool next to him. She cleared her throat. 'I'm sorry, okay? I really didn't have a choice. I've got to treat the charity like a business. If the meeting had gone ahead without me it would have been a disaster.'

Daniel turned to face her, his jaw set in a hard line. 'You didn't even bother to text me, Em. I assumed you'd be at the airport and you weren't. You didn't answer your phone when I rang. Imagine if that had been you waiting. You'd have been worried sick, just like I was. Why didn't you contact me?'

Emma couldn't meet his gaze. Simone was right, she was an awful liar. 'I thought you'd be mad at me.'

'That's not a good excuse. I'm madder now than I would have been.'

'You would have said I couldn't go, and I really couldn't miss today.'

Daniel sighed. 'I wouldn't have said you couldn't go, I would have said I'd prefer it if you didn't. I wanted to see you. You've been away all week and I've missed you.'

'I've missed you, too, and I'm sorry about today. It was important that I was there. There's a lot to go through for this kind of event. Sponsors to organise, venue details to confirm, menus to run through, guest speakers to contact. The list goes on and on. On top of getting through the actual agenda, I've then got to deal with all the questions and stupid interruptions from the other volunteers. Keep in mind that most of these women are wives of successful businessmen who are doing this to justify their existence.' She smiled. 'You wouldn't believe the amount of complaining about the meeting being on a Saturday: the number of manicures and spa treatments that had to be postponed was ridiculous.' Emma stopped, she was getting carried away.

143

'So why was it?' Daniel asked.

'What do you mean?'

'Why was it on a Saturday? It's an event being planned by a bunch of women you say loll around all week being pampered. You're in charge, so why did you make it on a Saturday? You could do it any day of the week and no one would have to cancel their essential spa or nail treatments.' Daniel stared at her.

Emma could feel her face growing hot. That was a good point; other than attending events, they never organised them on the weekends. 'Partly because I wasn't going to be there all of last week. I really need to be at the meetings. It's too far to commute from the Bay for a meeting and I couldn't leave early from there either.'

Daniel nodded. 'Makes sense, although your first meeting was scheduled before we knew your mum was sick, wasn't it?'

Emotion raged inside Emma. Her web of lies was getting out of control. Something bothered her more than this though.

She stared at her husband. 'You know, instead of grilling me over where I've been or what I'm doing, you could give some thought to asking me how Mum is. It's my priority right now.'

Daniel raised his eyebrows and took another swig of his beer. 'Really? Everything suggests this charity is your priority right now.'

Emma didn't respond. Instead she got up and opened the fridge. She could feel Daniel's eyes on her as she poured a glass of wine and took it out through the back door and down to the pool. The air was warm and the cicadas were making a racket, signalling summer had nearly arrived. A cane toad hopped out of her way as she opened the pool gate. Ugh, that and humidity were the only downsides to a Queensland summer, as far as she could see. The pool lights twinkled and Emma sank down on to one of the sun loungers and sipped her wine.

A few weeks ago Daniel had been the number-one focus in her life. Her life revolved around his and she was happy – or at least

144

she'd thought she was. The first trip back to Golden Bay had woken something inside her. An urging that she needed to do something for herself. Something of value. Even helping at the aged-care facility seemed important. She was making a contribution where it mattered, not just planning dinners and making sure she and her house were well groomed. She'd had the discussion about her working or doing something for herself with Daniel before. Each time he'd talked her out of it. Convinced her that they were a team and her role was as important as his when it came to securing clients. She no longer agreed.

She pulled herself up off the lounger. She was tired. She needed something to eat and then she was going to bed. She still had to tell Daniel she was going back to the Bay the next night. She decided to leave that news until the morning. He was already mad enough with her as it was.

Emma stretched out, pleased to be back in her own bed. The bed at her parents' house was comfortable, but she hadn't slept in a single since leaving home. She rolled over; the other side of the bed was empty, and by the looks of it hadn't been slept in. Daniel had taken himself off to the media room and was watching a movie when she'd come back in from the pool last night. She'd made herself an omelette and gone to bed. She wondered if he'd fallen asleep watching the movie. The reclining chairs were so comfortable she wouldn't be surprised if that's exactly where he was.

She sat up and pulled on her robe. She still needed to tell him she was going back to the Bay. After the reception she'd received the previous night, she could only imagine how that was going to go down. She took a few deep breaths. This was her mother, her family; in this situation, they came first. She went downstairs and into the kitchen. Dirty dishes sat on the bench. She walked down the hallway to the media room. The room was dark. She tiptoed in, not wanting to wake Daniel. It was so dark she had to walk right up to the chairs to see if he was there. He wasn't.

Emma retreated from the room and walked further along the corridor to their guest wing. She'd like to think that he'd slept in a guestroom so as not to wake her but knew him better than that. The fact they'd been apart for almost a week and he hadn't wanted to have sex with her last night indicated just how upset he was. His clothes were still on the floor of the second guestroom and the bed was a mess of tangled sheets. The curtains were open and he wasn't in the bathroom. Was he using the gym or the pool? Emma checked the home gym – no sign of him. Most likely he was swimming laps. She went back to the kitchen and switched on the coffee machine. She'd make some coffee and take it out to the pool. A peace offering.

The City Cat sped through the calm waters of the Brisbane River, its passengers mostly up on deck taking in the river views, enjoying another beautiful spring day.

Emma leant back in her chair, watching as the ferry went by. She saw a girl in her mid-twenties, blond hair blowing in the breeze, looking up, laughing at something the man she was with said. How nice it would be to be so happy and carefree. She picked up her coffee cup, suddenly brought back to the present, aware that Cass was sitting across from her, waiting for her to continue. 'I still haven't spoken to him. He wasn't out at the pool. I finally used my brain and checked the garage and his car was gone. Who knows what time he went out. His golf clubs were gone, too. Assuming he stays at the club for lunch after his round, he could be gone for hours.'

'And he doesn't know you're going back to your parents' tonight?'

Emma shook her head. 'No. I've left him a message but I doubt he'll return it until after his game – if he returns it at all. He's pretty upset that I didn't turn up at the airport.'

Cass opened her mouth and then closed it again.

'Have I given you extra ammunition to hate him more than you already do?' Emma asked.

Cass laughed. 'I don't hate him, I just don't like the way he treats you. Although this time I will give him some credit: you could have handled the airport better. Still, he's a grown man, for God's sake. You were out yesterday doing a good deed and he's going to hold it against you. It makes it hard to like him.'

'Good deed?' Emma smiled. 'That's one spin to put on community service.'

'Well, it's helping people, so it must be a good deed. And anyway, he thinks you are doing something for charity, so that would be a good deed. There's no point going around in circles about Daniel. Hopefully he'll be home before you go tonight and you'll sort things out. If not, it will have to wait until you come back again. Tell me about your mum. How long are you planning to go for?'

Emma filled Cass in on her mother's situation and her days spent in the Bay.

'Will they need you to help out for long?'

'I'm not sure. It will depend on what treatment she might need. I'll help out until she's ready to go back to work, assuming . . .' Emma stopped. The alternative was something she'd done her best to avoid thinking about.

Cass put her hand on Emma's arm. 'No need to think like that just yet. Wait until you know more. If it is cancer, hopefully it's early stages and your mum'll be back on her feet quickly. If it's not cancer then it might not be anything to worry about.'

Tears pricked Emma's eyes. She'd wasted so many years avoiding her family. If something happened to her mother now she wasn't sure she'd ever forgive herself.

'So, I've got some news,' Cass said.

Emma looked at her. 'What?'

'I interviewed this week for a professor exchange program with the university. If I get it, I might be going to the States for a few months.'

'Really? That's fantastic,' Emma said. 'Whereabouts?'

'California. But I'm not getting too excited just yet. There were about thirty other applicants so my chances are slim.'

Emma squeezed her hand. 'Your chances are as good as anyone else's. Make sure you keep me up to date with any news. Don't you dare leave the country without saying goodbye.'

Cass laughed. 'I'd hardly do that.'

After paying the bill they walked out to the car park.

Cass gave Emma a hug, with an extra-tight squeeze. 'Now let me know how everything goes with your mum, okay? I really hope it's all just been a big scare and there's nothing to worry about.'

'Me too. I'll give you a ring from the Bay. Perhaps we can have coffee again next weekend? You can update me on the professor exchange, too.'

'See how you go with Daniel; you might need to spend some quality time with him next weekend. You can always ring me last minute, like today. I'm pretty sure I'll be free.'

Emma waved to Cass as she climbed into her car. Her phone chimed with a text message.

Mum's home, feeling tired but otherwise in good spirits.
Have to go back to Brisbane on Wednesday for test results.
See you tonight. Love Dad.

Emma manoeuvred the Audi out of the car park. That was good news at least. Now she just needed to get home and try to get things back on track with Daniel.

Daniel was upstairs having a shower when Emma returned. She hoped his game of golf had put him in a better mood.

She lay down on their bed and mentally repacked her bag while she waited for him to come out of the bathroom.

The bed sank beneath Daniel's weight, and she turned her head. He was naked, his hair wet and tousled from the shower. He ran his hand up her body, looking into her eyes.

'Hey, wife, I've missed you.' He grinned, as if last night hadn't happened.

Emma responded as Daniel's body engulfed hers. He kissed her, again as if nothing had happened. She wanted him, but her mind wouldn't disconnect and just let her enjoy the physical pleasure. She pushed her hands against his chest.

He stopped kissing and looked at her. 'What's wrong?'

Emma sighed. 'What do you think? You were so cold last night and then you took off this morning without a word, and now you want sex. What am I supposed to think?'

Daniel pushed himself on to his knees, straddling her, and started to unbutton her shirt. 'You're supposed to think how good it is that your husband is ready to forgive you for not being at the airport yesterday or contacting him to let him know your whereabouts, and then you're supposed to lie back and enjoy being made love to.'

'You're not angry any more? We're not going to do this and then you get all upset with me again?'

Daniel shook his head. 'I wasn't angry to start with. I was disappointed you stood me up and didn't seem to care. Right now I

149

plan to make love to you once, maybe twice, then take you out for dinner. We are going to have a night with just the two of us.' He smiled at her, his blue eyes crinkling at the edges, his face soft. 'How does that sound, Mrs Wilson?'

It sounded perfect, except somewhere between now and dinner she had to break the news that she was going back to the Bay tonight.

'What's the problem?' Daniel stared at her. '"Lovely" would have been a suitable response, not clamming up.'

'Sorry. Yes, it sounds lovely, although . . .' Emma hesitated.

'Although what?'

Emma shook her head, deciding it could wait. She'd let him down enough this weekend already. She pulled him toward her. 'Nothing.' She cupped his face, losing herself in his passionate kiss.

'Tonight? You're going again tonight?' Daniel shook his head as he leapt out of bed. He slammed the bedroom door and stormed down the hallway.

Emma lay back on the bed, the intimacy of the previous hour shattered. With her fingers curled through his after the second time they'd made love, she'd worked up the courage and told him she would need to help her parents out for a little while, which meant returning to the Bay that night. The second the words were out of her mouth a vein in his forehead started to bulge.

Emma pulled herself up off the bed, slipped on her robe and followed him. They needed to have a proper conversation; he still hadn't asked about her mother. Where had all the previous concern gone? She could hear Daniel swearing as he crossed the kitchen and dining areas and went out on to the patio. Emma stopped as a loud crash came from the pool area. Her stomach contracted. He wouldn't have touched her lion, would he? She knew he was angry, but she was still sure he wouldn't ruin something he knew was so precious to her. She was almost afraid to look.

Emma took a deep breath and walked out through the French doors on to the patio. She stopped, seeing immediately what he'd done. Her beautiful lion, the first present Daniel had ever given her, now lay on the path, its head just one of the many broken pieces around it. She willed herself not to cry. Courage and strength, that was what the lion represented. It was what she needed now; however, this time she wasn't strong enough. Silent tears streamed down her face as she bent to pick up the broken pieces. Her tears turned to anger as she carefully picked up each piece, examining it to see if there was any way it could be fixed.

Emma could hear Daniel powering through the pool, taking his anger out on the laps. Why couldn't he have done that to start with? She walked back toward the house in search of a box to put the broken pieces in.

Ten minutes later she carried the box into the house and through to the garage. She put it down next to the cupboard that housed all the items she'd stolen. She really needed to get rid of them. Daniel would break more than a lion if he found her hoard. Community service must be working – she hadn't added an item to the haul since she'd been caught shoplifting. At least it appeared she could stop. She'd realised she'd been going out once, sometimes twice a week, enjoying the thrill and buzz her little adventures gave her. Life had been so much busier in the past few weeks that, even if she hadn't been caught, she doubted she would have had the time.

Emma returned to the pool area with the vacuum cleaner and got to work sucking up the last shards of the lion. She was conscious of Daniel watching as she finished cleaning up. When she was sure she'd cleaned up every piece she switched off the vacuum and unplugged it. She refused to acknowledge him. It was probably best for both of them if she got herself organised and left for the

Bay now. She carried the vacuum back into the house. She'd make a coffee and then pack her things.

'I'm sorry.' Daniel's arms slid around Emma from behind as she sat at the kitchen bench sipping her coffee. He nuzzled her neck. 'I'll buy a new lion. I shouldn't have taken my anger out on it; I know how much you loved it.'

Emma continued to sip her coffee.

Daniel released his grip on her and went around to the other side of the bench. 'Em, I was angry. I've hardly seen you and when you are here you're putting a stupid charity first. I was thinking about it when I was playing golf this morning and realised yesterday wasn't important but today is. We need a fresh start. I went to the effort of planning a nice night for us. There's no point even going if you need to drive to the Bay tonight. You'll need to go by eight, which kills dinner and the plans I had for after.'

Emma stared at him. 'My mother's sick, probably with cancer. I need your support right now, not this.'

Daniel hung his head. 'I know, and I'm sorry. Of course you need to go back and help out. Will you come back during the week or on the weekend?'

'I'm not sure, I'll have a better idea on Wednesday when we get the test results. Although Dad knows I have to be back for the weekend.'

'Have to?'

Emma looked away, this would no doubt start the next round with him. She was going to need to hold her ground. She had no choice: she had to complete her community service, but she couldn't let Daniel find out. It was one thing for him to be angry with her but she couldn't bear him to be disappointed or ashamed. She returned her gaze to meet his. 'Yes, I have to. I'm committed

152

to this event and I can't let them down.' She held up her hand, stopping him. 'It's no different from what you do, Daniel. When you make a business commitment you need to uphold it. It won't look good on me, or you, if I drop out only weeks before their gala dinner. The entire night will be a disaster, which is unfair to them and unfair to the charity they're supporting. It's a great opportunity to tap into a lot of wealthy people for donations.' Emma sighed. 'Don't forget, you're the one that pushed me into volunteering to start with; I shouldn't have to justify it.'

Daniel nodded. 'I guess I'd assumed your charity work would be during the week. You're right though, you can't just pull out. What does it mean, you'll be gone all day next Saturday, too?'

'Yes, but how about I organise it so that if I'm going back to the Bay I don't leave here until Monday, at the same time you head off to work. I'll do an afternoon shift rather than the early one and that way we'll still have all day Sunday together. Perhaps we could postpone the dinner you've booked for tonight and do it next Saturday or Sunday?'

'Okay.' Daniel came back to Emma's side of the bench. He pulled her into his arms and hugged her tight. 'And I am sorry about the lion. I'll get it replaced before you come back. I promise.'

Emma let him pull her to him. She was still upset about the lion, but it was just a thing. At least now she had Daniel's blessing to return to the Bay and she'd managed to cover her tracks for the next few weeks in relation to her community service. Her body responded to his as his hands slipped in through the front of her robe. She could finally relax. She'd have enough to worry about with her mother's situation in the coming week without worrying about her marriage, too.

Chapter Thirteen

LUCIE

Lucie tried to block out the noise of the schoolyard as she dropped an aspirin into the glass and watched it fizz. How on earth was she going to make it through the day? It hadn't even started yet. Her mouth tasted like a sour, day-old fish. Since when did Matt's beautiful wine leave this kind of taste? Granted she'd got a bit carried away the night before, and she vaguely recalled opening a second bottle but still, she should be able to handle that. Perhaps she was coming down with something – her pounding head certainly suggested that might be the case.

The details of the previous night were fuzzy. She remembered being on the phone, speaking to Brad for a little while. She'd rung him in pure defiance of Kate, under the guise of thanking him and checking she hadn't caused any problems for him. She'd half imagined Kate would overhear their conversation and hang up on her. But Brad wasn't at home, he was out having a drink. Oh God, no wonder she felt so rotten, he'd suggested she refill her glass each time he bought himself another round. They must have spoken for longer than she recalled.

'Morning.' Anna walked into the staff kitchen, lunchbox in hand, and opened the fridge. She put her lunch away before restating her greeting. 'I said, "Morning."'

Lucie turned and forced a smile. 'Sorry, million miles away. Morning.'

Anna raised an eyebrow. 'Aspirin? Big weekend?'

'Not really. I'm not sure if it was one too many wines last night or if I'm coming down with something. Anyway, this plus a coffee should do the trick.'

'Poor you.' Anna's face was genuinely sympathetic. 'No hurry if you want to drink it in peace before the bell rings. There's nothing urgent I need you for.'

'Thanks.' This time Lucie's smile was genuine. 'I appreciate it.'

'I'd better get to class, work out a few things for the day. I'll see you when you get there.' Anna opened the staffroom door to find Noah standing outside.

Lucie got up and walked over. Noah was fidgeting with his school shirt.

'Is everything okay?'

Noah's top lip trembled. 'Jack and Ricky are teasing me. Calling me a baby.'

Lucie pulled Noah to her and gave him a hug. 'Some boys are just meanies. The best thing you can do is ignore them, although I know it will be hard. Don't say anything at all, just go and find someone else to play with. If they keep doing it, you need to speak to Mrs Winthrop.'

'But I hate them. I want you to talk to them.'

'I can't, sweetheart. They are in the prep area so a prep teacher needs to talk to them. If I come in they'll probably want to tease you even more, they might say you run to your mummy for help.'

Noah looked confused. 'Mummies are supposed to help.'

155

'Of course they are, but at school it is the class teacher who needs to help. I can talk to Mrs Winthrop but I think it would be better if you did.'

'No, I want you to.' Tears were welling in Noah's eyes. 'She might not believe me.'

Lucie was suddenly aware of Jane Winthrop's presence; she was standing a little way down the corridor, listening to the conversation. She willed her away. At some stage Noah needed to learn to go to his class teacher, but right at this minute he needed his mum and she needed to be his mum, not a teacher at the school.

Jane didn't receive her silent messages and instead approached them and put her hand on Noah's shoulder. 'You can come to me about anything, Noah. When you're telling the truth I'll always believe you. Together we can work out a way to stop our friends from being nasty. Would you like to have a talk with me?'

Noah shook his head.

Jane smiled. 'Really? Because I've heard that Jack and Ricky can be a bit mean at times but unless I see it for myself, or one of my good, honest students like you comes and talks to me, then I can't do a lot about it.'

'See, Noah? Mrs Winthrop wants to hear about it from you.' Lucie stood up. 'How about you go back to class with her? You might get me into trouble. You know you're really only supposed to come and find me during school time if it's an emergency.'

'It *is* an emergency. What if they find out I've told on them?'

'Come on. You asked me a few minutes ago to come and get them into trouble. Why are you now being silly about talking to your teacher?' Lucie's head pounded; her aspirin solution was only half drunk and her coffee was turning cold.

Jane took Noah's hand. 'Come on back to the classroom with me. We can have a little chat if you want to, or we can play a game. There are only a few minutes left before the bell rings. We need to leave Mummy to get organised – she looks like she might need her coffee.'

'No.' Noah pulled away from Jane and clung to Lucie's leg. 'I'm not going to school today and you can't make me.'

Lucie tried to detach Noah from her leg. 'Noah, you do not talk to your teacher like that. Let go of me immediately and apologise to Mrs Winthrop.'

Noah clung to Lucie even tighter. 'Can't make me. I hate her and I hate you. You're all meanies, just like Jack and Ricky.'

'Sorry,' Lucie mouthed to Jane. Jane didn't say anything, just stared at Noah. She looked shocked at his behaviour. It was embarrassing. It was bad enough when he behaved like this at home, but at school, at her workplace? Anger bubbled inside her. She took Noah's hands in hers and broke his grip from her leg. He started to wail. 'Oh, for goodness' sake, Noah, stop it.' He cried louder. Lucie tightened her grip on his wrists. She wished Jane would get on with her day and leave them alone. Having someone else witness this little scene was making her even angrier. She could feel Jane's judgemental eyes boring down on her.

Lucie got down on her knees, released her grip on Noah's wrists and placed her hands firmly on his shoulders. 'Listen to me,' she said. He rubbed his wrists as tears streamed down his face. 'You cannot behave like this. Mrs Winthrop is offering you help and you are being very rude. You need to stop immediately.' The firmness of her voice must have done the trick, as Noah's tears turned to whimpers.

Jane Winthrop cleared her throat. 'Come on, Noah, let's leave Mummy to her coffee. She sounds like she needs a little break before she starts the day.'

This time Noah went straight across to Jane and took her hand.

Lucie stood up and stared after them. What had just happened? She'd finally calmed Noah down and now she'd been made to feel like she'd done something wrong. She watched as Noah walked off with Jane, neither of them bothering to acknowledge her. She sighed. This was not what she needed this morning. She turned back to her drinks, finished the aspirin and picked up her coffee. The cup was cool. The bell rang just as she considered making a fresh cup. She sighed again, picked up her cold coffee and hurried toward the Year Two classroom.

It was well after five by the time Lucie walked across the school car park. The monthly staff meetings were a pain, especially when added to what had already seemed like a ridiculously long day. She'd had four cups of coffee and had contemplated, but decided against a fifth. She'd never sleep if she did. She hoped Jane had sorted out the nasty boys and that Noah's day had improved. She hated that she'd had to discipline him in front of his teacher. She needed to talk to him, work out a better strategy for dealing with problems at home and at school.

Lucie sang along to the songs on the radio, willing herself into a better mood as she made her way to her in-laws' house. She didn't know what she'd do without their help. After-school care, she supposed. She dismissed the thought. Luckily it wasn't relevant.

She pulled into the driveway, smiling as she heard Noah's excited scream of 'Goal!' She got out of the car and walked straight around to the back garden. Noah was kicking his soccer ball toward Walt. It appeared Walt was the goalie, with chairs placed a couple of metres either side of him. Lucie clapped as Noah kicked the ball between Walt and the chair.

Noah turned to her. 'Oh, Mum. Why are you here? I'm not ready to go yet.'

Jan's voice rang out from the kitchen. 'Glass of wine, Luce? I'm just pouring myself one.'

'I'd love one, thanks,' she called. She smiled at Walter. 'How's it going? I hope he hasn't been too much trouble.'

'Trouble?' Walt's booming laugh filled the garden. 'My Noah would never be any trouble, would you, matey?'

Noah grinned at Walt and shook his head. 'Come on, Grampy, I'm going to kick another goal.'

Lucie watched them as Noah ran off again with the ball. Grampy – that was a new one. She smiled and walked in through the French doors to be greeted by Jan, wineglasses in hand. She took hers gratefully.

'Come and sit down.' Jan pointed to the wicker chairs in the sitting area. 'How was your day?'

Lucie sat down and sipped her wine. The effect was better than coffee. Instant relaxation. She should have had a glass before she left for school this morning, hair of the dog and all that. She shuddered. No, that wasn't her style. 'Day was okay. How about you? How's Noah been this afternoon?'

'Fine, love. He was a bit quiet when we picked him up but he's perked up since he's been here. He said he'd had a horrible day, but wouldn't elaborate. You might need to chat to him about it later, see what's going on.'

Lucie nodded, taking another sip of her wine. 'He was being teased this morning. Hopefully the class teacher sorted it out. I'll chat to him tonight and find out.'

Jan smiled. 'He's lucky to have you at the school, able to look out for him if something happens.'

Lucie looked down at her feet. Jan might not think Noah was quite so lucky if she'd heard her tell him he could only come to her in an emergency. She really hadn't handled it well.

'How's the broken window? Have you had it fixed yet?'

Lucie lifted her eyes to meet Jan's. 'No, hopefully next week. It's fine with the board, I just haven't had a chance to call anyone.'

'Lucie.' Jan lowered her voice and moved forward on her seat. 'If you need some help paying for it, Walt and I can always loan you some money. You know that, don't you?'

Heat flushed Lucie's cheeks. She couldn't look Jan in the eye. She appreciated all of their help but she was too proud to admit the extent of her financial situation, just how stretched she was. 'Oh no, it's not the money, it's more about being home to let the tradesmen in. Working full-time isn't very conducive to that.'

'I can let them in for you, anytime you need. Just give me a days' notice and I'll pop around.'

'Thanks.' Lucie smiled at her. She knew Jan was only trying to help but she wished she'd drop it. Her financial situation was her own problem.

'I hear Kate paid you a little visit. I'm sorry about that.'

'Why are you sorry? It had nothing to do with you.'

'I know,' Jan sighed. 'But she is my daughter – my headstrong, outspoken, speaks-before-she-thinks daughter.'

Lucie snorted. 'An accurate description.'

'I hope she didn't upset you?'

Lucie was curious. 'Why would you think she'd upset me? I can handle Kate.'

'I'm sure you can. It was just that, well, from what she said to me, she was concerned as to why Brad had spent so long at your house. I got the impression she was accusing you both of . . . of something a bit untoward. I was worried that would upset you.'

'It probably should, but I've known Kate for long enough. Matt warned me about his strong-willed sister before I'd even met her.'

'Good, well, I'm glad. I told her nothing would be going on. That there was no way you'd risk your relationship with the family by doing something stupid with Brad. I was also surprised that she thought Brad might cheat on her. They've got two children. He wouldn't do anything to jeopardise that.'

160

'Of course he wouldn't. Kate's imagination is very vivid.'

'You can see it from her point of view though, can't you?'

Lucie realised Jan wasn't ready to drop it. Did she actually think something had happened? 'Jan, Walt sent Brad around to do a job I'd asked Walt for help with. I wasn't expecting him. He was very good to me: he helped fix the window and then he spent some time with Noah. Noah loved every minute of it – a man putting him to bed, reading him a story for a change. After he'd done all of that of course I felt obligated to offer him something to eat. I had no idea that such an innocent evening would become such an issue. To be honest, it makes me wonder about Kate, about why she doesn't trust Brad. Perhaps she doesn't trust him because she's been doing things she shouldn't.' Lucie was sure it was the wine giving her the courage to speak up. Jan was being subtle in her suggestions but was definitely making her message clear.

The colour drained from Jan's face. 'You think Kate might be having an affair?'

Lucie sipped her wine. No, she doubted that very much. Who would be crazy enough to get involved with her high-maintenance sister-in-law? 'I have no idea. I'm just saying that people who accuse others irrationally often have something to hide.'

Jan nodded. 'I think I'd better speak with Kate.'

Lucie stood up. 'Thanks for the wine, and for looking after Noah. I'm so grateful for all you do – you do know that, I hope.'

Jan leant forward and hugged Lucie. 'Of course we do and it's our absolute pleasure. Now, we'll see you on Saturday. How many more weeks are there of your course?'

'Three, I think, and yes, we'll be here at eight.'

'Hold on a minute.' Jan walked over and opened the pantry door. She pulled out a chocolate frog and handed it over to Lucie. 'Bribery – use it to get Noah out of here without an issue. Tell him it's for his dessert but Granny said he has to be good right up until then.'

Lucie smiled. 'Thanks.' Anything for a calm night was worth a shot.

Lucie sank down on to the couch, a glass of wine in one hand, the TV remote in the other. She had to hand it to Jan, the chocolate frog had worked a treat. Noah had run happily to the car and chatted all the way home about his soccer game with Grampy. Lucie smiled as she listened to him talk about how he would be good enough for the World Cup in about ten years if he kept practising. She wanted to ask him about school and the rest of his day but decided to leave it. She could always talk to his teacher if she believed there was still an issue. They'd eaten dinner together companionably and then, after his chocolate and his bath, had read three stories. He'd gone straight to sleep.

She flicked on the TV. She hadn't watched anything in ages. It was nice to have a night to herself. She was feeling much better than she had that morning. The wine had definitely worked its magic. She settled on an episode of *Survivor*, wondering how she'd get on, stuck on a beach for thirty-nine days without any food. It would probably be easier than dealing with a five-year-old. Some days it would even be preferable to dealing with him. She watched as one team won a reward challenge, enabling them to stuff themselves silly at a pop-up beach taco bar. Who would want to drink a margarita after not having had any food for nineteen days? They must be mad, all chugging them down.

Just as the votes were about to be read, a gentle knock on the front door made Lucie jump. It was almost nine thirty; who would be calling so late? She tiptoed past Noah's room and down the hallway. Peeping through the window, she saw Brad. He was dressed in sports clothes, his hair sweaty. Was he completely crazy? Kate would kill him – and her.

She opened the door. 'Hello, what brings you here so late?'

Confusion quickly wiped the smile from Brad's face. 'Sorry, didn't we have plans?'

'Plans?' What was he talking about?

'You know, last night when we were chatting. You said to drop in for a drink on my way home from squash.' He spread his arms wide and grinned. 'So here I am.'

Jesus. No wonder she had felt like crap this morning. She knew she'd spoken to him but had no recollection of organising this. She obviously hadn't been thinking. Okay, she'd let him in for one drink and make it clear this would have to be the last time. Sneaking around was not her style. She attempted a smile and opened the door wider. 'Of course, come in. Don't mind me, it's been a long day. Wine?'

Brad nodded as he followed Lucie to the lounge. 'Sounds great.'

Lucie retrieved the bottle and another glass from the kitchen. When she came back she found Brad had made himself comfortable on the couch. She passed him the glass of wine and topped up her own at the same time. 'How was your game?'

'Great. I didn't win, but it was a good workout. The guy I play with is ultra-competitive so it gives me a good run around.'

Lucie nodded, trying to think of something else to ask him. She was still thrown by the fact she'd organised this and had no recollection of it. She looked at her wineglass: she needed to slow down. She didn't want another hangover or a situation where she woke up tomorrow not recalling their conversation. She would pace herself. Her thoughts were broken by Brad staring at her. He was probably waiting for her to say something. She assumed the conversation had flowed more naturally the night before.

'I can go, if you like? You look uncomfortable.'

Lucie sighed. 'Sorry, I'm just a bit worried about Kate. I'm assuming she doesn't know you're here?'

'No, but I usually go out for a drink after squash; I just decided seeing you would be nicer than sitting across from a sweaty bloke who'd just whipped my arse for the last hour.'

Lucie laughed. 'That conjures up an interesting image. I think we might need to make this the last visit though. I don't want any more trouble with Kate or Jan.'

'More trouble?' Brad looked confused. 'There's been trouble?'

Lucie nodded. 'Didn't Kate mention her little visit to me the morning after you fixed the window?'

'No, she didn't.'

'She basically warned me to keep my hands off you. I then had Jan reinforce it this afternoon. You'd better watch out when you next see Jan – it'll be your turn. I'm surprised Kate didn't tell you.' Kate was normally so outspoken she was amazed she hadn't made it very clear to Brad that she'd warned Lucie off. 'They obviously think you are capable of an affair if Kate's that worried.'

Brad sipped his wine. 'Everyone's capable.'

His eyes searched Lucie's, causing a ripple of nervous energy to run through her. He wasn't really suggesting they had an affair, was he?

'Just not everyone acts on it,' he said.

Lucie gulped her wine. Brad was completely off limits. There was no way she'd cross that line.

Brad smiled. 'Anyway, tell me about your day. How was school?'

Lucie relaxed, quickly forgetting the awkwardness between them. It had been a long time since anyone had shown real interest in her. Sure, they often asked her how Noah was, but no one seemed interested in her. The conversation wound its way from discussing their days to talking about music, what they loved to listen to and then on to their favourite movies and television shows.

It turned out they had a lot in common, particularly their love of reality shows.

It was after eleven by the time Lucie suggested she make them both a cup of tea. So much for one glass of wine. 'What time do you usually get home from squash?'

Brad glanced at his watch. 'By now. I probably should give the tea a miss and get going. Kate might start to get worried.'

Suspicious, more like. She stood up ready to walk him to the door. She needed to get to bed; this was a late night for her, especially with school tomorrow. When they reached the door, Brad leant toward her and engulfed her in a bear hug. 'Thanks, Luce. I've really enjoyed the past couple of nights talking to you. I feel like I've made a new friend, a really decent one.' He pulled away from her, smiling. 'Now, I'd better get home before Kate jumps to any wild conclusions.'

'I assume you won't be telling her you were here?'

Brad laughed. 'No. If she's got it fixed in her head that we're having an affair, it's probably not a good idea. Thanks again. I'll drop in next Monday after squash if you feel like some company?'

She knew she should say no. It was a shame though. She and Brad got along so well; it was nice to have someone interested in her. And to have an intelligent adult conversation in the evening was a rarity. No matter what seeds of doubt Kate and Jan were trying to plant in her head, like her, Brad was only looking for friendship. He'd hugged her like a brother would hug a sister. 'Okay, but if Kate finds out about tonight let me know and we'll cancel. At least I'll be ready for you this time.'

Brad raised an eyebrow. 'Sounds ominous.'

Lucie's cheeks grew hot. 'I'll be expecting you is what I meant.'

Brad winked. He was definitely enjoying her embarrassment. 'Mm, better not let Kate hear you talking that way, she'll cotton on to the fact it's making me excited.'

She swatted his arm. 'Get out, you. It's late and the wine is twisting my words. Turn up Monday if you want. Is that better?'

'Yes, a much better exchange of information between two friends. I think that would be considered acceptable, even by my wife.'

'I wouldn't count on that.'

They both laughed as Brad walked down the path to his car.

Chapter Fourteen

EMMA

Emma ran through the checklist in her head. The tables out the front of The Café had been cleaned, the umbrellas were up, the specials of the day had been handwritten with chalk on the blackboards, and the fruit and vegetables had been cut up ready for the juicer. She had two experienced staff in the kitchen preparing food and Kristen, a junior, was out front with her, ready to make coffee and wait and clear tables. She took a deep breath, trying to calm the butterflies in her stomach. She reminded herself that it was just a café and the worst-case scenario was someone would get the wrong order or be made to wait too long. Neither of which were the end of the world.

Kristen smiled at her. 'Ready?'

Emma was grateful for the support. At seventeen, Kristen could probably run the place single-handedly. She'd been working full-time for over a year now and knew the processes inside and out.

The ring of the little bell as the front door of the café opened made Emma jump. She turned, ready to smile and serve her first customer. Her body relaxed as Simone walked in. Good, a guinea pig to practise on. 'What are you doing up so early?'

Simone laughed as she waddled toward the counter. 'Thought you might need some moral support – first day and all that. It's a bit daunting getting to know all of the systems, isn't it?'

Emma nodded.

'I'll have a coffee and toast, thanks,' Simone said.

Emma wrote down the order and then looked up at Simone. 'Is there some sort of family rate or do I charge you full price?'

Kristen called out to Emma before Simone had a chance to answer. 'Family rate is on the house. There's a button, bottom left of the till, just push that and then the orders. It will ring them up at zero cost but we can still keep track of what we've sold.'

Emma studied the till: the button on the bottom left read 'Family'. She keyed in the order and then took the docket and passed it through to the kitchen. 'First order done. Take a seat, if you like.'

Simone sat down at the table closest to Emma. 'How was your trip home? Was Daniel okay with you coming back to help?'

'Yes, he's as worried about Mum as we are.' On cue, Emma's phone beeped. She took it out of her pocket and saw the message was from Daniel.

Hope all goes well on your first day, you're an amazing wife and daughter. I love you and can't wait to see you. xxx.

Emma smiled and slipped the phone back into her pants. 'Daniel?' Simone asked.

Emma nodded. 'How did you know?'

Simone laughed. 'Your face lit up like it did when you were sixteen and heard from a boy. That's so lovely, Em, that he still makes you feel that way. I can't think of the last time Johnno did anything that had me feel that spark. He's like a comfy pair of jeans. Don't get me wrong, I love him to bits, but a bit of excitement wouldn't go astray.'

Emma laughed. 'Looking at that huge belly you're carting around I think you've probably got enough excitement coming your way in a few weeks.'

The café door opened and a couple came in. Emma greeted them and took their order. Another three people came in and she got into the swing of taking orders and passing them through to the kitchen. Kristen was pumping out the coffees and once the kitchen started to ding their service bell she carried the meals across to the tables. A steady flow of customers continued until just before nine.

'Coffee?' Kristen called out to Emma. There were a few full tables out the front but inside was currently empty, Simone having left half an hour ago.

'Yes, please.' Emma's stomach rumbled.

Kristen placed a coffee in front of her. 'You seem like an old pro already,' she said. 'We must have served at least thirty people and all the orders were correct and served within the timeframe your dad likes us to stick to. He'd be pretty impressed, I'd say.'

'I don't think I can take too much credit for any of that. All I'm doing is taking the orders. You three are doing everything else. It would be pretty hard for me to mess that up.'

Kristen laughed. 'Oh you'd be surprised. Just ask Simone. You've got everything under control; some other family members aren't always so well organised.' She winked as the café door opened and two grey-haired ladies, one with a walking frame, came in. Kristen greeted them before heading outside to clear a table.

One of the ladies stopped before she reached the counter, and stared at Emma. 'Little Emma Jean? Is that you?'

Emma smiled at the two old ladies – they looked familiar. 'Emma Wilson now, but yes I was Emma Jean before I married. I'm terribly sorry, but I can't remember your name.'

The woman looked at her companion. 'Do you hear her, Elsie? Can't remember my name. All that time we spent helping her with her homework and she doesn't remember us at all. Not that it should be a great shock to me, throwing away her education and taking off out of town without even a goodbye.'

Now Emma remembered who they were. The Thompson sisters, Maude and Elsie, teachers who lived next door to her parents. God, they'd aged. Of course they had, she hadn't seen them for seventeen years, so they must be in their eighties. 'Miss Maude, of course I remember. I'm sorry I didn't recognise you, everything is a bit overwhelming today.'

Miss Maude frowned, shaking her head. 'You nearly killed your poor mother, you know that, don't you?'

Emma hesitated. What was she talking about? 'Excuse me?'

'Running off like that, leaving your parents on their own, never contacting them. It broke your mother's heart.'

A lump lodged in Emma's throat and she felt a ridiculous urge to defend herself. 'I'm sorry, but I think you might have the wrong idea. My parents were well aware that I wanted to leave school. I certainly didn't run off. I was seventeen and both myself and a friend chose to start building our careers in Brisbane. I spoke with my parents most weeks and visited a number of times a year. I'm not sure what information you seem to think you have on me, but I can tell you right now it isn't true.' Emma attempted a smile. 'What can I get you two ladies?' This was one of the reasons she'd left the Bay in the first place. Small-town gossips and busybodies. She'd hated growing up in a place where everyone knew your business. The town itself might have had a facelift and moved into the modern world, but if this was anything to go by, the small-town mentality of the residents certainly hadn't changed.

Miss Maude turned to her sister. 'I don't think we'll be able to eat here today, or any other day *she's* serving.' She turned back to Emma. 'It makes me sad to think of what you put your poor mother through. You say you kept in touch but I've heard otherwise. Married Harvey's hotshot of a son, got too big for your boots and ignored your parents altogether. It took your parents' wedding anniversary to drag you back here, didn't it? Wonder when we would have seen you otherwise?'

Emma just stared at her. Had her mother really spoken about her in this way? Had Emma's behaviour really upset her mother enough that she'd confided in these old biddies?

A deep voice interrupted her thoughts. 'Now, now, ladies. This hardly sounds like the type of conversation that is being supportive of Maggie.'

Emma had been so focused on the Thompson sisters she hadn't noticed Drew approach the counter.

'How about you order your cups of coffee and one of those delicious looking cakes, like you do every Monday, and head to your table outside? There's no one sitting there – it's waiting especially for you.' He smiled, his face warm and friendly.

The two sisters shook their heads. 'Thank you, Drew, but as much as we'd love to continue with our usual Monday morning routine, we feel we can't this week, or in fact any other day this girl is working here. I don't think you have any idea of the awful things she's done.'

Drew put up his hands. 'Again, are we here to support our friend Maggie, or tear strips off her daughter?' He winked at Emma. 'I can only assume you are not aware that Maggie is very unwell, undergoing tests at the moment. Being a small town we must get behind the family and support them. I'm sure you could enjoy your coffee and cakes outside in the cool breeze and discuss in great detail all the awful things Emma's done. I'd hate to be the one to tell Maggie that you were abandoning her in her time of need. Family's everything to Maggie and the fact that the business is still being run by the family is providing her with a lot of comfort. I'd also hate to hear rumours around town that you'd encouraged anyone else not to come to The Café while Emma is here.' He was still smiling, but no one could miss the warning in his voice.

'Fine, two flat whites and a piece of mud cake to share.' Miss Maude dumped a pile of coins on the counter and turned, clunking her walker against the floorboards as the two moved toward the door.

Drew laughed as the old ladies sat themselves at the table furthest from the entrance. 'That's not their usual table so they've obviously got some further discussions to have about you. What did you do, set fire to the town or something?'

Emma shook her head. 'No, but I'm beginning to think I should have. Gossiping old bags.' She took a deep breath and managed a weak smile. 'Thanks for the support. What can I get for you?'

'Just a juice; a red rocket, thanks, with extra celery. Actually, another smile would be good, if you've got one going?'

Emma looked up from her notepad. 'What?'

'A smile. You almost gave me one before. Your face looks like it could totally transform from the usual pissed-off look you throw my way.' He cocked his head to one side. 'I'm still not completely sure what you have against me, but it would be nice to start afresh.'

Emma passed the juice order over to Kristen, who was grinning madly. She'd probably seen more drama in The Café in the past ten minutes than she had in the last two years.

'Look, I appreciate you stepping in with the old ladies but I have no desire to become friends. I'm here for a short time to help out my family. I'm not interested in befriending the local hippie surfer-cum-business entrepreneur. I realise that might come as a shock to you, having wrapped everyone else in the town around your little finger.'

Drew considered her response and smiled. 'Wow, harsh. You do realise you're missing out, don't you? I'm funny, I'm charming, I love long walks on the beach and, look, I'm already defending you. What more could you ask for?'

'I'm not sure telling two old biddies to head outside and discuss my awful actions is completely defending me, and I'm not on the lookout for someone who's charming, funny or likes long walks.' She held up her left hand. 'I'm happily married, if you hadn't noticed.'

Drew's smile had all but faded. 'I had, and that's why I'm surprised at your reaction toward me. I'm just trying to be friendly, Emma. I've become good friends with your parents in the past few years, and Simone and Johnno, too. I was hoping to get to know you. From what I've heard from Maggie we have quite a lot in common. You may have noticed the Bay has a rather ageing population. Having someone younger to chat to would be a novelty.'

Kristen placed his juice on the counter.

'Thanks.' He picked it up and took a sip. 'Hopefully this will reinstate my powers of charm; they certainly don't seem to work around you. I'm afraid I've let Maggie down.'

'Let Mum down? What are you talking about?'

Drew hesitated. 'Nothing. Don't worry about it. I'd better be off.'

'No, hold on. I want to know what's going on.'

'Nothing much. Maggie just asked me to keep an eye out for you. This was before I knew who you were and had already pissed you off by flattening you. She thought you might need a friend while you were here, someone who wasn't family to talk to occasionally. Seems she was wrong.'

Emma picked up a cleaning cloth, ready to wipe down the bench. 'Yes, she was. There's no need to try to be friendly moving forward. I'll explain to my mother that she doesn't need to ask

173

people to be my friend. I have plenty already and certainly don't need one that pities me.'

Drew stared at Emma for a moment. 'I'll be off then. Enjoy your day.' He turned and walked out of the café.

Emma furiously wiped at the bench. What was her mother thinking? She wasn't five, for God's sake. Other than the fact she found Drew arrogant and annoying, the last thing she needed was Daniel finding out she had a new, good-looking, male friend.

Emma pulled into a car park outside the pharmacy. Her first shift was done and she'd survived. In fact, the job itself had gone very smoothly. If not for the run-in with the Thompson sisters and then Drew, the day would have been a complete success. Bloody small towns – neither of those incidents would have happened in the city.

She went into the pharmacy to pick up some eye drops. Her eyes had been dry and a little sore all day. It reminded her of her teenage years. Something about the beach and the associated winds didn't agree with her eyes or lips. Growing up she was forever putting in eye drops and applying lip balm.

Emma came back out of the shop, stopped and drew in a breath. Harvey was walking toward her. His butcher shop was only a couple of doors up from the pharmacy. His face lit up with a beaming smile.

'Emma, what are you doing back here so soon?'

After everything Emma had learnt recently about Harvey, she wasn't so pleased to see her father-in-law. 'I'm helping out my parents. Mum's not very well so they need a bit of a hand.'

Harvey's smile was replaced with a frown. 'Nothing serious, I hope.'

'We're not sure yet, waiting on some test results. Hopefully she's just a bit tired. I'd better get going, she'll be expecting me.'

'Oh.' Harvey took a step backward. 'Danny's okay with you being here then?'

'Yes, he is.' Emma didn't elaborate.

'Oh, good. That's really good. He's usually so keen to avoid the town I thought he might not like you being here either.'

Emma raised an eyebrow. 'Harvey, from what Daniel has told me, he has very good reason to avoid the town. I'd probably do the same if I were in his situation.'

'Oh?' Harvey hesitated. 'I'm sorry, Emma, when we chatted at your parents' anniversary party you gave me the impression you were going to ask him to get in touch. I'd been hoping I might hear from him.'

Emma shook her head. 'I doubt you'll hear anything. Daniel's told me the full story about why he left the Bay and why he doesn't visit or stay in touch. I don't blame him and I totally support him.'

Harvey stared at Emma. She could tell he hadn't a clue what she was talking about. Was she really going to have to spell it out for him? She sighed. 'Look, he's still very upset about what happened when his mother died. The fact that you sent him off to a school camp and then brought her home to die is something he's unlikely to forgive. That, and then having to pretty much fend for himself for the next three years. Both of those experiences are enough to leave anyone feeling bitter and resentful.'

Harvey's eyes focused on the ground. 'There are things Danny doesn't know,' he muttered. 'Things I couldn't tell him.'

'If you want any sort of relationship with your son, and I can't guarantee that is going to happen anyway, then I suggest you tell him. He was fourteen, had just lost his mother and he felt like he was on his own. The town didn't help either. He told me how your wife used to organise meals and support for any family who needed it, yet when she died it sounds like no one did anything.

Daniel was left to cook and clean for you while you wallowed in your own grief.'

'I wouldn't call it "wallowed".' Harvey spoke quietly. 'My wife had just died after a battle with a horrible illness. Until you go through something like that you have no right to comment.'

Emma immediately thought of her mother. She hoped she wasn't about to get first-hand experience.

'To be honest I never really understood the townswomen's behaviour. Caroline had always been the first to organise the meals and cleaning rosters for any family in need. Most of the women in the town would get behind them. We were brought meals before she died but once she was gone that was it. No help at all. Living off Danny's toasted sandwiches and bowls of cereal was hardly ideal.'

Emma tried unsuccessfully to control herself. 'You're kidding?' Her voice was loud and even though she was aware that a couple of women had stopped and were hovering nearby she couldn't help herself. 'You're complaining that your fourteen-year-old's efforts weren't up to scratch? If you'd pulled yourself together and been a father to him you could have done it together. Cooked something healthy, looked after your son. Instead your actions, or lack of them, drove him out of town. Do you really wonder why he chooses to avoid you? First you take away his opportunity to say goodbye to his mother and then you let him be the one to pick up the pieces, rather than you being a father. I'm sorry, Harvey, but I'm going to agree with my husband on this one; if it had been me, I wouldn't have waited until I was seventeen to leave. And, like Daniel, I doubt I would ever have come back.'

Harvey recoiled as if Emma had slapped him. He turned his back on her and, shoulders slumped, walked slowly toward his shop.

Emma's stomach churned as she watched him go. Confrontation wasn't something she enjoyed, but Harvey had needed to hear that.

What he'd done was unforgivable. Emma's legs trembled as she walked back to her car. She was aware of the eyes of the two old ladies following her. They'd be dining out on that bit of gossip for weeks. She'd been back in the Bay for less than twenty-four hours and in that time she'd managed to have run-ins with the Thompson sisters, Drew and now Harvey.

She got into her car; it was time to go back to see her parents. Her mother had a few questions to answer about setting her and Drew up as friends. She hoped that wouldn't turn into her fourth run-in.

Maggie was propped up in bed against a wall of pillows, her make-up done, hair neatly brushed and colour back in her cheeks. She looked completely transformed from when Emma had seen her in the hospital the previous week.

Emma smiled at her mother and sat on the edge of the bed. 'Wow, you look fantastic. How are you feeling?'

'Much better, love. A couple of nights back in my own bed was what I needed. I could get up and head back to work right now, if only your father would let me. He seems to think I need to stay in bed, regardless of the fact the doctors said I could do whatever I wanted.'

'They did not.' Brian walked into the room carrying a cup of tea. 'They said you could move about as long as you didn't tire yourself.'

Maggie rolled her eyes. 'I don't think they meant move about within the confines of my bed. I think they meant move about like a normal person, around the house, out in the town.'

'You can get up tomorrow. For now I want you to rest. You've had a day full of visitors. You'll probably be tired out from that.'

'Yes, love.' Maggie's voice dripped with sarcasm. 'I'm sure chatting and laughing will have done me in.'

Brian sighed. 'I'll leave you to it.' He retreated from the room.

'I'm sure he's just trying to help, Mum.'

'I know. He's terrified, that's the problem. Terrified of what the results are going to be on Wednesday. I shouldn't give him a hard time, but if I'm too nice it will probably scare him even more.' She grinned. 'I'm trying to act my normal, difficult self in order to protect him. Now, tell me all about your day. How did you get on?'

'It was good. I seem to have the hang of the ordering system and the till. It was fairly constant with customers.' Emma rubbed her feet as she spoke and decided not to mention her run-in with the Thompson sisters. 'I'm certainly not used to standing around like that all day. I'm going to need a hot shower to loosen up.'

'That's wonderful. I knew you'd take to it like a duck to water.' Maggie patted Emma's hand. 'You know how grateful we are that you're helping, don't you? With Simone about to pop, we can hardly expect help from her. We could employ someone else but it just isn't the same. It's a family business so having family run it is just wonderful.'

'That's what Drew said.'

Maggie smiled. 'Drew came in today?'

'I think you probably already guessed he would, didn't you?' Emma raised her eyebrows at her mother.

Maggie had the good grace to blush. 'I think it would be nice if you two became friends. He's a friend of the family already and such a nice person.'

'Mum, I appreciate you wanting me to feel welcome in the town, but I'm here purely to help you and Dad out. I don't have the time or the inclination to be making new friends. Particularly good-looking, male friends. Daniel wouldn't be too happy about that.'

'Good-looking? I hadn't noticed.' Maggie tried to appear innocent.

'Oh, come on. He's got that whole surfer thing going on: the tan, the floppy hair, the rippling muscles. How could you not notice? He even talks in that sexy, laid-back way. To top it off, he's got those dimples that make him look like he's twenty-five, not pushing forty. You must have noticed.'

Maggie's eyebrows had raised. 'It certainly sounds like *you've* noticed how good-looking he is. It wasn't something I considered at all when I thought he might be a nice friend for you. I'm not trying to set you up, just make sure there's someone else you can lean on if you need to. Drew's intelligent, successful and great fun. Why wouldn't I want him to be your friend?'

Emma's cheeks were warm. 'He might be all of those things but he's not friend material for me, okay? Daniel would have a fit.'

'Really?'

'Really. He's a man – he gets jealous. He's supportive of me being here, but that won't last if he thinks I'm out having a good time with some other guy.'

'Supportive? That's a surprise. I assumed he might be put out about your visits.'

'No, he thinks I should be here. Family is very important to him. You don't know him so you wouldn't know that.'

Maggie laughed, a wry little laugh.

'What?'

'We didn't see you for five years and yet you say family is so important to your husband. He's met us a handful of times and has no contact at all with his own father.'

Emma was silent. The bitterness in her mother's voice was obvious. 'I bumped into Harvey this afternoon, actually.'

'Oh?'

'Yes, I popped into the pharmacy to get a couple of things on the way home and he was out on the street.' Emma hesitated. 'I think I might have created a bit of town gossip.'

'Why? What did you say to the poor man?'

'Poor man? Mum are you aware of what he did to Daniel? Why Daniel wants nothing to do with him? He is completely responsible for Daniel leaving the Bay.'

Maggie looked uneasy.

Emma stared at her. 'You know what he did, don't you?'

'I know his wife died and he was left to raise a son on his own. I know how difficult that would have been; it's a shame Daniel can't appreciate that.'

Emma shook her head. 'That man stopped his son from saying goodbye to his mother. Sent him off on a school camp and brought his wife home the next day, knowing she was going to die. How do you think Daniel coped, coming home to that news?'

Maggie pulled the blankets around her. 'I'm sure he would have been very upset. Now, love, I am getting a bit tired. Do you think we could finish this conversation another time?'

Maggie's face had completely drained of colour. Damn, she should've let her rest. Asked her another day, when she was stronger. She'd looked so well when Emma arrived she hadn't given it another thought. She stood. 'Of course. I'm sorry, Mum, I shouldn't have brought this up today.'

'No, it's fine. I guess your dad was right after all: a few visitors has made for a tiring day. We can talk more later. I just need a little rest.' She closed her eyes.

Emma turned back to look at her mother when she reached the bedroom door. Maggie had one eye slightly open and shut it the moment Emma turned. Was she really using her illness to avoid the conversation? Emma shook herself. Regardless, her mother was sick; the last thing she should be doing was grilling her.

Emma's second shift at The Café ran smoothly, this time with the added bonus of no confrontations. The old ladies hadn't appeared today, neither had Drew, and she was fairly certain Harvey wasn't likely to take time away from his own shop to drive over to The Café.

Emma had asked Kristen to show her how to use the coffee machine, mainly so she could make her own coffee. The shop was quiet so she made herself her second cup of the day – some extra energy to get through the next hour before her shift was over.

Simone walked in just as she sat down with her cup. 'Want one?'

Simone shook her head. 'I'm limiting how many I drink this far along. I'll have a juice though, if there's one going.'

'I'll get it,' Kristen called out. 'Why don't you take a break, Emma? I can look after the shop for a minute. Go and enjoy your coffee.'

Emma smiled at her. 'Great, I will. Thanks.' She led Simone to a table outside, noticing a customer raise her eyebrows to her companion as she did. Simone noticed, too.

'Talk of the town, I believe.'

'What?'

'You apparently made quite a spectacle yesterday, tearing strips off Harvey in the middle of the main street. You didn't really hit him, did you?'

Emma spluttered her coffee. 'What? Who told you that?'

Simone laughed. 'Small town, sis. Words don't just get around, they fly at about a million miles an hour. You can't breathe here without someone noticing. Johnno stopped to pick up some chops on his way home last night. Apparently old Dora Cromwell was in the shop, trying to be supportive of poor Harvey.'

'She must be one of the two old bags that stood by, watching.'

Simone shook her head. 'Don't think so. Johnno said it sounded like she'd heard the news from her neighbour that the horrible Jean girl was back stirring up trouble and Dora decided she needed to come and check on him immediately. So anyway, what really happened?'

Emma explained to Simone why Daniel had left the Bay when he was a teenager and exactly what she'd said to Harvey. 'He can't go around acting like he's been wronged and his son has deserted him when that's their history. I wanted to make that quite clear.'

'Sounds like you did.'

'What, you think I was out of line?'

Simone shook her head slowly. 'Not out of line, perhaps just not the most appropriate place to have that discussion. The progressive side to the town – the new shopfronts, the upgraded look – has certainly modernised its appearance, but when it comes to small-town mentality and gossip, I can tell you right now it has probably gone backward. Next time, do it in private, that's all.'

'There won't be a next time. I have no reason to speak to him again and by the looks of it'– Emma nodded toward the two women sitting at the other table, who were obviously listening – 'he'll hear that through the gossip vine later today.'

Simone laughed. 'Probably. Do you know, when I first told everyone I was pregnant some smart-arse made a joke about Johnno not being the father because he was working away so much. I had bloody Mum come to me demanding to know who the father was and what this meant for my marriage. It took her months to convince the town that I was a reputable, upstanding married woman, as she liked to put it. I helped actually – told one of the old biddies that Johnno was away a lot but when he was back we were at it like rabbits so of course it was his. I'm sure that made the rounds.'

Emma laughed. 'You think they'd have something better to do with their time, wouldn't you?'

'That's half the problem. They haven't. Gossiping gives them something to do. Now, what time does Mum get her results tomorrow? Do you think we should all go or should we wait until they get home and go over to the house?'

'Let them go, digest whatever information they're given. I'll be here until four tomorrow. How about I pick you up on the way home and we can go and see them together?'

Simone's eyes filled with tears. 'Face the music together, you mean.'

Emma squeezed her hand. 'Hopefully it will be happy music.'

Emma had been delayed at The Café and didn't arrive at Simone's until close to five the next afternoon. 'Sorry,' she called as she climbed out of the car. She walked around to open the passenger door as Simone carefully heaved her bulk down the driveway.

'No worries,' Simone puffed. 'I spoke to Dad; they only got home an hour ago and wanted some time to themselves. Mum's pretty tired.'

'Did he tell you anything?'

Simone looked at Emma, her eyes full of fear. 'No.' She pulled herself into the car. 'Remind me once this baby is born to avoid pregnancy. We'll buy the next one if we want one. Everyone makes out it's supposed to be a beautiful, sensual experience. There's nothing beautiful about feeling like a hippo, and looking like a large one.'

Emma laughed. 'You look amazing. You definitely have the glowing skin going on. You shouldn't complain. There are many people who'd kill to be as hippo as you are right now.' Emma tried to cover the wistful tone of her voice with another laugh.

They pulled up outside their parents' house and Emma helped Simone out of the car. 'Just hold on a sec, I've got some food in the boot I need to bring in.' Emma took out the two platters she'd had made up at the shop.

'Yum. Is that for us?'

'Yes, I thought it would do as an early dinner.' Emma grinned. 'Or a snack for a hippo.' She ducked out of Simone's reach.

'Hey, not fair, don't tease the wildlife.' Simone pouted. 'Wait for me. I might look like a hippo but I move at a snail's pace.'

Emma waited and the two of them walked up the stairs to the front door. Emma opened it and called out to her parents. 'Only us.'

The house was quiet. She looked at Simone. 'Maybe they're having a sleep?'

Simone shrugged. 'Maybe. I guess we just wait and see when they appear. It's been a tiring couple of weeks, they're probably knackered.'

The moved quietly toward the kitchen and Emma put the platters of food down on the bench. 'Glass of wine?'

'I'd love one.' Simone laughed and rubbed her belly. 'However this one might not appreciate it quite so much. Cup of tea would be great though.'

Emma flicked the kettle on. 'Sorry, wasn't thinking. I'm going to have one if you don't mind?'

'Pour me one too love, a big one.' Emma turned as her father walked into the kitchen, his eyes sagging with exhaustion.

'You look awful. Have you had any sleep at all?' Simone asked.

'Thanks, love. I feel awful, too. It's been a rough few days.' He sighed and took the glass of wine Emma offered. 'Come and sit in the lounge. Mum will be down in a minute.'

Emma glanced at Simone as their father retreated from the kitchen. She looked as scared as Emma suddenly felt. Brian had aged twenty years overnight. He looked like an old man: a weary, sad old man. Emma squeezed Simone's hand and led her into the lounge. Whatever news they were about to receive, they would hear it together.

Simone sat across from Emma, her mouth hanging open, at a loss for words. Emma knew how she was feeling. How could her beautiful, healthy mother have lung cancer? It just wasn't possible.

'But you've never even smoked, have you?'

'No, love.' Maggie sipped her wine. She smiled at the girls. 'Ah, heaven. Cramped up in that car all the way to the hospital and back; I need something to relax me.'

Simone caught Emma's eye; the fear that had been there earlier had returned. Other than the occasional glass of celebratory champagne at Christmas or on birthdays, Maggie didn't drink. Their father liked a beer every now and then but wasn't much of a drinker either. Their father's glass was already empty.

'Okay, you'd better tell us,' Emma said. 'You're scaring us.'

Maggie and Brian exchanged a look. 'Do you want me to tell them?' Brian asked his wife.

Maggie shook her head. 'No, I will.' She took a deep breath. 'There's good news and there's bad news. The bad news is the tests have confirmed I have a cancerous tumour on my right lung. The good news is the tumour is early – stage one – and very treatable. It doesn't appear to have spread anywhere else. If they can remove it I should be fine. Other than being a nuisance for the next month or two, long-term nothing will change.'

Emma looked at her father, a lump catching in her throat. Tears were rolling down his cheeks. 'So why is Dad crying?'

Maggie looked at her husband and smiled. 'Because he's a big softy and it's been a long day. I have to have a few more tests later this week, which will determine my treatment. The most likely scenario, according to the oncologist, is that they will operate and

185

remove the tumour. The test this week will confirm the exact size of it and that will determine whether or not they'll do some chemo after the operation.'

'Some chemo? How much?' Simone asked.

'I don't know exactly; it would go in a three-week cycle and it was suggested I might require two, possibly three cycles.'

The room was silent.

Simone broke the silence. 'If you have chemotherapy, what does that mean for the baby? Don't you have to stay away from pregnant women and babies?'

Maggie shook her head. 'No, that's radiation therapy and I won't need that, thank goodness. Don't you worry, I'll be the first person demanding a cuddle of my new granddaughter. Nothing, not even stupid cancer, will stop me from doing that.' She waggled her finger at Simone. 'Just you make sure you don't have that baby while I'm being operated on. That will make me very cross.'

Simone managed a smile.

'When do they think they'll operate?' Emma asked.

'Possibly next week. They'll do the final tests this week and then schedule it. They don't muck around.' Maggie smiled at them both. 'Now, I'd better go and rustle us up something to eat.'

'No need,' Emma said. 'I brought a couple of platters home. Not that I could eat anything anyway. But I'll bring them in, you should eat something.'

'No,' Brian said, standing up to help Emma. 'Let's take them out on to the back deck, sit and enjoy the view. It's going to be a beautiful sunset, we might as well enjoy it.' He turned to Maggie and Simone. 'You two stay here. We'll call you out when it's ready.'

Emma followed her father into the kitchen and slumped against the bench. 'I can't believe it. Lung cancer?'

Brian nodded. 'I know. It's awful, I'm really not sure what to do.'

Emma saw the fear in her father's face, the glistening tears in his eyes. She went to him and hugged him. 'I guess there's not a lot we can do, just listen to the doctors and support Mum. You're already doing a wonderful job of that.'

'With your help, love. I'm not sure what I'd do without you. Taking on the shop like you've done is an amazing help.'

'I can stay as long as you both need.'

'Sounds like it might be a while. If she has the operation at the end of next week we've probably got at least six to eight weeks of chemotherapy.' He pushed his hand through his thinning hair. 'I was reading about the side effects of that – it's going to be miserable.'

'Still, we need to look at the bigger picture. If it gets Mum through this then what does it matter what we have to do?'

Brian nodded. 'You're right, love. We need to focus on the end goal, not the road that gets us there.' He smiled at Emma. 'I don't know what I'd do without you right now. Thank you for coming home.'

Emma's eyes filled with tears. Why had she avoided her family for so long? She'd let Daniel convince her that all they needed was each other. It was hard to believe she'd gone for five years without seeing them. For the first time since she was a little girl she felt like she was part of a family, that she was home again.

Chapter Fifteen

LUCIE

Climbing on to a chair, Lucie hung the Year Twos' stories from the decorative ropes that criss-crossed the ceiling in the classroom. She had to admit, Anna's room looked good. The parents were always blown away when they came in, seeing the quality of the written work and the detail in the artwork. Lucie couldn't remember producing any work like this when she was at school.

'Looking forward to the holidays?' Anna looked up from her desk where she was marking homework books. The kids were off at their music lesson, giving Anna and Lucie forty minutes to get some jobs done. 'You and Noah going anywhere?'

'No, not this time,' Lucie said. 'You?'

Anna rolled her eyes. 'Apparently we're spending four nights at the Gold Coast. Each day spent at a different theme park. I'm thinking I'll let Tom and the boys go to the parks and I'll laze about by the pool with a book.'

'Sounds wonderful.' What Lucie would give for four days to herself with a good book.

'It does, but it's probably not realistic.' Anna laughed. 'I bet I'll get dragged to every park and will stand at the bottom of the rides, holding hats and drink bottles.'

Lucie's phone beeped. She jumped off the chair and retrieved it from under the desk. It was Brad, suggesting he come over that night.

'Everything okay?'

Lucie looked up to find Anna staring at her. She slipped the phone back into her bag. 'Yes, fine.' Her face was hot.

'Mm, methinks you have a new man.'

'What makes you think that?'

'The smile as you read the text message for a start, and then the guilty red face I'm now staring at. Tell me, who is he?'

Lucie cleared her throat. 'No one, just my brother-in-law. He boarded up a broken window for me last week and wanted to check if the glass had been replaced yet.' The lie rolled off Lucie's tongue.

'Oh. That's not very exciting. Never a good idea to steal extended family – kind of ruins the family Christmas.' Anna raised her eyebrows. 'Could get yourself into a lot of trouble.' She turned her attention to the books she was marking.

Lucie climbed back on to the chair and continued hanging the children's stories. Anna was right: she was setting herself up for trouble. While she enjoyed Brad's company and friendship, the lying and sneaking around was not who Lucie was. She needed to put an end to it before any further problems were caused with Kate or her in-laws. She felt a sense of relief. The decision was made. She would text Brad during her lunchbreak.

A kilometre from home, Lucie pulled the car over to the kerb and turned to face Noah. 'Kick my chair one more time and I'll put you out on the footpath and you can walk. Do you understand me?'

Noah stuck out his tongue and kicked Lucie's seat as hard as he could. 'You can't do that, you'd get in trouble.'

Lucie undid her seatbelt and got out of the car. She went to open Noah's door, but he'd locked it. He was sitting on his booster, pulling faces at her through the window.

Part of her wanted to laugh, he looked so ridiculous. If it were a one-off incident she probably would have, but every day Noah seemed to go out of his way to push her buttons. She needed to find some way of getting him under control.

She pressed the unlock button on her car key and opened his door. His face fell immediately. 'Get out.'

'No.' Noah grabbed the sides of his booster seat, determined to stay in it. Lucie leant forward to undo his belt and he brought his knee up into her chest.

'Ow, Jesus!' Lucie rubbed her chest and backed away from the car. 'That hurt.'

Noah started to cry.

Lucie took a deep breath. What had she been thinking? Was she really going to manhandle him from the car and then drive off? Of course not. She might as well just ignore him and go home. The whole incident had started in the supermarket when she was buying ingredients to make pizzas for dinner. He'd wanted an ice cream and she'd said no. He'd already had a cupcake for afternoon tea and she didn't want him to be sick.

Lucie got back into her seat and started the car. She didn't say anything to Noah as she pulled into the traffic and continued the drive home. She ignored as best she could the gentle kick, kick, kick on the back of her seat. Tomorrow she'd move his car seat to the passenger side of the car.

When they pulled into the driveway she got out, collected the bags and walked up the path. She left Noah to get himself inside. She wasn't in the mood to deal with more outbursts. She'd run the bath for him, get herself a glass of wine and hope they'd both be relaxed and happier by the time it came to having some dinner.

A knock on the door forced Lucie from the kitchen stool where she was enjoying her glass of wine. She smiled as she passed the bathroom. Noah's squeals of delight and splashes confirmed she'd made a good choice.

She opened the door, her smile slipping as she faced Brad. He grinned. He held a six-pack in one hand and wine in the other.

'Brad, what are you doing here?'

'What do you mean? We have plans, don't we?'

Lucie shook her head. 'No, I sent you a text saying I wasn't comfortable with the idea. You must have received it.'

Brad shook his head. 'No, I didn't hear back. I assumed it would be okay to just come over. I'm sorry.'

Lucie smiled. 'It's no problem. I'm sorry you've come all this way to be turned around again. I can't hang out with you if Kate doesn't know about it. It's not fair to Kate and I don't want to do anything that could jeopardise my relationship with Jan and Walt. That's what my message said.'

'Okay. I'll head off then?'

Lucie nodded. 'Yes, sorry.'

'Uncle Brad!' Noah's excited cry filled the passageway. He ran to the front door, a towel wrapped around his waist, drops of water flicking from his hair.

'Hey there, little matey.' Brad put the drinks down and scooped Noah into a bear hug.

'Have you come for dinner and to read me stories again?' Noah asked.

'Um, I'm not sure,' Brad said. 'We might need to ask your mum if that's okay.'

191

Lucie stared at Brad. Why had he said that? Now she had to be the bad guy and tell Noah no.

'Please, Mum, please? I can share my pizza with Uncle Brad if there's not enough, and I promise I'll go straight to bed after dinner if he can read me my stories. And I'm sorry I kicked your chair, I won't do it again.'

Lucie sighed. Noah had said all the right things. She swallowed, letting Brad in for an hour would be okay. She wasn't doing anything wrong; she just couldn't bear the invitation to be misconstrued.

'Please,' Noah begged.

The two faces in front of her were full of hope.

She nodded. 'Yes, of course he can.'

Noah shrieked with delight, high-fived Brad and pulled him into the house behind him.

Lucie bent down to retrieve the beer and wine. This was going to be the last solo visit from Brad. She needed to make that very clear.

Lucie smiled at the laughter coming from Noah's room. Regardless of her reservations, they had enjoyed a lovely evening. Brad had grabbed the soccer ball and taken Noah outside and kicked it back and forth while she made the pizzas. She'd stood at the kitchen window, glass of wine in hand, watching on wistfully.

Dinner had been a huge success and the pizzas were delicious. Brad had kept them both entertained with stories of when he was a boy scout. Noah had hung on every word and then rushed off to brush his teeth before jumping into bed, ready for his stories.

Sitting in the family room with her glass of wine, Lucie enjoyed hearing the noisy story time, but wished the deep, booming laugh was coming from Matt, not Brad. It was a small taste of what life could have been like. It should have been Noah and Matt kicking the ball, waiting for dinner. Noah should be looking forward to Matt coming home from work, being excited that he'd made a pizza to share with his dad. It was something he should look forward to every day. Instead, what did he normally have to look forward to? A screaming match with his mother. Lucie shook herself. She was being silly. It wasn't a screaming match every afternoon, although sometimes it felt like it. It was amazing to see the transformation in Noah when a man was around the house.

Lucie's thoughts were interrupted when Brad returned to the family room. She stood up. It had been lovely but she needed the evening to end.

'He's a great kid, Luce.'

'Thanks. He loves having you around.'

Brad's smile mirrored her own. 'Good, I'm glad. I love hanging out with him.'

'I'll grab the leftover beers for you to take.' Lucie moved to the kitchen.

'Really?' Brad said. 'You're throwing me out already?'

Lucie handed the beers to him. 'Yes. You need to go. Noah will probably tell Ruby you were here and it will filter back to Kate. It won't look as bad if she knows you left after reading the stories.'

Brad placed the beers on the bench. 'Does it really matter what she thinks? I enjoy your company, Luce; we're friends. Why don't we have a drink together and unwind a bit?'

Lucie shook her head. 'No, sorry. You've given Noah a great night and I appreciate it, but that's where it ends. I don't think you realise what a big part of my life Jan and Walt are. I can't do anything to jeopardise that.' Lucie shifted uncomfortably. Brad was staring at her. Why wasn't he picking up the beer and leaving?

'I'm disappointed, Luce. I thought there was something kind of special between us. Something bigger than Kate or Jan or Walt.'

Lucie's cleared her throat. 'Come on, it's time to go.'

Brad shook his head and moved toward her.

'What are you doing?' Lucie's mouth was dry.

Brad smiled and took her hands. 'Something I know deep down you really want.' He pulled her to him and kissed her.

Lucie jerked her head away and tried to free herself.

He tightened his grip on her hands. His eyes were hard as they drilled into hers. 'Now, we both know you want this. You're dying for it, in fact, so there's one of two ways it can go. You comply and we both have the best night of our lives, or you don't and I give you a good night anyway.'

Lucie's legs and arms had begun to shake. 'No, Brad, please. Please leave.'

'Not until you give me what I came for.' He yanked on her blouse, laughing as it ripped open. The buttons scattered on the kitchen floor.

Tears escaped Lucie's eyes. She wiped them roughly with the back of her hand. She should never have encouraged his visits, never have allowed Noah's excitement to sway her judgement and let him in tonight.

'Don't cry, Luce. I'll make this good for you.' He pushed her up against the fridge, his hands exploring her body.

Noah's voice broke into the room. 'What are you doing, Uncle Brad? Can I play, too?'

Brad let go of Lucie and turned to Noah. 'Of course you can, little matey. We're playing a game of hide-and-seek. I caught Mum so now she's it. How about you go and hide and Mum can find you. I have to get going.'

Noah grinned and took off down the hallway.

Lucie pulled her shirt around her, unable to control her trembling body. 'Get out,' she spat through clenched teeth. 'Don't ever come near me or Noah again.'

'Or what? You'll tell Kate?'

Lucie would have loved to smash the smirk off Brad's face. She opened the kitchen drawer and took out a knife. 'I said get out.'

Brad laughed and collected his beer from the bench. 'Yeah, great move, Luce. Stab me and end up in jail. Leave Noah with no father or mother; well thought through.' He turned and walked from the kitchen, calling out a goodbye to Noah as he went.

Lucie sank to the kitchen floor as she heard the front door shut. The knife clanged on the tiles as she curled into a ball and rocked back and forth.

'Mum, are you coming to find me?' Noah called.

Lucie stopped rocking. Noah. She needed to pull herself together. He couldn't see how terrified or affected she was. She wrapped a cardigan around her shoulders and went in search of her son.

'Can I hide again?' Noah asked a few minutes later when Lucie found him hiding in the laundry basket.

She smiled. 'Tomorrow, hon. We'll play lots of hide-and-seek tomorrow, okay?' She pointed to the laundry basket. 'That is the best hiding spot I've ever seen, by the way; do you think I'd fit in it?'

Noah laughed and ran to his room. 'Of course not, you're way, way too big.'

Lucie followed him into his room, turned the light down and sat on his bed.

Noah frowned as he looked at her. 'Are you okay, Mummy? You look sad.'

Lucie tried to smile then pulled Noah to her.

'I love you, Mummy.' Noah's muffled words came from where he leant against her chest.

Tears rolled down Lucie's cheeks as she hugged him tight.

Chapter Sixteen

COMMUNITY SERVICE

Emma sat on the hard chair in the middle of the foyer, waiting for the other prisoners to arrive. The newly applied 'Prisoner' signs on the chairs suggested Rodney wasn't getting sick of this ridiculous, degrading waiting area. There were only four chairs out today. Emma assumed some of the people must have finished their work orders. Her thoughts drifted back to the last few days at the Bay and her mother's tests. They had all been done now but they wouldn't have the results until early next week. Emma sighed. She was looking forward to seeing Daniel. He was flying back from Darwin at four so would be home by the time she'd finished her community service.

Emma was brought back to the present as Lucie sat down beside her. She looked tense, a vein throbbed in her forehead. 'You okay?'

Lucie mustered a smile. 'Yes, thanks. You?'

Emma nodded.

They sat in silence for a few minutes until two young women reported to Rodney and were sent to sit next to them. Emma smiled at them but received no response.

'Okay,' Rodney snarled as he checked his clipboard. 'Put your bags away and get into the kitchen. You and you' – he pointed at Emma and Lucie – 'show the newbies the ropes. Have everyone ready in five minutes.'

Emma nodded. 'Where's Florrie?'

Rodney shook his head. 'I don't respond to questions that aren't phrased correctly.'

Emma sighed. God, he was such a little prick. 'Sorry, Warden.' She heard a snigger from one of the new girls. 'Excuse me, Warden, could you please tell me where Florrie is today?'

'That's better.' He checked his clipboard. 'No, I can't tell you that. I can confirm she won't be with us today and that is all.'

'Arsehole,' Lucie murmured, making Emma grin.

They led the new girls into the kitchen and showed them where to put their belongings, where to scrub their hands and to put on aprons and hairnets.

The morning dragged for Emma. It seemed like hours before she was sitting outside having a cup of coffee. Lucie sat with her while the other two women found a bench to themselves.

'Not very friendly, are they?' Lucie looked over to them.

'No,' Emma said. 'Not that it matters. I wonder where Florrie is? I got the impression she never misses a session.'

'Yes, I hope she's all right. Perhaps she got herself that gun and is now doing hard time somewhere.'

'I wouldn't put it past her. I hope for her sake the food's good if she is. Sounds like that was her only requirement.'

They both laughed. Emma was pleased to see Lucie beginning to relax. 'You look like you needed that. Everything all right? You were looking pretty stressed this morning.'

Lucie's smiled faded. 'Something happened last night that I'm not sure how to handle.'

She told Emma about the difficulties she'd been having with Noah and how Brad had helped them out the other week by fixing the window. She told her about Kate and Jan's reactions and warnings to stay away from him. 'He turned up last night after I'd said no to coming over and then . . .' A tear rolled down Lucie's cheek.

Emma took Lucie's hand. 'What happened? Are you okay?'

Lucie closed her eyes.

'Did he . . . Did he hurt you?'

Lucie shook her head and opened her eyes. 'Luckily Noah interrupted him before he could do more than scare me.'

Emma clenched her fists. 'The arsehole. Did you call the police?'

'No. You're the only person I've told. He shouldn't have been at my house in the first place. I can't let my in-laws find out.'

'Lucie, he can't get away with it either.' Emma sat thinking about Lucie's situation. She tried to put herself in the same place: what would she do? 'The guy, what did you say his name was?'

'Brad.'

'He's a total bastard. I'd say he's seen you as easy prey. You're widowed, lonely, struggling with your son, and he's decided to take advantage of that. He's obviously counting on you not telling his wife or your in-laws.'

'I know. He'd lie through his teeth and then it would be my word against his. I'm pretty sure I know which side they'd take.' Lucie sighed. 'School holidays start in a few weeks and Noah will be expecting to spend a lot of time with his cousin, Brad's daughter. It's going to be a nightmare.'

'You should think about going away for the holidays. Sounds like you need a break. It might be good for you and Noah to get away from your normal routine.'

'It's a nice idea.'

'But?'

Lucie looked away. 'But not financially viable.'

'Oh.' Emma hadn't considered that. She couldn't imagine being a single mother. The two women sat silently, finishing their morning tea. Emma wished she could help, but other than handing Lucie a wad of cash for a holiday, which probably wasn't a good plan, she couldn't think of any ideas.

'Looks like the warden is about to crack his whip.' Lucie picked up her plate and cup. 'We'd better get back to it.'

Emma glanced at the big clock on the wall of the industrial kitchen. It was finally lunchtime; she couldn't believe they still had the entire afternoon to get through. Why was the day dragging so much? It hadn't felt as long on other Saturdays. She looked across at Lucie, whose face was a picture of absolute misery. The bastard brother-in-law – he shouldn't be allowed to get away with what he'd done.

While she'd been peeling the dozens of potatoes the warden seemed to think it was hilarious to give her each week, Emma had come up with a solution to Lucie's holiday problem. She really needed to discuss it with Daniel first, but could at least run it by Lucie to see if she'd even be interested.

She waited until they were sitting back at the table, lunch trays in front of them. 'I was thinking, I might have an idea of how you could get away for part of the holidays without having to spend much money.'

Lucie looked up from her sandwich. 'How?'

'Well, I might have a place where you and Noah could have a little holiday.' Emma explained about Maggie's illness and her need to commute to and from the Bay. 'I think I'll be doing it for at least two to three months and I can't stay at my parents' that long. I had a bit of a look around this week and found a three-bedroom townhouse that I can rent month to month. It's part of a new development so it's very modern. It's fully furnished so there would be a room for you and for Noah. The only snag is I haven't had a chance to discuss it with my husband yet – not that I expect him to object as I doubt he'll be coming up to stay.'

Lucie shook her head. 'I couldn't impose like that, especially when your mum is going through such a hard time. You'll probably want your own space at the end of the day. A five-year-old isn't likely to give you that.'

Emma smiled. 'I'd say the distraction is exactly what I'll need. I'm sure he'd love Golden Bay. My parents have fishing gear, kayaks you can take out in the bay, and the surf around the headland is fantastic. There's plenty to do without having to spend any money, other than food of course. You'd be buying that here so that really isn't an additional expense.' Emma could see Lucie hesitate. It was understandable as they hardly knew each other, but she liked Lucie. She seemed like a caring, nice person who'd obviously suffered a lot since her husband died and could use a break. 'I haven't rented the place yet, but hope to confirm with the agent tomorrow after I've spoken to Daniel. It was empty and clean so, ideally, I'd like to move in on Monday when I go back. Give me your number before we leave today and I'll ring you tomorrow and let you know whether I've rented it or not. There's no pressure to come and stay, but you'll have it there as an option.'

Lucie nodded. 'It's so generous of you, thank you.'

Both women looked up as one of the younger girls approached their table. She was holding a note. She handed it to Emma. 'Some old lady asked me to give you this.'

Emma unfolded it. 'It's from Florrie.' She started to read the handwritten note.

Hi lovelies,

Sorry to miss out on seeing you today, I'm so disappointed. You mustn't have many weeks of jail left. Perhaps go and commit another crime so you'll still be there when I'm back. I'm a bit under the weather at the moment so not sure when or if I'll see you.

Love, Florrie.

PS: Did you think I'd got the gun and was in jail?

Emma smiled. 'She's such a character. What a shame; hopefully she'll be back before our work orders are finished.'

Lucie turned to the girl who'd delivered the note. 'Where did you get the note from?'

The girl looked away. 'Can't tell you. Sorry.'

'Why?' Emma asked.

'Made a promise to an old lady.'

'Who?' Emma held up the note. 'Florrie?'

The girl shrugged. 'Dunno her name but she made me promise to give you the note and say nothing more.'

Emma stared at the girl. Something wasn't quite right. 'Was there anything in it for you?'

'What do you mean?'

'Did she pay you to keep quiet?'

The girl laughed. 'I wish. No, she just asked, that's all.'

'If I gave you fifty dollars would you break your promise and tell me how you got this note?'

The girl's eyes widened. 'For real? You'd give me fifty dollars?'

Emma nodded, reached into her bag and pulled out her purse. She opened it and took out a fifty-dollar note. 'So?' She held it up.

The girl reached out and took it. 'Thanks. The old lady is in room twelve in the Koala Wing. She's in bed, looking a bit sick. I had to take her some dry biscuits. She asked if you two were here helping and when I said yes she made me wait while she wrote you that note. That's all I know.' She pushed the fifty dollars into her pocket and turned and walked away.

Emma looked at Lucie. 'She's a resident. So much for the armed robbery story.'

Lucie smiled. 'She's a classic.'

The warden was approaching their table. Lunchtime was over.

'I'm amazed he goes along with it,' Emma said. 'He's such a bastard. I can't imagine him sharing that secret with Florrie.'

'Shall we visit her?'

'What? Now?'

'No, after we've finished this afternoon. We could surprise her.'

Emma smiled. 'I'd love to, although I'm not sure if Florrie will be happy that her cover's been blown.'

'She'll just have to live with that one. At least it means she'll have some visitors.'

They stood up before the warden reached their table.

'Okay, Rodney, keep your clipboard on, we're coming.' Lucie winked at his horrified face as she walked past.

Lucie experienced a twinge of guilt as she entered Florrie's room. The old lady was sitting up in bed watching television. Her face lit up at the sound of visitors and then instantly crumpled the moment she recognised Lucie and Emma.

'So, my cover's blown. How disappointing.'

'We were worried we might not see you again. We've only got a couple of weeks left on our work orders.' Emma pulled a plastic container out from behind her back. 'I swiped these for you.' She handed it to Florrie. 'I seem to remember you have a sweet tooth for jam tarts.'

'Thanks, love.' Florrie took the container. She sighed. 'So that young girl couldn't keep a secret then?'

Emma blushed. 'I made it a bit difficult for her.'

Lucie laughed. 'Emma bribed her. Your secret was worth fifty dollars, in case you were wondering. How are you? You don't look very well.'

Florrie took a sip of water. 'I'm okay, love. Just a silly cold. They always get worried that it will turn into pneumonia so make a bit of a fuss. I should be up and about in a couple of days.'

'How long have you been in here?' Emma asked.

Florrie sighed. 'Eleven years. Eleven bloody years.'

Lucie glanced at Emma; she wasn't really sure what to say. She looked around the small room. It lacked Florrie's colour and vibrancy, however the many photo frames Florrie had on the shelves of the bookcase and the window ledge gave it a personal touch. 'You've been in this room for eleven years?'

'Yes. Not exactly the Ritz, is it?'

'I thought you didn't have any family?' Emma was standing over at the window looking at the photos that adorned the ledge. She picked up a photo and brought it over to the bed. 'Who are all of these people?'

Lucie looked at the photo. A younger version of Florrie was sitting among a small family. A little girl, who must have been about two, sat on her lap, while a boy of about Noah's age stood next to Florrie, grinning and making rabbit ears above the little girl's head. Behind them stood a man and woman in their thirties, arms around each other, their smiles bright.

Florrie took the photo from Emma. 'That's my Laila.'

'Your daughter?' Emma asked.

'Yes, and her husband and their two beautiful children.' Florrie's eyes filled with tears as she studied the photo. 'Becky would be thirteen now and Jacob, the little monkey, would have been sixteen.'

Lucie squeezed her hands together. Would have been. Oh God, she almost didn't want to hear the rest.

Florrie looked up from the photo. 'A drunk driver. A bloody drunk driver took my family away from me. All four of them wiped out, just like that.'

'Oh, Florrie.' Tears rolled down Lucie's cheeks. She could see Emma's eyes glistening, too. 'I'm so sorry, I don't know what to say.' Her own problems suddenly seemed so trivial. She fleetingly thought of the night she had picked up Noah, Ruby and Liam from the pool. She had been over the limit. Probably only just over the limit, but imagine if she'd done something like this to another family? She shuddered and did her best to push away the thought.

Florrie patted her hand. 'Thank you, love. There really isn't anything to say. I moved in here after it happened because it was suggested that I needed looking after. My friends got worried about me, decided I needed help. They were right, of course; not that I wanted to move in to start with. Anyway, that was all a long time ago.' She smiled weakly. 'I still have my memories of them to treasure.'

Lucie and Emma were silent. Neither seemed to know what to say. The vibrant, cheeky woman they'd met a few weeks ago wasn't at all who she'd portrayed herself to be.

'Why does Rodney go along with your charade of being a prisoner?' Emma finally asked.

Florrie chuckled. 'Rodney is a product he and I created. His name is actually Leonard James; we call him LJ. He's a lovely, lovely man. He let me join in with the community service group the first week I realised it was on. He was far too nice, making cups of tea for everyone – they walked all over him. I had to give him a real

204

talking-to. Make him realise that these people are all felons. This gig was too cushy and it gave them no incentive not to be repeat offenders. So we got tough and he got tougher. I think he's doing a wonderful job now, don't you? He's very convincing.'

Emma started to laugh. 'I can't believe you did that. It was all your idea – the "Yes, Warden, no, Warden, three bags full, Warden," and calling us all prisoners.'

Florrie nodded. 'Did you like the signs on the chairs today? I thought they were rather good. Bev's great on the computer so I got her to print them out for me.'

Lucie's mouth dropped open. 'I can't believe you got him to go along with all of that.'

'I haven't managed everything I've wanted. Some of the ladies sewed him a uniform and we wanted to make orange ones for the prisoners, like they have on television, but he refuses to wear it. I'm still working on him with that one.'

Lucie still couldn't believe it. That horrible little man was an act he'd agreed to go along with for the sake of a lonely old woman. She'd be seeing him through different eyes from now on. 'So, tell me, do you still see all of your friends? Do you get to go and visit them? Go on outings?'

Florrie shook her head. 'I rarely go out. Occasionally there's a bus trip somewhere and I might go on that, but most people get out when their family come and take them somewhere. I don't have that option. Three of my friends do visit – it used to be four, but Doris died.'

'They don't take you out?'

Florrie shook her head. 'None of them drive, and they're old too. They don't go out a whole lot themselves.'

Lucie nodded. This wonderful, vibrant woman was wasting away. Her main entertainment was playing with the minds of those carrying out community work orders. It was so sad. 'I've got a five-year-old who'd love to meet you, Florrie. Perhaps when you're feeling better we could come and collect you, take you out somewhere or to our house for the day. I'd love the company, and so would Noah.'

Florrie's face lit up and tears welled in her eyes. 'Oh love, that's the kindest thing anyone's suggested in such a long time. Thank you. Of course I couldn't impose on you like that, but just the very offer has made my day.'

'You wouldn't be imposing, I'd love to have you.'

'Yes, go on,' Emma said. 'You can never have too many grandmas. I'm sure Lucie's son would love another one.'

Lucie smiled. 'She's right. Come and be our adopted grandma, even just for a day. You can help me tame Noah. You'd actually be doing me a favour, and him. We probably wouldn't yell at each other if we had a visitor.'

Florrie nodded. 'If you really mean it, I'd love to. I'm sure I'll be better in a few days.'

'Good, that's settled then,' Lucie said. 'I'll ring you on Monday and see how you're going. Perhaps we could do something one afternoon later in the week. Then if you like us enough we could always have a Sunday together.'

Florrie was beaming at the suggestion. She turned to Emma. 'Now you've been awfully quiet. Tell me all about what you've been doing. How's that husband of yours? Stolen anything nice for him lately?'

Emma laughed. 'No, sorry to disappoint you. I've been too busy to continue my day job.'

Lucie listened as Emma told Florrie about her mother and the outlook for the next few months, with surgery and possibly chemotherapy. The cheeky twinkle in Florrie's eye had been replaced with understanding and compassion. She glanced at the happy, innocent faces of Florrie's grandchildren. What a devastating thing to have happened.

Her own thoughts transferred to Noah. It could happen to her – he could be gone instantly, just like Matt. She shuddered. You always heard people saying things like 'make the most of every day' and 'treat every day like it was your last'. When she considered all the arguments she'd been having with Noah lately, it would be awful if something happened and they were the memories she was left with.

Hearing Florrie's story also left her in no doubt that she needed to put the incident with Brad behind her. Dwelling on it wasn't going to achieve anything and it would be her word against his if she spoke up. Whether anyone would believe her was irrelevant. She wasn't going to put herself through the trauma of finding out.

Chapter Seventeen

EMMA

A contented smile formed on Emma's lips as Daniel curled his body around hers. The reception she'd received after being apart from him for close to a week was very different from the week before. The moment she'd arrived home he'd whisked her off her feet and carried her to their bedroom. He'd undressed her slowly before making love to her. His kisses had been passionate and full of love, rather than urgency. She just hoped his mood wouldn't change when she discussed her ideas about commuting between home and the Bay for the next few months.

An hour later they sat out by the pool, sipping champagne in the moonlight.

Emma was sitting between Daniel's legs, leaning back on him on the sun lounger. 'Are you sure you don't mind?' Daniel's reaction to Emma's news that she wanted to rent the townhouse for at least the next two months had been a pleasant surprise. He'd been full of concern during the week when she'd told him her mother's diagnosis and possible treatment plan.

'No, it makes no difference to me whether you stay with your parents or somewhere else. Chemotherapy's not very pleasant so it would probably be best for both you and your mum if you're not there. Give you both some space.'

Emma laced her fingers through Daniel's. 'Did your mum have chemo?'

'Yes. Not that it worked for her; they found her cancer too late. They used it to prolong her life. She said at the time if she'd realised how awful it was going to be she wouldn't have had any. There are heaps of different chemo drugs so it won't necessarily be as bad for your mum.'

Emma shivered. She knew they needed to look at the bigger picture, that they were trying to save her mother's life, but it was still scary.

Daniel pulled her closer to him. 'Don't worry, your mum's a tough old bird and you've got me and the rest of your family to get you through it, too.'

'Do you think you'd be able to come up and see me? I'll still try to come home on the weekends but once the gala event is finished I won't have any more commitments down here.' Once Emma's last two community service days were done, Daniel would be the only reason she'd need to come to Brisbane.

Daniel's body stiffened. She'd pushed him a step too far. God, she was stupid. They'd had such a beautiful evening and she had to go and put her foot in it. Of course he wasn't going to come to the Bay. How many times had he told her that he never wanted to set foot in it again? Her body tensed, waiting for the verbal blow she was about to receive.

'Maybe,' he said. 'Let's see how things are going with your mum and take it from there.'

Emma turned to face him. 'Really? You'd really think about coming?'

Daniel nodded.

Emma leant forward and kissed him.

Daniel responded, kissing her, and at the same time he took her champagne and placed it on the table next to his. He tugged at the rope on her robe, his hands pushing away the silky material as the front parted. Emma groaned as Daniel's tongue explored her mouth, his hands caressing her body. The slow lovemaking of earlier was forgotten as an urgency to have Daniel inside her again overtook Emma. She needed him, she needed the closeness and love of her husband. She tugged at his shorts, his hands never leaving her as he expertly stepped out of them. Laying her back, he looked deep into her eyes. His own urgency was obvious as his hardness pressed against her. She pulled him down on top of her – she needed him and she needed him now.

The little black Audi travelled virtually on autopilot north from Brisbane toward Golden Bay. This was Emma's fourth trip in a matter of weeks. She smiled as she thought back to the time she and Daniel had spent together. They hadn't been able to get enough of each other. It reminded her of when they'd first started dating. Daniel had stocked the fridge before Emma returned and they made themselves meals as they needed them, remaining in their robes right up until the moment Emma realised she needed to have a shower and go. There had been no objections at all from Daniel about her leaving. He'd told her how much he'd miss her and then laughed, saying he'd need a week to recover. Her heart swelled just looking at him. He loved her so much and right now he was supporting her exactly how she needed. It was likely to be a tough week ahead if Maggie had surgery, and having Daniel on her side was a huge relief.

She pressed the auto-dial button for Cass as she drove past the signs to Noosa signalling she was almost halfway.

Cass's voice was loud over the car speakers. 'Hello?'

'Hi, it's me. I was hoping to come and see you today, but ran out of time. I'm so sorry.'

Laughter echoed through the car. 'God, don't worry about that. I hope you ran out of time because you were enjoying your husband rather than fighting with him.'

Emma smiled. 'Yes, that's exactly why I ran out of time.'

'That's great. I'm pleased. He's okay with you helping your parents?'

'Yes, he is. In fact, it's why I'm ringing. I'll be up there for the next few months, I think, and am renting a place today with plenty of room. If you feel like a getaway let me know and come up for a few nights.'

'I'd love to, but I've got news, too. I got the gig in the States. I'm going to California for six months to exchange with a professor at UCLA.'

Emma was stunned. 'Six months? You never said it was six months.'

'I know. It changed last week. Was supposed to be two but got extended to six. It's all happened really fast. I'm leaving on Wednesday.'

'Wednesday? Why didn't you tell me? I would have come and visited before I left this morning. I don't think I can get back down before you go. You promised you wouldn't leave without saying goodbye.'

Cass laughed. 'Don't stress. It's only six months, and this is me saying goodbye. With everything going on with your mum, that time will fly past. I'll keep in touch while I'm away. Tell me, how many more Saturdays have you got to do?'

'Two more, then I am officially free.'

'Good. So . . .'

Emma sensed Cass's hesitation. 'No, I haven't stolen anything since the day I was caught.'

Cass let out a breath. 'Sorry, I shouldn't have even asked. I'm sure community service is enough of a deterrent.'

Emma immediately thought of Lucie and Florrie. The actual work on a Saturday had become mind-numbingly tedious but she did look forward to seeing those two and would miss them afterwards. She wouldn't, however, miss lying to Daniel or the Saturday commitment.

They spoke for another ten minutes, promising to keep in touch before saying goodbye. Emma still couldn't believe Cass was going to America so soon.

She drove faster as she sang along to Adele. She was looking forward to getting back to her parents and to work tomorrow. Who would have thought? She, the girl who absolutely refused to work in the shop as a teenager, now couldn't wait to get there.

The waves crashed against the rocks, sending up a spray that drenched Emma. She moved further along the walking track, enjoying the cool relief the water brought. She looked out over the ocean, sure she'd seen something rise up out of the water two hundred or so metres offshore, but it disappeared again. It might have been the hump of a whale. Emma continued walking along the track as it weaved its way around the rocks before taking her back on to the sandy beach. Kicking off her shoes, she enjoyed the warmth of the sand as it scrunched between her toes.

She glanced at her watch. Three o'clock. Maggie would still be in theatre. She'd offered to come with them but her father had said no. He needed her back at The Café. There was no point them all sitting around waiting. He would call as soon as he had some news.

Since arriving back in the Bay, the days seemed to have blurred into one long one. Receiving the news late Sunday night that Maggie's surgery was scheduled for Tuesday was probably a good thing. It had given them only a short amount of time to worry about the procedure and possible outcomes.

Emma walked down to the edge of the water, testing the temperature with her toes. It was cool yet inviting. Further down the beach the lifesavers had set up flags and people were swimming and boogie boarding. She continued along the shoreline. It was still unthinkable that her mother had cancer, and lung cancer at that. For someone who'd never smoked in her life it was incredibly unlucky.

'Hello there.'

A deep voice interrupted Emma's thoughts. She spun around. Drew. That was all she bloody needed.

He grinned at her. His surfboard was tucked under one arm, his wetsuit rolled down to his hips. His hair was messy but dry. His dimpled cheeks made him look like a teenager.

'Sorry, didn't mean to scare you. Just saw you walking down here. Wanted to say hello. How's your mum?'

Emma turned back to look out to the ocean. 'They're operating now. We should know some more later today.'

'Sorry. I didn't realise it was today.'

'Sorry? Why are you sorry? The quicker they get this bloody tumour out the better.'

'I meant I was sorry to interrupt your walk.'

Emma looked at him. 'That's okay. I'm just filling in time until Simone's home. We wanted to be together when Dad rings with any news.'

'Feel like some company?'

'I don't know. Have you been asked to come and find me today?'

Drew smiled. 'My surfboard isn't a prop – I was heading out for a surf when I saw you here. Nothing pre-planned.'

'Surf looks good. Don't let me stop you.'

Drew walked away from Emma and placed his board on the sand a few metres from the shoreline. 'Surf will be there later. Let's go for a walk, shall we? See if I can win you over with my sparkling charm.'

Emma was about to say something sarcastic in response but stopped herself. This wasn't the day to be prickly. He was only trying to be nice. She could use some company to take her mind off her mother. She stepped into line next to Drew, enjoying the breeze on her face as they walked toward the lighthouse end of the beach. 'So what's your story then?' she asked. 'Other than trying to be my knight in shining armour, everyone tells me of the miracles you've been performing since you got here, but no one seems to know what you're actually doing in the Bay.'

Drew laughed. 'Not sure about miracles, but nice that you say that.'

'Really, though, why are you here? Didn't you have some fancy job in Melbourne or something?'

Drew's smile dropped. 'Sydney. I grew up in Sydney and lived there all my life until I came to the Bay.'

'What made you move?'

Drew sighed. 'A friend died. A very close friend. I'd known him since I was a kid. We went to school and uni together. We surfed together on the weekends, went out drinking. All the stuff that mates do.'

'I'm sorry.'

Drew gave her wry smile. 'Yeah well, we had plans to meet for drinks one night and he didn't show up. Didn't answer his phone. It was really unlike him. I went around to his place. I had a key so figured I'd take some beers and wait until he came home. He was dead on the couch when I walked in.'

Emma gasped. 'That's awful.'

Drew nodded. 'It was an aneurysm. Anyway, his computer was on the coffee table in front of him. He'd been making, or maybe adding to, a bucket list. I didn't know he had one. He had about thirty things listed that he intended to do but the one he had highlighted said he planned to persuade me to leave Sydney, find a town with good surfing and enjoy life. Stop working so hard, find a nice woman each and settle down. I decided if he couldn't follow his dream then I could. He'd worked so hard only to end up dead on his couch two months before his fortieth birthday. All his dreams ended, just like that.'

'What about your friends, your family? What do they think of you moving?'

Drew sighed. 'They all think I'm crazy. That I'm still grieving for Luke and I'll come back to Sydney, keep making them all rich.'

Emma raised an eyebrow.

'I worked in financial markets for many years before getting into commercial property marketing. I made a few good investment suggestions that my family and friends benefited from. I stopped though – it got too stressful when I realised the potential downside for all of them if one of my recommendations went the other way.'

'Do you go back to Sydney often?'

'I've been back a few times, to see the family, but now that I'm living here I find it hard to relate to my friends who are still all stuck on the working treadmill. Luke's death was a real eye-opener. If he hadn't died I'd still be doing exactly what they're all doing. There's no way he would have been able to convince me to give up what I had and move somewhere like this.'

Emma nodded. 'Why the town overhaul?'

Drew raised his eyebrows. 'Don't you like it?'

'I like it, it's just that for someone with the aim of getting away from the rat race and relaxing, it looks like you've been pretty busy since you got here.'

Drew laughed. 'Yeah, I'm not sure I'm quite ready for retirement. I met lots of interesting people when I got here. They were so friendly, so welcoming. Your parents were part of the welcoming committee. I realised I wanted to stay here and saw some opportunities to help them and help the town become more sustainable. These small towns get tired and shops close down. With a bit of a facelift I figured we'd keep them alive for another ten years, then we'll need to do it again.'

'It's very good of you.'

Drew grinned. 'Not completely altruistic, I'm afraid. The town was seriously lacking in some of my creature comforts: nice cafés, good coffee, juice bar, wine bar. Other than the wine bar, so far I've managed to tick all of those boxes.'

Emma laughed. 'You'll get some objection from Kenney's and its punters if you try to get a wine bar up and running. That pub's an institution. I'd say the brownie points you've racked up would be quickly diminished.'

'Yes, I'm well aware of that. But I'm working on it. You wait and see. I'll get it up and running and it will be a success.'

Emma rolled her eyes.

'You don't believe me, do you?'

'It won't work in a town like this. They like their pub, end of story. Don't forget the majority of the town are older; I'm not sure paying fourteen dollars for a glass of wine will do it for them. Most of them cringe at paying those sort of prices for a bottle. Also, they're probably in bed by ten o'clock. I doubt they'll be slipping out after eating their Meals on Wheels for a late night at the wine bar.'

'Sounds like a challenge to me. I'll prove to you I can do it and on the first night we're open you'll come as my guest to enjoy a glass of the most expensive champagne we have. How does that sound?'

'Great, but it has to be a proper wine bar – piano music, tables, chairs, the whole thing. If you turn up at my door with a bottle you've bought at the shop and suggest we drink it on a park bench I'll be saying no.'

Drew laughed.

They continued walking along the beach in a comfortable silence.

'So you're still looking for your nice woman to settle down with.'

Drew shrugged. 'Eventually. There's no hurry for that. Gotta make sure she's the right one. Someone intelligent, fun, good sense of family values. Long blond hair, sparkly blue eyes. Finding that here might be a bit tricky – what do you think?'

His tone was light so she assumed he was joking. He'd just described her. She decided to keep the moment light, play along.

'I'd say she sounds perfect to me. Almost too perfect, in fact. Those perfect ones are usually out of bounds, happily married, living the dream.'

Drew chuckled. 'I'm sure they are – lucky them. How about you, Emma? Are you living the dream?'

Emma looked away, considering the question. A few months ago, bored and reduced to shoplifting for excitement, she would have answered no. But now, a second chance with her family, the opportunity to work in the shop and do something useful, and with Daniel's blessing, life was good. Right now, other than a clean bill of health for Maggie, she didn't want anything to change.

She nodded and glanced at her watch. 'God, I'd better get going. I said I'd be at Simone's by now. Dad might have rung.'

'Sure, I'll walk back with you.'

They turned and walked briskly down the beach to where Drew had left his board.

Emma smiled. 'Thanks for the walk, it was nice to chat to you.'

'You too. I might pop in and see you in the morning, if that's okay? Get a coffee and find out how Maggie is.'

'Of course. It's a café, you don't need to ask.'

'I know, but I've enjoyed our chat. It would be nice to do it again.'

Emma nodded. 'Yes, it would. But right now I really should get going.' Emma could feel his eyes on her as she walked across the sand and toward the car park. An image of Daniel filled her mind. She knew Drew's flirty comments were just a bit of fun but, after what had happened to Lucie, she needed to be careful.

Emma put the milk back in Simone's fridge and picked up the two cups of tea. She walked back into the lounge and handed one to her sister. 'You okay?'

'Yeah.' Simone rubbed her belly. 'Just uncomfortable. I guess it gets painful as they grow bigger.'

'Nothing's wrong though?'

'No, I think she's just moving about, testing out her footy kicks at the moment.'

Emma sat down and sighed. 'Dad's news was good news.' Brian had rung half an hour earlier. Maggie was in recovery, resting comfortably. The tumour had been removed and it appeared that there was no sign the cancer had spread. The doctors were recommending two cycles of chemotherapy to follow up the surgery and increase the odds of it not returning.

'What a relief.' Simone put her tea down on the coffee table and continued to rub her stomach. 'Let's just hope the chemo isn't too awful and it gets rid of it once and for all. I did a Google search on lung cancer, did you?'

Emma nodded. 'Yeah, and then wished I hadn't.'

'Me too. Although they got it early so there is a good chance it won't reappear.'

'Are you okay?'

Simone's face had turned red and she was wincing. 'Yeah, she's just moved into a funny position. I can't get comfortable. Feels like she's got a knife in there and is going to town with it.'

Emma put her own tea down. 'I don't think it's supposed to feel like that. Why don't we go to the hospital just in case?'

Simone laughed. 'It's fine. All just part of the process. I've been having pain like this the last couple of days. It comes and goes, it's just more coming than going at the moment.' She suddenly drew in a sharp breath, the smile wiped from her face.

'Look, it might be normal, but I'd feel better if we got you checked out. At least let me call someone. Do you have a doctor or midwife you're supposed to ring to ask questions?'

'On the fridge.' Simone gasped between each word.

Emma went and got the number and her phone. Just as she was beginning to key in the numbers a shriek came from the lounge. 'Shit, Emma! Shit!'

She rushed back into the room. Simone was standing, legs apart, a pool of fluid at her feet. 'I think my waters just broke.'

Emma drew in a breath. The look of terror on Simone's face hurried her into action. 'Come on, let's get you to the hospital. Can you walk? I'll get a towel for the car – I don't want you leaking on my leather seats.'

Simone was glued to the spot. 'What about Johnno and Mum? They're both supposed to be here. I can't have the baby unless they're here. Mum will kill me.'

'Not much choice, Sim. Your baby is coming. I'll ring Johnno on the way to the hospital. There's no point ringing Mum, she definitely can't get here. Do you have a bag or something?'

'In the bedroom, first cupboard, at the bottom. Why are you so bloody calm? We're supposed to be panicking!'

Emma looked at Simone: her sister's eyes were filled with fear. Emma's insides were anything but calm but one of them needed to

219

be strong. She'd be panicking, too, if she had to push out the huge lump that was inside Simone's stomach. She had the easy job – she was about to meet her niece and she couldn't wait. 'Sim, the baby's unlikely to just fall out. It will probably take ages. Let's get your stuff and get you to the hospital for a nice calm birth.'

'Easy for you to bloody say. Don't you watch all of those programs where people have them on the kitchen floor or on the way to the hospital?'

Emma laughed. 'No, I don't, and as the hospital is only about a four-minute drive, I think we'll be right. Don't even think about having a baby in my car. You'll be buying me a new one if you do.'

'Oh fuck.' Simone bent double, her face contorting in pain.

Emma took it as her cue to get organised. She really didn't want this baby born on the floor or in her car. She cursed her hands as she dashed into Simone's room, willing them to stop shaking. She managed to pick up the bag Simone had prepared for the hospital and then stopped at the linen cupboard for towels for the car. While she couldn't wait to meet her niece, she knew nothing about childbirth. With Johnno a four-hour drive away and her mother in hospital, it looked like she was going to be launched into the position of Simone's birth partner. She rushed back to the lounge. 'Do you want some fresh clothes to put on?'

Simone was still bent double. 'No, just get me to the fucking hospital.'

'How long do you think we've got?'

'How the fuck should I know? I've never done this before.'

'But you would have read up on it or something. Surely they give you some kind of idea?' Emma looked at her sister's red face and quivering lip. Time to stop asking questions and get her to the hospital. She took Simone by the arm. 'Come on, let's go. Time to meet your daughter.'

Emma sat in the armchair in Simone's hospital room, nursing the precious little bundle. She'd fallen in love the minute the screwed-up, screaming little face had shot her way into the world. Simone may have never given birth before but she was right in thinking the baby was coming while they were standing in her lounge. She'd been checked by a midwife as soon as they arrived at the hospital and was already eight centimetres dilated. They'd been whisked straight to the birth suite and fifteen minutes later Mia was born. Simone had been amazing, grunting and groaning and pushing with extreme effort. There'd been no screaming, yelling or even abuse. Emma had watched her little sister in absolute wonder at what she and her body were capable of.

Simone appeared from the small en suite. A delighted grin spread over her face as she came out to see Emma holding her daughter. 'I can't believe she's here.'

'I can't believe how gorgeous and tiny she is and what a brilliant job you did.' Emma shifted to the front of the chair. 'Here, do you want her back?'

'No, you hold her for a bit longer – you've earnt your cuddle.'

Emma arched an eyebrow. 'No, I haven't. I did nothing.'

'Yes, you did. You got me here and you were so calm. I was shitting myself and you acted like we were going out for coffee. It helped, made me think I was overreacting.'

Emma laughed. 'I put on a good act. I was shitting myself, too. What if you'd had her at home? What on earth would I have done?'

'Called an ambulance, I guess. Like you pointed out, we were only minutes from the hospital. I wish Johnno would hurry up. He's going to be so upset he missed it.'

'No, he's not.' Johnno walked into the room holding a massive pink teddy bear. He walked straight over to Simone pulled her to him and kissed her. 'Are you okay?'

'Yes, I'm fine. A bit tender in places but nothing to worry about.'

'I'm so sorry I wasn't here.'

Simone put her finger to her husband's lips. 'Don't worry about it, we're two weeks early. I had no idea I was in labour or I would have called you. Come and meet Miss Mia Maggie Jones.' Simone's eyes met Emma's as she announced her daughter's name. 'Do you think Mum will approve?'

Emma nodded as tears formed in her eyes. 'I think she'll be honoured.' She handed Mia to Johnno, who scooped her up so naturally you'd think he worked with babies. Tears began to roll down Emma's face as she saw the sheer joy and awe on his face as he stared at his daughter. She stood up and wiped her eyes. 'Coffee,' she mouthed to Simone. This moment was so special, so intimate, one she knew her mother would be heartbroken to have missed, but she didn't want to intrude. The new little family needed time to get to know each other.

The black Audi came to a stop in front of Simone's house. It was astonishing to think she'd only spent one night in the hospital after Mia's birth. Emma had imagined she would be exhausted, certainly not up for the trip to Brisbane to see their parents. She walked up the driveway, half expecting to hear the sounds of a screaming baby. Hearing nothing, she knocked quietly in case they were still asleep.

Simone opened the door, dressed in a beautiful blue dress, her eyes sparkling. 'Hey sis, come in.'

Emma followed her into the house as the smell of freshly baked muffins wafted from the kitchen. 'What's going on?'

'What do you mean?'

'I mean you had a baby three days ago, you're dressed beauti-fully, you don't look tired and what, you're baking, too?'

Simone laughed. 'I think I'm still running on adrenaline. Johnno says we should make the most of it before I turn into a zombie.'

'Where is Johnno?'

'Here.' Johnno appeared in the kitchen doorway, wearing a pair of boxer shorts. He stretched his arms above his head and yawned.

Emma laughed. His hair was a ruffled mess and he looked like he'd been out for a big night. 'Now this is more what I expect you both to look like.'

'Yeah, coffee. I need coffee.' He kissed Simone as he passed her. 'That little girl is one hungry baby with very strong lungs. How many times was she up in the night?'

'Only three.'

He rolled his eyes. 'Only three. Far out. How many were you expecting?'

'One of my friends from the prenatal group said her baby only sleeps for twenty minutes at a time.'

Johnno stopped and stared at his wife. 'You're kidding? I'm going to have a word with Miss Mia. If she gets any ideas in her head we'll have to send her back. Make sure you keep her away from your friend's baby, in case it rubs off.'

Emma laughed. 'I'm glad to see you guys are coping so well. Can I have a peek at her?'

'Of course, she's in her room, trying out her bassinet.'

'You said you were having her in your room?'

'We did the first night, but then I was taking her into her room to feed her last night so figured she might as well just start there. It's nicer for me, going into the big comfy chair. I fall asleep with her feeding.'

Emma tiptoed down the corridor and pushed the door to the nursery open. She swallowed when she saw the tiny bundle, dark hair poking out of the muslin wrap. She was so gorgeous – like a beautiful little doll. She was only her aunty yet she had so much love for this tiny creature. She couldn't begin to imagine the overwhelming emotions she would feel if this were her baby. She pulled the door shut and took a deep breath before re-entering the kitchen. 'She's gorgeous. Looks like she's always been here.'

Simone nodded. 'It is so weird. I look at her and she's so tiny but looks so wise, like she's been around for years and knows more than any of us.' She bent down and opened the oven, taking out a tray of muffins. 'Mum's favourite. We'll take a few to cheer her up. Dad said she's been feeling a bit miserable.'

Emma laughed. 'I think Mia's enough to cheer her up. I don't think you needed to bake muffins, too. Not that I'm complaining, assuming there's one for me?'

'Of course. We'll give them ten minutes to cool then pop them in the basket and get going. I feel great now, but who knows? By this afternoon, I might need a nanna nap.'

'You coming, Johnno?' Emma asked.

He shook his head as he poured hot water into his coffee mug. 'No, I'm going to let you girls do the family thing, if that's okay. I thought I'd stay here, clean up a bit, get a meal ready for tonight. It appears I'm married to superwoman but on the off-chance it doesn't last I think one of us should be prepared.'

'Wow, what a great husband you've got, Sim.'

Simone laughed. 'What he's just told you is code for I'm buggered and will be spending my day out on the verandah in the hammock. I'll get some takeaway for tonight and possibly empty the bin in the kitchen to suggest I've been cleaning.'

Emma laughed.

'In fairness, he's not as useless as he sounds. He did forget to mention that he spent most of yesterday afternoon at Mum and Dad's mowing the lawns and tidying the garden so Dad wouldn't have to do it. Mia and I slept the entire four hours he was gone.'

Johnno grinned. 'See? I have justification for my lazy day. I will, however, help you get Miss Mia and all of her baby crap in the car.' He turned to Emma. 'Hope you've got a trailer – she comes with a lot of stuff.'

Half an hour later they placed a sleeping Mia into the car seat Emma had purchased that morning. 'It's part of my present to you guys – it will be useful to have a second one. You might want one in both of your cars or to leave with Mum and Dad in case they're looking after Mia at any stage.'

'But you've already given us way too much,' Simone said. 'A cleaner for three months and all of those clothes – they're amazing presents.'

'The cleaner is so you can enjoy Mia, hopefully get rest when you need it and not worry about a dirty house. Everyone says that even having a shower when you have a new baby is virtually impossible. Although, looking at you this morning, I'm beginning to wonder what they're all going on about. Looks pretty easy to me.'

Maggie was sitting up in bed, her hair freshly brushed and a smatter of make-up recently applied to her pale face. Their father stood up to greet them, his hair neatly combed, as they came into the room.

'Oh my, she's so beautiful,' Maggie cooed, rocking Mia in her arms.

Brian hugged Simone. 'Well done, love, you've done a great job. She looks just perfect.'

'And you,' Maggie added, looking Simone up and down, 'you look more glamorous than Emma today. You're not supposed to look that good when you have a three-day-old baby. You're supposed to look like a sleep-deprived wreck. Let me tell you, I know.'

'She's amazing, isn't she?' Emma said. 'Poor Johnno looks exactly how you've just described.'

Maggie smiled. 'The men find it more difficult than the women. And half of the time their only complaint is they had broken sleep because they heard crying, not because they actually had to do anything. Has he changed a nappy yet?'

Simone nodded. 'Yep, and he's bathed her. He's doing really well, isn't he, Em?'

Emma thought back to the hospital when Johnno had taken Mia from her for his first cuddle. 'He's a complete natural. You're really lucky. So's Mia.' She turned to her mother. 'How are you, Mum?'

Maggie smiled. 'I'm fine, love. A bit tender and a bit tired from all the drugs, but the excitement of knowing I was about to meet this little girl has pulled me through.' She stroked Mia's cheek. 'She's so beautiful. She looks just like you did, Simone. Doesn't she, Brian?'

Their father nodded. 'Just as beautiful, with the same button nose.'

They continued to admire Mia until the perfect sleeping bundle finally stirred. Her little arms squirmed and her face crinkled up as her lips made sucking motions but received nothing but air.

'Time for a feed.' Maggie handed her back to Simone. 'Are you okay in the chair here?'

'Do you want me to go?' Brian asked, shifting uncomfortably from foot to foot.

Simone laughed. 'No, Dad, you can stay. Don't worry, I've got it all worked out.' She sat down as Mia's cries became louder, more demanding. Her top was unbuttoned, Mia placed against her nipple and a muslin wrap draped over her, giving her privacy and removing any distractions for Mia.

'That's it?' Emma asked. 'She's feeding?'

'Yep.' Simone had Mia cradled in her arm, the other arm draped lightly across her back. She looked like she'd been feeding babies for years, not two days.

'Okay, I honestly can't wrap my head around this. How can you be such an expert already? Aren't you supposed to have cracked, bleeding nipples and all sorts of issues?'

Simone nodded. 'I've been so lucky. Considering all the stories you hear about horrible labours, exhaustion, feeding issues, so far' – she tapped her forehead – 'we're cruising.'

'Your mother was the same,' Brian added. 'Made it look sickeningly easy. All her friends hated her. It must be in your genes.' He winked at Emma. 'At least you know how easy it can be if you decide to have kids.'

'You'd better get on with it, Em. Mia's going to need some cousins that are about the same age. You could pop one out within a year if you get moving.'

Emma shifted uncomfortably on the edge of her mother's bed.

'Okay, that's enough,' Maggie said. 'Let's leave Emma to determine her own schedule if she chooses to have children. I'm sure we've all got enough to keep us occupied without worrying about that. Mia won't want any competition just yet; she'll expect us all to dote on her for quite some time.'

Emma was grateful to be rescued. She didn't want to discuss her baby-making, or lack of, with her family. 'So what have the doctors said about you?'

Maggie sighed. 'Not a lot. They won't have the results from the lobectomy for at least ten days. I'll be home again before that so then we'll have to traipse back in for the results and to find out if I need further treatment.'

'The chemo?' Emma asked.

'Yes. It sounds pretty certain I'll have to have it.'

'Will you have to come in here?'

'Hopefully not. The doctor mentioned it might be possible to take an oral dose. We'll see. It does mean I probably won't be up and around for another month at least. Is that going to be a problem for you with Daniel?'

Emma shook her head. 'No, he's happy for me to stay as long as I need. In fact he said that now I'm renting a place he might come up for a weekend. I still have to get back to Brisbane this weekend and the next, but after that I'm free of my Saturday commitment.'

'It would be lovely to see him, it's been far too long.'

Simone finished feeding Mia, moved the wrap up on to her shoulder and then leant Mia up against it and rubbed her back. A loud burp escaped, followed by a trickle of milk. Simone wiped Mia's mouth before removing the milky wrap. 'Can you take her?' She held Mia out to her father.

He scooped her up, chatting softly as he stood at the window and described what he could see. Simone put away the wrap and pulled out a nappy. 'She needs to be changed. Dad, I'll take her off you in a sec, before you get wet.'

Brian handed Mia straight back, making Maggie laugh. 'I think I can count on one hand how many nappies your father changed when you were little. It definitely wasn't his most favoured task.'

Simone lay Mia on her change mat and expertly applied a fresh nappy.

'Are you sure you haven't got a bunch of babies stacked away somewhere?' Emma was amazed by the expertise her sister was showing. Simone had Mia's clothes off, nappy changed and was handing a clean baby back to Brian within a couple of minutes.

Simone laughed. 'Yeah, I keep them all in a cupboard. Wind them up and bring them out to do party tricks. I don't know why it seems so easy; maybe it's just because she's been easy so far. The midwives told me to expect her to be really sleepy and easy the first few days, as she'd be exhausted from the birth. At least it's given me a couple of days to get the basics down. The one thing I can tell you is this feeding makes me starving. Em, where did you put the muffins?'

Emma retrieved the basket and handed them around. She sat in the heart of her family, enjoying the closeness. Unexpected tears pricked the back of her eyes. Simone and her mother were laughing over the indignity of childbirth while her father continued to be mesmerised by Mia. Emma was exactly where she wanted to be, where she needed to be. She'd undervalued her family and their importance for seventeen years. What sort of person was she? It had taken cancer for her to spend quality time with them. She'd felt a sense of obligation to help out. If it weren't for Maggie's illness she would have missed all of this. She would have driven up for a day to visit Simone and Mia and that would have been the extent of her involvement. While she wouldn't wish illness on anyone, especially not her mother, she had cancer to thank for giving her back her family. Her fingers were clenched so tight her nails dug into the palms of her hands. With everything she had cancer to thank for, she now needed to pray that Maggie was in the clear, that it wouldn't take her mother away.

Chapter Eighteen

LUCIE

'He's a delightful little boy,' Florrie said as she sipped her glass of wine.

Lucie smiled as Noah rode his bike in circles around the large mango tree that dominated their back garden. She and Florrie were sitting at the old table the previous tenants had left behind. Lucie had added some cushions to Florrie's chair and laid a cloth on the table to try to make it look a bit nicer.

'And this wine. I'm not sure what to say, it's just delicious. You'd better not give me too much more though, or I'll need a wheelchair to get me back into Treetops. You'll have to tell me what it is. I might have to get myself some.'

'I'll give you some. This is Matt's wine.' She cleared her throat. 'My husband, he was in the wine industry. We have a few investments in wineries and as part of our agreements we get quite a few cases of wine a year. I've got boxes of it in the garage. I'll never get through it and the whites do need to be drunk. The reds will last longer of course, but if you like this Pinot Grigio we'll take a few bottles back for you. I can always restock them when you run out.'

'You must miss your husband.' Florrie's eyes were full of sympathy and understanding.

Lucie nodded. 'Every day. Having Noah is wonderful but he's also a constant reminder that Matt's not here. He looks so much like Matt. The older he gets the more obvious it is that I'm not enough and won't be enough.'

Florrie patted her hand. 'You will be enough. You're what he's got and that's what's important. Of course he'd like to have a dad, but he doesn't, so you will make do. My husband died when Laila was twelve. I know what it's like to be widowed. You never recover, but over time it does get easier.'

Lucie looked at Florrie: this wonderful old woman had been through so much. 'How do you keep going?'

'It's not always easy, love. After Harry died I thought I was going to die. If it hadn't been for Laila I probably would have. I made myself get up each day, just like you probably do because of Noah. I'd take her to school and come home and cry. Some days I'd lie on the couch from the moment I got home from drop-off until I went back at pick-up time. I hardly ate; in fact I got so thin even I ended up getting worried. Coffee became my best friend – I think some days I'd drink eleven or twelve cups.'

Lucie nodded, she could understand that completely. 'I think work has probably pulled me along. I couldn't afford to take much time off after it happened so I had no choice but to try to block it out and get on with my day.'

'Doesn't work, does it? You forget for a minute, an hour, half a day, and then the exact moment you remember it's like being hit by a ten-tonne truck, again and again. Are you doing anything for yourself? Getting some time out, a break from Noah?'

'Like what?'

'I don't know, having coffee with a friend, going for a walk or doing a class?'

Lucie smiled. 'At the moment my only me time is spent doing community service. I look forward to it just to get a day off. That's terrible, isn't it?'

'No, love. Kids are hard work. We all need some time to ourselves.' Florrie stopped talking and smiled as Noah came running over to them, his bike now propped up against the base of the mango tree.

'Florrie,' he said, 'can we play a game of snakes and ladders?'

'Snakes and ladders? I'd love to.'

Noah smiled at her. 'You're a cool old lady, you know that?'

Florrie chuckled. 'Well, that's not something I've ever been called before. Why don't you get the game and bring it out here? Mum can enjoy her wine while I see if I can beat you.'

Noah ran back into the house in search of it.

Half an hour and three games later, Florrie sat back and sighed. 'I think I'm too old for this, Noah, or you're just too good at it. Now, I think I'd better just pop to the bathroom.'

Lucie helped Florrie to her feet and pointed her in the direction of the bathroom before returning to Noah. 'Come on. It's time we packed up the game and took Florrie home.'

'No.' He looked up at Lucie, his face set in a defiant look. 'We are having another game.'

Lucie leant over and picked up the board. 'Florrie wants to be back by six.'

'Why can't she stay for dinner? She only just got here.'

Lucie got down on her knees next to Noah. 'Look, Florrie hasn't been very well so today's visit was for afternoon tea. We'll invite her back again for a weekend day when she can stay longer. Right now, I need you to pack up the game and then come and help me take Florrie home. You'll get to see where she lives.'

Lucie waited while Noah considered what she'd said. His bottom lip poked out and he wrapped his arms around himself. 'No, I want to play another game.'

Lucie sighed. She started to put the game back in its box. It looked like Florrie was going to see the other side of her son.

Noah stood up and stamped his feet. 'No, no, no! I want to play another game. I want to play with Florrie!'

Lucie put the last piece in the box and stood, ignoring Noah's cries. She turned to go back to the house when a sharp pain at the back of her leg stopped her. He'd kicked her. He'd bloody well kicked her!

She turned to face him, just as he lashed out at her with his fist. She grabbed his wrist, stopping the punch from connecting. 'Stop it.' Her voice was firm.

He tried to pull his hand away, lashing out with his feet as he did. That was enough for Lucie; she'd had it with him. She released her grip on him and brought her hand down on his legs, smacking them hard. 'You are to stop right now, do you hear me?'

Noah froze. His face was white as he stared at Lucie.

She regained her composure. 'I'm sorry, but you left me no choice. You need to listen when I speak to you.' Her lip trembled. She'd just hit her son, and hit him hard. Noah started to cry, large sobs wracking his chest. She pulled him to her but he pushed her away and ran into the house. Lucie took a deep breath.

'You okay, love?' Florrie stood at the garden door.

Lucie's stomach clenched. It was bad enough that she'd hit Noah, but to have someone else witness it? 'Yes, sorry you had to see that. Like I mentioned, he's getting out of control. I'm not sure what to do with him.'

'He's very upset, sobbing his little heart out in there.'

Lucie sighed. 'I know, that didn't exactly go to plan. Anyway, let's get you back home, shall we?' She smiled. 'Perhaps we could have you over another day, try again.'

Florrie patted her arm. 'Of course, love. I'd enjoy that. I've had a lovely afternoon. Noah's probably a bit tired and by the looks of it he's good at pushing your buttons. Don't you worry about me. An afternoon out of jail with delicious wine and great company cannot be spoiled, not even by a five-year-old.'

'I'm glad.'

'But, love,' Florrie said carefully, 'we might have to start thinking about how to discipline him. If you're whacking him like that and he's still going out of his way to be defiant then I'd say it's time to find another approach.'

Lucie took a step back from Florrie. 'I've never hit him like that before. I just don't know what to do. He's hitting, punching, kicking and screaming every time he doesn't get his own way. He's driving me insane.'

Florrie chuckled. 'In my day we used the strap, our hands, shoes – even washed their mouths out with soap. You don't have to explain to me the overwhelming desire to give someone a good whack, I completely understand it. I'm just suggesting that he's five, he's missing his dad and if one type of discipline isn't working then perhaps it's time to look at some other methods of getting through to him.'

Tears welled in Lucie's eyes. 'If only I knew what they might be.'

'Leave it with me, love. There's someone I think you should meet, someone who will be able to help you with Noah. I'll give her a call tonight and then let you know. She specialises in difficult situations like yours. Now come on, let's see if that little monkey is up for a game of I Spy in the car. I think I've even got some chocolates in my room back at Treetops that I can bribe him with.'

Lucie followed Florrie toward Noah's room, her stomach churning. Florrie was right, nothing she was doing was helping Noah. Even though she liked to believe Matt's spirit was around them, at times like this she hoped he wasn't witnessing how badly she was failing their son.

'You staying for the staff meeting, Luce?' Anna asked as she finished tidying her desk.

Lucie looked up from the pile of spelling books she was correcting. 'I didn't realise it was optional?'

Anna laughed. 'It's not. I've just noticed that a few of the other teacher aides seem to think it's okay to miss them.'

'I'm hoping my attendance is being noted by the powers who renew my contract. I can't afford to not be renewed, so yes, I will definitely be there.'

'What's Noah going to do?'

'His grandma, Matt's mum, is picking him up. He's got swimming lessons and she's offered to take him and his cousins.'

'That's handy.'

Lucie nodded, ticked the last line of spelling words and restacked the books in their place.

'So, how are things going with Noah? You said he was being difficult a couple of weeks ago.'

'That hasn't changed. I never knew I had so many buttons he could push. I think more must be growing each day and he's dancing with joy, rubbing his hands together thinking, oh wow, another one, let's see what it does.'

Anna laughed. 'Yes, it can be fun, can't it? Joel, my third, has always tried his hardest to make life difficult. My other three combined aren't as much work as he is.'

'Listen to me! I've only got one and I can't seem to handle him, and you've got four.'

'Yes, but only one is a real handful.' Anna shuddered. 'Imagine if it was the other way around – three handfuls and one nice, complacent child. I'd probably kill myself, or them.'

Lucie laughed.

'If you need a hand just let me know. You can always send him over to my place, give him a chance to be around some older boys, some brothers. He won't get his own way in that bunch but they'll make sure he has a good time.'

Lucie was touched. She knew Anna's offer was genuine. She was about to respond when she noticed Jan standing at the door. Jan should have left by now for the pool. The kids would be late for their lessons. She hurried over. 'Is everything okay?'

'Yes, I'm about to go, Ruby was running a bit late. The kids are over there.' Jan pointed to the playground. 'I told them I needed two minutes for a quick chat.'

'Anything wrong?'

Jan took a deep breath and looked across to the storeroom where Anna was selecting supplies for the next day. She lowered her voice. 'You've put me in a horrible situation, you know that, don't you?'

Lucie stared at Jan. What was she talking about? Had she found out about the community service order, that Lucie had been lying to her about her whereabouts? 'Let me explain.'

Jan stared at Lucie. 'Explain what? Your face is like a beetroot, that's all I need to know. You know I really hoped you would be able to look me in the eye and tell me Kate was imagining that something was going on between you and Brad. But you can't, can you? You're guilty as hell.'

'Hold on – what? There's nothing going on between me and Brad.'

'Not any longer perhaps, but something did, didn't it? Don't lie to me, Lucie. Kate asked Brad outright and he admitted it. In fact, he told her everything.'

Lucie opened her mouth and closed it again. She didn't know what to say. What had Brad told them? Obviously not that he'd tried to force himself on her.

'I'm very disappointed, Lucie. Surprised and disappointed. I know you're lonely; we all miss Matt, but to upset the family so much – it's unforgivable.'

A lump rose in Lucie's throat. 'Jan, I didn't encourage Brad. In fact it was quite the opposite. I need to explain what happened.'

Jan put her hands up. 'No, I need to take the kids to their lesson. You've said and done enough. There's no excuse for any of this. I'll drop Noah home after swimming; you don't need to collect him. You will be home by six, won't you?'

'Yes.'

'Good. For the moment I'd like to keep our contact to a minimum. We'll see Noah as much as usual, but I'd like to just pick him up and drop him off, no hanging around. Same on Saturday when you leave him with us. Make it quick. I haven't told Walt, and don't intend to.' Her eyes misted over. 'He'd be so disappointed he'd ban you from our lives altogether. I'm not doing that but right now I need some distance.' Jan stared at Lucie one last time before turning and walking toward the playground.

Tears filled Lucie's eyes as she watched Noah and Ruby run toward Jan, eager to get to their swimming lessons. Moving to Brisbane to be closer to the family wasn't turning out at all as she'd expected.

'Everything okay?' Anna reappeared from the storeroom.

Oh God, she'd forgotten Anna was even in the room. Had she heard that exchange? That's all she needed.

Anna must have read her mind. 'I didn't hear much and wouldn't repeat anything even if I had.'

Lucie forced a smile. 'Thanks. For the record, I didn't encourage him and didn't consent to anything that went on.'

'Didn't consent? Luce, what happened?' Anna's genuine concern opened the floodgates.

Tears poured down Lucie's face. 'Not what you're thinking.' She wiped away the tears. 'He tried, but I stopped him before he did anything but scare me.'

'So why has he led his wife to believe something's going on between you?'

'I have no idea. I thought once he left that would be the end of it. I'd put it behind me, avoid him at all costs and move on with things.'

'Seems he has a different plan. You'll have to tell them what really happened. You can't let your in-laws think you've done something wrong. You're the victim here.'

Lucie nodded.

Anna pulled her into a hug. 'You poor thing. He's going to want to hope he doesn't cross my path any day soon, I can tell you that much.'

'You wouldn't say anything, would you?'

Anna shook her head. 'Not if you don't want me to, but I'll want to kill him, I can promise you that much.'

Lucie smiled. 'Thank you. It means a lot to me.'

Anna laughed. 'What, that I'm willing to kill for you?'

Lucie nodded.

'If you need to talk about anything, let me know, won't you? Why don't you bring Noah over on Saturday? He can play with the boys and you and I can have a relaxed lunch.'

Lucie was touched. 'I'd love to, I really mean it, but I have a commitment on Saturdays at the moment that I can't change. Noah spends the day with his grandparents.'

'Okay, but if anything changes let me know. I mean it, I'm a good listener.' Anna picked up her bag. 'Come on, let's get to the staff meeting. Hopefully trying to keep our eyelids open for the next hour will distract us from thinking about that bastard.'

Chapter Nineteen

COMMUNITY SERVICE

The warden glared at Emma as she strode through the foyer of the retirement village and took her seat next to Florrie. This was her second-last day of community service, thank God. She grinned at Florrie, pleased to see the old lady back with them. While she looked forward to her work order being completed, she would miss Florrie and Lucie.

The warden continued pacing up and down with his clipboard, checking it constantly and making notes. What he was doing, Emma couldn't imagine. He had five chairs out, so that suggested they were waiting for Lucie and two others. Surely he just had to tick the box to say they had arrived.

'Crosswords,' Florrie whispered.

'What?'

'The warden, he's doing crosswords.'

'You're kidding?'

'Nope. I give him one at the start of each day. His challenge is to get it back to me by the end of his shift. I'm making them harder and harder but he usually gets them done. Drives him nuts when he misses a clue.' She chuckled. 'If he's in a horrible mood after lunch you'll know I've stumped him.'

Emma shook her head; Florrie was hilarious. 'How are you feeling?'

'I'm fine, thanks, love. Much better than last week. I even had a special outing during the week – went and visited Lucie and little Noah. Was a lovely treat. We had some beautiful wine and a lovely chat. Although . . .' Her face clouded over.

'Although what? Was there a problem?'

Florrie shook her head. 'No, but I think Lucie might be having a hard time. She needs some help. It's not easy being a single mother, particularly a widow. At least if you're divorced you get a break from your children while they are with the other parent. I think perhaps Lucie needs a break, a change of scenery. I've got a friend I'm hoping she'll agree to talk to. I'll give her the details later on.'

Just as Florrie finished talking Lucie hurried through the door, a man and a woman trailing close behind. Rodney looked up briefly from his clipboard before moving past her and intercepting the two new people. Lucie sat down on the other side of Florrie.

'Morning,' Emma said. 'You okay? You look a bit pale.'

Lucie mustered a smile. 'I'm fine; just had a slightly awkward morning.' Dropping Noah off with Jan had been very uncomfortable. Lucie knew she needed to sit down with Jan and try to explain what had happened, but it was incredibly difficult and that morning had certainly not been the right time to do it.

'Noah okay, love?' Florrie asked.

Lucie nodded. 'He's fine – he loves you by the way.'

'Silence, prisoners.' Rodney cut the conversation off, pointing the two new inmates to the vacant chairs. 'Take a seat, we need to get on with the day.' He went through his normal drill, ensuring everyone knew he was in charge and that he considered them to be the scum of the earth. Once he'd finished belittling them, they were sent into the kitchen to get started on lunch for the residents.

'See you at morning tea,' Emma whispered to Lucie as they donned their aprons, ready to start.

Two hours later Emma carried her coffee cup over to their usual table, nicely shaded at this time of day by the large mango tree. Lucie and Florrie were already deep in conversation.

The conversation stopped as Emma reached the table. 'Oh, sorry, have I interrupted?' She watched as Florrie looked over at Lucie.

Lucie shook her head. 'No, Florrie's just suggesting I have a chat to a friend of hers. I'm just not sure if it will be any help.'

Emma sat down and stirred some sugar into her coffee. 'Who's the friend, Florrie?'

'Mary's a psychologist,' Florrie said. 'I was very reluctantly dragged along to see her when Laila died. Actually, it was about six months after, when I was in the depths of a very dark depression.' Florrie's eyes were far away as she spoke about the time following the accident. 'A friend of mine knew I needed to talk to someone who could help me try to make sense of everything – not that it was really possible, but it did help me. I started getting up each day again, whereas before I'd lie in bed, the television blaring away, and I couldn't have told you what I'd watched. I'd stopped seeing my friends, stopped going out, stopped caring about anything. Mary got me going again.' She turned to Lucie. 'I know you're nothing like that, love, but I think you could use a hand at the moment. It's hard work being a single mum, especially when you're grieving still.'

'Matt's been gone for three years.'

Florrie put her hand on Lucie's. 'I know, and in that three years, how many days have you had to yourself? To cherish your memories, to love Matt, to say goodbye?'

Lucie's eyes filled with tears.

'You need that time, the opportunity to heal. With a five-year-old driving you crazy that's not going to happen. Now, I won't take no for an answer. I've booked you a session with Mary next Thursday. It's all paid for and so are the next twelve weeks, if you decide you want to continue seeing her. No arguments. I may not look it in my prisoner garb, but I'm a rich old bird. Gives me something to spend it on, other than crossword books to stump our warden friend with.'

Emma could see Lucie struggling with her emotions. She'd been thinking about Lucie all morning as she chopped vegetables and prepared soup. 'When do the holidays start?' she asked.

'End of next week.'

'Good. Then you and Noah are to pack your bags and come up to the Bay for a few days, a week even if you'd like, sometime the following week. The house is all set up and you'll probably have it to yourself most of the time; I'm often only there at night. You need a break, Noah probably does, too. What do you think?'

Lucie stared at her, open-mouthed. 'I didn't think you were serious last time.'

'Well, I was. Like Florrie, I'm not taking no for an answer. Let me know what day and what time you expect to arrive and I'll give you directions to The Café or the house, depending on where I'll be.'

The tears that had been threatening rolled down Lucie's face. 'You two are amazing. Here I am doing something as a punishment and I've got you two looking at ways to improve my life. If I'd known I'd have the chance to meet you I'd have sped around the streets a long time ago.'

Emma and Florrie's laughter was cut off by the presence of the warden. 'Back to work, prisoners. There's far too much chatter and laughter going on here. We might need to separate you if this continues.'

Emma picked up her coffee mug; it might all be a show but it was still annoying. She turned just in time to see Rodney smile and wink at Florrie. The grin that Florrie returned softened Emma's attitude. He might be annoying but he was giving Florrie a reason to get up in the morning and for that she was grateful.

Chapter Twenty

EMMA

Emma turned to Daniel who was straightening his tie. 'Can you zip me up?'

He walked over and carefully pulled up the zip on her Alex Perry midnight-blue cocktail dress. 'You look stunning.' He ran his hands down her sides, letting them linger on her hips. 'Just gorgeous.' He leant in and nuzzled her neck. He groaned. 'Oh God. You smell delicious, too. How am I supposed to contain myself until after dinner?'

Emma turned to face him. 'You don't have to. Feel free to undress me right now.'

Daniel kissed her deeply and then pulled away. 'Don't tempt me. I'd much rather be doing exactly that than sucking up to this lot on a Saturday night.'

Emma wrapped her arms around him and pulled him to her. The last thing she wanted to do tonight was make small talk with Elise and Jerry. She was tired from her stint at community service. 'Why don't we cancel, say I'm sick or something?'

Daniel shook his head. 'We can't. Jerry's bringing a potential client and his wife. They're worth a fortune and we need to impress them. And that means I need you to impress Mrs Fortune with your witty banter.'

Emma smiled. 'Elise could do that.'

Daniel rolled his eyes. 'If we want knock-knock jokes that she can't remember the punch line to, we'll call on her.' He looked at his watch. 'Come on, shoes on, we need to go. That way we'll have time for a drink and a chat before they arrive.'

Thirty minutes later Daniel and Emma were shown their seats by the maître d' at Aria. Their table overlooked the twinkling lights of the Brisbane River. Daniel ordered champagne before taking Emma's hand. 'Sorry, I know we've hardly seen each other, but work goes on, as do these schmoozy dinners. We've got half an hour before they're due to arrive so fill me in on everything. How's your mum?'

Emma told Daniel everything she knew so far about Maggie. The main concern was the lobectomy results they were still waiting for.

Daniel fiddled with his glass. 'Do you think she'll be having chemo?'

Emma nodded. 'Probably. If the results from the lobectomy show anything unexpected I guess that might change. The doctor did suggest she could have it orally so no need to go to the hospital every day.'

'That's good.' Daniel's eyes had a faraway look as he spoke. 'Mum hated that. Especially having to drag herself in for more when she already felt awful.'

Emma took his hand and squeezed it.

He smiled and then stood as Jerry and Elise approached the table.

It was all smiles and air kisses with Elise. She was dressed in a short black skirt that barely covered her bottom and a plunging, gold, sleeveless slinky top. If she'd been fifteen, the outfit would have looked great. At forty-five, it didn't.

'How are you, Emma?' Jerry had a silly grin on his face, the look he usually had when he'd drunk too much.

Emma narrowed her eyes. She couldn't imagine he would turn up drunk, so there was something else going on. 'Good, thanks, and you? Been back to Perth lately?' Jerry had grown up in the Margaret River wine region and always spoke wistfully about the beauty of the area and how much he missed it.

He shook his head. 'No. I have good intentions to get back but never seem to find the time.' He laughed. 'I need to organise more clients in Perth and add some weekends to my trips.'

Elise pouted. 'But then I'd miss you, Snooks.'

Daniel caught Emma's eye and grinned. It was hard to picture balding, slightly podgy Jerry as *Snooks*.

Jerry turned back to Emma, the glint still in his eye. 'Been shopping lately? Elise mentioned she sees you at the shops occasionally.'

Emma forced a smile. She hoped the heat rising up the back of her neck was not displayed on her cheeks. 'No, I haven't had a chance.'

Daniel unintentionally rescued her, briefly explaining Emma's current family situation.

Jerry locked eyes with her. He looked like he was debating whether to say more.

She silently begged him to stop.

He smiled at her, just as the waiter arrived. 'I'm sorry to hear about your mum.' He turned to Elise. 'Darling, next time you're shopping, *buy* something nice for Emma's mum from us, something to cheer her up.' He turned to Daniel. 'So, how was your game today? Do any damage to that handicap?'

Emma let out a breath. She'd love to wipe the smirk off Elise's face but her main concern was ensuring she didn't tell Daniel.

She turned to Elise, willing herself to remain calm and friendly. 'What a stunning outfit. You look so young. Where did you find that amazing top? It's such a beautiful colour.'

Emma was conscious of Elise's mouth moving, speaking with animation about her recent clothing purchase, while on her other side Jerry's booming laugh muffled out Daniel's words. The one night they had to spend together this weekend and this was what they ended up with. Hopefully the other couple who were joining them tonight would be more bearable. Emma quickly realised, as the maître d' escorted a smiling couple to their table, that it was unlikely.

The woman looked like a clone of Elise: stick thin, dressed expensively but again in fashion meant for teenagers, not women in their forties. What did they do? Walk into Alannah Hill and ask for a midlife crisis in size six? Emma sighed and sipped her champagne as the two women excitedly discussed their handbags. Her mind wandered to Florrie. She wondered what the old lady was doing. She was probably exhausted from her community service day and tucked up in bed. She was such a feisty old bird. Emma shuddered, thinking of Florrie's family, lost so tragically. She couldn't even begin to imagine how awful that would be. Lucie, too, her husband gone, without warning. It made Emma appreciate how lucky she was. People always said you needed to live each day as it came, that you often didn't have warning of changes or tragedies ahead. Maggie's illness had given Emma a second chance to reconnect with her family and had also brought her closer to Daniel. She knew she was incredibly lucky.

Emma was reluctant to get into her car. She was enjoying the sensation of Daniel's body engulfing hers. She kissed him again, slowly pulling away. They'd been standing on the driveway kissing like teenagers for over ten minutes. At this rate they should probably go back inside and revisit the wonderful place they'd spent most of the morning. They'd arrived home late last night after the other two couples had opted to go on to a jazz bar for more drinks after dinner. Daniel had smiled apologetically at Emma when he agreed to go. She knew it was all business, that building the relationship with a potential investor was exactly how he gained their trust. Still, it was annoying to feel like the third wheel between two superficial women. She wished he'd find some investors who valued intelligent women and thus paired themselves up with one. The only thing she could be thankful for was that neither Elise nor Jerry had referred to her shopping again.

'I was thinking,' Daniel said. 'Wednesday and Thursday will be pretty quiet for me this week but then I have to get organised for going away on the weekend. There's that corporate weekend in the Blue Mountains I promised I'd attend.'

Emma had completely forgotten about it. She was supposed to be going, too.

Daniel shook his head. 'Don't worry, I cancelled your spot a couple of weeks ago when I realised you wouldn't be able to make the Saturday. Bad timing for both of us.'

Relief flooded through Emma. According to her made-up schedule, the event she'd been so busily planning for her non-existent Saturday charity was scheduled for this coming Saturday. She'd been trying to think up an excuse as to why Daniel couldn't go. Now she wouldn't need to.

'Anyway,' Daniel continued, 'I could come up Tuesday night to the Bay and stay until Thursday, if you'd like?'

'You'd really do that?' Emma was unable to hide the surprise in her voice.

Daniel pulled her close. 'Of course. I want to see you and I want to meet my new niece. I'll bring a present for your mum,

249

too. But' – his face hardened momentarily – 'I'm not interested in visiting my dad, or anyone else, so don't mention my visit if you see him, okay?'

'I wouldn't.'

Daniel kissed her again. 'Okay, you'd better get going, I don't want you driving too late. I'll see you Tuesday night.'

Emma opened the car door and slipped into the driver's seat. She smiled at Daniel. 'I love you.'

He leant in through the open window and kissed her. 'Ditto.'

Emma wiped down the outside tables before stacking and carrying the dirty dishes through to the kitchen. Kristen was taking a late lunchbreak so she was managing alone. They'd had a steady day so far: the usual coffee and juice rush early morning, the cake-and-coffee brigade for morning tea and then a constant stream of customers throughout the lunch period.

The bell on the door jangled as Emma walked back from the kitchen to the counter. She smiled. 'I was just thinking about you.'

Drew ran his hand through his damp hair. He was wearing board shorts and a huge grin.

Emma wondered if he ever wore a shirt. His tanned chest suggested it was a rarity.

'That's good to hear. And exactly what were you thinking?' He winked suggestively.

Emma laughed. 'Nothing like that, let me set that straight. I was just thinking about how much better my parents' lives are, not being committed to working every afternoon and evening like they used to. We've got a lot to thank you for.'

Drew shook his head. 'No, of all the townspeople I think your parents would have done this anyway. Your dad was one of the few people who jumped at the idea, saying he'd been thinking of similar changes for years.'

'Yes, but the difference is he was just thinking it, he wouldn't have actually done anything about it.'

Drew shrugged. 'We'll never know, but I'm glad it's worked out for them. How's Maggie?'

Emma made Drew a coffee as she updated him on her mother's progress. 'She's going back into the hospital tomorrow so we'll have the results of the lobectomy then and will know if she's having further treatment.'

'Good. She's tough. If anyone's going to pull through, she will. How about you? What's going on in your busy city life? Any gossip?'

Emma laughed. 'You sound like a nosy old woman. What, are you bored?'

Drew shook his head. 'No, just interested. What did you do for your weekend?'

'Nothing out of the ordinary. Some volunteer work on Saturday and then dinner with my husband and some of his work colleagues on Saturday night.'

'Volunteer work? That's very noble of you.'

Emma swallowed; she couldn't wait until her work order was complete and she could stop lying about it. 'Noble? Says the king of noble. I think with the amount of volunteer work you've done in this town you'd expect nothing less from us mere mortals.'

Drew laughed. 'Fair call. What about your girlfriends? You must have a ton of them. All beautiful, intelligent and ready to settle down in a little bay with a gorgeous fellow.'

'I've got one that fits most of those criteria.' She thought of Cass. 'But I can't see you two hitting it off. She's an academic and pretty set in her ways. She's also in America at the moment.'

'How many cats does she have?'

'Three, I think.'

Drew nodded. 'Okay, she's out then. Any others? Or am I going to have to get back to my mission of chasing you after all?'

Emma blushed. 'You'll need to be careful if you do. Daniel will be here tomorrow and he'll come after you with a shotgun.'

Drew's eyes widened. 'Your husband's coming here? To the Bay?'

'Yes. Why are you so surprised?'

'Sorry.' Drew looked sheepish. 'Maggie likes to chat, that's all. She mentioned Daniel had some issues with his father.'

'She's got a very big mouth, that mother of mine. Is there anything about me she hasn't told you?'

Drew grinned. 'Let me see: shoe size, tick; dress size, tick; favourite drink – champagne, tick; favourite food . . . um, now I'm stumped. I'll have to go and see Maggie, get the list finalised.'

Emma swatted him on the arm. 'Idiot. So when's this wine bar opening?'

He rubbed his hands together. 'Not long now. After our discussion last week I've oiled the wheels and it's all about to roll. I will, of course, need to know your favourite food so I can ensure it will be served on our date.'

'In the unlikely event you get a wine bar up and running, and convince me to have the drink I've promised with you, I can confirm it will in no way be a date. In fact, I might even bring Daniel with me – there was nothing in the terms and conditions of our bet that said I had to come alone.'

Drew laughed. 'No, there wasn't. Might be a good idea anyway. Make sure he doesn't get the wrong idea about me.'

Emma rolled her eyes. 'Because you don't flirt or act inappropriately around me.'

'I act like this around everyone, Em.' He stared at her for a minute. 'Seriously, it's how I am. The fact that you aren't available makes it more fun. If you were available I'd be a lot less flirty. Wouldn't want you to get the wrong idea. The truth is, at this stage, a woman would have to be simply amazing, and of course single, for me to be interested.'

Emma smiled. 'That's good to hear, but don't you have some place you need to be? I need to get cleaned up before Kristen gets back.' She glanced at the clock. 'The moment my shift finishes I'm off to see Simone and the gorgeous Mia.'

Drew stood up and retreated from the table. 'Okay, hint taken. Although I'm not sure driving customers out of the store was part of my pep talk to your parents. You might want to think about your business acumen before you come in tomorrow – you're supposed to be helping their business, not killing it.'

Emma threw a scrunched-up napkin at him. 'Get out.'

Drew grinned and pushed open the door. 'See you, Em. Can't wait for our date. Make sure you've got a slinky dress all ready for me to drool over.'

Emma smiled and started tidying up the counter. Her parents were right. He was a good guy, someone she could be friends with. Having him confirm he was just messing with her, flirting because he could, was a relief.

Emma stepped over a pile of baby paraphernalia as she manoeuvred her way from the front door of Simone's house to the kitchen. 'What happened to the cleaner?' she called.

'She only comes once a week.' Simone's voice came from Mia's room. 'I'll be out in a minute, make yourself a coffee if you can find a cup. I'll have a tea, thanks.'

Emma stopped in the doorway of the kitchen and sucked in a breath. Dirty plates were stacked high, boxes of cereal standing open on the bench. The bin was overflowing with take-out contain-ers. 'When did she last come?'

'Who?'

'The cleaner.'

'She comes on a Friday.'

It was only Monday and the house looked like a bomb had hit it. How was it possible to make such a mess in three days? Emma walked over and opened the dishwasher. She could at least pile the dirty dishes in it for Simone. It was full of clean ones. Emma unpacked it. She then collected up all of the dirty dishes from the benchtops. She could see coffee cups and plates strewn all through the open-plan lounge area. It appeared things had changed in the few days since she'd last seen Simone. She finished collecting the dirty dishes and switched the dishwasher on again. She was just finishing spraying the benchtops when Simone walked in, Mia gurgling in her arms.

Emma dropped the cleaning cloth and smiled, doing her best to hide the shock at seeing her sister so transformed from the week before. She walked over and gave Mia her finger to grasp. 'Hello, beautiful girl, how are you today?'

Simone handed her to Emma. 'Feel free to take her, if you like. I could use a break.'

The dark rings under Simone's eyes, her messed-up hair and the vomit all down the back of her shirt suggested she could. 'Sim, you need a new shirt. I think Mia's brought up some milk on that one.'

Simone looked down at her top. 'I just put it on, it looks fine.'

Emma laughed, her hand going to her mouth when Simone didn't smile. 'Sorry, it's just down the back, that's all. There's a fair bit, so I wouldn't sit down if I was you.'

Emma could hear Simone muttering 'shit' as she walked out of the room. She reappeared in a clean blue T-shirt moments later. 'Thanks for that. I usually know when she's chucked.'

'How are you going? You look a bit more tired than last week.'

'A bit? Jesus, I look like shit and we both know it. I reckon I've had one full hour of sleep in the past four nights. Someone's been screaming every bloody hour on the dot. Johnno's a wreck and he had to go back to work today.'

'Why do you think she's screaming?'

'Because she's a fucking baby, that's why.' A large tear escaped the corner of one eye and rolled down Simone's cheek.

If Emma hadn't been holding Mia she would have pulled her sister close and hugged her. 'Oh Sim. Why don't you go and have a lie down?'

'How can I?' Simone wiped the tears from her face.

'You've just fed her, haven't you?'

Simone nodded.

'Fine, go. I'll play with her and then I'll put her back to bed when she's tired.'

'She'll want more food then.'

'Really? That soon?'

'Every bloody hour.'

'Okay, well go and have an hour's sleep. If she needs a feed, I'll wake you.'

Simone rolled her eyes. 'Her screaming will wake me.'

'Then stop wasting time and go and lie down. Come on, Mia. Let's go for a walk and let Mummy have a rest.'

'The pram's out the front.' Simone walked toward her room. 'Nappies are in the back if you need one.'

Emma smiled at Mia. A whole hour to themselves; now this was the good part of being an aunt.

Emma continued to chop the vegetables she'd picked up on her walk with Mia. She'd used the last hour while Mia was asleep to tidy the house for Simone and then decided to start on dinner. Looking at the overflowing bin of microwave dinners and pizzas, it appeared everything had gone downhill in the past few days. She was humming to herself when Simone appeared, hair wilder than before she went to bed, a look of panic on her face.

'Thank God you're here.'

Emma smiled. 'Where did you think I'd be?'

'Where's Mia?'

'In her bed, having a sleep.'

'But . . . but, I went to bed hours ago. How did you get her to sleep?'

Emma grinned. 'Took her for a walk, gave her a cuddle, changed her nappy, wrapped her up and put her in the bassinet. Figured that was what I was supposed to do. She agreed and went straight to sleep.'

Simone shook her head. 'She fed every hour last night. I couldn't get her back to sleep for more than half an hour at a time. Now she's gone for three hours without a feed.'

'She was probably tired. Maybe she was having a growth spurt last night?' Emma suggested. 'That happens, doesn't it?'

'I guess so.' Simone groaned. 'My boobs are like rocks. That's what woke me, they're killing me they're so full.'

Emma pointed at her shirt. 'They're leaking, too.'

Simone looked down at her chest as milk seeped through her shirt. 'Jesus, I'm a freak. I'd better wake her up and give her a feed, do you think?'

'I have no idea, but don't they say never to wake a sleeping baby? Can't you express a bit, make it a bit more comfortable until she wakes up?'

Simone nodded. 'I can try. I haven't expressed yet.' She moved around the kitchen and collected the breast pump and equipment she needed. 'Has Dad rung?'

'No, which is beginning to worry me. Wasn't their appointment at one?'

'It was. Do you think we should go round?'

Emma shook her head. 'No, I'll give him a ring in a minute, find out what's going on.'

Emma put the food she'd been preparing in the fridge and picked up her phone. Brian answered on the first ring.

'Sorry, love, I've been meaning to call. It's been a long day.' Sadness tinged his words. Emma tapped her fingers nervously on the benchtop. Had they been given bad news?

'How's Mum?'

'She's doing well. The doctors are very confident they removed all of the cancer and have given her the first round of chemotherapy to take at home.'

'She can have the oral one?'

'Yes, thank goodness. She starts tomorrow. She's so tired though, I wish we could leave it for one more day.'

'Can you?'

'The doctors said no, we need to get on with it immediately for it to have the best results. Hopefully the side effects won't be too bad.'

'How are you going, Dad?'

Brian sighed. 'I'm fine, love, just worried about your mum.'

Emma spoke to her father for a few more minutes before she switched her phone off and slipped it back into her bag.

'What did he say?' Simone asked.

'Not a lot. They're both really tired. Good news though. They are pretty certain they got all of the cancer and Mum can have the oral chemo at home. She starts tomorrow.'

'That soon? They don't muck around, do they?'

Emma shook her head. 'No, I think that's what makes it all so scary. That one day, or one hour, will make such a difference.'

'It probably does. Thank God they got to it quickly. Imagine, Em, imagine if . . .' Simone's voice trailed off, tears welling in her eyes.

Emma walked over and pulled her close, tears wetting her own cheeks. 'I know, I can't even imagine it.'

'It'll happen one day though,' Simone said. 'We'll be dealing with this one day for both of them.'

Emma released Simone and looked at her. 'Yeah, we will. Hopefully not for a lot of years.'

Simone nodded. 'Hopefully. And Em, I'm glad you're here.'

Emma pulled her back into another hug. 'Me too.'

Daniel bounced up and down on the end of the bed. He pulled Emma toward him. 'It appears the most important part of the townhouse is comfortable, although we might need to give it a good try out, just to make sure.'

Emma laughed. Daniel had arrived just as she walked in the door from her shift at The Café. He'd originally said he would be coming that night so she was surprised and delighted when his car pulled into the driveway just before four. She'd given him the grand tour of the townhouse, which took about a minute, and they'd ended up in the bedroom.

An hour later they pulled their clothes back on and made their way downstairs. 'It's a beautiful afternoon,' Emma said. 'Why don't we go for a walk over on the beach and pick up some Thai on the way back? There's a good Thai restaurant next to the pharmacy.'

Daniel remained quiet.

'Is something wrong?'

'No, I'm just trying to remember what was next to the pharmacy before. Wasn't it a bottle shop?'

'Yes, that's gone. There's a big one attached to the pub and that's it. Their prices are so good no one can compete. We should stop there on the way back as well, get a bottle of wine, or some beers, if you'd prefer.'

Daniel opened the passenger door of the BMW for Emma and she slid in. He got in beside her and started up the car. 'I'm pretty sure I can remember the way.' Daniel manoeuvred the car into the street and followed the road until they reached the town centre. He slowed as he drove down the main street. 'You weren't kidding when you said the place had been done up. It's hardly recognisable.'

'I know. Looks amazing, doesn't it?'

Daniel nodded, his foot pushing down harder on the accelerator as they neared his father's shop.

They arrived at the beach. Spray filled the air as the surf crashed against the rocks. Daniel took Emma's hand as they walked from the car toward the dunes. He inhaled. 'I can't remember the last time I smelled the beach. It was the one part of growing up here I actually loved. Funny though, it still wasn't enough to draw me back.'

Emma squeezed his hand. 'Tell me about your week. What's been going on?'

Daniel talked as they walked, filling Emma in on the various investors he'd been meeting with and opportunities that were currently available to them. 'This weekend six potential investors will be at the Blue Mountains retreat. It's a shame you won't be able to come. Their wives could certainly use some of your magic.' He laughed. 'Unless they're only interested in handbags and shoes, I can't see Elise adding a whole lot of value to the weekend.'

'Elise is going?' Emma's stomach clenched. She shook herself. Elise would have told Daniel already if she'd planned to. She certainly wouldn't tell him in a situation where they were surrounded by potential clients. She was dumb, but not that dumb.

'Yes, of course. Jerry wouldn't miss this. Actually, Elise was asking about the charity event you've got happening on Saturday. She's offering some help if you need it.'

'She'll be at the Blue Mountains so that wouldn't work.' Elise offering help – that was suspicious, if nothing else. 'Tell her I said thanks for the offer, it's very generous of her.'

They continued walking until they reached the lighthouse and then turned back the way they'd come. 'Race you.' Daniel dropped Emma's hand and ran toward the surf. 'Let's dip our toes in.'

She chased him down to the water, smiling as he splashed around like a little boy. It was so nice to see him in a pair of shorts, looking relaxed and happy. She never imagined she'd see him in Golden Bay enjoying the experience.

They walked hand in hand back along the beach. As they neared the dunes a surfer appeared, board under his arm. Even from a distance Emma knew it was Drew.

'Emma!' A delighted smile highlighted his dimples as Drew walked toward them. 'Great to see you.' He turned to Daniel and held out his hand. 'You must be Emma's husband. I'm Drew, Drew Myers.'

Daniel smiled and shook his hand. He looked from Drew to Emma. 'How do you guys know each other?'

'Drew's the guy I've been telling you about,' Emma said. 'He's transformed the town since he got here.'

'Ah, the facelift guy. Nice job – the place looks great. I haven't seen Maggie and Brian's yet, but the main strip looks like a completely new town, very modern.'

Drew smiled. 'Glad you like it. Your dad has a shop there, doesn't he? The butcher? You're that Wilson, aren't you?'

Daniel's face hardened. 'I guess I am. Any more plans for the town, or has the magic wand dried up?'

The sarcasm in Daniel's voice didn't go unnoticed. It only took the mere reference of his father to annoy him.

'I've got a few projects on the go, haven't I, Em?'

Em? Oh great, she could already imagine Daniel's reaction to that familiarity. 'Have you? I thought you said you'd finished, that you were getting a bit bored, even.'

Daniel squeezed her hand. It wasn't a friendly, loving squeeze. It was a come-on-let's-go squeeze.

'Actually, I have a bet with Emma. She doesn't believe I can pull off my latest venture.'

Daniel raised his eyebrows. 'Really? What's the venture and what's the bet?'

Drew looked at Emma. 'Sorry, I thought you would have mentioned it. You said you were hoping to bring Daniel with you if I won the bet.'

'Bring me where?'

Emma turned to Daniel. 'It's nothing,' she said. 'Drew's bet me he can open a wine bar in the town and I don't believe there's a market for it.'

'And if he does?' Daniel asked.

'Then I have myself a date, don't I?' Drew winked at her. He turned to Daniel. 'Actually, she made it very clear it wouldn't be a date and she'd be bringing you, too. I hope you'll still be around for the opening?'

'Unlikely,' Daniel replied.

Emma laughed, trying to lighten the moment. 'I think we can both concede that it isn't going to happen. You'd be throwing away a lot of money to start up something like that in this town. Now we'd better let you get to your surf.'

'Sure, nice to meet you, mate.' Drew earnt himself a grunt from Daniel. 'I'll see you soon, Emma. Tell Maggie I plan to drop in over the weekend to visit her, unless she's not up to it.'

Emma nodded.

He tucked his surfboard under his arm and whistled as he walked down the dune toward the surf. Just as she let out a breath, glad he'd finally left them, he called back over his shoulder.

'Start thinking about what drink you're going to order, Em. I reckon you'll be drinking it much sooner than you would imagine.'

Emma sighed as Daniel stormed away from her toward the car park.

After ordering their takeaway Thai, Emma led Daniel to the pub to get some wine while they waited. 'They've got a surprisingly good selection here. What do you think, a white to go with the food?'

Daniel nodded. He'd hardly said a word since they got in the car. Emma had tried to explain that she barely knew Drew but Daniel's lack of response made it very clear he didn't believe her. She'd given up in the end. Hopefully some dinner and a couple of drinks would relax him.

They pushed open the door to the busy bottle shop. Emma walked over to the fridge – she'd need a bottle for herself if Daniel didn't snap out of it soon.

'Oh, Jesus. The day just gets better,' Daniel muttered behind her.

'Danny?'

Emma turned to see Harvey approaching them. She took a deep breath; this was not going to brighten Daniel's already dark mood.

'It's been a long time, son,' Harvey said. 'How are you?'

The vein in Daniel's forehead began to throb. 'Good. You?'

'I'm doing well. Did you see the shop?' Harvey's face was hopeful.

Daniel shook his head. 'No, only just got here. We've had a walk along the beach and now we're waiting for some Thai.'

Harvey's face lit up. 'Thai? The shop's directly across the road from the Thai.' He looked at Emma. 'I'm surprised you didn't point it out to Danny.'

'Daniel, my name is Daniel, and Emma doesn't need to point out the shop. After seventeen years of living here, I can probably find it myself.'

Harvey nodded. 'Sorry. I'm just excited to see you, that's all. How long are you here for?'

'Not long,' Daniel replied. 'Just enough time to see Emma before I head to Sydney for the weekend.'

'Any time to catch up with me? Come over to the house for a beer?'

Daniel shook his head. 'Doubt it.'

Harvey's face fell. 'Oh, okay. Well if you change your mind let me know, won't you?' He looked from Daniel to Emma, his eyes full of sadness.

Daniel opened the wine fridge and selected two bottles of wine. 'Come on,' he said to Emma. 'The Thai's probably ready. See you around.' His tone was so casual you'd assume he was talking to an acquaintance, not his father.

Harvey nodded. Emma could feel his eyes following them as they walked to the counter to pay. The afternoon that had started so well wasn't turning out to be such a success. Daniel picked up the wine and walked toward the exit. When they walked out on to the street he handed Emma a brochure he'd been given with his receipt.

She looked at it. The headline screamed, 'Wine Bar – Grand Opening'. He'd bloody done it. The wine bar was opening the following weekend as a separate section to the pub with a piano bar and selection of the world's finest wines and champagnes. She scrunched the brochure up in her hand. Bloody Drew – now she really would kill him. She wanted to kill Harvey, too. It had been such an achievement to get Daniel to visit and within a few hours the trip had already been ruined. She imagined he'd leave first thing in the morning and, to be honest, she wouldn't blame him.

Emma woke to find Daniel staring at her. She pulled the doona up over her, the cool draught of the ceiling fan causing her to shiver.

He smiled at her. 'Sorry.'

'Why are you sorry?' She'd fully expected Daniel to be up early, heading back to Brisbane. He'd hardly spoken the night before. Instead he'd found a movie on television and knocked back about three times as much wine as he normally would. He was snoring on the couch by the time the movie finished, the second wine bottle half empty.

'Last night, I behaved like an arsehole. It's not your fault my dad's a disaster and this town makes me crazy.'

Emma smiled. 'Drew didn't help with his arrogant insinuations.'

'No, but I meet guys like that all the time. I know you know how to handle them. I wanted to punch him though, and I'd prefer you didn't go to his stupid wine bar. He probably only set it up to try to impress you.'

Emma laughed. 'Don't be silly. He's hardly going to go to that expense and trouble to have a drink with a woman he knows is happily married.'

Daniel rolled his eyes. 'You'd be surprised what lengths some people will go to to get laid. Anyway, enough about him.' He pulled Emma to him. 'Let me make up for last night. I drank way too much and I'm sorry.'

Emma kissed him. She knew the pressure he had put himself under by coming to the Bay. Before Maggie became sick, even the mention of the Bay was enough to have him explode with anger or shut down completely. Maggie's illness had changed something in him.

'I love you.' She looked into his eyes. 'You are an amazing man.'

Daniel smiled. 'Let me show you just how amazing.' He pushed her back on to the pillow and moved his body on top of hers.

'The town might have changed, but this still looks the same,' Daniel said as he and Emma walked up the driveway to her parents' house.

Emma squeezed his hand, her body still tingling from their morning's activities. They'd eaten a late brunch and now planned to spend part of the afternoon with her parents.

The front door opened as they reached the top of the stairs. Simone stood in the doorway, surprise registering on her face when she saw Daniel.

'I did mention Daniel was coming,' Emma reminded her.

Simone smiled. 'Sorry, I know. I just haven't seen you in ages.' She came over and hugged him. 'It's great to see you; you look fantastic.' She squeezed his bicep. 'I think you need to have a chat to Johnno – about time he started lifting something other than a stubby.'

Daniel laughed. 'Where's this gorgeous niece of mine – I can't wait to meet her.'

Emma felt light and relaxed for the first time in months. To see Daniel happy and genuinely interested in Mia was lovely. She took his hand. 'Let's find Mum and Dad first, shall we?'

'Actually, I'd leave them. Mum's on day three of the chemo and she's feeling rotten. Dad said she comes good by mid-afternoon. Come and meet Mia in the meantime and then I'll make you a cuppa.'

Simone led them through to her parents' spare room. A beautiful, white wooden bassinet was set up in the corner with a mobile featuring colourful animals hanging over it. 'Recognise this?' Simone asked Emma.

'Was that ours?'

'Yeah, Dad restored it, bought a new mattress and set it up here to surprise me. It's great and means I don't have to lug stuff over here every time we visit.'

Emma noted the small bookshelf next to the bassinet, stacked with nappies, wipes and spare clothes. It was a perfect set-up.

They peered into the bassinet and were rewarded with a gurgle. Mia was awake, staring at the mobile.

Emma heard Daniel suck in a breath. She turned to look at him. He was staring at Mia, fixated. 'She's beautiful,' he said.

'Would you like to hold her?' Simone asked.

'Oh, no that's okay.' Daniel laughed. 'I'd probably break her.'

'I'm sure you wouldn't, she's pretty tough.'

Simone moved to the bassinet and picked her up. She held her out to Daniel. 'Go on, say hi to your niece.'

Daniel looked unsure. 'I've never held a baby. What do I do?'

Simone gently placed Mia against his chest, showing him how to support her head. 'Just keep one hand on the back of her neck and the other on her bum.'

Daniel nodded and followed Simone's instructions. Mia was now snuggled against him and he stroked the back of her head with the hand supporting her neck. He smiled at Simone. 'She's amazing.'

'Would you like to sit in the rocking chair? She loves the rocking motion.'

Daniel moved cautiously across the room and eased himself and Mia into the chair. The chair rocked back and forth as he continued to stroke Mia's head.

'We'll leave you two to it,' Simone said. 'Give us a yell when you've had enough and I'll take her off you.'

Daniel smiled, his attention focused on Mia.

Emma and Simone stood in silence outside the nursery door, listening as Daniel started singing softly to Mia.

'Now that is unexpected,' Simone whispered.

Emma nodded. It sure was.

'You might find he's a bit clucky after this trip.'

'Who's clucky?'

Emma and Simone turned around. Brian was helping Maggie into the family room.

'Mum,' Emma exclaimed. 'How are you feeling?'

'Like shit.'

Emma laughed, her hand instantly flying to cover her mouth. 'Sorry.'

Maggie smiled. 'I'd rather you did laugh and make a joke out of this whole bloody awful experience. I feel worse today after taking that pill than I did after the surgery.' She ran her hand through her hair. 'Still, my hair's intact and I've kept most of the food I've eaten down today so I'm doing better than some. Now, tell me what you were talking about when we came in. I want to know, who's clucky?'

'No one,' Emma said. 'Daniel's in the nursery with Mia. He's enjoying some time with her on his own. He's never held a baby before so we are a bit surprised, that's all.'

Maggie squeezed Emma's arm. 'Now that's a turn up for the books. How on earth did you get him up here?'

Emma shrugged. 'I'm not sure what's more amazing: his performance with Mia or the fact he's actually in the Bay. He's making such an effort.'

'That's wonderful love, I'm looking forward to having a chat with him. It's been far too many years.' Maggie slowly made her way back to her chair. 'Now, who's going to make me a cup of tea?'

Daniel called Simone into the nursery ten minutes later. 'She's started to grizzle so I'm assuming she needs something I can't give her.'

'What? Like a boob?' Simone laughed and took Mia from him.

Daniel grinned. 'Or a nappy change.'

Emma watched the exchange, still amazed at her husband's willingness to cuddle Mia.

'Daniel, how wonderful to see you.' Maggie sounded genuinely delighted when he appeared in the lounge.

He crossed the room to give her a hug. 'You too, Maggie.' He shook hands with Emma's father, who then went to organise drinks for all of them. Daniel returned his focus to Maggie. 'How are you?'

'Okay, just need to hit this stupid cancer on the head and get life back to normal. Give you back your wife. She's been so good to us.'

Emma smiled. 'Anyone else would do the same.'

Daniel's look of delight when handing Mia back to Simone was replaced by a hard look, not unlike the one he'd given his father the night before. 'Not everyone, Em. You're going above and beyond what most people would do, so don't minimise it.'

Emma shifted uncomfortably in her seat. They weren't talking about her, or Maggie. He was talking about his situation; what people hadn't done for him when his mother died.

Brian returned to the lounge with the tea. 'Simone said she'll be out soon, she's feeding Mia in the spare room.' He handed Emma and Daniel their cups. 'So, how's business?' he asked.

Emma breathed a sigh of relief and sent a silent thanks to her father. This was definitely safer ground. Daniel gave them a brief rundown of what he was doing before turning the conversation back to them and the changes to the town and shop.

'Emma took me into the shop this morning. It looks great. I'm really impressed.'

Maggie smiled. 'We have Drew to thank for everything.'

'He's a young hotshot from the city who's turned the town around,' Brian added.

Daniel nodded. 'Yes, I met him yesterday.'

'Have you seen your father?' Maggie asked.

Emma held her breath. Why couldn't they stay on safe topics? Hadn't they seen Daniel with Mia? He had been so happy, so amazingly paternal only minutes ago. This line of questioning would probably have him leaving town any minute. She gave her mother a look that clearly said 'shut up'.

Maggie ignored her. 'I feel a bit sorry for Harvey. He's quite lonely in that big house by himself. I think he lives for work and his golf and that's about it.'

'We bumped into him last night,' Daniel said. 'He looked happy enough, said business was thriving. I think he's fine.' The bitterness in Daniel's voice was obvious.

'I'm sure he'd like to see you more, love,' Maggie said.

'Mum,' Emma warned.

'What? I'm just saying he would be missing you. We've missed you so much Emma, and now you're back we feel like the luckiest people alive. But then you were just off doing your own thing, you weren't staying away because of unresolved issues.'

'My issues can't be resolved or forgiven,' Daniel spoke calmly. Emma knew his demeanour was at odds with what he was feeling. 'My father made a decision when I was fourteen that changed our relationship forever. I won't forgive him, any more than I would expect forgiveness if I did the same thing to someone else.'

Maggie nodded. 'I don't think what he did was meant to hurt you. I think he had his reasons.'

Daniel stared at her. 'What would you know about it? You weren't there.'

'No, but we were friends, your mother and I. She wanted to die at home without you being haunted by that for the rest of your life.'

'That backfired, didn't it?' Daniel sipped his tea, a faraway look in his eyes.

'None of us knows what dying is like. I think your mum wanted to spare you that.'

'Maggie, that didn't mean she couldn't warn me, give me a chance to say all the things I needed to say to her. He robbed me of that. Let me go off on a bloody school camp while my mother died. When I came back most of the town acted like nothing had happened. I had my father curled up in the fetal position for twelve months and a town that said hi to me as if it were just a normal day. I'm sorry, but my dad fits right into this awful place.'

Emma closed her eyes, wishing they'd just stayed at the townhouse, enjoying their own company.

'Son, I think Maggie is trying to say that not everything is always as it appears. Your dad was devastated when your mum died and doubly so when you left town. He realised he'd helped drive you away but you've never given him the opportunity to properly explain the situation to you.'

'You keep saying *explain*. Like there is an actual explanation for stopping a fourteen-year-old from saying goodbye to his mother. There's no explanation for that, any more than there is for your own behaviour.'

Maggie was looking paler than she had when she'd come into the room.

Daniel stood up. 'I'm sorry. I didn't mean to upset you, Maggie. In fact, I had no intention of talking about my father or my past. I think we might go, leave you to relax. You've got enough going on right now.' He smiled. 'There's really no point revisiting old memories when they're not pleasant ones.'

Maggie nodded. 'I'm sorry, too. I agree that no one behaved well at that time but there is more to the situation than you realise. You shouldn't be so hard on Harvey.'

She looked away, her eyes watery.

Emma looked at her with mixed emotions. Her poor mother was going through chemo. She didn't need anything more right now than comfort and support. However, she had stirred the pot with Daniel and he didn't take that kind of thing lying down. She knew her mother was holding something back. Something that Daniel probably needed to know.

She followed her husband out to the car and slipped into the seat beside him. The veins on his hands were clearly visible as he gripped the steering wheel. They didn't speak as Daniel drove the car away from her parents' toward the townhouse. Emma remained deep in thought. Maggie had a secret. If it was something that had the slightest chance of putting Daniel's memories of his mother and hatred toward his father to rest, then she needed to find out what it was.

Emma woke the next morning to find Daniel's arm snug around her.

He stirred at her touch and pulled her closer into him. 'Good morning, beautiful wife.'

Emma turned and kissed him gently on the mouth. 'I'm sorry about yesterday – about what Mum said.'

Daniel pushed the hair from her eyes. 'It's not your fault, but it's one of the reasons I hate coming here. When we're in Brisbane I don't have to think about my past. It's not in my face the whole time. I don't want to dredge up all the old stuff. Being in the Bay makes it impossible not to.'

Emma nodded. 'Next time we'll just keep to ourselves.'

Daniel smiled. 'We could hang out with Mia. She doesn't say anything I don't want to hear. Other than you, she's my new favourite member of your family.'

Daniel leant forward and kissed Emma.

She felt him harden against her leg.

'I think it's time, don't you?'

Emma laughed, reaching down and stroking her husband. 'Certainly feels like it might be.'

He groaned and then removed her hand.

'No, not that. Well, yes that – sort of. I mean, I think it's time to start our own family. Make a baby. Just imagine how beautiful it will be with you as its mum.'

Emma stared open-mouthed at Daniel. Had she heard correctly?

'Yes.' He laughed and pulled her on top of him. 'I'm ready, now let's get to it. We're going to need a lot of practice if we're to make the perfect baby.'

Emma leant down and kissed him, tears falling on to his chest. Of all the things that could come of Daniel's visit to the Bay, this was not one she would ever have considered.

Chapter Twenty-One

LUCIE

Lucie almost relaxed as she sank into the comfortable tan leather armchair. It reminded her of the one her father had sat and smoked his pipe in when she was a little girl. She glanced around the office, taking in the other furnishings. The beautifully carved mahogany desk, bookshelf and coffee table were at odds with her image of what a psychologist's office should look like. The bookshelves were overflowing with a mixture of textbooks and novels, all piled together in no particular order. It appeared Mary Fowler had a love of psychological thrillers and crime stories. Perhaps they were research – an entertaining way to get to know her clients better. Lucie hid a smile; it looked like the sterile white office with a long, black couch and doctor carrying a straightjacket would only be found in her imagination.

Lucie jumped as Mary entered the room and placed a glass of water in front of her. 'So, how are you, Lucie?'

Lucie didn't know what to say. Was she supposed to launch into her feelings about Matt and losing him, or her troubles with Noah? Or was this just a normal question? She was completely out of her depth. She appreciated Florrie's gesture in organising this appointment – it was incredibly generous – but now she was here, she wasn't sure it was the right place for her.

Mary sensed her discomfort. She smiled. 'I'm literally asking how you're doing this morning, nothing more than that.'

'Oh, fine, fine thanks. You?'

Mary laughed. 'I'm good, too. Tell me, how do you know Florrie? She's such a wonderful old lady, isn't she?'

Lucie nodded. She didn't really want anyone to know how she'd met Florrie, but then again Florrie might have told Mary already.

'You're really not comfortable at all, are you?' Mary asked.

Lucie shook her head. 'No, sorry, I'm not. This was Florrie's idea, not mine. I've never visited a psychologist before. I'm not sure I want to share anything with a total stranger – no offence.'

'None taken. A lot of people feel like you do, initially. You don't know me. What right do I have to give you advice? I'm not part of your life; how would I know how you feel or what's going on? That sound about right?'

Lucie nodded.

'Okay, well let's start from the beginning. Let me tell you a bit about me, then you might see why Florrie has suggested you come for a chat.'

Five minutes later, Lucie had tears in her eyes and wanted to hug Mary. The poor woman had lost her eight-year-old, fifteen years ago. Having had to make the horrendous decision to turn off his life support after he'd fallen from a motorbike – a motorbike he should never have been on – she then had to deal with her distraught husband – now her ex-husband – who had gone against her wishes and allowed their son to ride the bike.

'While we come from completely different scenarios, I understand loss, Lucie. I'm not here to preach wise sayings to you. I'm here to listen to your story, how you've been coping, or perhaps struggling, since Matt died. I'm here to offer some constructive suggestions to help you move on when you are ready.'

Lucie nodded.

'Why don't we start with Noah? Tell me about him. How has he been coping since Matt died?'

Lucie found it easy to talk about Noah; much easier than talking about herself. She told Mary about his moods and his anger.

Mary listened and Lucie told her a little of how she found herself reacting to Noah and the times she wanted to shake him until he stopped. After confirming Lucie wasn't actually shaking her son, Mary had assured her that over the next few sessions they would devise coping strategies to help Lucie stay calm and deal with Noah.

An hour later Lucie took the lift from Mary's office down into the basement car park. She climbed into her car and sat without turning the key in the ignition. Tears streamed down her face. The conversation had moved from Noah to Matt. It made her realise she didn't talk about Matt enough. She loved talking about him. She could lose herself, imagining him sitting across from her smiling, as she sung his praises. Talking about his death, however, brought back all of the feelings. The feelings of shock and disbelief resurfaced immediately. Having to tell Noah his father was not coming back and comfort him when all she wanted to do was throw herself to the ground and scream was the hardest thing she'd ever had to do.

She started up the car and wiped her eyes with a tissue. Time to face the music. She needed to pick Noah up from his grandparents and it was time to tackle the Brad situation head on. He'd already spun a web of lies and she could only hope that when she explained what had really happened that Jan would believe her.

Lucie knocked on the front door of Jan and Walt's house. She didn't feel comfortable going around the back and letting herself in through the kitchen like she normally would. Jan had made it very clear that her involvement in the family was to be kept to a minimum. She could hear Noah's laughter as she waited for someone to answer.

When the door opened Lucie found herself staring at Kate. She shifted uncomfortably and willed her legs to stop trembling. Telling Jan was one thing, telling Kate that her husband had tried to force himself on her was another.

Kate's expression was calm but her eyes flashed with anger. 'Come in. Mum had to go out so I'm looking after Noah.'

Lucie couldn't muster the courage to spit out the words she needed to. Instead she focused on Noah. 'Thank you for looking after him. I'll get his things and get out of your hair.'

She moved toward the TV room where the laughter was coming from.

'No,' Kate said. 'I want to speak to you. Come to the kitchen so the kids can't hear.'

Lucie turned back to look at Kate. 'I really should be going. Jan's made it quite clear she'd prefer that I keep my visits to a minimum.'

Kate walked toward her. 'I'm sure she has. But for now I'm in charge. I've spent the past two hours looking after your son so you can do me the courtesy of coming into the kitchen and listening to what I have to say.'

Lucie's stomach churned as she followed Kate into the kitchen. She felt like she would vomit any minute. How on earth had she ended up in this situation?

Kate put her hands on the bench and looked directly at Lucie. 'How could you do this to me?' Her voice was calm, devoid of any anger. 'I thought we were friends.'

Lucie coughed. 'Kate, I haven't done anything to you.'

'Fine, so you did it to my husband – you know exactly what I mean.'

'No, you've got it wrong. What happened between Brad and me was not something I asked for.'

'What's that supposed to mean? You've been ringing him, having him over to your house, what, eight or nine times, and suddenly the affair isn't something you want? It's a bit late.'

'There has been no affair, Kate. I promise you that. Brad fixed the window and then dropped in two other times, once invited, once not.'

'How many times have you had sex with him? All three times?'

Lucie shook her head and took a deep breath. 'You need to believe me when I tell you this. I've never had an interest in having sex with your husband.'

'That's not what he's told me. He came home really agitated last Friday night, pretty much threw me down and had his way with me. It was incredible. He was so dominating, so in control. He usually learns something new when he's been with someone else, but this time it was so different I wanted to know why. After much interrogation and holding back of sexual favours he told me it was you – that everything he was doing he'd learnt from being with you.'

Bile rose in Lucie's throat. She hurried past Kate to the bathroom, shuddering as the contents of her stomach emptied into the toilet bowl. She flushed then rinsed her mouth and washed her face. How and why would he lie like that? And what did Kate mean that he learns something new when he's with someone else? She made her way back to the kitchen and sat down.

Kate handed her a glass of water.

'Thanks.' She sipped it slowly. 'I need you to listen, Kate. You need to know exactly what happened and then you can decide what you need to do.'

'Okay.'

Lucie riffled through her bag and pulled out her phone. She opened up the contacts and found Brad. She handed the last messages between them to Kate to look at. 'Brad sent me a text at school on Friday, as you can see, wanting to come over. I said no.'

Kate nodded. 'Okay, so that's what your message says. How come he told me he was at your house?'

'Because he was. He turned up just before Noah and I had dinner. He said he never received the message asking him not to come. I told him he couldn't come in but then Noah heard he was there and desperately wanted him to stay for dinner and then read stories to him. I stupidly said yes.' Lucie took a deep breath. 'After he finished reading to Noah, I asked him to leave. I also told him that it was the last time he was to come over on his own.' Lucie ran her hands through her hair, willing herself not to cry. 'He grabbed me, tried to kiss me and got angry when I said no.'

Kate shook her head. 'No way?'

Lucie nodded. 'Yes, he then ripped my shirt open and pinned me against the fridge. He gave me the option to comply with his plans or be forced.'

Kate's hand covered her mouth. 'He didn't – please tell me he didn't rape you?'

Lucie wiped the tears that had spilt on to her cheeks and shook her head. 'Noah was still awake and came in thinking we were playing a game. He wanted to join in. Brad threatened me and then left.'

Kate moved around the counter next to Lucie and pulled her to her. 'I am so sorry, Luce. So, so sorry.'

Lucie gulped. 'It's not your fault, but I was too scared to tell you. I didn't want to cause problems in your marriage and I wasn't sure if you'd believe me anyway. I was just going to try to forget about it.'

'I'm glad you've told me and I do believe you. He'll never come near you again, that much I can guarantee.'

'But what about you and him?'

Kate sighed. 'I'm not sure. Things are complicated. Our marriage isn't quite what it appears.'

Lucie waited for Kate to elaborate.

'We have an open marriage. But we have rules, standards which we live to.'

'An open marriage?' Lucie shook her head. 'So why did you get so angry when you thought Brad had been visiting me to have an affair?'

'We don't have sex with people we know. That's when it becomes cheating. I was so upset because you're my friend, Luce, and to think you'd do something like that was just so hurtful.'

'Really? So your issue was about Brad being with me, not the fact he might be having an affair?'

Kate nodded.

'I didn't realise you considered me a friend,' Lucie said.

'Of course I do – you're the only sister I have.'

'But you're the first to put me down, make me feel like an idiot. You've pointed out so many times how Noah and I are burdens on your parents, with the school fees and even the swimming lessons. You gave them as a present but then make me feel indebted. I honestly assumed you considered me an inconvenience.'

A look of horror crossed Kate's face. 'Of course I don't, you're just too sensitive. You can't take a joke.'

'A joke? The digs at my situation are a joke? Kate, you've shown no compassion toward me or Noah since Matt died. You act like we're some charity case that you've been stuck with because you were related to my husband.'

Tears welled in Kate's eyes. 'I didn't know I came across like that. I don't think that at all. You're the closest thing I've ever had to a sister. You and Noah are our links to Matt. Of course we want you in our lives. I never meant to make you feel like that. Shit, you must hate me.'

'No, I've just never really understood you.'

Kate nodded. 'Can we put everything behind us, start again?'

'I'm not sure that I can put what Brad did behind me. I can't be around him.'

Kate nodded. 'I understand and I need time to think. Time to talk to him.' She blushed. 'We sometimes act out scenarios, just for fun, and Brad forcing himself on me is one of our games. I know it sounds terrible, but it's not when it's by our rules. I honestly never dreamed he'd force himself on someone else.'

'Well, he did.' Lucie stood up. She needed a glass of wine. First the psychologist, and now this. She definitely should have done these two meetings the other way round. 'I'd better get Noah and head home. I am sorry about what's happened, Kate, please know that.'

'I know, and I am, too. I'll tell Mum so you don't need to worry about her any more.'

'You'll tell her what Brad did?'

'I'm not sure. I'll tell her that it was a misunderstanding and nothing happened between the two of you. I'm not sure if I'm ready to admit what he's done though. I need to come to terms with it and what it means for my marriage. Is that okay?'

Lucie nodded. 'So long as Jan knows I've done nothing wrong and Brad keeps away from me, I'll be happy.'

'And Luce,' Kate called as Lucie made her way out of the kitchen. 'No more jokes about you and your situation. I promise I'll be nicer.'

Lucie nodded and managed a small smile as she went in search of Noah.

Lucie turned the television on for Noah, headed into the kitchen and poured herself a large glass of red wine. Her muscles relaxed as the magical substance flowed through her veins and around her body. What a day. She was now glad Kate had been the one looking after Noah. A weight had been lifted from her. That and the appointment with Mary had left her feeling quite different.

She had to thank Florrie for introducing her to Mary. She could see that visits to her were going to be beneficial. Today had only been a starting point, but it already made her realise that she hadn't had the chance to grieve properly and neither had Noah. They had got on with their lives – different lives, but still busy and moving forward, rather than spending enough time on what they missed, who they missed.

Noah appeared at the kitchen door. 'I'm hungry.'

Lucie smiled. 'I bet you are. How about I make us both some scrambled eggs?'

Noah pulled a face. 'Yuk. I want spaghetti or hot dogs.'

'I haven't got either. We can make spaghetti tomorrow night if you want. Tonight your choices are eggs or toasted sandwiches. You can have some ice cream for dessert if you eat up your dinner first.'

Noah considered his options. 'Why can't you cook a proper meal? Aunty Kate was making roast chicken. We never have roast chicken. She said she loves making it, that it's a real family meal. Is that why you don't make it for us, because we're not a real family?'

Lucie came over to him and got down on her knees, her face drawing level with his. 'Of course we're a family, you and me. We're a small family but we're still a family. I don't make roast chicken because you don't normally eat it. You only eat the potatoes. It seems like a waste to go to all the effort to make a chicken that I have to eat.'

Noah stamped his foot. 'I want one and I will eat it.'

Lucie thought back to her conversation earlier in the day with Mary, to her own observation that her reactions to Noah were at times quite extreme. This was a good opportunity to practise staying calm, resolving the issue without resorting to raised tones or threats. She smiled at Noah. 'Good, then how about we get all of the ingredients tomorrow and make one on the weekend? They take a while to cook so we'll have to start preparing it early if we want to have it for dinner.'

Noah looked like he was thinking about this idea. 'Okay. But I want something better tonight. How about sausages?' He looked at her hopefully.

She ruffled his hair. 'Sorry, matey, it's eggs or toasted sandwiches. I've got ham and cheese if you'd like that?'

Noah kicked the cupboard next to him. 'No, I don't want a stupid toasted sandwich, I've already told you that.'

'Hey, don't kick the cupboard, you'll wreck it.'

Noah walked closer to the cupboard and opened the door, slamming it suddenly before opening and slamming it again. He opened his mouth and screamed, 'I want sausages or spaghetti!'

Lucie walked over and removed his hand as gently as possible from the cupboard. 'Go to your room, please, until you've calmed down. I'll call you when you can come out.'

'No, get your hands off me. You're a bitch. Aunty Kate told Grandma that and she's right.'

'Noah! You don't speak like that.' Did he even know what 'bitch' meant? Damn Kate!

'Why not? That's what Aunty Kate said. She said you were a total bitch and she couldn't believe you had done what you did. What did you do? Did you do something mean?'

Lucie shook her head. 'We had a misunderstanding, that was all. You saw Kate when we left. She was very friendly.'

'Yeah, but Grandma wasn't. Maybe she thinks you're a bitch.'

'Stop saying "bitch". I'm sure Grandma doesn't think that.'

'Make me.'

'What?'

'Bitch, bitch, bitch, bitch, bitch. Mummy's a bitch!' Noah started running around the island bench, chanting the word at the top of his lungs.

Lucie watched him. No wonder she usually lost her temper. He was completely out of control. Would it be different if Matt was here? Of course it would. She sat down and sipped her wine as he ran in circles. What was the point? She might as well try to relax. Her thoughts had been with Matt a lot following the appointment with Mary, and the wine she was drinking was one of his favourites. It was funny how she sensed Matt's presence when she was having a drink. It was something special they had shared, something she could always rely on, like she had relied on Matt prior to his death. She couldn't imagine her son would be running around the bench screeching obscenities if Matt were still alive.

It must have been at least five minutes before Noah stopped running and stopped chanting. He looked surprised to find Lucie sitting watching him. He walked around to Lucie's side of the counter. He looked like he'd finally calmed down.

Perhaps this was the approach Lucie needed to take. Let him work it out of his system rather than intervening. She sipped her wine. Stopping and watching, rather than reacting, seemed to be working; had she finally had a small breakthrough?

'Bloody hell!' Lucie dropped her wineglass, the glass shattered and red wine pooled on the bench. She rubbed her shin. Noah had just killed any idea of a breakthrough by lining up in front of her and kicking her as hard as he could. Her leg was coming out in a bruise already.

'Get me my dinner, you mummy bitch!' he screamed.

That was it. Lucie got up off the stool, grabbed him by the arm and dragged him to his room. She kicked open the door and man-handled him inside, ignoring his screams. She managed to avoid his wildly lashing limbs and pushed him on to his bed. She pinned her legs against his and held his arms so he couldn't move. 'Look at me,' she instructed him. 'Noah, look at me right now.' His eyes flickered over to hers. 'You will stay in your room. I'll bring you something to eat then you will put on your pyjamas and go to bed. There will be no more television and definitely no stories.'

'Let go!' he screamed at her. 'You're hurting me and you're not allowed to do that. Mrs Winthrop said.'

Lucie let go of Noah and stepped back from his bed. 'What? What did Mrs Winthrop say?'

'She asked me if you hurt me and told me that it wasn't okay for mummies to do that to their kids. You hurt me all the time. You scream and yell and then you squeeze and hurt me.'

Lucie's jaw hurt. She opened her mouth, realising she'd been grinding her teeth. That explained the strange looks and dismissive behaviour Jane had shown toward her. Did Noah's teacher really suspect her of abuse? She needed to sit down. The enormity of an accusation like that was incomprehensible. No, she hadn't worked out an effective way to discipline Noah as yet, but she wasn't abus-ing him.

'Don't be silly, I do not hurt you. When you've behaved badly or are out of control I need to restrain you, that's all. I'm not hitting or deliberately hurting you.'

Noah curled up in a ball on his bed, cuddling his beloved soft toy cat to his chest. 'Yes, you do. You squeeze me and you hurt me and I hate you.' He turned toward the wall, his thumb planted firmly in his mouth.

Lucie retreated from the room and went back to the kitchen. She would talk to Jane Winthrop tomorrow. Filling Noah's head with the idea that she was hurting him was not on. Ignoring the smashed glass and wine-soaked bench, she took a fresh glass from the cupboard, reached for the wine bottle and refilled it.

Lucie rubbed her jaw as she watched Noah run off toward the playground. If she didn't stop clenching her teeth she'd be trying to find money for the dentist next. She'd send the bloody bill to Jane Winthrop. She was still reeling from Noah's words the previous night. She took a deep breath: she really needed to calm down before she spoke to her. She had fifteen minutes before she was due in Year Two. She took another deep breath and turned toward the prep classroom.

Jane was engrossed in something on her computer when Lucie walked into the room. She cleared her throat.

The teacher looked up and a smile quickly replaced her look of surprise. 'Gosh, sorry, I didn't hear you come in. Everything okay?'

Lucie hesitated. She'd built Jane up into some horrible woman overnight, but that wasn't who she was at all. 'It's Noah. I need to speak to you about Noah.'

Jane stood up, coming around the desk to where Lucie stood.

The look of concern on her face made Lucie question what she had to say. This woman genuinely cared about her son.

'What is it Lucie? Is Noah all right?'

Lucie nodded. 'Yes, he's fine. It's about something he said last night. I felt I needed to discuss it with you.'

'Okay.'

'He said you've been asking if I hit him, if I hurt him.'

Jane nodded. 'Yes, I did ask him some questions along those lines.'

Lucie waited. Surely she was going to say more, give her an explanation? Jane continued to stare at Lucie.

'I don't.'

Jane nodded again. 'Okay, so is there anything else or was that all you wanted to say?'

'Is that it?'

'What do you want me to say? You know the school's policy. If you think there might be a problem, you find out what you can and then report the situation to the school's child protection officer.'

'And have you?'

Jane shook her head. 'No. Look, I realise this is hard to accept but this isn't personal. I'm looking out for all of the kids in my care. I have to, just like you have to with your class. Imagine if something was happening to one of the kids and I missed it. How would I feel? Noah's a bright, lovely little boy. You've done a wonderful job with him, I can see that.'

'So why are you questioning him?'

Jane sighed. 'I questioned Noah after he made a comment that Mummy would get very angry with him again if he did something wrong. The way he said it, his expression, he seemed scared. I've seen you get angry with him myself, so I wanted to check he was safe.'

'He's safe.'

'Lucie, I'm sure he is. If there's nothing more, I need to get ready for the day and you probably do, too.'

'Are you planning to question him again?'

Jane stared at Lucie, her eyes hard. 'I hope not. I will, of course, if I feel there's a reason to.'

Lucie swallowed. 'There won't be. Thanks for your time.' She turned and strode toward the classroom door.

She cut through the playground and dropped a kiss on Noah's head as she passed him. 'Have a great day, hon. I'll see you this afternoon.'

'You too, Mummy.' He squealed and ran off to the sandpit.

Lucie took a deep breath and walked across the courtyard in the direction of the Year Two classrooms. Noah was acting like nothing at all had happened the previous night. She guessed that was one thing she could be grateful for – that he lived in the moment and didn't appear to hold a grudge. She rounded the corner of the building and stopped. Her gut clenched. Brad stood directly in front of her.

'Bastard.' She clenched her fists; how she'd love to punch him. Instead she released her fingers and willed herself to relax.

'What?'

'You, you're a lying bastard. What did you think you'd achieve with your lies?'

Brad took a step back. 'Look, I don't want to argue with you. There's not really any point.'

Lucie stared at him. 'Really? That's it? That's all you've got to say?'

'What were you expecting?'

Another voice spoke before Lucie had the chance to answer. 'I'd suggest she's looking for an explanation.'

Lucie turned to find Anna standing behind her.

'Mr Graham, I suggest you give her one. It might stop her from calling the police and reporting you for indecent assault.'

Brad's face reddened. 'You call me a liar, Lucie, yet you wanted it, you know you did. All the teasing and flirting – what was I supposed to think?'

'You were supposed to know that when I said no, I meant it.'

Brad shrugged. 'Oh well, no harm done.'

'I don't know if Kate agrees with that.'

'My marriage to Kate is none of your business. I suggest you stay right out of it.'

'And you make sure you stay away from Lucie,' Anna said. 'I appreciate that you have children at this school but from now on I suggest you use the drop-off zone rather than come into the school grounds. I'll make sure your name is mud if you even dare say hello to Lucie, do you understand me?'

Brad shook his head and muttered to himself.

'Mr Graham, do you understand?' Anna repeated her question.

Brad nodded.

'Good,' Anna said.

Their discussion was silenced by the bell. Lucie didn't want to hear another word out of his mouth. With Anna behind her, she pushed past Brad and continued to the classroom.

Chapter Twenty-Two

COMMUNITY SERVICE

Emma walked through the front doors of the retirement village, glad that this was the last time she'd be forced to come here. She wondered whether her work order would have been enough to have stopped her from shoplifting if she hadn't been so distracted with Maggie and everything happening at the Bay. She hoped that it would have been, but didn't trust herself completely. She still hadn't removed all of the stolen items from the garage. She would do that tomorrow while Daniel was away.

Florrie and Lucie were already deep in conversation when Rodney ushered Emma to a vacant seat next to them.

She sat down. 'Everything okay?' Lucie's face was tense and Florrie certainly wasn't her usual bubbly self.

'I had a run-in with Noah's class teacher yesterday. Seems to be my week for causing problems.'

'Really?' Emma asked. 'What happened with the teacher?'

Lucie looked like she was about to say something and then changed her mind. 'Issues with Noah,' she said. 'He's out of control and I'm not sure what to do. The teacher wasn't much help.'

'Well, I know nothing about five-year-olds, but I do know how to have a lot of fun at the beach. Your holidays started this week, didn't they?' Emma said.

Lucie nodded. 'Yesterday.'

'Good. No excuses. I want you and Noah to come up to the Bay for a holiday. I'd love to have you. You could both do with a change of scenery.' Emma could see Lucie hesitating. 'I really mean it. I'm not home a lot so you'll need to be pretty self-sufficient, but it is a beautiful place. Heaps to do for a five-year-old. The town-house that I've rented is nice, with plenty of room. I'm sure you'd be completely comfortable there.'

'Go on, love,' Florrie urged her. 'I'm sure Mary would agree that it is a good idea.'

'Mary?' Emma looked at Lucie.

'I saw Florrie's psychologist during the week,' Lucie explained. 'It was only the first session but she has already made me realise a few important things.'

'That's great.' Emma stopped talking as Rodney approached the group. Three other prisoners sat down on the chairs beside them.

Rodney went through his usual routine, barking at them to ensure they knew they were inferior beings. 'And you two,' he said, pointing his clipboard at Emma and Lucie, 'I expect you to work twice as hard as usual if you want your work orders signed. Do you hear me?'

'Yes, Warden,' Emma called out in a loud, clear voice, making the new prisoners jump.

Rodney clapped his hand against the clipboard. 'Finally! It's taken, what, five weeks, but finally you've learnt how to respond. Well done, prisoner Wilson. Now you' – he turned to Lucie – 'you could learn from your inmates. Make sure you do an exceptional job today, or you'll be back again next week.'

Lucie nodded, causing Rodney to shake his head. 'Yes, Warden,' she added.

'Okay, get to work.'

Emma turned to Lucie as they entered the kitchen area. 'Have a think about what day you want to come up. I'd really love to have you both.'

'No talking!' Rodney yelled out. 'Show the new criminals the ropes and get on with it.'

Emma indicated to the new people to wash their hands and put on their aprons. She was already looking forward to the following Saturday, when she wouldn't be here.

'What about Florrie?' Emma asked. She and Lucie sat at the picnic table nursing their cups of coffee. 'Do you think I should invite her as well? There's plenty of room. Or would it be a hassle for you and Noah? You'd be the one spending the most time with her.'

'It's fine with me, and it would probably be a lovely break for Florrie, too.' Lucie had agreed that she and Noah would go up on Tuesday and stay until the weekend, possibly longer if it was working out for everyone. She suddenly clapped her hand over her mouth. 'How did she organise this?'

Emma turned around to see what Lucie was gaping at.

Florrie walked toward them holding a chocolate cake covered in sparklers. She had a huge grin on her face. 'Couldn't let you two go without making some sort of a fuss.' She put the cake down on the table. Emma laughed as soon as she read the inscription: 'Happy Escape Day'.

'I'm not sure if the warden will allow this,' Lucie said.

Florrie winked at them. 'Don't worry, he's sorted. I'm going to miss you two. You've brightened things up the past few weeks for me.' Her eyes lit up. 'I know, perhaps you could go on a shoplifting spree together and get another work order. That would be great.'

Emma laughed. 'How about we don't and we just visit you instead, like regular people would?'

Florrie reached over and removed the used sparklers. 'You two are busy enough, I'm not expecting visits. But I do think we should have some cake and enjoy our last day together.'

Emma looked at Lucie, who nodded at her. 'Actually, we were wondering if you'd like to escape from here yourself?'

Florrie looked up. 'What do you mean?'

'Lucie and Noah are going to come up to the Bay for a week, or a few days, whatever they decide. Why don't you come, too?'

'Yes, do,' Lucie added. 'Noah would love you to come and so would I. We can pick you up and all travel together. What do you say?'

Florrie's eye's filled with tears as she stared at the two women. She took out a handkerchief and wiped her eyes before blowing her nose. 'You are both far too kind. Of course I can't come. But thank you, just asking me means so much.'

'We're not just asking you to be polite,' Emma said. 'We want you to come. The Bay is beautiful. You can breathe in some nice fresh ocean air and even meet my family if you'd like to. I'm sure Mum could do with some extra company if she's feeling up to it. From what Dad's said she's complaining about being bored already.'

'And I'd love some help with Noah,' Lucie added. 'We need a change of scenery but we also need a change to our dynamic. Having you there would be great for us, too.'

Florrie sat in silence. She looked from Emma to Lucie and back again. 'I'd love to come, but I'm still worried I'd be in the way.'

'It's only a four-hour drive,' Lucie said. 'We can come back any time we need to. If you aren't having a good time we'll just come home. It's no big deal.'

Florrie laughed. 'I doubt that will be an issue for me, love. My guess is you'll be dragging me kicking and screaming back here.' She looked over to where Rodney had walked into the outdoor area and was heading toward their table.

'Oh great,' Lucie said. 'I think we're about to be ordered back to work.'

Rodney approached the table. His eyes widened as he saw the cake sitting uncut between them. 'Who is responsible for this?' he demanded.

'I am, Warden.' Florrie got to her feet and saluted Rodney.

Emma laughed out loud. She quickly covered her mouth with her hand. Florrie was hilarious.

'This is not at all acceptable. You should know better. Please rectify the situation immediately.'

Florrie reached down and picked up the knife she'd brought out with her.

Emma held her breath as Florrie cut an enormous slice and put it on a plate. She held out the plate to Rodney, who took it from her and inspected the cake as if he were examining evidence.

'Fifteen minutes, ladies. You're due back in the kitchen in fifteen minutes, and make sure this cake is dealt with in an appropriate manner.' He winked at them and turned, his tongue running over his top lip as he walked away from the table.

Florrie grinned. 'Come on, ladies. The man's just given us fifteen minutes extra and permission to eat this cake; we should obey him.' She picked up the knife and cut three generous portions. 'With a holiday to look forward to, I really do feel like I have something to celebrate.'

Chapter Twenty-Three

EMMA

Emma hummed along to the Verve as she manoeuvred the black Audi through the frangipani-lined street toward home. A calmness had settled over her as she'd driven away from the aged-care facility. Her work order had been signed off; her community service was complete. She could stop lying to Daniel.

She smiled as she thought about her husband. She still found it hard to believe that he wanted to start a family. Finally. She had Mia to thank for that. Magical little Mia. The moment he'd laid eyes on her he'd fallen in love.

She slowed the car as she approached their house. The garage door was open. Her heart rate increased. She was sure she'd shut it that morning; she never forgot. She stopped at the base of the driveway, relieved to see Daniel's car. He must have cancelled his trip. Was he as keen to get on with making a baby as she was?

Emma parked in the driveway and reached for the door handle. She hesitated. She was still in her cargo pants and T-shirt. Hardly the clothes she would have worn to organise the gala ball.

It was too late to do anything about it. Daniel appeared at the garage door. His arms were crossed, his face hard as he waited for her.

A lump formed in her throat and she immediately forgot about her clothes. Was it Maggie? Had something else happened? She climbed out of the car. 'What is it? Is it Mum?'

Daniel shook his head.

'What is it then? What's wrong?'

He stared at her. 'Where have you been?'

'What?'

'I said, where have you been?'

Emma's eyes darted around the garage. *Quick, think of anything, anything at all.* He couldn't find out, not now that it was over. She swallowed, forcing herself to meet Daniel's gaze. 'Final preparations for the ball. It's tomorrow night, you know that.' Hopefully he wouldn't pick up on the change of date.

He shook his head. 'You mean tonight?'

'No, tomorrow.' Emma moved closer. Was he buying it? God, she hoped he was. Her baby was in reach; she couldn't lose it, not now. Time to distract him or at least change the subject. She put her arms around him. 'Why are you home? Aren't you supposed to be at the retreat by now?'

'I needed to see you.'

She moved her hands lower and caressed his thigh. 'So we can spend the rest of the weekend making Daniel junior?'

Daniel didn't respond. He continued to stare at her. 'I'll ask you again; this time, I'd prefer it if you didn't lie. Where were you today?'

Emma swallowed as he shook himself from her and walked over to the large storage cupboard. No, please, this could not be happening.

Daniel pulled the sliding door across and revealed the neatly stacked boxes. He turned to face her, his eyes cold, the vein in his forehead throbbing. 'Now we've established how you spend your days. What's the bigger thrill? The stealing or the lying?'

Emma reached for the wall. She needed support.

He walked over to her car and opened the boot. 'Where's today's haul? I'm assuming that's where you've been and why you are wearing those clothes.' He pointed at her pants. 'What? Are you less suspicious dressed like a teenager?'

'I haven't— I didn't . . .' Emma couldn't find the words.

'Slim pickings, was it?' Daniel slammed the empty boot shut. 'I can't believe you've been using the façade of a charity to go out every Saturday to steal stuff. God, you don't even use it. Just shove it all in a cupboard. What the hell is wrong with you?' He gestured to his BMW and her Audi. 'Buy whatever you want, just use your fucking credit card next time. You realise I'm a laughing stock, don't you?'

Emma cleared her throat, willing her words to make sense. 'If anyone's a laughing stock it's me, not you. It's not about you.'

Daniel slammed his fist against her car, making her jump. 'No, this reflects on me. I can tell you right now, there's no way I could show my face at the retreat after Elise decided to fill me in. They'd be checking my bags on the way out.' He calmed a little and faced her. 'Em, what's going on? Tell me what made you do this.'

Emma shook her head. She couldn't speak. There was nothing she could say to make this better. She couldn't bear to look at Daniel. Disappointment and hurt were etched on his face. Anger she could cope with. This, she couldn't. She turned and walked toward the house.

'Where are you going?' Daniel asked. 'Em, stop, we need to talk.'

Emma turned and forced her eyes to meet his. 'Talk? All you're doing right now is yelling at me. Worrying about how everything reflects on you. It's all about you, Daniel, isn't it?'

Daniel stared at her. 'What do you mean?'

Emma waved her hands around them. 'This. Cars, houses, money, success. Our lives are all about that. About how you're going to achieve it all. What about me? What am I in all of this?'

'You? What do you mean? You're integral to it all. Our success is because of us, not just me. We're a team.' Daniel glanced at the shelves of stolen goods. 'Well, I thought we were, anyway. Right now I don't think I even know who you are.'

Emma sighed. 'No, I don't think you do. In fact I'm not even sure I do right now.'

Daniel stared at Emma. 'So that's it? You're not going to even try to explain to me why you've been shoplifting? Give me a reasonable explanation that I can use with our friends, our colleagues?'

Emma shook her head. 'That's still the most important thing to you, isn't it? How this reflects on you?'

'Yes. No!' Daniel held his head in his hands. 'Oh shit. I don't even know what to think Emma, I just need you to tell me what's going on.'

'Not right now.' What could she say? She'd lied to him and deceived him for months. Her lies went far beyond the actual shoplifting. Community service, the fabricated charity meetings; she'd woven an entire life of lies. How did you explain that? She'd thought everything would be okay, that he would never know. She wiped her eyes with her sleeve as she walked into the house. How wrong she'd been.

Emma woke to the early morning songs of the kookaburras. She'd fallen into a fitful sleep fully clothed on the top of the bed covers.

Her stomach rumbled and she was in desperate need of a shower. Food, or at least coffee, was her first priority. She assumed Daniel had slept in the spare room. Nothing less than she deserved. Of course she was in the wrong, she knew that. She'd shoplifted, been caught and then covered it up with a trail of lies. He had every right to be upset. If the situation were reversed, she would probably walk out on him.

That thought played on her mind as she made her way through the house to the kitchen. Would Daniel be able to trust her again? She made herself some coffee and walked out to check if he was in the pool; he wasn't. She sipped her drink and watched the ripples on the water's surface. She sighed. What she'd give to be able to reverse the clock to the day she was caught shoplifting. To not have stolen the cufflinks. To have stopped the stealing immediately. The caring, loving version of Daniel would have reappeared when Maggie got ill and she wouldn't have had any need to lie to him. They'd be busy making their baby. Life would be perfect.

The salty sea breeze welcomed Emma back to the Bay a little after three. Before leaving Brisbane, she'd found a note on the kitchen bench from Daniel saying he'd gone to play golf and they'd talk when he returned. Emma decided she wasn't ready to talk. Instead, she left her own note, asking him to give her some space, that she'd call him in a few days.

She went through and opened up the windows of the townhouse. A breeze blew in and cooled the house. She inhaled. While she loved their house in Brisbane, there was something very relaxing about the quiet, slow pace of Golden Bay. It had none of the hustle and bustle of the city. She was back much earlier than she'd planned, which gave her the afternoon and evening to fill in. She debated visiting her mother or Simone and, deciding on her mother, she picked up the phone. She hung up a few minutes later, having learnt from her father that Maggie was asleep and would probably remain so for a few hours. The chemo had really knocked her around the last few days and she had very little energy. Brian suggested she stop in after dinner if she wanted to say a quick hello.

Emma dialled Simone's number next and got her voicemail. After leaving a message she wandered around the house, her mind on Daniel, wondering what he was doing. She needed to get out, do something. A walk would give her some exercise and hopefully a chance to clear her head.

Ten minutes later Emma found herself walking at a brisk pace along the beach. It felt good. The wind blew through her hair, the salty spray cooled her face. She imagined Daniel was taking his frustrations out on the golf course. She almost pitied the ball.

'Hey, Emma.'

She looked up to see Drew smiling at her. She must have been walking toward him for quite some time and hadn't even registered another person on the beach.

'How come you're not in Brisbane?'

She smiled. 'Came back early; wanted to visit Mum and Simone. However, as surprise visits often tend to go, no one was up for a visit.'

'Good for me then.' He grinned. 'Can I join you?'

'Sure, I'm just walking – needed to clear my head.'

'Anything wrong?'

God, where would she start? Imagine the field day the town would have if they got hold of her gossip. 'No, nothing's wrong.'

Drew laughed. 'Your face tells a completely different story. It's not Maggie, is it? I popped in on her yesterday and she was tired but seemed okay.'

'No, she's okay, other than dealing with the side effects of chemo. I've just got a few things on my mind.'

'I'm a good listener.'

Emma stopped and stared at him. 'Actually, you're a good stirrer – you really pissed Daniel off the other day, you know.'

Drew laughed. 'I was only kidding around. He knew that. I told him the date was a joke and that we expected him to come, too. You said he hated coming to the Bay so I thought I'd try and lighten things up a bit.'

'It had totally the opposite effect. Getting him to the Bay was a big enough deal in itself, your contribution really didn't help.'

'Sorry.' Drew looked anything but sorry. 'Why doesn't he like coming here?'

Emma shook her head and continued walking. 'Too long a story.'

'Like I said, I'm a good listener. Have to be, actually. The wine bar opened last night and I've decided to do a few shifts. Everyone likes spilling their guts to the barman, or at least that's what I've heard, so I really need to sharpen up my listening skills. I could get you to give me some practice – go on, try me out.'

Emma laughed at his persistence. 'Fine, I got myself into some trouble. I lied to Daniel and he found out.' Emma's phone rang at just that moment. She pulled it out of her pocket and saw it was Daniel. 'Just a minute,' she said to Drew. 'This is important.'

'Hello,' she said.

Daniel's voice was harsh. 'I'm just calling to let you know I got your message and for now I agree, we need some space. I have no idea why you went on a shoplifting spree, in fact I don't even really care. What I care about is the detail you went into in order to lie to me, and then you ran back to the Bay before even telling me what's going on. I can't trust you and I don't even want to look at you.'

'Daniel, I love you.'

There was silence at the other end of the phone.

'I'm so sorry, I know what I've done is unforgivable but I need you to give me a chance. I can make it up to you. You can trust me, I'll prove it to you over time.' Emma waited for his response. She'd turned her back on Drew and had momentarily forgotten he was there until she heard him clear his throat.

She turned, putting her finger to her lips, asking him to be quiet.

'Who was that?'

'What? No one. I'm on the beach, there's just noise about. It's quite windy.' Another lie.

'Anyway,' he continued, as if she hadn't spoken, 'it sounds like we both need some time to think. I'll call you later in the week, we can work something out then.'

'Maybe I can come back next weekend?' Emma held her breath; she had to see him, they had to make up, she just didn't know how to do it.

'Em,' Drew called out. 'I've got to go. Why don't you meet me at the wine bar later, let me buy you that drink?'

Emma immediately put her hand over the phone.

'Fuck! I can't fucking believe this!' Daniel's anger came through loud and clear. 'For fuck's sake, you just told me I could trust you and you're standing there lying to me as you're saying it. That was that arsehole Drew, wasn't it?'

'Yes,' replied Emma. 'But he just turned up, I hadn't planned to meet him.'

'But you lied to me again – that wasn't the wind, was it?'

Emma screwed her eyes shut, wishing for once timing would work in her favour. 'No, no it wasn't.'

The phone went silent. Daniel had hung up. Emma put it back in her pocket, swearing to herself. Bloody Drew. Bloody timing. She took a deep breath. She'd get through this. *They'd* get through this. She needed to be patient, give Daniel some time and space, then sit him down and talk through exactly what she'd done and, more importantly, why.

The next two days passed slowly for Emma. She worked her shifts at The Café, dropped in to visit both Maggie and Simone and spent some time organising the house ready for the arrival of Lucie, Noah and Florrie. She'd rung Lucie the night before, suggesting they come a bit later in the day so that she would be home to welcome them. Being rostered for the early shifts, she'd be finished a little after three.

Drew had come into the café for breakfast that morning, seeming put out that she hadn't turned up on Sunday night at the wine bar.

'Why would I?'

'Because we had a bet.'

'Drew, I'd just told you I was having some issues with Daniel and you have to go and yell out so he knows we're on the beach together.'

Drew had laughed. 'So what? We weren't doing anything wrong. We're just friends.'

'Of course we are, but Daniel's a jealous kind of guy and I just don't need any extra aggravation with him at the moment. He doesn't trust me, so hearing you in the background when moments before I said I was alone just added fuel to that fire.'

Drew rolled his eyes. 'You started that fire, not me. Why not just be honest to start with, then you wouldn't have these issues?'

He was right, but he was also annoying. He asked her again to come and try out the wine bar. In the end she'd relented. 'I've got some friends coming to stay. We'll all come if I can get a babysitter for Noah. He's only five.'

'Just bring him. There's a kids' area with an Xbox, a TV and a whole bunch of games and books. He'll have a ball.'

'You have a kids' area in a wine bar?'

'It was already part of the pub so now it will be shared by the pub and the wine bar. I did listen to you; that most of the residents in this town are in bed early so a wine bar would never work. It opens at three o'clock. So far we're doing our biggest trade between three and six. It's become an afternoon wine bar.'

Drew paid for his meal and, before he left the café, made Emma promise they would come. 'You're the main reason I set the bloody thing up. I can never back away from a challenge so you'd better come and have a drink soon, just in case you're right and it does close down as fast as it opened.'

Emma finally agreed to go; it would be a good chance to take Lucie and Florrie out somewhere.

Now Emma surveyed the townhouse. It was ready for visitors. She'd just finished cleaning the kitchen and putting away the groceries. She wasn't really sure what five-year-olds liked to eat so had bought a selection of items that looked kid-friendly. She'd also stopped at the bottle shop and bought some champagne and wine.

A little before four Lucie's old Toyota Corolla pulled into the driveway. Emma dashed outside to greet her visitors. The back door of the car flew open and out jumped a small boy. She grinned as she caught his eye. He was a cute kid, his baseball hat carefully positioned backward on his head, temporary tattoos on each arm – he was definitely cool. However, under one arm he had a beaten-up soft toy cat, completely at odds with the look he was trying to pull off. Emma's heart swelled the moment she saw that cat. He was still such a little boy. One that she was looking forward to getting to know.

'Hi, Noah,' she called. 'Why don't you open Florrie's door for her? She could probably use a hand.'

Noah went to the door and opened it. At the same time Lucie climbed out of the driver's seat.

Emma went around and gave her a hug. 'I'm so glad you've come. I've been looking forward to this all week.'

Lucie laughed. 'So have we, let me tell you. Noah's itching to do everything. The beach, the rockpools, the park, everything.'

'And so am I,' Florrie called. She steadied herself with the side of the car as she stood up. 'My body is disagreeing right at this second but I can't wait to get to the beach either.'

Emma gave her a hug; it was really lovely to see her.

'You okay, love?' Florrie's face was full of concern.

'Of course. Why?'

'You look a bit tired, not at all like your usual self.'

Emma's eyes instantly filled with tears. No one else had noticed how she looked. Her parents, Simone – they were all so caught up with their own lives they probably wouldn't have noticed if she'd grown an extra head. Not that she blamed them: cancer and a new baby certainly trumped an argument and a few sleepless nights.

Florrie squeezed her arm and looked over at Noah. 'How about you get us settled in and then we can have a chat. I'm sure Lucie and Noah will want to go exploring.'

'You have to come, too, Florrie. We have to see the beach at the same time; we agreed, remember?'

Florrie laughed and ruffled Noah's hair. 'That we did. Let's take our bags in, I'm sure we can work something out.'

Twenty minutes later Emma pulled up in the car park at the beach.

'Wow!'

Emma looked in the rear-view mirror. Noah had taken off his seatbelt and was staring out at the crashing waves, his little face mesmerised.

'He's not been to a surf beach since he was a toddler. He probably doesn't remember it,' Lucie said.

'Really?' Emma was surprised. Living in Brisbane, most people commuted to the Gold Coast or Sunshine Coast regularly. 'Why not?'

Lucie's face had turned red. 'We're just busy most of the time, that's all.'

'And petrol costs too much,' Noah added. 'Can I run on the sand?'

'Of course,' Emma said. 'Jump out and go down with your mum; I'll just get a few things from the boot and help Florrie.'

'Are you sure you don't need a hand?' Lucie asked.

'No, we'll be fine.'

Emma opened the boot and took out the picnic rug and hamper she'd prepared earlier. 'I've got a chair here,' she said to Florrie. 'What would you prefer?'

'Picnic rug is fine. I'm not so old I can't sit on the beach. Although,' she chuckled, 'you might have to help me up at the end.'

They walked down the embankment and on to the sand. Noah was already down at the water's edge, running in and out, squealing with delight.

'I think this holiday will do those two the world of good,' Florrie said. 'They need something nice in their lives.'

Emma nodded. 'I hope so.' They walked until they were halfway between the car park and the water's edge. Emma put down the picnic rug. 'Now, I've got some afternoon tea here. Lucie,' she called. 'Do you want a champagne? We should celebrate that you're here.'

Lucie walked over. 'I'd love one. Wow, look at you and that hamper.'

Emma had opened her hamper, showing two bottles of champagne, a juice box for Noah and a wonderful spread of dips, antipasto and cheeses.

Emma opened one of the bottles of champagne and poured them each a glass. 'To friendship.' She raised her glass.

'And criminals,' Florrie added. 'May they continue to commit crimes so that I find more friends.'

They all laughed and sipped their drinks.

'So, what's been happening, love?' Florrie asked. 'On Saturday you looked alive, in fact you were buzzing with excitement and I'm sure it was more than just finishing your work order that had you so excited. That spark has completely left you.'

Emma's eyes filled with tears. She wiped them. 'Sorry, I'm tired and a bit emotional.' She told them what had happened with Daniel. How they'd made the decision to finally start a family and the very next day he'd found out about the shoplifting and lying. How she'd been unable to give him a proper explanation and run back to the Bay before they had had a chance to talk.

'He'll come around, love. It's not the end of the world what you've done. You didn't kill anyone or cheat on him. They are about the only two things that are hard to forgive in my books. He probably just needs a bit of time.'

'It was made worse though.' Emma explained about Drew and his comments on the beach.

'But you haven't done anything with this Drew, have you?'

'No, he's just a friend, and I'm not even sure that I'd call him that now. He went out of his way to stir up Daniel last week and hearing I was with Drew on Sunday didn't go down well. If he's got trust issues, me being with another man in any capacity, particularly an intelligent, good-looking one, won't help.'

'Intelligent and good-looking?' Lucie asked.

Emma nodded. 'He's pretty hot actually, not that I should say that, or even notice it.'

'You're married, love, not dead,' Florrie said. 'You are allowed to notice these things, you just don't flirt and you definitely don't touch. Those are the rules I lived by when my Harry was alive.'

Noah came running up to the group, his face pink with excitement. 'Mummy, this is so good. Can we stay here forever? I saw a fish and tomorrow I want to catch it. We can eat it for dinner.'

Lucie laughed. 'I'm not sure about forever, but certainly for a few days. We'll have to see if we can get a hold of some fishing gear and try to catch that fish. Now, Emma's put together some nice food and there's a juice box here for you. Would you like some?'

Noah peered into the hamper and turned his nose up. 'It's a bit yucky for me.'

'Noah!'

Emma laughed. 'No, he's right. Don't worry about it. If I were five I'd think this was all pretty yucky, too.' She handed Noah the juice box, slipped her hand into the side pocket of the picnic basket and pulled out a plastic container. 'There are some normal biscuits and cheese in here, if you'd prefer?' She opened the lid and Noah squealed in delight.

'Mum, Emma's got my favourites. How did she know?' He took a handful and ran off toward the water.

'Thank you,' Lucie said. 'You've made his day already.'

'If all it takes is biscuits and cheese, it should be pretty easy.'

The three women sat back and enjoyed their champagne as they watched Noah tear about the beach. The sun went down behind the dunes and the air cooled. 'Why don't we take the other bottle back to the house?' Emma said. 'Noah might want to watch a DVD and we can organise dinner.'

'Sounds good,' Lucie said. 'Although getting Noah to come is going to be a battle – he's loving it too much.'

'Leave it to me,' Emma said. 'Finish your champagne, you look like you're enjoying it.' Lucie was on to her third glass and it was nice to see her relaxing.

Moments later Emma walked back up the beach, hand in hand with Noah. They helped Florrie up and walked toward the car. Emma could see Lucie shaking her head. 'You okay?'

Lucie smiled. 'I'm fine, better than fine. How on earth you managed that without a tantrum I'll never know.'

'It was easy.' Emma grinned. 'Bribery. I've got a huge box of chocolates at home for dessert, and Noah's getting two if he'll be my helper between now and dessert time.'

'That was the easiest night I've had with Noah in ages,' Lucie said. 'Thank you.'

Emma smiled. 'He's a great kid, he didn't exactly make it hard.' She'd tucked Noah and his cat into bed half an hour ago and they hadn't heard from him since.

'That's because you're so organised. Spaghetti – his favourite – then the DVD, chocolate, the books; he's never going to want to leave.'

The three women were sitting in Emma's lounge, enjoying a bottle of red wine Lucie had brought with her. She'd brought a case of twelve bottles. Some to drink and some for Emma to keep.

'This wine is beautiful,' Emma said. 'Is this one of . . .' She hesitated. '. . . of Matt's?' She wasn't sure whether Lucie would want to talk about him or not.

She soon got her answer. Lucie started telling them about Matt and his love of wines. How he'd turned her from a teetotaller to now really appreciating and enjoying select vintages. 'I feel a connection to him when I'm drinking his wine,' she explained. 'It was something we shared. He taught me all about the different grapes and how to distinguish between flavours. Sometimes when I'm having a glass I feel like he's sitting next to me, about to ask if I can smell the hint of passionfruit or gooseberries.'

'What else did he like doing?' Emma asked.

Lucie's face lit up as she talked about Matt and his daredevil side. He'd had her bungee jumping in New Zealand, white-water rafting down the Zambezi River. They'd sandboarded, snowboarded, parasailed and zip-lined their way through many countries when they'd travelled before settling down. 'The only thing he couldn't convince me to do was skydive,' Lucie said. 'He practically begged me. I kind of wish I had now – another memory to have.'

Emma noticed Florrie didn't contribute. She sat listening quietly. She hadn't said much since dinner. 'You okay?' she asked.

Florrie smiled. 'Okay? I couldn't be better. You've got no idea how this afternoon contrasts to my usual evenings. For starters, dinner at a table with intelligent conversation beats dinner on a tray in front of the television. Fine wines, fancy food.' She sighed. 'I'm with Noah, I'm never going to leave.'

Emma and Lucie laughed. 'Good, I'm glad you feel at home. It's so lovely to have you all here. I was thinking tomorrow afternoon we might go down to the pub, get Drew off my back about visiting the wine bar.'

'If you think it's a good idea?' Florrie was studying Emma closely.

Emma was surprised. 'You don't?'

'Love, you suggested that he was causing problems between you and Daniel. How will Daniel feel if he knows you're at the wine bar?'

'It's about the three of us having an afternoon out, not about me and Drew. Golden Bay doesn't offer a whole lot of choice when it comes to enjoying a wine or two.' She turned to Lucie. 'He said they have a kids' area with an Xbox and TV and stuff. There'd be plenty for Noah to do.'

'Sounds wonderful.' Lucie stood up and stretched. 'If no one minds, I might go to bed. Noah will be up around six. I'll keep him quiet so he doesn't wake anyone.'

'I start work at six thirty so he won't wake me,' Emma said. 'Make yourselves at home, won't you? The fridge and cupboards are stocked. Use anything and everything. You might want to take a picnic somewhere for lunch. I should be back just after three. Don't hurry back though, I'll see you when I see you.'

Lucie yawned. 'Great. Now I'll leave you two to finish Matt's wine and see you in the morning. Night.'

With Lucie gone, Emma and Florrie sat in a comfortable silence.

'She's had it tough,' Emma said.

Florrie nodded. 'She has, but unfortunately I get the feeling Noah's had it tougher.'

'What makes you say that?'

Florrie sighed. 'Losing a husband is awful – I know I've been there. But for a child it is world changing. All of the comfort and security that's been built up to make them feel safe is stripped away. It's much harder for them to come to terms with the fact that a parent is never going to return. I think Noah's dealing with that and perhaps a few other issues.'

'Like what?'

Florrie held up her glass. 'Like this. Lucie puts it away like it's water. I know she says it's her connection to Matt but I think you'd probably find it's a crutch for her. Makes her day more bearable.'

'I'd say that was fair enough under the circumstances. It can't be easy grieving, working and being a single mum.'

'No, it's not. The problem is she's hidden behind the wine and hasn't grieved. She's angry about Matt's death, and so she should

310

be. But have a few drinks and that anger can spiral out of control. I have a nasty feeling Noah's dealing with that, too.'

Emma glanced toward the stairs and lowered her voice. 'You think she hurts him?'

'Not intentionally, but I think it's possible he stirs her up until she snaps. I had a glimpse of it last week when I went over to visit.'

'Should I hide the wine while she's here?'

Florrie laughed. 'No, I don't think so, she'd probably get a bit suspicious. I'm hoping the counselling sessions with Mary will help her. I'm going to go in and see her myself when we get back. Mention some of my concerns.'

Emma nodded. 'I can't believe it. He's such a happy little boy. You'd never pick up on it.'

'Not today perhaps, but he's also a stubborn little boy. He's excited today, had his own way for most of it, been made a fuss of. You watch what happens if we have a day where he's not the centre of attention. I might be wrong, and I hope I am, but my gut tells me there's a bigger problem here than him just being without a father.'

Emma's thoughts were occupied by Lucie as she worked at The Café the next day. She found it hard to believe that Lucie would hurt her son. She seemed so level-headed. She wondered if Florrie had different standards of discipline than Lucie did? Surely it was normal to raise your voice if your child was being naughty? Emma knew that people had moved away from smacking children, but again, there must be times when you had to get a bit physical, even if it was just to stop them from doing something dangerous. Then there was the drinking. Yes, Lucie had drunk more than she or Florrie had, but it still wasn't an excessive amount. Many of the wives of investors that she and Daniel dined with could hardly stand by the end of the night and no one blinked an eye.

She checked her watch. She wanted to stop in and see her mother before going home. She wanted some answers about what had really happened when Daniel's mother died. Emma finished clearing up the counter before handing over to the afternoon staff. She'd been helping in the café for four weeks now. She knew the routines backward. She had all the ordering down pat and was now organising the staff rosters and ensuring all the financial information was being sent to the bookkeeper. Initially her father had popped in a few times a week to check on the running of the business, but over the past ten days he had left it up to Emma. She drove past Simone's on the way to her parents' and dropped off a large platter of food for Simone and Johnno's dinner. She only stayed for a few minutes, long enough to peek in at Mia, who was sleeping peacefully, and to admire Simone's clean house.

'The cleaner just left.' Simone laughed. 'I don't know what we'll do when she leaves, probably get used to living in a pigsty.'

Emma made a mental note to call the cleaner and contract her for a twelve-month period. 'If you're free, I might organise a get-together on the weekend. I've got a couple of friends staying with me.'

Simone raised her eyebrows.

'What?'

'I can't imagine any of your glamorous city friends will want to hang out with me and Johnno.'

Emma decided not to even discuss it. 'Look, I have to go. Just be free, okay. You might be surprised.'

Emma walked from the house and climbed back into her car. She started it up and continued the drive toward her parents' house. She could guarantee Simone would be surprised if she found out how she'd met Florrie and Lucie. She'd have to think up a good story before Saturday. Emma hesitated as, minutes later, she pulled up outside the old Queenslander. Another lie? Was she really going to tell another lie to cover her tracks?

Maggie was sitting up in bed surrounded by at least a dozen brightly coloured cushions when Emma entered the room. She was instantly hit by a wonderful perfume emanating from a huge arrangement of pale pink roses standing on the dressing table.

Maggie herself looked terrible. Her face was pale and thin, her eyes surrounded by dark rings. She managed a thin smile for Emma.

Emma came and sat on the bed. 'How are you, Mum?'

Maggie gave a little laugh. 'Having had the misfortune of looking in the mirror this morning I hardly think you need ask that question. This' – she waved her hands up and down indicating her face and body – 'pretty much tells the story.'

'Can I get you anything?'

Maggie shook her head and sighed. 'No, but I assume you're here for answers. What really happened when Caroline died. Am I right?'

'Yes, I'd like some answers. But only if you are up to it. I don't want to tire you more or upset you.'

'There's not a lot I can tell you.'

'Why not? You were very clear to Daniel that he didn't know everything. You suggested he'd feel differently if he did, but then didn't tell him anything.'

'I know, and I still can't.'

'Why?'

Brian entered the room carrying a cup of tea for Maggie and a glass of water for Emma. 'Your mother made a promise – one I doubt she'll ever break.'

Emma looked at Maggie. 'To who?'

'Caroline, Daniel's mother. She had very set instructions for her death. She made Harvey promise to carry out her wishes, and some of her friends, too. In hindsight it was an awful thing to do to us. She'd made assumptions about the consequences, but she got it wrong. Harvey was too distraught to do anything but follow her wishes.'

Emma stared at her mother. 'It was Caroline who decided she didn't want Daniel to be there when she died?'

Maggie nodded.

'But why didn't she say goodbye before he went on camp?'

'I think she did, in her own way. She didn't want him worrying about her. She wanted him to remember her cheerful and loving. She certainly didn't want him to see her die. Anyway, I've said too much.' She laughed softly. 'Caroline is probably sending daggers down from heaven. This is Harvey's story to tell. The fact he's never told Daniel says a lot about him. I don't think he wants anything to change Daniel's opinion of his mother.'

'But it's cost him his relationship with his son, doesn't he see that?'

'I'm not entirely sure. I think he believes there's more to it. That Daniel's a bigshot now, that he's embarrassed by his roots.'

Emma shook her head. 'He hates everything about this town, but it's because of his mother's death. That he was prevented from saying goodbye and then left on his own to basically care for his dad.' She stared at Maggie. 'Was that all part of Caroline's plan, too?'

Maggie was even paler than when Emma had arrived. 'Sorry, Mum. I'm not meaning to upset you, I just need something to take back to Daniel. We're having some problems and if I can answer these questions for him it might help fix other issues.'

314

'What's wrong? I thought everything was good between the two of you. The fact he came to the Bay after all of these years told me how much he loves you.'

Emma looked away, not meeting Maggie's eyes. 'Things were good, but I've messed up. I've lost his trust and, before you ask, no I didn't cheat on him, but I did lie and it was to protect myself, not him. I've been a bit stupid.'

'But you'll work it out?'

Emma really wasn't sure. However, she didn't want to worry her mother so she smiled. 'Yes, of course. He just needs a bit of time.'

'I can't tell you any more; I've said too much already. If you want answers you need to talk to Harvey. This is his business, not mine. Caroline was my friend, my very good friend, and I made her a promise. I've broken part of that today already.'

Brian stood up. 'Yes, love, time to get back to your friends. Give Mum a rest. She's tiring really easily at the moment.'

Maggie smiled. 'When am I going to meet these friends of yours? How do you know them anyway?'

Emma hesitated. Here she was demanding Maggie tell her the truth when she was about to tell more lies. It needed to stop. But they would be horrified.

'Are they the wives of Daniel's business partners?'

Emma shook her head and let out a deep breath. Here goes nothing. 'I got myself into some trouble recently.' Her fingers dug into the palms of her hands as she watched their faces turn from interest to concern.

'What kind of trouble?' Brian asked.

She swallowed, unable to meet her parents' eyes. 'I was caught shoplifting.'

Maggie gasped. Her hand flew to her mouth. 'Emma!'

Emma unclenched her hands; it was too late to stop now. 'I know, I know. It's awful – I've no excuse.' She took another breath.

'Long story short, I was sentenced to do community service at a retirement village. I tried to appeal the sentence but there was no way they would let me just pay a fine.'

'So these friends, they were doing community service at the same time as you?' Brian asked.

'Lucie was only there because she couldn't afford to pay a speeding ticket so she was working off the fine, and Florrie is a resident. Don't worry, they're not criminals, even though Florrie tried her best to convince us all she was.'

Emma's face flooded with heat as she looked at her parents' shocked expressions. She pushed her hair back and this time looked them in the eye. 'The shoplifting was stupid. I was bored and unhappy and it gave me something to do. The shock of being caught and then the stories I've concocted to keep Daniel from knowing are enough to ensure I'll never do it again.'

'Is this why you and Daniel are having problems?' Maggie asked.

Emma nodded.

'He was upset about the community service?'

'He doesn't know about it, he's only just found out about the shoplifting.'

'You need to tell him, Emma,' her father said. 'Before he hears it from someone else.'

Emma sighed. 'Yes, I know you're right, and I will. I'd better go, I've promised to take Florrie and Lucie to the wine bar tonight.'

'Is that a good idea?' Maggie looked concerned. 'The way Daniel spoke the other night suggested it might be dangerous territory . . .'

'Daniel's not talking to me at the moment so it really isn't relevant. I'm not going there to see Drew, I'm going to take my friends out. Also, I mentioned to Simone I might organise a catch-up on the weekend for all of us if you are up to it. I don't think I'll be going back to Brisbane so it would be a good chance for you to meet Florrie and Lucie.'

Maggie nodded. She appeared to be at a loss for words.

'I'm sorry, Mum, really I am.' It was as if she were twelve years old, not a grown woman. She almost preferred Daniel's anger to the quiet disappointment her parents were showing.

'You don't have to apologise to me, Emma. It's your life. I just hope you can make smarter decisions moving forward.' Maggie lay back on the bed. 'Now go on, have a good night and tell Drew thanks for the fruit basket.'

'Fruit basket?'

'Yes, it arrived this morning. It was very thoughtful. Your dad's eaten most of it already so he certainly agrees. Don't you, Brian?'

Her father nodded. 'No point it going to waste when all you want is dry biscuits.'

Emma hugged her parents before letting herself out of the house. She knew they were disappointed in her. They weren't the only ones – she was disappointed in herself. She almost couldn't believe now that she'd done it at all. The one thing she knew for sure was she wouldn't be doing it again. She sat in the car for a few moments before starting the ignition. Telling the truth had been humiliating, but she was glad she had. No more lies. Her thoughts turned to Daniel. From what Maggie had said it wasn't Harvey or the townsfolk who'd made Daniel's life hell. It was his mother. How could she convince Harvey to tell her, or Daniel, the full story?

Chapter Twenty-Four

GOLDEN BAY

Lucie squeezed Noah's hand as they followed Emma and Florrie through the side door of the pub into the wine bar. Jazz music engulfed them as they entered the darkened room. Soft lighting and candles on every table added to the atmosphere. It was close to five and most of the tables were occupied with people laughing and enjoying generous glasses of wine. They could be in the middle of the city, not in a small country town.

'This takes me back to my twenties,' Florrie said once they were seated, a faraway look on her face. 'Wine bars weren't a huge thing back then, but there was one in the area we lived in. They'd have jazz bands or someone playing the piano and Harry and I would go there for a drink if we were celebrating.' She looked at the walls, which were covered with pictures of famous singers. 'Not unlike this. I'm not sure if the selection of wines was so impressive though.' She passed the menu to Lucie. 'Have a look at this.'

Lucie took the menu from her, opening it to reveal four pages of wines. She looked up at Emma. 'Your friend knows his wines. This is an impressive list.'

'Thank you.'

Lucie turned to find a tall, well-groomed man standing behind her. He smiled, his dimples creasing his tanned face.

Lucie drew in a breath; Emma was right, he was gorgeous.

'Hi.' His gaze fixed on Lucie. 'I'm so glad you could make it.'

Emma introduced them all.

So this was the Drew Emma had spoken of. The one who'd caused issues for her and Daniel. No wonder – those dimples would suck anyone in. His caramel-coloured eyes were warm and full of humour. Looking at him, Lucie had a strange feeling: an urge to know everything about him. She shook herself. It must be the sea air – she hadn't even had a drink yet and she was thinking crazy thoughts. She turned to Noah. 'Do you want to have a look at the kids' area?'

He hesitated. There were some older children already over there, which she knew he'd find intimidating. 'I'm sure the other kids are friendly.'

Drew didn't give him a chance to answer. He held out his hand to Noah. 'Come on, mate, I can show you the ropes, introduce you to some of them, if you like. There's a great car-racing game on the Xbox you might like to have a go on.'

Noah smiled and took the hand Drew offered him without hesitation, something he'd never done with a total stranger before. Lucie didn't blame him – she half wished he'd offered his hand to her. She shook herself. This was getting ridiculous. He was just a person in a nice package, that was all.

'Why don't you ladies have a look at the wine list? I'll set Noah up over there and come back and take your orders. Have a look at the pinot noir range if you like a red – there are some beauties.'

'Now, he's rather scrumptious,' Florrie said. She winked at Lucie. 'If I was thirty years younger I'd have a go at that one myself.'

Drew returned to the table moments later. 'He's made himself some friends.'

Lucie cleared her throat. 'Thank you. He can be a bit shy.'

Drew smiled, his eyes locking with hers. Lucie's stomach flip-flopped. Was he flirting with her? The next moment he was smiling and chatting with Florrie, suggesting a wine she should try. She must have imagined it.

'Oh, I don't know, love, there's too much choice here. Why don't you just bring me something you recommend? I'd probably prefer a sparkling if you have one.'

'Of course,' Drew said. 'What about you ladies? I did promise you a champagne too, Emma, so do you want to all start with sparkling and then perhaps try one of the reds?'

Emma nodded. 'Sounds lovely.'

Drew flashed another smile at them before returning to the bar area to organise their drinks.

Lucie watched him go, his shirt pulled tight across his broad shoulders, his jeans slung low on his hips. She became conscious of Florrie and Emma looking at her.

'You right there?' Emma asked.

Her face grew hot. 'Sorry, he's a bit distracting.'

Emma laughed. 'Yes, he is. Thanks for both coming with me. It gets this obligation out of the way and he's not going to sit down and expect me to have a conversation with him. I know it's all perfectly innocent, but every now and then he throws in a comment to unsettle me. He thinks it's hilarious. In saying that, he's been so good to Mum and Dad, so I can't really get annoyed with him.'

'You can if he's stirring up trouble for you and Daniel, love. He might think it's all a big joke but it sounds like Daniel doesn't.'

'It's not Drew's fault,' Emma said. 'I've definitely handled things badly, that's all.'

'Have you heard from Daniel today?'

Emma shook her head. 'No, he needs some time out. I think I might have found out something interesting today though, something that might help us get back on track.' She explained what Maggie had told her and her need to now speak with Harvey. 'Daniel carries so much anger and resentment toward his father and the town, it would be nice if he could put all of that to rest.'

Drew interrupted them as he placed their drinks on the table. 'There you go, ladies. Enjoy. Give me a shout when you're ready for another or to try something else. There's some food on its way, too.' He looked at Emma. 'All complimentary tonight – I'm coming good on our bet.'

Emma shook her head. 'No, you offered to buy me a glass of champagne, not provide all three of us with a night out.'

Drew shrugged. 'If you have a good night, you might all come back. Now that would make me happy.' He winked at Lucie as he turned away from the table.

'So tell me what you got up to today,' Emma said.

It was close to seven by the time they decided they should go home. None of the women needed a meal. Drew had sent plate after plate of antipasto, bruschetta and beautiful cheeses to the table. They'd enjoyed their champagne and then he'd made some recommendations of reds that would go well with the food. Noah hadn't reappeared the entire time they'd been there. Lucie could see him chatting and laughing with the older children in the kids' area. She'd glanced across at one stage to see him sitting with them, eating a burger. He was completely at home.

She sighed. Why couldn't life be like this all the time? Noah happy and carefree. No pressure of work or school, or being judged by bloody Jane Winthrop or anyone else.

'You look miles away,' Emma commented.

Lucie smiled. 'Enjoying this escape from reality. This is only our second day and Noah looks like he's lived here all his life. It's just so nice to have a break. Thank you, again.'

Emma stood up. 'No need to thank me. I'm loving having you all. But we'd better go; if I have another glass we'll all be walking home.'

'Let's just thank that nice young man,' Florrie said. 'He's given us such a lovely night.' She walked over to the bar where Drew was laughing with a couple who were sitting at it, enjoying their wine. He excused himself and came around the bar when he saw them approaching.

'Off already?'

Florrie nodded. 'We wanted to thank you for a fabulous evening.'

Drew smiled. 'You're very welcome. I hope you'll come back again during your stay.'

Lucie thought he looked at her when he said that. She shifted from foot to foot, sure she had imagined it. He was smiling at all of them.

'Are you sure you won't let me pay for anything?' Emma asked. 'We've rung up quite a bill with the wine and the food.'

Drew shook his head. 'Nope, tonight was on me.' He grinned. 'Hopefully you'll feel obligated to come back another night while your friends are here, that way I'll get to see them all again.'

'I'm sure we will,' Emma said. 'I still feel funny though, not paying a cent.'

Drew looked at her. 'It was my treat. However there's another way you can pay me.' His cheeks reddened. 'I'll have a chat with you another time, see if you approve.'

'I have a feeling I won't,' Emma said. She turned to Florrie and Lucie. 'I'll go and get Noah while you two head out to the car.'

'No wonder Emma's having trouble with Daniel.' Florrie shook her head as she and Lucie made their way out of the door. 'I'm surprised at him. He seems like such a nice young man. However, I'm not sure he'd dare to make such a suggestive comment in front of

322

Daniel. I think our girl needs to watch herself. He's too charming for his own good.'

Emma reflected on the previous night as she switched on the coffee machine and finished the opening jobs at The Café. She still hadn't heard from Daniel and had decided not to go home for the weekend. It would give her more time to spend with Florrie and Lucie, which would be a good distraction. Going home to a house full of people was a nice change. Even in Brisbane Daniel was away a lot. She liked her own space but it was nice to share it from time to time.

She'd wanted to kill Drew, again, for his comment last night. She hadn't encouraged him – in fact quite the opposite – yet he had said things that implied there was something going on. That she could pay him another way. She could just imagine Daniel's reaction to that one.

Her bigger worry, however, was Lucie. She was beginning to think Florrie's concerns had some merit. When they'd arrived home from the wine bar, Lucie had selected another bottle of red wine from the stash she'd brought for them to try. Both Emma and Florrie had declined, they'd had enough already, but it hadn't stopped Lucie from opening it. After she'd put Noah to bed she'd joined them in the lounge and they'd continued to chat and laugh about things. It was very nice, except for being so conscious of Lucie refilling her glass. Emma had gone to bed before the other two as she had to get up early for work. When she had got up this morning, she'd found the bottle, three quarters empty, on the kitchen bench. Adding that to the three glasses Lucie had had at the wine bar made a lot. She wondered how she would be feeling today.

Emma's thoughts moved back to Daniel. She really needed to speak to him. She hated the silence. She wondered whether he was missing her at all, or whether he was just angry.

A steady stream of customers had kept them on their toes all morning and lunchtime came around very quickly. Emma was contemplating taking a break when Drew walked in.

He grinned. 'Hope your friends enjoyed themselves last night.'

'They did, thanks. What can I get for you?'

Drew looked surprised at Emma's curt tone. 'Um, just a juice, number seven, thanks.' He held out ten dollars to her.

'Why don't you hold on to that? I owe you for last night. Make the next five juices on the house.'

Drew shook his head. 'No, don't be silly. Last night was my treat, there's no need to pay me back.'

'That's not what you suggested last night.'

Drew stared at her. 'What do you mean?'

'You said I could pay you in another way.'

'Oh.' His face coloured, as it had the night before. 'Well, that doesn't matter. I probably wouldn't be comfortable asking anyway, might make things a bit awkward.'

Emma rolled her eyes. 'I'd say it definitely would and my answer would be no. I believed you when you said you were joking with me. I'm such an idiot.'

Drew's face went a darker shade of red. 'Oh, okay. Well, I wondered if that might be the case, that you might not be okay with it. Let's just leave it.'

Emma stared at him, wondering for a moment whether they were talking about the same thing. 'Take a seat, I'll get your juice organised.'

'I can do it.' Kristen took the order from her hand. 'Trying something new today, hey Drew?'

He nodded, still looking uncomfortable.

She'd thought they were friends, so why was he set on stirring up trouble? All she was interested in at this stage was Daniel and how to fix her marriage.

Emma's attention was diverted by a movement out the window. Harvey was walking a dog on the footpath on the other side of the road. 'Kristen,' she called out, 'I've got to pop out for five minutes. Can you look after things?'

'Sure.'

Emma pulled off her apron and hurried out the door. She crossed the road and increased her pace to a jog to catch up with him. 'Harvey!' she called from behind. 'Wait a minute.'

Harvey turned around, surprise registering on his face. 'Emma, you're still here?'

She nodded and pointed to the shop. 'Yes, Mum's still not well.'

'Oh, I'm sorry to hear that.' His face took on a faraway look. 'It's an awful bloody thing, cancer.' He looked at her. 'Although I hear Maggie's on top of it, that things are looking good.'

'Yes, they are, and it's kind of what I wanted to talk to you about.'

'Oh?'

Emma looked at the dog, who was now snuffling around the base of a tree. Where did she start? 'It's about Daniel. I think a lot of his anger and resentment toward you and the town could be sorted out if he knew the truth about what happened when his mum . . . when Caroline died.'

'The truth?'

Emma nodded. 'Mum won't say much but she's suggested that a lot of what went on around the time she died was Caroline's own wishes. That she'd made you and her friends promise to do things a certain way – a way that she thought would work out for the best but perhaps didn't.'

Harvey pushed his hand through his thinning hair. 'That's right. She also had us promise we'd never tell Danny what had been said.'

'But wouldn't it help your relationship with him if you did? He thinks you kept him from saying goodbye to his mum. That's not what happened, is it?'

Harvey's face filled with pain and he shook his head. 'No, not exactly.'

'So why don't you tell him that?'

'I made a promise to my wife when she had a few days to live. Her life ended so many years before it should have. It was the least I could do to honour her.'

'But it's ruined your relationship with your son. Is that what you think she would have wanted?'

Harvey shook his head. 'No, I think she assumed her plan would strengthen it. In hindsight it didn't.'

'But you could fix things now; explain to Daniel.'

'No, Danny's not interested. He left town when he was seventeen, couldn't wait to get out of here. Hasn't looked back since. He's embarrassed by his roots, by me. Nothing I say will change that.'

Emma stared at him. That's what he actually believed? That Daniel left town because he was embarrassed. That had certainly been her reason for leaving town – she couldn't wait to get out of here and not be associated with a greasy fish and chip shop any more, but it wasn't Daniel's.

'He's not embarrassed,' she said. 'He's the first to admire people like you who work hard and make a success of themselves. He's well aware that his own work ethic comes from you.'

'Sorry, love, I don't agree. You don't take off and not look back unless you want to pretend something never existed.'

'He resents you, Harvey. He resents the town. His mother died when he was fourteen and he wasn't given a chance to say goodbye.

On top of that he was expected to look after you with very little help. He resents the hell out of you and everyone who dared call themselves your friends. That's why he left and that's why he doesn't like coming back. He's angry, and I think with very good reason.'

Harvey pulled at the dog's lead. 'We'd better get going. Danny's not going to change his attitude to me or the town no matter what I say to him. He's too big for us, too successful. I think you might have your wires crossed. While it might be nice to think that his mum is the entire reason he left, you're wrong. Think about your own reasons for leaving. I think you'll find you and Danny are very similar.' He continued walking down the road, leaving Emma to stare after him.

Emma pulled into the driveway of the townhouse to find Lucie loading bags into the car. What was she doing? They'd only been here two nights, surely they would at least stay for the weekend? She opened her door and climbed out. 'Hey, what's going on? Leaving already?'

Lucie nodded. 'Yes sorry, we need to get home.' She walked back inside the house before Emma had a chance to question her further. Sobs were coming from the back garden. She let herself in through the side gate and found Noah sitting on the grass, tears streaming down his face. Florrie was sitting next to him, rubbing his back.

'What happened?' Emma asked.

'I'm afraid I've rather spoiled things,' Florrie said.

'Oh?'

She nodded and turned to Noah. 'Why don't you pop inside, love, get your little cat and bring him out? I think he needs a cuddle, too.'

Noah wiped his face on his sleeve and got up and walked toward the house.

Florrie sighed. 'Noah spilt some milk this morning and Lucie got angry, beyond any reasonable level of anger. It was an accident, yet she reduced him to tears and then dragged him off to his room when he wouldn't help clean it up. I didn't blame him to be honest. He tried to say it was an accident but she wouldn't hear it, just kept telling him how naughty he was and he wouldn't be allowed to come again if he didn't look after things.'

'Poor little guy,' Emma said. 'Then what happened? Why is she packing up the car?'

'I started to clean up the milk, told her it was no big deal and wondered if she had perhaps overreacted. She didn't like that, which is fair enough – no one likes their parenting to be criticised. Anyway, one thing led to another and I mentioned that her tolerance level might be a bit low this morning after drinking so much last night. That was it. She accused me of being an interfering old lady and told me to mind my own business, that I was as bad as her sister-in-law, judging her all the time.'

'Slight overreaction,' Emma said.

Florrie nodded. 'She's got a problem. I think she knows it, too. Admitting it, however, is another thing.'

Noah returned from the house, his beloved cat in his arms. He came and sat back down next to Florrie and snuggled against her. It was obvious to Emma that he'd found a safe place with Florrie.

'It's such a shame,' Florrie said. 'We've been having such a lovely time. Me and my big mouth.'

'No,' Emma shook her head. 'You needed to say something. Can you keep Noah entertained for an hour or so? I'm going to take Lucie down to the beach for a walk, see if I can convince her to stay.'

'Of course, love. But I wouldn't get your hopes up, she's pretty angry.'

Lucie packed the last bag into the boot and slammed it. Bloody Florrie. She'd been having such a nice time, feeling that she'd got away from people who judged her and whammo! Florrie had unrolled her own agenda. She had a drinking problem and was bullying her own son. Not exactly Florrie's words, but Lucie could read between the lines. She wasn't going to stay around for another serving. She needed to get Noah, thank Emma and then they could go. Florrie would have to find her own way back to the city. She wasn't going to share a long car drive with her.

She was just going to find Noah when Emma came out of the front door. She walked toward her car and opened the door. 'Come on,' she called to Lucie. 'Get in.'

'What?'

'I said get in. Florrie's keeping an eye on Noah, and you and I need to have a chat.'

Lucie shook her head. 'I'm sorry but we're going. Florrie's probably told you that already. I appreciate your hospitality but I'm not going to stay and be spoken to like that. I'm going to get Noah and we're heading back to Brisbane now.'

'No, you're not,' Emma said. 'You're my guest and it would be incredibly rude of you to go without at least listening to what I have to say. Come on, jump in. We'll go over to the beach and have a walk – a bit of fresh air would do us both good. Give you a chance to calm down. I don't want you risking your or Noah's life driving while you're angry.' She smiled at Lucie. 'Come on. I'm not going to move my car until you're in it, so you have no choice anyway, unless you plan to drive over the top of mine?'

Lucie smiled, she couldn't help it. 'Okay, but I want to leave soon. It's going to be a late night as it is.' She walked over and climbed into Emma's car.

Five minutes later she kicked off her shoes and followed Emma down on to the beach. The sand squished between her toes. It was cool and inviting.

They walked in silence for a few minutes before Emma spoke. 'She didn't mean to upset you, you know that, don't you? She cares about you, we both do.'

Lucie didn't respond.

Emma continued. 'You've had an awful few years. Matt dying, relocating, all of the emotional and financial stress and changes that come with that. Your in-laws welcoming you on one hand and being a pain on the other. Single parenting can't be easy: no time for yourself, a child who's angry that his father's not here any more. Luce, you need to take a step back and try to see things from Florrie's perspective. She's been in your shoes, she knows better than anyone what it feels like.'

'There wasn't a whole lot of empathy coming from her this morning,' Lucie said.

Emma stopped and turned to face Lucie. 'Do you think you've got a problem?'

'What do you mean?'

'With Noah? With your drinking? Do you think there's a problem? I know the wine is your connection to Matt, and it's totally understandable that you'd want to sit and drink and think about him and happier times, but does it affect how you respond to Noah? How you feel the next day?'

Lucie focused her gaze out on the water. The waves were crashing on to the beach, spray shooting toward them. 'If anything it relaxes me, helps me cope with Noah and his defiance.'

Emma nodded. 'I'm sure it does. You mentioned when we were doing community service that Noah can be hard work. Is that why you got so angry with him today? Florrie said it was a bit of an extreme reaction for an accident. She wouldn't have made a big deal of it except she said it was similar when she was at your house the other week.'

Lucie's stomach tightened. 'She's just an interfering old busy-body. Sees me discipline my son twice and thinks she knows everything.'

'Yeah, I agree, she's a cow. I've known that all along. She really hasn't been interested in us, just wants to judge us, be superior to us. We shouldn't have invited her.'

Lucie turned to Emma. 'Really? That's what you think?' Up until this afternoon she'd loved everything about Florrie.

Emma sighed. 'No, of course she's not like that. I know that, but wasn't sure if you did. Look, you know your life better than anyone. If you honestly think there's no problem then great, I'll support you. But if you think there might be even a hint of one then we need to work out what to do about it, get some help if need be. Life is for enjoying – you can't spend your days wishing your problems away until it gets easier, because it never will unless you fix them now.'

Lucie could feel her eyes prickling with tears.

Emma put her arm around her shoulders. 'Come on, life's hard and you've been served a rotten deal. If Matt were here things would be different, we both know that. But he's not and you've got a little man who's counting on you to be Mum and Dad. You've got to be at your best to be able to do that.'

Tears ran down Lucie's face. 'Florrie's right.'

Emma hugged her tighter.

'There are times I want to kill Noah. I want to shake him until his teeth rattle. I'm doing everything I can for the two of us to get by and he just winds me up. I don't shake him, by the way, but there are times when I'm probably a little bit rougher than I need to be. Then I have a glass of wine afterward to calm me down.'

'You started seeing Florrie's psychologist. Have you told her any of this?'

Lucie nodded. 'We talked a little about the issues I'm having with Noah, but it was the first session and the conversation quickly turned to talking about Matt and ways I can deal with my grief. At the end of the session she said she wanted to talk about Noah more next time so we can devise proper strategies to cope with my frustration. I guess I need that session as soon as possible.'

'Maybe Noah needs to speak to someone, too?'

Lucie looked at Emma. 'What, about the way I treat him? I'm not that bad.'

Emma laughed. 'No, you donkey, about Matt. Has he had any counselling?'

'No, I couldn't afford it.'

'There would be free counselling available for him, I'm sure. Why don't we have a look into it later? You might as well take advantage of any help you can get. It can't hurt.'

Emma let her arm drop from Lucie's shoulder. 'You know we just want to be your friends, Florrie and I. She's not judging you; she sees what she thinks is a possible problem, that's all. It's often a lot easier to look from an objective point of view into someone's life and see things that need to change. We're often too close to it all ourselves.'

Lucie sighed. 'Maybe you should have been a psychologist: what you're saying makes a lot of sense. I'm not sure I want to give up the wine though. It's my connection to Matt.'

'No one is asking you to give it up, perhaps just try to cut it back a bit. You can't have woken up feeling too good this morning.'

Emma was right – Lucie had woken up with a horrible taste in her mouth and a pounding headache. A couple of Panadol had fixed the headache but her head was still fuzzy. Noah's energy was not very welcome on mornings like that. 'No, not the best.'

'I'm sure Matt loves that you have your wine and think about him, but you've got more connections to him than just his wine. Think of all of the things you've told us that you two used to do together. You've got those memories and you've got Noah – he's the biggest connection you're ever going to have.'

Lucie nodded. 'You're right, of course he is.'

'Get him to talk to someone, Luce. I think that's what you both need. Keep going to Florrie's psychologist and organise someone for Noah. You both need to grieve properly.' Emma glanced at her watch. 'Now, we'd better get back, they'll be wondering where we are. Let's go and unpack the car and take Noah to the park. Then we can come back and make hamburgers for dinner. I haven't even tried the barbecue out the back yet.'

Lucie turned to follow Emma. Noah would be happy they were staying and, if she were honest, so was she.

Chapter Twenty-Five

EMMA

Emma introduced Florrie, Lucie and Noah to her parents and Simone and then left them in the family room together as she went to help her dad organise drinks. She was glad that her mother had been well enough for the morning tea. In fact, Maggie had insisted they have it. 'It will give me something to look forward to,' she'd said. 'Take my mind off feeling awful and get me out of this bloody bed.'

Johnno came up the back stairs of the house and into the kitchen as Emma pulled the cups down from the shelf. He had a football in his hands. It looked brand new. He grinned at Emma. 'Where's the little matey? I've got strict instructions from Sim to show him a good time.' He spun the football between his fingers.

Emma pointed to the lounge. 'He's in there, probably bored out of his brain already.'

'Excellent.' Johnno walked through to the lounge. Emma could overhear him interrupting the conversation. 'Noah,' he said, 'I'm Johnno, Mia's dad. Come with me, we've got man stuff to do. Let's leave these women to their tea and gossip.'

'Can I, Mum?' Emma heard Noah ask.

She must have said yes as the next minute Johnno walked into the kitchen with a beaming Noah, out the back door and down the stairs to the garden.

'He's sorted.' Brian chuckled. 'Mia's going to be one hell of a football player if Johnno's got anything to do with it. They'll be gone for hours.'

'How's Mum doing, Dad? She tells us she's fine but she looks awful.' Emma had been quite shocked to see Maggie this morning. On top of the pale, drawn face, her hair was beginning to fall out. She'd aged at least ten years overnight.

'Don't tell her that, love, it's the side effects of the drugs. The main thing is we stop this cancer from coming back; the next few months are just part of that process.'

Emma poured the boiling water into the cups. 'It's so awful.'

'No, love, I think we've escaped lightly. It could be awful, but she's a survivor, she'll get through this – we all will. Anyway, tell me some of your news. What are you doing here on a Saturday? Shouldn't you be trying to patch things up with Daniel?'

'He needs some space. I thought it was better that we have a weekend to ourselves. I doubt he would have hung around in Brisbane if I'd gone home.' She sighed. 'I'm the last person he wants to see right now. I've handled it all so badly.'

Brian patted her shoulder. 'Give him some time and when you do see him, be honest. Lies are never good for a relationship.'

Emma nodded. 'So I've learnt. Let's get these cups of tea handed around; it sounds like bedlam in there.' They could hear shrieks of laughter from Maggie and Lucie. Florrie was no doubt holding court.

Brian smiled at Emma. 'Just what she needs, love.'

They came back into the lounge to find Maggie smiling and chatting, a beautiful turquoise scarf now wrapped around her head.

'Gorgeous scarf, Mum,' Emma said. 'Where did you get it?' She certainly hadn't been wearing it when they arrived.

'It was a gift from Florrie and Lucie. Such a lovely present,' she added.

'We saw it at the market down by the wharf yesterday,' Florrie said. 'It was so cheerful I nearly got one for myself. I'd have no luck making it sit like your mum does though.'

Maggie laughed. 'That's because you've a head of beautiful curls, not a thinning, balding head like mine.'

'If it were me, I'd look at it as a wonderful chance to buy lots of gorgeous scarves and wear them like you are now,' Florrie said. 'Make the most of it.'

Simone came back into the room holding Mia. 'Fed, changed and ready for cuddles,' she announced. 'Anyone keen?'

Florrie put her cup down. 'I'd love to hold her, if you'd let me?'

'Of course.' Simone handed Mia over to her.

'Oh, what a gorgeous baby.' She looked up at Simone. 'What a clever thing you are, producing a baby this beautiful. Well done.'

Simone laughed. 'Not sure I had a lot of control over any of that.'

There was a knock on the door. 'I'll get it,' Simone said. She disappeared while the others smiled at Florrie cooing away to Mia.

'Emma?' Simone reappeared in the doorway. 'Daniel's here.'

Emma's gut clenched. 'Daniel?' He was here?

His head appeared behind Simone's. 'Oh, sorry,' he said, seeing Florrie and Lucie. 'I didn't mean to interrupt. You weren't at the townhouse or at The Café so I hoped you might be here. I'm Daniel,' he added and smiled at Florrie and Lucie.

'You up for the weekend, son?' Brian asked.

Daniel looked over at Emma, his eyes hardening. 'No, just for a chat. Emma and I have a few things to discuss.'

Emma let out a breath.

'Why don't you two head off to the beach or somewhere private?' Maggie suggested. 'We can look after Florrie and Lucie, and Johnno's got things under control with Noah. Take your time.'

'Thanks, Maggie,' Daniel said. 'And thanks, too, for . . . Well, for you know what.'

Maggie nodded.

Emma looked from her husband to her mother. What was all that about?

Her dad interrupted her thoughts. 'We can drop Florrie and Lucie back at your place later, love, so take as long as you like.'

Daniel was looking questioningly at Emma. Of course he was; he'd never heard of Lucie or Florrie. 'Shall we go?'

Emma nodded.

Daniel turned to Florrie and Lucie. 'Nice to meet you both.'

'You too love, look after that gorgeous wife of yours won't you?' Florrie said.

Daniel didn't respond. He took Emma's hand and led her to the front door. 'The beach sounds like a good idea. We need to talk.'

A lump lodged in Emma's throat. She doubted from his tone that this beach walk was going to be one she'd want to remember.

The high tide crashed against the rocks as Emma and Daniel arrived at the beach. There was no sand to walk on.

'We could walk along the bike track, if you want to?' Emma reached to open her car door.

Daniel put his hand on her arm. 'No, wait. Let's just sit here; there are a few things I need to say.'

Emma's heart pounded as she sank back into her seat. Was this it? Was he actually going to end their marriage? She wouldn't be surprised. Most things were fairly black and white to Daniel – second chances were not something he usually entertained.

'So,' Daniel began. 'I had a phone call from my dad yesterday.'

'Your dad?' This was the last thing Emma had expected.

'Yes. After the chat you had with him during the week he decided it was time to clear up a few facts for me.'

'Oh, he gave me the impression he wouldn't say anything.'

'I guess he changed his mind. I drove up last night and went to his place. He told me about the promises he'd made to my mum when she was dying. She wanted to spare me the pain of watching her die, she wanted me to remember her from that last day, chatting normally, as if she was part of my life. He told me he'd tried to talk her out of it, to have her say goodbye properly, but it wasn't what she wanted. She couldn't say goodbye forever, she just couldn't do it.' A tear escaped the corner of Daniel's eye. He wiped it away roughly. 'She made him promise not to tell me, to let me believe that she would make it. That way she would never have to say goodbye.'

Emma placed her hand on Daniel's leg. 'That's a lot to ask of someone. She put Harvey in a horrible position.'

'He thinks she didn't realise what she was doing. She even asked all of her friends to not help us once she died. She'd filled the freezer full of meals, which lasted the first few weeks but that was all. She assumed if Dad was forced to look after me he'd have something to keep him busy, help him get on with his life. She also seemed to think it would give us something to bond over.'

'But if he knew about that, wouldn't he have acted on it?'

'He didn't know anything about it until yesterday. You spoke to him and a few hours later he had a phone call from your mum. She filled him in. Said you'd been asking questions and, really, it was time to put my mother's wishes aside as they seemed to have backfired spectacularly. I think that's what she told him.'

'So no one helped you at the time because your mum had asked them not to?'

Daniel nodded. 'Apparently.'

'But couldn't they see that you were struggling?'

'Thinking about it, probably not. Your mum used to come into the shop all the time to check up on Dad, he told me last night. He said his standard response to everyone was to smile and pretend life was great. Then he'd pretty much go home and curl up in the fetal position for the rest of the night. That was the dad I dealt with. He was lost without her. I think everyone assumed we were doing fine, that Mum's plan for us had worked. Then I took off and they all saw me as a bastard for deserting Dad; they had no idea what we'd been through.'

'How are you and your dad now?'

Daniel smiled. 'Surprisingly good, although I imagine he's got quite a hangover this morning. It took him about seven beers to get through the entire conversation.' He looked at Emma. 'Do you know he believed I was embarrassed by him? That I left town because I thought he was a loser?' He shook his head. 'Sure, I was angry at him about Mum but not about his life. He's done amazingly well. He took me around to the shop this morning; it's a little goldmine.'

Emma squeezed his leg. 'I'm so glad. What about your mum? Are you okay with what she did?'

Daniel sighed. 'I should be really angry at her, but I'm old enough to realise she did what she did to try to protect me. She just misread the situation. There's no point being angry at her now.'

They sat in silence. Emma was so pleased for Daniel. He'd carried anger and resentment around with him for such a long time and hopefully now a lot of that would be put to rest. Unfortunately she was following in his mother's footsteps of screwing up spectacularly. She doubted he was going to be so forgiving of her.

'So who are Florrie and Lucie? And why are they staying with you?'

Emma swallowed and then met Daniel's gaze. 'I met them doing community service.'

'Community service?'

'Yes, that's where I was all those Saturdays I said I was organising the charity event. I was preparing meals for elderly residents of a retirement village. The court refused to allow me to pay a fine. The clerk basically told me I was a disgraceful rich bitch who needed to be taught a lesson.'

Daniel stared at her, his expression mirroring that of her parents' shocked faces earlier in the week.

Emma continued. 'Lucie's a widowed single mum – she was there for unpaid speeding tickets – and Florrie's a resident.' Emma smiled. 'She's quite a character, tried to have us believing she was in for armed robbery and was actually a criminal rather than a lonely old lady who needed some company. They deserved a break so I brought them up here for a few days.'

Daniel shook his head. 'They're not even in your league of crime then? You were the worst offender of the three of you?'

'I guess you could say that.'

Daniel turned to her. 'I still can't wrap my head around why you were stealing stuff. We've got plenty of money. I don't care how much you spend, you know that.'

Emma nodded. 'I know. This is going to sound pathetic, but it gave me something to do, and a bit of a thrill at the same time.'

'You needed something to do so badly that shoplifting was all you could think of? What about all the charity work?'

'You've seen what those women are like: they're not real. All rushing off to their manicures and day spas after mournfully discussing the underprivileged and how much they're doing to help. I can't stand them. My days were spent going from those types of meetings to dinner with your colleagues, whose wives were mostly just as plastic.'

Daniel's mouth was still set in a hard line. 'Let me get this straight. You were so fed up with all these fake people that the only thing you could do that you found any meaning in was to steal stuff? I still don't get it.'

Emma sighed. 'You didn't want me to work, you didn't want to start a family. Of course I didn't set out initially deciding it was going to be my new day job – it just kind of happened. I did it once and it was exciting. Me, wife of a wealthy, successful businessman, doing something illegal. It gave me a weird buzz. On days I had nothing to do I found myself attracted to the shops. I don't expect you to understand, I don't really myself, but that's the best I can make of it.'

'You were that unhappy?' Daniel's face softened.

Emma nodded. 'I just had nothing that was mine; nothing I wanted to be doing. I had you, when you were around, but I needed more.'

They sat in silence for a few minutes, then Daniel took her hand. 'I'm a shit.'

'What?'

'First I take off on my dad and act like he never existed. Then the last few days I've been feeling like the reason you couldn't tell me why you'd done it was because you'd deliberately screwed me over, deliberately set out to embarrass me.'

'I didn't.'

He squeezed her hand. 'I'm realising that. I didn't listen enough when you spoke about working or having a family. I'm sorry.'

Tears rolled down Emma's face.

'Hey, don't cry.' He gently wiped the tears away with his fingers. 'I'm trying to fix things, not upset you.'

'They're tears of relief,' she said. 'I thought you'd come to end our marriage.'

Daniel cupped her face in his hands and brought it close to his, kissing her.

She responded, kissing him back, the tension of the past week leaving her body. She had her mother and Harvey to thank for this turnaround. She sent them both a silent thank you as Daniel deepened the kiss.

He pulled away. 'I love you, Em. I don't care about what you did any more, but I do care why you did it. We need to make some changes when we get home. Find you something you want to do.' He put his hand on her stomach and gently caressed it. 'And get on with making our own little Mia.'

More tears escaped Emma's eyes. This was like a dream. She half expected someone to wake her up at any minute and tell her it was.

A thumping on her window made her jump. The loving look on Daniel's face turned to anger.

'What the fuck does *he* want?' He opened his car door before Emma had a chance to say anything.

Drew was standing outside her window. She pushed open her door and got out.

He was smiling at them both. 'Sorry to interrupt, but I had something I needed to ask Emma.'

'Bad timing, mate,' Daniel said. 'What do you want? And if it's about that bloody drink, I'm telling you right now, give it to someone else. Emma won't be joining you.'

Drew looked confused. 'Um, no it's not about that. I think the girls drank enough the other night to say the bet is well and truly paid.' He laughed. 'Actually it was about that though. I wondered if you'd got the wrong idea yesterday, Emma, when I said I had a way that you could even us up.'

'What? Mate, you are aware that I'm standing right here, aren't you? She's not interested.'

Drew looked from Emma to Daniel. 'I think we've had a bit of a misunderstanding all along and I wanted to clear that up.'

Daniel crossed his arms and waited.

'I have no interest in your wife. Sorry, but firstly she's not my type and secondly she's married – and happily, from what she's told me. What I wanted to ask Emma was whether she'd mind me asking out her friend Lucie. The other night I was joking that she could pay me in kind; it fell flat at the time as she misunderstood. It's Lucie I'm interested in, not Emma. I've only ever been interested in Emma as a friend. I'm truly sorry if our wires have been crossed.'

'You want to ask Lucie out?' Emma smiled. 'Really?'

Drew nodded. 'Yes, but I wanted to check first that it was okay. I wasn't sure what her situation was.'

Daniel shook his head and laughed. 'Jesus, what a mess. I'm going down to dip my toes in the water. You two work out your matchmaking and then come and join me.' He held out his hand to Drew. 'No hard feelings.'

Drew shook his hand.

'Lucie's single,' Emma said as they watched Daniel walk toward the water's edge. 'But she's recently had a guy scare her off men. You'll need to tread carefully.'

'Okay. I wanted to check it was okay with you – your friendship is really important to me.'

'To me, too.' Emma smiled. 'I've got to catch up to Daniel. You can do whatever you like with Lucie, but she's pretty fragile so if you do anything to hurt her you'll have me and Florrie to answer to. Keep that in mind.'

Drew grinned. 'I will.'

Emma looked at him one last time, returned his grin and ran after Daniel.

'Now if that doesn't make a baby, I don't know what will.' Daniel kissed Emma before rolling off, sweat dripping from his hair. He took her hand in his as he lay back on the pillows, slightly out of breath. 'That was amazing.'

Emma curled her leg over his, her spare hand making circles on his chest. 'I almost hope that doesn't make a baby,' she replied, 'I'd be quite happy to practise that until we can perfect it.'

Daniel smiled, his hand running through her hair. 'Mm, definitely. Give me five minutes and we can practise again, if you want to.'

Emma laughed. 'We'd better not. I'm sure Dad will drop the others back soon. We don't want to scar Noah for life.'

'I'm willing to take the risk,' Daniel said. 'Forget the five minutes, I'm ready.' He rolled back on to Emma, kissing her passionately. 'It's good to be back here, Mrs Wilson.'

'Mm,' she murmured. Her legs tingled as he ran his fingertips down the inside of her thighs. 'I agree, Mr Wilson, I definitely agree.'

Daniel silenced her. Pressing his lips firmly against hers, his hands parted her legs. She kept her eyes locked with his. Thank God they'd found their way back.

Chapter Twenty-Six

LUCIE

'You look like a princess, Mummy.' Noah's eyes shone as Emma spun Lucie around in front of him. Emma had lent her a dress and done her make-up and hair for a date with Drew.

Lucie had been surprised when Drew had called her. She'd definitely felt something the night they'd met in the wine bar, but she'd imagined it was probably just lust, after all he was gorgeous. What he saw in her she couldn't imagine. Her stomach was doing somersaults. She hadn't been on a first date since Matt. She swallowed a lump. She'd nearly said no to Drew, guilt setting in immediately. But then she'd looked over at Noah, who'd been chasing bubbles in the garden; they both needed a fresh start and perhaps going out with someone was part of that.

She glanced at the clock. Seven already – he'd be here any minute. On cue, the doorbell rang.

'I'll get it.' Florrie had been hovering by the door for the past ten minutes.

Emma raised her eyebrows at Lucie. They heard the door open and then muffled whispers.

'What on earth is she saying to him?' Lucie asked.

Emma shrugged, just as Florrie appeared with Drew behind her. 'Look who's here, love.' She ushered Drew into the room.

He blushed as he saw them all staring. 'I wasn't expecting a welcoming committee.' He turned and sought out Noah. 'Hey, buddy, how are you going?'

Noah smiled shyly at him.

'Are you collecting the soccer cards by any chance?'

Noah nodded.

'Great.' Drew handed him a plastic bag. 'A mate of mine had a whole stack, said he didn't want them.'

Noah looked inside the bag, his eyes lighting up. 'Wow, thank you. There are tons in here.'

'My friend's involved with making them. He asked me if you had the book to put them in, but I wasn't sure.'

'No, I don't,' Noah said. 'They cost too much.'

'Yeah, you're right, they do. I'll mention that to my friend, see if he'll send you one, if you like. I think he's probably got a few spare.'

'Thank you. That'd be awesome.' He turned to Lucie. 'Is it okay if I open these now?'

Lucie ruffled his hair. 'Of course. Now remember, Emma and Florrie are in charge, so whatever they say goes, okay?'

Noah nodded.

Lucie bent down and hugged him. 'Have fun and I'll see you in the morning.'

He nodded, his focus completely on the bag of soccer cards.

She turned to Drew. 'Let's go, shall we?'

Drew winked at Emma and Florrie. 'Have a good night, ladies.'

He turned to Lucie when they were sitting in his car. 'You look gorgeous. I'm so glad you said yes to coming out tonight.'

A flutter in her stomach reminded Lucie how nervous she was. 'I should warn you, it's been a while since I went on a date.' She just hoped she didn't make a fool of herself.

Drew grinned. 'My only expectation is that you enjoy yourself.' He turned on the engine. 'I thought we might get out of town and drive over to Brimby – there's a lovely restaurant on the bay there. Is that okay?'

Lucie nodded, glad she'd let Emma convince her to borrow a nice dress.

Fifteen minutes later Drew pulled into the car park of Henri's, a floating restaurant that sat right on the water. 'They do beautiful seafood. I hope you like it?' Drew said.

Lucie nodded. She loved seafood, but other than fish, it wasn't something she could usually afford.

Drew guided her along the jetty toward the restaurant. A number of small boats bobbed on the water and people were scattered about fishing, the lights of the restaurant giving them just enough light to fish by.

Drew opened the door of Henri's and guided Lucie inside. Soft music mixed with the murmurs and laughter of the other diners created a relaxed and inviting atmosphere. The floor-to-ceiling glass windows showed off the twinkling lights of Brimby. Lucie imagined they would give lovely views of the ocean and the rolling hills when it was daylight.

Once they were seated, Lucie stared around the large room. 'This is beautiful. Do you come here often?'

Drew shook his head. 'No, I've had a few business lunches here but I haven't actually been here for dinner.' He laughed. 'Other than The Café I haven't been out much at night since moving to the Bay.'

'What about your wine bar?'

'That gets me out, but it's a bit different. I'm usually working when I'm there and it's only been open for a few weeks.'

'Emma's told me about the changes you've made to the town. Sounds like you've done some amazing things.'

Drew laughed. 'Let's not bore you talking about me. First things first, champagne?'

Lucie hesitated. Normally she would say yes without a second thought. She didn't really think she had a drinking problem, but Florrie and Emma's concern had sunk in. 'That would be lovely,' she found herself saying. A couple of drinks wouldn't hurt. She needed one to calm her nerves anyway.

Drew signalled to a waiter and ordered a bottle for them to share. 'Now tell me all about Lucie Andrews,' he said once the waiter was gone. 'How do you know Emma and what brought you to the Bay?'

Lucie took a deep breath. 'You know, if I tell you all about me, you'll never want to see me again.'

Drew laughed. 'That I doubt very much. This is what I know so far. You're a gorgeous, intelligent woman with a great little boy. You've got good taste in friends, if Emma and Florrie are anything to go by, and the fact that you are here with me suggests you are single and therefore I am a very lucky man.'

Lucie laughed. 'Well, there you go, you know enough already.'

Drew smiled at her. 'I'd love to know more, get to know you.'

'Okay.' Lucie decided it was best to be honest. If he didn't want to see her again, that was fine. At least they wouldn't have wasted each other's time.

Drew reached across the table and took Lucie's hand as she told him about Matt dying and her decision to move to Brisbane to be close to her in-laws, which she now thought was a mistake, and the unresolved issues both she and Noah had about Matt's death.

'See, I told you.' She smiled at him. 'I'm a bit of a mess, probably best avoided.'

Drew squeezed her hand. 'I'm so sorry you had to go through all of that; I'm sorry for you and for Noah. I think you're doing the right thing though, having counselling.'

'Yes, well, that's all pretty new. It's only since meeting Florrie and having her set it up that I've started, and I'll be looking into something for Noah when we get back. That was Emma's idea, actually.' She smiled, thinking of the forceful conversation Emma had had with her on the beach. 'They're both really looking out for me.'

'You didn't say how you know them.'

'Oh, I thought I'd avoided that.' Lucie pulled her hand away. 'I might as well get it all out on the table. I was doing community service in lieu of paying speeding fines. I met them there.'

'Emma and Florrie were doing community service?'

Damn. Lucie realised she'd put her foot in it. If Emma hadn't even told her husband, she probably didn't want Drew knowing. 'They have volunteers doing work at a retirement village and Florrie lives there. I was the only one paying off my speeding tickets.' She hadn't lied outright, just implied that Emma was a volunteer.

Drew smiled at her. 'I'm having dinner with a crim. That's pretty exciting.'

'Hopefully that was a one-off.'

'I'm only teasing you. Speeding tickets are hardly a big deal. God, if you open up my closet about a hundred skeletons are going to fall out. Best we don't do that. How about we take a look at the menu – I've heard the oysters are superb.'

Two hours later, Lucie was still laughing at Drew's stories. It turned out they'd both travelled extensively and may have even crossed paths at a ski lodge in Canada ten years earlier. Drew had had all sorts of adventures, getting himself into difficult situations around the world. 'That's why I'm better off living in the Bay,' he said. 'Can't get myself stuck on a gondola or lost on a mountain in a blizzard. The surf is about the only dangerous place I visit these days. What are your plans? You'll be heading back to Brisbane soon I guess?'

Lucie nodded. 'Term four starts Monday week.'

Drew reached across the table and took Lucie's hand again. His fingers slipped in between hers. 'Brisbane's not that far you know. Perhaps I could come down and visit you and Noah?'

Lucie blushed. 'I think I'd like that.'

'Good.' He smiled at her again, his dimples making her insides melt. He leant across the table and kissed her lightly on the lips. 'I can't wait.'

On the last night of their stay, Noah was already in bed and the three women were sitting out the back, sipping their tea and enjoying the cool breeze that was coming from the ocean. The stars were bright, a sign of a clear night ahead. They'd had wonderful weather since arriving at Golden Bay, Noah's tanned little face and arms a true testament to that.

'You're very quiet tonight, Florrie,' Emma said.

'Just thinking, love. We've had such a wonderful time. I think we're all going to miss the Bay.'

Emma nodded. 'You might have some trouble getting Noah to leave tomorrow. I'm so glad you stayed longer; it has been lovely.'

'It has,' Lucie agreed. 'You've been so kind to me and Noah. We're going to miss you.'

'And Drew,' Emma teased.

After her date with Drew it had been an easy decision for Lucie to extend their trip. It had given her the opportunity to spend more time with Drew and for Noah to get to know him. He was an instant hit with Noah, teaching him how to bait his hook and then helping him reel in his first big catch. That and their mutual love of soccer bonded them. Drew promised to teach Noah to surf when he and Lucie came up to the Bay for a weekend.

Florrie sighed. 'Yes, it has. Back to jail for me tomorrow.'

Emma laughed. 'Only because you let it be jail. You don't have to help in the kitchen you know. I've seen the residents doing all sorts of activities. You could join in with some of them.'

'I know, but it just doesn't appeal. They all seem so old to me. I like being with younger people; it makes me feel younger. In that place I feel like I'm sitting around waiting to die.'

'Stay here then,' Emma suggested. 'I'll have the house for another couple of months at least. I love having you, and Simone and my parents will keep you company when I'm not around.'

'Oh, I couldn't impose any longer, love. What if Daniel wants to come up for the weekend?'

'He still can. It's more likely I'll be going down to Brisbane the next few weekends as we've got things on, but it's no problem if he does come up.'

'Why don't you stay?' Lucie encouraged. 'Noah and I will come up for the weekend if Emma's away and keep you company.'

Emma laughed. 'That's Lucie's way of saying she's going to need a babysitter so she can go out with Drew, so you'll be quite useful.'

Florrie smiled. 'Well, if I'm needed then I can't really say no now, can I? The only thing is getting around; Lucie's driven me about since we've been here.'

'Why don't you rent one of those buggy things from the pharmacy?' Lucie suggested. 'They've got one sitting out the front for hire.'

Emma clapped her hands together. 'Perfect; consider it done. That way you'll be able to get about. What do you think?'

'Sounds marvellous,' Florrie said. 'Are you sure?'

'Of course I am. You can keep me in line. Make sure I'm doing everything I should. Speaking of which, does anyone want another cup of tea?'

When Daniel had left the previous Sunday to go back to Brisbane, Emma had declared it was time she looked after her body as best she could while they tried to make a baby. She'd stopped drinking coffee and alcohol and started taking a folic acid supplement. Florrie had decided to support her and also stopped drinking alcohol for the week. Lucie wasn't stupid. It was Florrie's not-so-subtle way of making it harder for Lucie to have a drink. She went with it. She was in a good place. Noah was having a great time and her mind was on Drew most of the time. She found she could go without a drink more easily than she'd imagined. Around five o'clock she usually still felt like one. She wasn't kidding herself, but she had the self-control to say no and squeeze some fresh lime into some mineral water instead. She'd looked at the case of Matt's wine and part of her felt guilty that she wasn't having her evening chats with him, but the sensible part of her also knew it was time to try to move on. He'd always be a huge part of her, she'd always think of him and see him in Noah, but she couldn't live in the past forever. She needed to think of her future. It was much easier to do this when a future that included Drew Myers looked so inviting.

Six Months Later

Florrie's hands trembled as she tried to pin the brooch on to the front of her new aquamarine dress. Emma had talked her into buying it and she was glad now that she had. They were all going to so much effort. Her eyes were teary; she really didn't deserve such kindness.

'Do you need a hand, Florrie?' Daniel came into the kitchen. 'You look lovely, by the way. Very regal.'

Florrie gave a shaky laugh. 'While I appreciate the compliment, the word "regal" makes me feel old. But then again, I guess I am. It's hard to believe I'm eighty. If it weren't for my body telling me it's wearing out, I would say I wasn't a day over forty. You'll get to this age and see what I mean. You'll have a near heart attack every time you make the mistake of looking in a mirror.'

Daniel laughed. 'Don't worry, I have that now. I don't think I'm exactly what you'd call a classic beauty and I'll be very happy if I look half as good as you on my eightieth birthday. Now, I'd better get you down to Brimby; Emma will kill me if we're even a second late. She's a bit uptight at the moment.'

Florrie rolled her eyes. 'That's a very generous description. You'd think she was the first person to ever have a baby. Let's hope she calms down a bit once he's born.'

'Still convinced it's a boy?'

'Definitely. The way she's carrying screams boy to me. Her moods do, too – her body's not used to all that testosterone. You mark my word, Daniel junior will be here before you know it.'

Daniel grinned. 'Might have to call him Danny.'

'Your dad would love that. He told me you'd been spending quite a bit of time with him out fishing on the weekends.'

Daniel laughed. 'And he told me he's been spending quite a bit of time with you, too. I hear you've got him putting bets on for you.'

Florrie winked. 'Gotta have something to spend my money on. Who knows how much longer I have on this earth?'

'Neither of us will have much time left at all if we don't get a move on. Come on.' He took her by the arm and led her out the front door to the car.

Daniel drove carefully through the town and out on to the main road toward Brimby. Lucie had insisted they celebrate Florrie's eightieth in a private dining room at Henri's. It was by far the nicest restaurant in the area and, as she felt it had brought her and Drew good luck, she wanted it to do the same for Florrie.

Florrie stopped Daniel before he got out of the car to open the door for her. 'Thank you, love, thank you for everything. You and Emma have been so good to me. I still find it hard to believe.'

'Don't be silly, you're doing us all a favour. Tradewinds would stand empty most of the time if you weren't living with us. And I hate leaving Emma on her own, but now she's got you for company too. We should be thanking you.'

Florrie smiled at him. When Emma had told her they were buying Tradewinds – a house by the beach in Golden Bay – and wanted her to live with them, she'd not believed her ears. She, of course, had said no, that she couldn't impose, but Daniel had had none of that. He'd pretty much marched into the retirement village, packed her bags and marched her out. The only person who would miss her would be LJ. She wondered if he still put on his warden act. She sent him a crossword every week to stump him. The arrangement was working well. Daniel was in Brisbane most of the week but returned at the weekend. Occasionally Emma would go back with him, but she spent the majority of her time in the Bay. She still worked at The Café and loved it. Daniel had been talking about a business of their own in the area but with the baby due in three months had decided to put that idea on hold.

Emma wasn't the only one working at The Café. Maggie picked up Florrie twice a week and took her in, supposedly to help make the jams and preserves that they used in their menu, but within a few weeks this had turned into an afternoon tea for local senior citizens when the café would be overrun, with Florrie running the show.

Daniel helped Florrie into the restaurant; they were the last to arrive and the rest of the party, aside from Maggie who was looking out for them at the entrance, were drinking out on the deck overlooking the marina.

Maggie pulled Florrie into a tight embrace as soon as she reached the door. 'Happy birthday. You look wonderful.'

Florrie hugged her back. 'So do you.' And she did. Maggie had finished her chemotherapy three months earlier and had been given the all-clear, although she still needed checks every six months to ensure the cancer didn't return. She'd put the weight she'd lost back on and her hair had grown back – it was shorter now, but the new look suited her. But the colour in her cheeks was the main improvement: she was no longer the ghostly pale colour that she'd been when Florrie had first met her. Brian was looking better, too. The constant worry had aged him – he was now almost completely grey – but he looked happy. He had a spring back in his step.

'Come out on to the deck,' Maggie said. 'Everyone's waiting and the champagne is flowing.'

Florrie followed her through the dining room, stopping to admire the white-clothed tables that were adorned with stunning arrangements of lilies – Florrie's favourite flower – and the ceiling, which was a sea of aquamarine and silver balloons, before stepping out on to the deck. Her eyes filled with tears as she saw the excited faces turn to greet her. Noah was standing with Drew and Lucie, looking so handsome in his new shirt, his eyes shining. Florrie was delighted that things were working out for them. A big part of it, she was sure, was Lucie being so honest with Drew from the start about her issues with Noah, with the wine and her need of some help. He'd contacted a friend of his in Sydney who was a child psychologist and they had referred Noah to a colleague in Brisbane. He had started weekly sessions and was like a different child. He still got angry and threw the occasional tantrum, but that was unusual rather than the norm. Lucie had made a huge photo board for Noah with pictures of Matt, which was now in his room. Each night as she put him to bed she thought of a memory to share with him. Noah loved it and so did she. She'd told Florrie that it gave her the closeness to Matt that she used to get from drinking his wine; the benefit now was that she shared that closeness with Noah.

Emma came over and hugged Florrie. 'You look beautiful.'

Florrie smiled at her. 'Thank you, love, and thank you for organising all of this. You've gone to so much trouble.' She looked around the deck area, which had been decorated in a similar style to the private dining room, with vases of lilies, bunches of aquamarine and silver balloons, and birthday banners. 'It all looks amazing.'

Daniel came over and put an arm around Emma. 'Just like my beautiful, glowing wife.'

Emma swatted him away. 'I'm not sure about the glowing part; "growing" would be more accurate. Ooh!' She rubbed her stomach. 'Someone's just woken up.'

Daniel immediately placed his hand on her stomach, his face lighting up when the baby kicked. 'Noah's going to be happy – I'd say he's going to have a soccer buddy to play with soon.'

'Or a ballerina perhaps, to join Mia?' Simone joined them and kissed Florrie. 'You look wonderful.'

Florrie smiled. 'So everyone keeps telling me. Now I think I need a glass of champagne to calm my nerves. I'm not used to being the centre of attention.'

Daniel fetched her a glass. She lifted it in Lucie's direction, who lifted her own in turn. Florrie smiled, seeing the wedge of lime in Lucie's clear glass. She really had turned things around.

A few hours later Florrie wiped the corner of her mouth with her napkin. She sat at the head of the table and had just enjoyed the most marvellous five-course meal. She leant back, watching her new family chatting and laughing. There was a table full of presents behind them, all for her. She knew without opening any of them that she'd been given the best present of all the day Emma and Lucie had started community service. Her own family had been taken from her, her grandchildren lost before they'd had a chance to grow and enjoy life. But she had been given a second chance. A new family to love and be loved by.

She smiled as she watched Emma and Lucie laugh as they wheeled a huge cake toward her. Emma never did anything by halves, she'd give her that.

It was amazing to see such a crowd gathered for her birthday. Emma's family were there in full force: Maggie, Brian, Simone, Johnno and Mia. Even Harvey had joined them, standing proudly next to Daniel. Of course, Lucie and Noah were there. They were staying at Tradewinds, too. They'd woken her early that morning with breakfast in bed, Drew coming in half an hour later, pretending he hadn't been there all night. She didn't know who they thought they were fooling – it certainly wasn't her or Noah.

Her smile grew as everyone turned and started to sing in her honour. Leaning forward to blow out the candles, her heart swelled with love for this group who'd so generously adopted her. When she'd lost Laila and the grandchildren she'd never imagined she'd feel such love again. She'd been a prisoner. Sentenced to end her life alone, left only with the memories of her family. Now, with the love of Emma and Lucie, her sentence was over.

ACKNOWLEDGMENTS

I'd like to send a sincere thank you to the wonderful people in my life who continue to encourage and support each step of my writing journey. In particular, Ray, Judy, Robyn, Maggie and Stacey. I am also fortunate to be part of several writing communities from which I not only learn but am constantly inspired.

To the early readers of *Everyday Lies* – Jo, Judy, Kelly, Kylie, Laila, Maggie and Tracy – thank you for the invaluable feedback provided at various stages of the manuscript development.

Mel, thank you for sharing your knowledge and advice on the legal elements of the plot.

To Kat and Lana, thank you for your amazing contributions to *Everyday Lies*.

To the exceptional Lake Union Publishing team – a huge thank you!

ABOUT THE AUTHOR

Louise has enjoyed working in marketing, recruitment and film production, all of which have helped steer her towards her current, and most loved, role – writer.

Originally from Melbourne, a trip around Australia led Louise and her husband to Queensland's stunning Sunshine Coast, where they now live with their two sons, gorgeous fluffball of a cat and an abundance of visiting wildlife – the kangaroos and wallabies the most welcome, the snakes the least!

Awed by her beautiful surroundings, Louise loves to take advantage of the opportunities the coast provides for swimming, hiking, mountain biking and kayaking. When she's not writing or out adventuring Louise loves any available opportunity to curl up with a glass of red wine, switch on her Kindle and indulge in a new release from a favourite author.

To get in touch with Louise, or to join her mailing list, visit: www.LouiseGuy.com